Nicola Upson was born in Suffolk and read English at Downing College, Cambridge. She has worked in theatre and as a freelance journalist, and is the author of two non-fiction works and the recipient of an Escalator Award from the Arts Council England.

Her debut novel, *An Expert in Murder*, was the first in a series of crime novels whose main character is Josephine Tey – one of the leading authors of Britain's Golden Age of crime writing.

She lives with her partner in Cambridge and spends much of her time in Cornwall, which was the setting for her second novel, *Angel with Two Faces*. *Two for Sorrow*, the third book in the Josephine Tey series, was followed by *Fear in the Sunlight*.

Praise for Nicola Upson and the 'Josephine Tey' series:

'An ingenious concept, beautifully realised.' Reginald Hill

'Upson writes well, giving new life to a classic murder setting. The portrayal of Tey herself is both sympathetic and perceptive ... Upson is chillingly effective at showing how good intentions may lead to evil consequences ... a fine addition to a promising series.' Andrew Taylor, *Spectator*

'Upson legitimately uses [Tey] as an avatar to meld a golden-age plot with modern frankness, and Tey's creative process mirrors her own concerns about blurring fact and fiction.' *Financial Times*

'The ingredients in this latest "Josephine Tey" detective mystery are

Also by Nicola Upson

AN EXPERT IN MURDER

ANGEL WITH TWO FACES

TWO FOR SORROW

FEAR IN THE SUNLIGHT

The Death of Lucy Kyte

NICOLA UPSON

ff

faber and faber

First published in this edition in 2013
by Faber and Faber Limited
Bloomsbury House,
74–77 Great Russell Street,
London WC1B 3DA

Typeset by Faber and Faber Ltd
Printed and bound by CPI Group (UK) Ltd, Croydon CR0 4YY

A CIP record for this book
is available from the British Library

ISBN 978–0–571–28772–7

FSC
www.fsc.org
MIX
Paper from
responsible sources
FSC® C101712

2 4 6 8 10 9 7 5 3 1

71123

This story is dedicated to three remarkable women:
my godmother Pearl, Elizabeth MacKintosh, and Maria Marten.

I suppose you are more or less living at the cottage these days. That is an experience I must try just once, I feel – making a new home.

Josephine Tey in a letter to Marda Vanne, December 1934

Josephine looked at her watch and sighed. Outside, the rain continued to pour down into Church Street, forcing the stream of Friday afternoon shoppers into circuitous routes along the pavement to avoid the puddles. Even through the shifting façade of black umbrellas and raised collars, she was alarmed at how many of the passers-by she recognised, and suddenly she craved the anonymity of the city she had just left.

The walls of the solicitor's office were lined with photographs. Prize-winning catches from Ness Castle Pool vied with shooting parties and other events that marked the town's sporting year, more reassuring to most of the firm's clients than any proudly framed legal qualifications would have been. These faces, too, were familiar to her and, if she looked closely, she could probably have identified most of them from among her father's circle of friends – but she was far more interested in the papers that lay on the desk in front of her, tantalisingly undisturbed for the last ten minutes. Impatiently, she glanced over to the small outer lobby that functioned as reception and waiting room; still there was no sign of any purposeful life beyond the frosted glass, so she half-stood and pulled the blotter towards her until the top sheet was close enough to read. She had got no further than the initial formalities when the door opened behind her and she was forced to turn her attention unconvincingly towards a nearby paperweight.

'Janet Mackenzie, died peacefully in her sleep, September 1926. The way we'd all like to go.'

'I'm sorry?'

John MacDonald smiled and nodded at the heavy glass object by Josephine's hand. 'She left it to me as a thank you for all the changes to her will. Bloody ugly, I know, but I liked the old girl so I feel obliged to keep it. There's a drawer full of them at home. Why is it always a paperweight?' He smiled and gestured for her to sit down again. 'Sorry to keep you waiting, Josephine. Tea *is* on its way, I promise.'

The making of tea at Stewart, Rule & Co. was such a lengthy process that Josephine had often considered leaving a new kettle to the firm as part of her own final instructions, but such a gift would have carried with it a Greek quality and she had never had the heart. 'From the date on your letter, I've kept *you* waiting,' she said. 'I've been south for a bit, and I never have my post forwarded when I'm away. It would completely defeat the object of going.'

'England – ah, yes.' He said it with a wistfulness that most people reserved for Persia, or at least somewhere that required travel by sea. 'Business or pleasure?'

Josephine would have found it hard to categorise the events of the last two weeks, even if she had been inclined to. 'Both,' she said non-committally. 'It makes sense to fit as much in as possible when I'm there.'

'Quite, quite. Who knows what your father would get up to if you turned your back for too long? Is he keeping well?'

'Very well, thank you.' She was saved from further small talk by the arrival of the tea tray. 'You wanted to see me about my godmother's will, Mr MacDonald,' she prompted gently, aware that if anything was to be achieved efficiently this afternoon, the impetus would have to come from her. 'I was sorry to hear that she had died. My mother always spoke very fondly of her.'

'Indeed she did. They were great friends.' MacDonald nodded emphatically. He searched among his papers and removed a photograph from the pile. 'Let's get down to business, then. This was Hester Larkspur's home for many years. It's in a little village in Suffolk and she loved it there. Now it's yours.'

His directness was completely out of character and Josephine looked at him in astonishment, convinced she had misheard. Beaming, MacDonald placed the image in front of her with all the flourish of a sideshow conjuror. She imagined that moments like this were few and far between in the life of a small-town solicitor and, because she liked him and because he had always been kind to her family, she tried not to let her sense of anticlimax show. The house was ordinary, a modest thatched cottage on the edge of a wood, and even the soft shades of sepia could not flatter it into being anything other than run-down and badly in need of repair.

'I don't understand,' Josephine said. 'To my knowledge, with the exception of the christening, I never even met my godmother. Mercifully, she seemed to place as little importance on the role as I do, so I can't imagine what I might have done to deserve this.'

Her irony was more pronounced than she had intended, and the solicitor smiled. 'I know what you mean, but it's an old photograph and I gather it doesn't do the place justice. And you did meet her again, at least once. She was at your mother's funeral.' Josephine thought back over the years but the day was a blur to her, filled entirely with grief and with a selfish fear of how her mother's early death would change her own life. She had been in no mood to welcome strangers. 'You were upset,' MacDonald said gently. 'Too upset to remember or even to notice who else was there.'

His kindness made her suddenly vulnerable, and took her back to a moment she had not prepared herself to revisit. 'My mother often talked about her, though,' she said, trying to keep the sadness out of her voice. 'I remember how pleased she always was to get a letter. Etta, she called her. My youngest sister took the nickname from her, but we never actually knew her.'

'She'd moved south by the time you were born, but she and your mother kept in touch, as you say. They'd been friends from childhood – lived next door to each other, went to the same school. When Miss Larkspur's husband died, your mother became the main beneficiary. Now that responsibility has passed to you.'

His choice of words was interesting, Josephine thought, and appropriate. 'Isn't there anyone else?'

'No family, no, and very few close friends. There are a couple of smaller bequests, but nothing very substantial. Miss Larkspur lived a solitary life on the whole, more so as she got older.'

'A childhood friendship once removed still seems a very distant hand to entrust your life to.'

'Perhaps, but nothing would surprise me after all these years.' He shrugged, and poured her more tea. 'And what do you do if you die alone, without a next generation to look to and with no one close who cares about you or really needs your money? There's charity, of course, but it takes a particular strength of mind not to make at least some concessions to sentimentality. A will really *is* the last word, you know,' he added, tapping the papers in front of him. 'It's your chance to say what you think without any fear or pretensions or niceties. Some people use it to settle a score or underline a grudge, but it's more often the reverse. Lots of people force an emotional obligation in death that never existed in life, and it's only human to lay claim to a love that will still be there when you're gone – anything else smacks of failure.' He smiled. 'But I don't think that's the case here.'

'Why not?'

'Originally, in the event of your mother predeceasing her, whatever Miss Larkspur left was to be divided equally between any surviving children. She changed that relatively recently, because she knew by then that you were making a success of your life in a way that would have made your mother very proud – and, most importantly, doing what you wanted to do. I only knew her as a client, not as a friend, but I knew her for a long time and she would have admired that.' Touched, Josephine looked again at the photograph, trying not to let her growing excitement blind her to the gift's problems. There was a word in her head that was strong enough to transform the cottage, removing its flaws and imperfections before her very eyes, and the word was freedom. MacDonald reached for his glasses and glanced through the first couple of pages. 'Shall we get the formalities over? Then I'll try to answer any questions you have.'

Josephine nodded and listened as he began to read, hoping that the formal language of law would not obscure a personality that was beginning to intrigue her. 'Let's see, now. Here we are. "I, Hester Larkspur, residing at Red Barn Cottage, Polstead, Suffolk, desire that everything of which I die possessed, whether money, goods, property, personal possessions, or any other belongings whatsoever, shall, except as hereinafter provided, be given to my goddaughter, Josephine Tey, of Crown Cottage, Inverness, as a tribute to my long friendship with her mother and an acknowledgment of her own achievements.

"'The following personal gifts are those provided for in the first paragraph: To Dilys Nichols, of Wren's View, St Paul's Churchyard, I leave all my clothes, including theatrical costumes and furs (in storage at Debenham and Freebody's). If Dilys Nichols does not survive me, the said clothes to be given to any deserving London charity. No clothes of mine are to be disposed of locally. To Moyse's Hall Museum, Bury St Edmunds, I give outright the collection of artefacts and theatrical memorabilia at present lent to them by me. To Josephine's sisters, Jane Ellis and Etta (Mary Henrietta), I leave the gold ring of half-pearls and a brooch made of the same pearls, given to me by their mother.

"'I appoint as my executors Messrs. Stewart, Rule & Co., Inverness, who will know as much about my affairs as anyone has a right to. I leave instructions, separately, to Stewart, Rule & Co. about the disposal of my body, and I charge them to see that my instructions are carried out."'

MacDonald leaned back in his chair. 'There you are. All fairly straightforward so far.'

'Was Hester an actress?' Josephine asked, intrigued by the personal gifts.

'Yes. Didn't you know?'

'No, I had no idea. I don't really remember much of what my mother said to us about her, but the things I can recall are all to do with the town and their childhood.'

'Miss Larkspur left here to go on the stage. That's how she met her husband. They acted together until his death, and then she gave it all up. She once told me that she didn't have the heart to go on without him.'

'What was his name?'

'Walter Paget.'

Josephine shook her head. 'Strange that I've never come across either of them in the theatre.'

'Not really. Neither of them were ever top-tier, you understand. It was melodrama mostly, real populist stuff.'

'East End rather than West?'

'If you say so. I'm not sure I'd know the difference. It was the acting that took Miss Larkspur to Suffolk, though, I know that much. There's a connection between the village and one of the roles she played. I suppose I should remember which one, but I'm afraid I don't. It's not really my cup of tea, the stage.' His embarrassment at the admission amused Josephine. 'I have dug out a photograph for you, though.'

Eagerly, she took the black and white portrait shot that he held out to her. Hester Larkspur was in costume, but not even the trappings of the Edwardian stage – hat and parasol and a fringe she would probably regret – could hide the warmth and fun in the actress's eyes. It was an attractive face – 'charming' would probably have been the word used by critics – but there was an intelligence there, too, that spoke instantly to Josephine, and she felt she could easily have been looking at Ethel Barrymore or a young Ellen Terry. In the back of her mind, a half-formed memory began to nag at her, but it would not come forward when summoned and she turned her attention back to the will. 'What did you mean – "straightforward so far"?'

'Ah – this is where it gets interesting.' He smiled, mocking his own enthusiasm. 'I do wish everyone could be so creative with their final wishes. It would make my job much more exciting. Now – there are two codicils. The first goes like this: "It is my wish and I direct that my goddaughter, Josephine Tey, shall immediately on my death be given the keys of Red Barn Cottage and that she shall have the sole right of entry thereto until such time as she has cleared up my personal belongings and papers. She must decide, according to her discretion, what is and what is not valuable, to her or to a wider public – and, if she is her mother's daughter, she will know that I am not talking in monetary terms. It is a writer's gift to know what has meaning in a person's life, to decide what stories are worthy of being told, and I instruct – I ask – her now to do that for me." Josephine opened her mouth to speak, but he held up his hand. "'If, for whatever reason, Josephine Tey is unable or unwilling to undertake the above, it is my wish and I direct my Executors to ensure that Red Barn Cottage and its contents are destroyed in their entirety. No sale of the house or contents shall be permitted; nor shall any inspection of the house be allowed.'"

The room fell silent as Josephine thought about the implications of what she had heard. 'I see why you called it a responsibility,' she said eventually. 'It's not just a matter of tidying up the garden, is it?'

'No, I'm afraid not. But at least Miss Larkspur's was an interesting life – well, a life *you* will find interesting, I think.'

'You said there were *two* codicils?'

'That's right. Have a Garibaldi.' He glanced at the tea tray. 'Good God, a choice of biscuits. What can Miss Peck be thinking of? Still, I suppose it's not every day that we have a celebrity in the office.' Absent-mindedly, Josephine chose a shortbread, keen for him to continue. 'So, last but not least: "In addition to the arrangements made in my will, I bequeath to Lucy Kyte and free of all encumbrances the right to take whatever she most needs from the house as an acknowledgement of the great kindness to me, and in the hope that it will bring her peace."'

'Who is Lucy Kyte?'

MacDonald shrugged. 'Your guess is as good as mine. I haven't been able to trace her yet. Dilys Nichols is straightforward enough – she's a dressmaker whom Miss Larkspur knew from the theatre. Lucy Kyte is a mystery, but that's my problem, not yours – unless what she needs most turns out to be the kitchen sink, of course. Somehow I don't think so.'

'No, it sounds more personal than that. What was the great kindness, I wonder? Perhaps Lucy Kyte is someone from the village who looked after Hester?'

'That was my first thought, but apparently not. There was no one looking after her, and that was the way she wanted it. The local vicar told me that in no uncertain terms.'

Something in his tone made Josephine uneasy. 'How *did* Hester die? I haven't even asked you.'

'Oh, at home in bed.'

'The way we all want to go?' He smiled, but said nothing. 'Well, I'm glad of that, at least.' She looked at the actress again. 'What was she like?'

'Delightful. Gracious, charming and witty – the sort of person whose company you felt you were lucky to have, even for a short time. She rarely came back to Inverness, of course, and we didn't see her often, but there were certain things she asked us to look after over the years – investments, mostly, and the purchase of the house – and her appointments were always looked forward to.' He took the photograph back for a moment and stared at it fondly, and Josephine could imagine him forty years ago, a young man dazzled by a glamorous client, wanting to do his best for her. 'It would have been easier for her to use a London firm, I suppose, but her family had always been with us and loyalty seemed to be important to Miss Larkspur. She was old-fashioned in that way, and I like to think we served her well. She certainly had Miss Peck eating out of her hand and that is no mean feat, believe me.'

'I wish I'd known her.' She smiled at her own cliché. 'You must hear that a lot.'

'Yes, and not always from people who were strangers to each other. Don't get me wrong, Josephine – she wasn't an easy woman. That's what I meant about knowing her as a client and not as a friend: there was a "thus far and no further" quality to her. She knew how to keep people at arm's length, and she didn't give a damn if that offended them. She was a law unto herself and that hardly made her popular here, as I'm sure you can imagine.' He gave Josephine a knowing look which she chose to ignore. 'Or, I understand, in Suffolk. The funeral was the last straw.'

'Why? What instructions did she leave?'

'That on no account was she to be buried in Polstead. She wanted a private cremation, and her ashes to be placed with Walter's at St Paul's in Covent Garden, with a memorial service for them both. It's an actors' church, apparently.'

'Yes, I know it. That's reasonable enough, surely?'

'Not to her neighbours. If a village is good enough to live in, it's good enough to die in, and I suppose that's reasonable, too. It was viewed as something of a snub. No one likes to be denied a good funeral – especially when the war has cheated us out of so many. But, as I said, she didn't give a damn.'

'An actress who didn't need to be liked? That *is* impressive.' He laughed, and Josephine sensed he was enjoying the opportunity to talk about a woman he wished he had known better. 'I'm sorry I didn't get your letter in time to pay my respects,' she said. 'I can't imagine it was much of a memorial if she had isolated herself in the way you say. Did you go?'

'No. I was tied up here, so Miss Peck represented us. There was a reasonable turnout, apparently – fans who remembered Miss Larkspur from her heyday, old colleagues who went out of curiosity after so many years, even a few famous faces.'

'Oh?'

'Sybil Thorndike and her husband were there. And Tod Slaughter. That can't be his real name, surely?'

'The "Slaughter" part is. I believe his first name is actually Norman, but most people call him Mr Murder. Pick a villain and he's played it.'

'I see. Well, Miss Peck seemed particularly taken with him – said he was charm itself. Between you and me, I think she rather enjoyed herself. I dare say she'd be only too happy to talk to you about it if you've time. She's quite a fan.' He hesitated, as if there were something else he wanted to say, and Josephine waited to see what it was. 'Miss Larkspur

9

telephoned me a few months back,' he admitted eventually. 'She told me she was thinking of changing her will. I wondered then if she had another major beneficiary in mind.'

'And did she?'

'I don't know. She never really explained herself. In fact, she seemed very distracted. All she would say is that she wasn't sure if you would *want* the house. I told her to send me her instructions in writing when she'd made up her mind, but I never heard from her. In fact, that was the last time we spoke.' His voice was full of regret, and Josephine wondered what else he thought he could have done for his client. 'If she was right about that, and the cottage is more trouble to you than it's worth, I can get a local firm to clear the place and destroy the contents according to her wishes. The property itself is more problematic. She's made it impossible for you to sell, but I'm not entirely sure about the legality of wanton destruction. It may be that the house must just be left to die in its own good time if you don't want to keep it. But I'm rather hoping you will.'

'And you feel burdened by a paperweight? I can't help wishing my own benefactor had been less creative.' The word felt strangely Dickensian in her mouth and she looked again at the house, trying to imagine herself there.

'It's a lot to ask of someone, I know, but you don't have to decide immediately. Take some time to think about it and let me know what you'd like me to do.' He passed a heavy iron key across the desk with the photographs and paperwork. 'And this belongs to you.'

Josephine took it, already feeling like an intruder. She stood to leave, and MacDonald showed her out. To her relief, his secretary was on the telephone. As keen as she was to know more about Hester Larkspur, she needed time to think about this unexpected turn in her life; Miss Peck's notes from the wake could wait for another day.

'Give my regards to your father.'

'I will.' The summer rain showed no sign of relenting, and Josephine took her umbrella from the stand. 'Did my father know Hester?' she asked.

'As well as a man ever knows his wife's best friend, I suppose.' There was a twinkle in the solicitor's eye as he bent to kiss her. 'Or his wife, when she's with her.'

He left her with that thought, and Josephine walked out into the street, conscious of the key in her bag. She headed for Crown Circus, intent on getting home, then changed her mind and retraced her footsteps back into town. It was only three o'clock, and the library would be open for at least another hour; there was still time to finish the day with more information about Hester Larkspur than she had at present. Someone with more sense than she would be thinking about the practicalities of owning a cottage four hundred miles away rather than chasing the memory of a woman she would never know – but the actress had gambled on her curiosity, on the heart ruling the head, and she had been right. Josephine was less intrigued by the gift itself than by the woman who had made it, and the prospect of seeing a different side to her mother through their friendship only spurred her on.

The library was quiet, and Josephine found a table to herself in the reference room. She pulled out *Who's Who in the Theatre* and flicked through the pages, feeling the familiar sense of pride when she passed her own entry. Her godmother's record was lengthy, particularly for someone who had abandoned her career when it was still in full swing, and Josephine wondered again how she could have been oblivious to her achievements until now.

'Larkspur, Hester, actress; *b.* 15 September, 1871; *d.* of the late Robert Larkspur and his wife Helen (Milne); *e.* Inverness Royal Academy; *m.* Walter Paget (dec.). Made her first professional appearance on the stage in a sketch, "How Others See Us", at the Playhouse, Whitley Bay; played various parts with the Hull Repertory Company, and, after gaining further experience with a number of companies in the provinces, made her first appearance in London at the Criterion, 8 Apr., 1891, as Lady Blakeney in *The Scarlet Pimpernel*.' Josephine skimmed

11

through the long list of revues, comedy parts and tours that followed, before arriving at the role that had slipped John MacDonald's memory. 'In 1896, she played the eponymous Maria Marten for the first time at the Pavilion Theatre, Mile End, where she acted opposite Walter Paget in the story of the Red Barn murder. They married the following year and, over the next two decades, toured the country with popular revivals of "blood and thunder" melodramas, including *Sweeney Todd*, *Jack Sheppard* and *The Crimes of Burke and Hare*, as well as *Maria Marten*, a play that Larkspur has performed more than a thousand times in her career, and for which she remains best-known.

'After the war, the couple settled at the Elephant and Castle Theatre, South London, where Paget became actor-manager, attracting West End audiences for their productions and for a popular Christmas pantomime. In 1921, she surprised critics by joining the Little Theatre's "Grand Guignol" company at the invitation of Sybil Thorndike and Lewis Casson, appearing for more than a hundred performances in *The Old Women*. She retired from the stage in 1922 after the death of her husband. More than ten years later, she was persuaded to return to the Maria Marten story in a film of the same name, starring alongside Tod Slaughter, this time as the heroine's mother, but she withdrew from the production before filming started. She was replaced by Clare Greet. *Recreations*: books; gardening; the countryside; *Address*: Red Barn Cottage, Polstead, Suffolk.'

Josephine recalled the film – one of those cheap and cheerful crowd-pleasers left over from a different age, memorable for the shamelessly excessive performance of its male star and quite magnificent in its own dreadful way. The details of the story eluded her, but she was fascinated to learn that Hester's cottage – she could not yet think of it as her own – had a place in the real history of the crime.

'The wanderer returns,' said a voice behind her. 'Is it my imagination, or are you away in the south more often these days?'

Josephine glanced at Margaret MacDougall, the local librarian, and smiled. 'Twice in two months is hardly a defection.' The words were as indignant as she could make them, and she hoped that a firm denial would outweigh the truth of the observation. She resented feeling obliged to justify the time she spent away from the town, even to someone she liked, but it was a habit of which she had never managed to break herself.

'No, I suppose not.' Margaret peered over Josephine's shoulder. 'Ah – the errant Miss Larkspur. Now there was a woman with spirit. It's a shame we've lost her.'

The librarian was roughly Josephine's age, so the comment could only be based on reputation; even so, she had an exhaustive knowledge of local history, including anyone who had been born within a fifteen-mile radius of the town, and there was no one better to ask. 'What can you tell me about her?'

'That you're wasting your time with a respectable volume like that when you could be benefiting from the insights of our local rag.' She grinned and disappeared for a moment to rummage through a pile of newspapers. 'Here you are.' She handed Josephine a copy of the *Inverness Courier*, opened at the page that would interest her.

'Hester Larkspur, actress and former resident of Shore Street, has died at her home in Essex.' It wasn't a promising start, Josephine thought: once you left Scotland, you obviously relinquished your right to accuracy. 'Daughter of popular Inverness baker, Bob Larkspur, Hester attended the Inverness Royal Academy and was destined for a teaching career but failed to achieve the necessary qualifications. It is not known where her interest in the theatre began, but in 1890 she left her home town, intent on turning her hobby into a profession. A number of walk-on parts and minor roles in northern England followed, then a brief spell on some of the stages of outer London, where she met her husband, Walter Paget – a fellow actor, ten years her senior. When the capital refused to embrace their particular style of melodrama, the couple settled for a life of touring barnstorming productions to provincial stages, returning sporadically to Inverness with productions of *Maria Marten*, *Sweeney Todd* and even the occasional Shakespeare.

'After the war, they returned to London and took over a small venue. It was to prove an ill-fated move: in 1922, Paget died on stage while playing William Corder to his wife's Maria Marten, and there were ugly scenes in the auditorium when crowds objected to the production being cancelled short of the murderer's execution! By this time, melodrama had gone out of fashion on the serious stage and Miss Larkspur took the opportunity afforded by her husband's death to retire. In a typically theatrical gesture, she chose to live out the rest of her life in the village where the inspiration for her most famous role met her death. During her later years, Hester Larkspur was rumoured to be working on a memoir but this could not be confirmed at the time of writing. She had few friends in the town she turned her back on, and leaves behind no children.'

Josephine threw the paper down in disgust. 'We certainly know how to celebrate the achievements of our own, don't we?' she said acidly.

'Read and learn, my dear, read and learn.' She looked curiously at Josephine. 'Why the interest in Hester Larkspur?'

'She was my godmother,' Josephine said, enjoying the flicker of admiration that crossed Margaret's face. 'I just wanted to know more about her.' She considered confiding the rest of the story, but then thought better of it. 'It's a shame I didn't own her with such pride when she was alive, isn't it? I never dreamt we had so much in common.' She glanced again at *Who's Who*, and wondered about the role that had meant so much to Hester. 'Do you know anything about Maria Marten?' she asked.

Her friend shrugged. 'Innocent village maiden seduced by wicked squire in eighteen-something and killed in a barn.'

'That's it? Surely there must be more to it if Hester played her a thousand times? Something that made her different from all the other village maidens seduced by wicked squires?'

'Well, there's the killed in a barn bit,' Margaret said wryly. 'I don't think they were *all* bumped off. And there was something odd about how she was found. Her mother had a dream or something and told her father where to look.'

'How very convenient.'

'Yes, I suppose it was. But why are you getting carried away with Maria Marten? Isn't there another life you should be reading about? How is Bonnie Dundee, if you don't mind my asking?'

Josephine could have cried. She had recently accepted a commission from Collins to write a biography of John Graham of Claverhouse, nobleman and Jacobite hero, and it was proving to be the worst decision she had ever made. All she had to show so far was a neatly stacked pile of research books and some random notes, but professional pride would never allow her to admit as much, especially not to a woman who was the soldier's most passionate advocate – so much so that Josephine was tempted to tell her to write the bloody book herself. 'He's fine,' she lied. 'Coming along nicely.'

'Good. I'm looking forward to reading it.' So was Josephine, but that day was a long way off. She thanked Margaret and left the library before a more penetrating question could expose the biography's true lack of progress.

Outside, the rain had cleared and the soft blue sky promised an evening whose beauty would make up for the day. She walked home to the Crown, deep in thought, looking up only when the polite ring of a bicycle bell told her that she had strayed from the path. As she opened the front door and walked into the hall, she was more sensitive than usual to the peace inside. Her father would not be back for another hour, and everything was just as she had left it when – late to see John MacDonald – she had rushed from the house without a thought for tidying up. She went from room to room, seeing her home through the eyes of a stranger: the morning's bills thrown hurriedly onto her desk, next to a photograph of Archie and a half-written note to her agent; flowers from Marta with a card propped up against the vase, its message beautifully discreet but open to a dozen interpretations; drawers full of postcards from friends, and books hiding letters that no longer held the urgency of love, but still stirred an affection too precious to be casually thrown away.

Then her bedroom – the jewellery given to her by her parents, clothes that carried her scent, notes left in pockets that seemed private and safe. She imagined her neighbours viewing the house after she was gone, knowing where she had worked and lived and slept, destroying the privacy she had so jealously guarded. In death, she would have no defence except a trust in someone to do as she had asked, and the peculiar terms of the will suddenly presented themselves in a new light: what had seemed both a mystery and a challenge could just as easily be a plea for decency, and Josephine knew then that whatever she eventually decided to do about the house, she could not allow Hester Larkspur's life to be disposed of by a stranger. Holding the key in her hand for luck, she picked up the telephone and hoped that Miss Peck would be diligent enough to stay late on a Friday afternoon.

2

The bus pulled out of the pretty Suffolk town, leaving behind the ancient half-timbered houses and present-day bustle of a Wednesday market. It was a beautiful day, clear and seasonably warm, but Josephine suspected that her own mood would have transformed even the dullest of mornings into something worth celebrating. After the early train from London, the bus seemed interminably slow, but she was glad of the opportunity to savour an adventure that would only come once. In the few days that had passed since the meeting with her solicitor, the mystery of Hester Larkspur's will had only intrigued her more and – although she had made no plans other than this fleeting, exploratory visit – she wanted desperately to like what she found.

Her father's reaction to her unexpected inheritance had been characteristically sanguine; if he had harboured any selfish concerns about what it might mean to his own life, he had not shown them. They had had ten years to settle into their respective roles and, in hindsight, Josephine realised that her original decision to return home was driven more by a personal sense of duty than by any great expectations on his part: he was an independent man with a life of his own, and he afforded her the same courtesy. By that time, both her sisters were married and living in England, scarcely more than visitors to the town they were raised in, and that life could have been hers if she had wanted it. But she had not, and her own journeys south – though frequent – had never held that quality of permanence. This one should have been no different – and yet it was, because *she* had changed: success was addictive, and the popularity of her books and plays had created other opportunities that she wanted to explore; and her love for Marta, still so new, had brought joy to her life whilst completely destroying its former contentment. As she booked her ticket and packed her case, Josephine had vowed to keep Hester's gift in perspective; but the solidity of bricks and mortar, so far away from all that was familiar to her, had subtly transformed idle thoughts into real possibilities. The sunlight sparkled on the road ahead, and she could not decide if fate was blessing her with different choices, or daring her to make something of them.

The weather must have been fine for some time. Some of the corn had been gathered in already, and where it remained, the countryside was a rich, deep yellow, pure and unspoilt. Away from the town, the landscape seemed increasingly at peace with itself, Josephine thought, happy to amble through the years and caring little if it kept pace with the rest of England. From the window of the bus, her impressions grew section by section, rather like a jigsaw puzzle. She longed for a hill or any sort of vantage point that would allow her to take in more of the area at a single glance, but Suffolk refused to make itself known in that way. 'Wait,' it seemed to say: 'I'll show you when I'm ready.' It was not a county for the lazy, it seemed, and she suspected that it hid its finest secrets away from the main road, down tiny lanes and myriad footpaths. What she *could* see hinted at an attractive independence: irregular-shaped fields; random, solitary oak trees that dared her to question their position by their very magnificence; hedges of blackthorn and hazel, wild and unruly and growing entirely as they pleased. As they rode, she wondered if she would find the landscape's strength of will reflected in its people, and if she would ever truly come to know either.

Eventually, the names she had studied on a map began to appear on signposts – Bower House Tye, Whitestreet Green, Polstead. The bus descended a slope, then slowed as it entered the village and turned left by a large pond. The road climbed again, past the water pump, and Josephine looked in delight at the well-kept houses on either side. For a village scarred by murder, Polstead certainly knew how to show itself off: a more perfect picture of rural tranquillity was hard to imagine. Its green was a triangle, fronted by an old inn, and a couple of the other passengers got off with Josephine when the bus pulled up. They looked curiously at her, but said nothing as they parted and went their separate ways. It was lunchtime, and somewhere nearby she could hear the sound of a children's playground. The inn was open and seemed the obvious place to ask for directions, but she wasn't yet ready to announce herself in such a public way; instead, she made her way to the opposite corner, where a small garage – the forge in its past life – stood under the shade of a splendid chestnut tree. A man was working under the bonnet of a car, and he glanced up as he heard her approach. 'Can I help?' he asked.

His tone seemed to suggest that it was unlikely, but she had already committed herself. 'I'm looking for Red Barn Cottage. Do you know it?'

It was a ridiculous question in a village this size, but the mechanic didn't hold it against her; if anything, he warmed a little. 'Miss Larkspur's old place?'

'That's right.'

'Yes, I know it. Are you her goddaughter?' Josephine's surprise must have been obvious because he added quickly: 'I don't mean to speak out of turn, but she mentioned a goddaughter and you've got her accent. If I've got it wrong . . .'

'You haven't got it wrong and you're not speaking out of turn.' Josephine interrupted the apology, although she found his knowledge disconcerting. 'I just didn't expect people here to know much about Hester, let alone about me. Someone told me that she didn't have anything to do with the village. He was obviously wrong.'

'No, it's true enough. Miss Larkspur liked her own company, but I suppose I knew her better than most round here. A car that doesn't start very often has a knack of bringing people together.' He wiped his hand on his overalls, but the grease was too stubborn to be shifted and he made do with a smile instead. 'Albert Willis,' he said. 'Everyone calls me Bert.' He didn't wait for her to introduce herself, and Josephine wondered if that was because he already knew her name. She listened carefully to the directions he gave her but they were impossible to fol-low, as directions always are when none of the landmarks are familiar. 'It's not as difficult as it sounds,' he added, 'but I've got to drop this car back at Shelly when I'm done. If you can wait ten minutes, I'll run you over there.'

Josephine hesitated, reluctant to be in debt for a favour so soon after her arrival. 'I don't want to put you to any trouble.'

'It's no trouble. I'm going that way.'

'Then a lift would be lovely. Thank you.' There was no such thing as too long a wait on a balmy August day. She sat patiently on the green while Bert finished his work, happy just to look around and enjoy the peace. The children's voices drifted away as they were herded back to their classroom, and the soundtrack of the afternoon reverted to birdsong and the occasional stifled curse from the garage. A couple of men glanced in her direction as the pub closed its doors on them; oth-erwise, she was beautifully undisturbed. After about twenty minutes, Bert closed the bonnet of the Ford and coaxed the engine gently into life, then gave her the thumbs-up and lifted her cases onto the back seat. As they drove off, a woman watched them from the house next door and Josephine guessed that her chauffeur would have some ques-tions to answer before he packed up for the day.

They went back down the hill and turned left at the bottom, a con-tinuation of the route she had come in on. The main road wound to the right, but Bert chose a tiny lane in the opposite direction, barely more than a farm track, and Josephine realised that – in spite of its tidy green – the village wriggled and straggled away from its centre. 'Is that the cottage?' she asked, looking ahead to a gable end that resembled the photograph she had been given.

'No. That's Maria Marten's old house. They're similar, but Red Barn Cottage is further up here.'

Intrigued, Josephine peered through the hedge and saw a pretty garden, filled with apple trees and roses. 'I'm afraid I don't know much about your murder,' she admitted, 'and I suppose I should, considering that's what brought Hester here.'

'You're probably the only person who *doesn't* know about it. Whenever a stranger turns up in the village, that's usually what they're after. Sometimes I think the rest of us might as well not exist.' The comment was amused rather than bitter, but Josephine would not have blamed him for resenting an obsession with Polstead's past when its present seemed so lovely. 'If I were any sort of guide at all, I'd have shown you Corder's house. It's the big timbered place on the hill.'

'And the barn?' she asked, falling into the trap herself. 'I assume from the name that it's near Hester's cottage?'

'It was, but it burnt down a few years after the murder. There's nothing left of it now.'

'Oh, I see.' Josephine was ashamed of her disappointment: there was nothing very laudable in glorifying murder sites, even if you could claim a professional interest in crime, but Bert seemed used to her reaction.

'Someone could make a fortune by rebuilding it,' he joked, then added more seriously: 'Miss Larkspur once told me that she'd dreamed of putting a theatre there, but that was when her husband was alive. She was quite taken with Maria, you know. She fought her corner, and not many people do that.'

Hester Larkspur wasn't the only actress to develop a passionate attachment to the character she played, Josephine thought. Her own friend Lydia Beaumont had embraced Mary Stuart with far more righteous zeal on stage than Josephine had ever felt when writing the play, and it was just as well that she had: impartiality was anathema to a good performance. 'What was she like?' she asked, keen to find out as much as possible while she had the chance.

'Oh, not the innocent she's painted. She'd had three illegitimate kids by the time she died.'

'What?' Josephine stared at him in astonishment.

'Maria Marten. Three children by three different men. One of them was William Corder's older brother.'

Josephine burst out laughing, then was quick to explain when he looked offended. 'I'm sorry, Bert. I meant what was Hester like? I never knew her, and it's special for me to meet someone who did.'

He smiled too, embarrassed at his mistake. 'She was lovely, Miss. Someone like her – well, you wouldn't think she'd give the time of day to a garage man, but she was so kind. The twins loved her, too. She told the best stories, they always said. Thanks to her, my Lizzie won't talk about anything but going on the stage, and she's only ten.' He tried to sound exasperated, but there was a pride in his voice as he spoke. 'We didn't see much of her, even less these last few months. Still, they miss her. *I* miss her.'

His sadness was the same in its way as John MacDonald's and, once again, Josephine found herself mourning a woman she had never known. It was a disconcerting emotion, a mixture of sadness, frustration and – although the fault was not hers – of failure. More than ever, she was glad at the decision she had made: clearing the cottage was the only thing she could do now for her godmother, and getting to know her in that way might, in part, make up for a relationship of which she was now beginning to feel cheated.

Bert stopped at a junction and put the handbrake on. 'There it is,' he said, pointing down to his left.

Red Barn Cottage lay at the bottom of a long, sloping field, nestled into the edge of a wood and facing back towards the village. There were some outbuildings to the rear and a small pond on the left, its surface glittering in the sun. The sheep grazing nearby were the final touch to a pastoral scene so perfect that she could easily have been looking at a canvas, but Josephine's overwhelming impression was one of isolation and loneliness. 'It's not exactly central, is it?' she said after a moment or two. 'Which county are we in now?'

He laughed. 'I've given you the wrong impression coming round by the road. There's a direct route over the fields, only half a mile or so, and a lovely walk on a day like this.' Not quite so lovely in the driving rain, Josephine thought, or at night. The setting was far more remote than she had expected, and she was suddenly glad of the list of guest houses that Miss Peck had insisted on looking out for her in case she wanted to spend her days at the cottage and her nights in comfort. Bert lifted her cases out onto the verge. 'That cart-track's a bit rough for the car, but I'll carry these down for you if you like?'

She shook her head. 'No, I'll be fine. They're not heavy.' Despite her reservations, Josephine wanted to be alone when she first walked into the cottage. It was the closest she could ever be to Hester Larkspur, and she didn't want it spoilt by conversation and distractions. Bert seemed to understand that, and Josephine liked him all the more for it.

'If you need anything while you're here, let me know,' he said. 'We live just behind the workshop and I'm usually about.'

'Thank you, Bert. You've been very kind.'

'Will you keep the old place on?' he asked, shrugging away her gratitude. 'There's a lot of history there and it'd be nice to see it come to life again.'

'I don't know,' she said, looking doubtfully across the field. 'I've come down for a few days to get the feel of it and to sort some things out, but I haven't thought any further ahead.' She tried to imagine herself making the cottage her own and wondered if she could ever truly be comfortable with such a solitary existence. Like many things that were the opposite of all she had known, a country life – away from the gossip of a small town and the celebrity of London – had seemed idyllic; faced with its reality, she was less sure, and she wondered how Hester had adapted to growing old alone in the house she had bought with someone she loved. 'When did you last see her?' she asked.

Bert hesitated, distracted by a kestrel that hovered twenty or thirty feet above the earth, poised in the air with quivering wings; she watched it dive headlong towards an unsuspecting victim, then rise again, unsatisfied, to hover over a more distant patch of ground. When her companion still didn't answer, she asked the question again. 'Some time in May,' Bert said vaguely, getting back into the car. 'I used to find an excuse to drop in on her now and again. There always had to be a reason for it – she didn't welcome social calls and she was a difficult woman to help, but I could get away with bringing the odd bit of shopping or dropping off her post if I didn't make a fuss about it.' He started the engine, bringing their conversation to an end before Josephine could ask any more questions, then thought better of it. 'Listen, Miss,' he said, 'your godmother gave me her car a few months back. She said she didn't have any more use for it, and I might as well keep it because it spent more time with me anyway.' He smiled to himself, remembering. 'She wasn't far wrong there, either. If you like, I could give it the once-over and have it ready for when you come back. If you come back. It might make you feel a bit less isolated, and it's probably yours by rights anyway.'

Josephine was touched, but she shook her head. 'You don't need to do that, Bert. She wanted you to have it or she wouldn't have given it to you.'

He grinned. 'It was kind of her, but it's a bit of a ladies' car, if you know what I mean. I'll fix it anyway, then it's there if you want it. If not, the wife can use it so I won't be wasting my time.' She thanked him and said goodbye, wanting now to be on her own, but he called her back. 'You *will* ask if you need anything, won't you? Anything at all.' Josephine nodded, trying not to let his kindness irritate her. It was ungrateful of her, but the sooner Bert realised that she was no more sociable than her godmother, the better they were likely to get on.

The track led only to Red Barn Cottage and, as Bert had said, was rough and little used. She walked slowly down the slope, picking her way carefully through the grass and nettles that had been quick to cover the traces of Hester's driving days. As she drew closer, the house had no choice but to be honest about its imperfections: the thatch was thin and brittle where the sun had scorched its ridges, or held together by moss at the more sheltered end; very little of the white-washed stone lived up to its name; and the garden – which had looked so lush and picturesque from a distance – was actually a wilderness, a daunting battle of wills between flower and weed. The curtains were drawn across at all the windows and yet, in Josephine's imagination, the cottage seemed watchful and wary of her approach, as though the appraising glances she gave it were mutual. When she put her hand on the gate to open it, she half-expected it to resist, but the only objection was a faint creak from a badly oiled hinge.

There was a tiny porch over the front door, added, she guessed, during Hester's tenure, and she set her cases down inside, admiring the herringbone pattern of the floor tiles. Just above her head, a rusted horseshoe hung on a nail and she wondered if the gesture had its roots in the traditions of the countryside or in Hester's chosen profession; Josephine had never known an actress who did not bow to superstition when she wanted something, and she brushed the iron with her fingertips, hoping that it had brought Hester the luck she had asked for and happy to absorb some of it herself. Still doubting her right to be there, she decided to make a full circuit of the house before going inside. The plot was bigger than she had expected: the cottage itself sprawled long and low, and the land around it was generous. Even in its overgrown state, it was easy to see that Hester had loved her garden and had known how to get the best from it. The borders at the front of the cottage were carefully planted to provide colour all year round: Michaelmas daisies, Chinese lanterns and heavily scented phlox had taken over from the early summer flowers, ensuring that the view from inside would be a mass of mauves, pinks and reds well into the autumn. If she ever had time, she would love to restore the garden to its former glory, but she tried not to promise herself the joy of seeing it in each new season. Instead, she made a mental list of the repairs that needed doing – the wooden name plate that was hanging off the wall, a missing pane of glass from one of the downstairs windows; then, as the repairs grew bigger and the list grew longer, she stopped that as well and was content just to look.

A wide gate at the end of the hedge led out to the pond and a footpath, presumably the direct route to the village that Bert had told her about. This shadier area, partially covered by trees at the edge of the wood, was taken up by a large timber workshop and Josephine guessed that it was where Hester's car had been stored. She pulled the door open and walked inside, and the rustle of dead leaves underfoot sounded unnaturally loud in the cool, quiet interior. Sunshine filtered through the ivied windows to create a pleasant half-light, and one or two oil patches on the floor testified to Bert's assessment of the troublesome vehicle. A set of dining room chairs was stacked just inside the door with some other bits and pieces of furniture and an old bicycle, but she was more intrigued by what lined the walls – rows of tall, flat objects, covered mostly with dustsheets but revealing just enough of themselves for her to recognise stage scenery. The backdrop she could see most clearly was an old-fashioned fairground, beautifully painted onto wood, and she made her way round the rest, apologising to the spiders whose homes she disturbed as she lifted the sheets. The series of settings – village green, cottage hearth, forest, drawing room, barn and prison cell – gave her a good idea of the play's story, even without a script. There was a trunk at her feet and she bent down to open it, startled at first by what she saw until she realised that she was looking at a pair of stage pistols, piled on top of other props – a spade, violin, and baby doll. The whole production was stored here, ready to take to the road again at any minute, and for the first time Josephine truly understood what a labour of love Hester's style of theatre was. It had been her life, hers and Walter's; no wonder she had not wanted to continue with it after his death.

She closed the trunk before it could absorb her attention completely and went back outside. This functional end of the garden had suffered most from being left to nature: the vegetable patch had gone to seed, although the herbs – lavender, rosemary, thyme – still beckoned her with their scent; the old beehive had rotted away; and the trees in the small orchard seemed burdened rather than blessed by their fruit, their branches bowed low with no one to appreciate the effort they had gone to. She reached up to pick an apple, realising suddenly how hungry she was, and ate it in the sun. The rear gardens looked out across open farmland, separated only half-heartedly from the fields by a crumbling red-brick wall, and were a larger version of the colourful maze that had greeted her at the front. Nothing had been tended for months, and Josephine wondered if Hester had been ill for a long time before her death or if the land had simply become too much for her; even so, everywhere she looked there were small touches that spoke strongly of her godmother's bond with her home, and she realised then that the sense of desolation she felt came not from neglect but from love. In revealing its secrets one by one, the house seemed to be mocking Josephine, questioning her right to be sad when its own loss was so much greater.

The gable end of the cottage was flanked by cherry trees, and she sat down on a wrought-iron bench, uneven and twisted with age but still warm from the heat of the day. There was a little more order here, she thought: an old variety of climbing rose had been given its head for years, covering the cottage wall and obscuring a good deal of both windows, but its roots were not choked with weeds like every other plant in the garden and she wondered if it had been a favourite or if its proximity to the back door made it easier to care for. She sat there for a long time, unsure of what she was waiting for but in no hurry to move. The isolation she had felt when first looking at the cottage was less extreme now, perhaps because she felt Hester's presence here so strongly, and she thought about the peace that had replaced it and what that might bring to her life.

Apart from spending some time with Marta and Lydia at their cottage in Essex, her only real experience of the countryside was as a child, when her family had taken their summer holidays in Daviot, a small village not far from Inverness. They had stayed in the same house every year, taken the same walks, shared the same memories, and the predictability of the holiday had been part of its joy, an affirmation of their importance to each other. Years later, when she had left home and was living in England, her mother wanted the whole family to go again, but Josephine was busy with her own life and had refused, claiming work as an excuse, promising next year. She had not understood that it was her last chance, that her mother would be too ill by the following summer to ask again – and she had never entirely forgiven herself for not going, or her mother for not telling her why it mattered so much. The family had made the trip without her, and a small part of Josephine would always resent her sisters for having memories rather than imagined pictures of those few precious days. It kept her awake at night sometimes, the thought that her absence might have made her mother doubt her love. So much of what she remembered about their relationship was marred by guilt, and that in itself was a betrayal: it was the last thing her mother would have wanted, but she could not help it and guilt invited itself. It was here with her now, more than ever, because this should have been her mother's cottage, her mother's journey. The strength of her own anger took Josephine by surprise, and it was all she could do not to walk away from a vulnerability that she rarely felt at home. The place might be strange and new to her, but how quickly her ghosts had found her there.

She stood up, eager to be distracted by more practical considerations. The first decision she had to make was where she was going to spend the night, and she couldn't do that until she knew the state of the cottage. She found the key in her bag and used it with as little ceremony as possible, trying to calm her nerves by acting as if this were normal. The door opened straight into a kitchen-parlour, cast in shadow now that the sun had moved round, and she went to the windows to pull the curtains back. There was a range at one end with an armchair either side, and it wasn't hard to see which Hester had favoured: the cushions on the left were flattened and misshapen from years of use and a small rosewood table stood next to the chair, piled with day-to-day necessities – a magnifying glass and some indigestion powders, knitting shoved unfinished into a bag and a cup and saucer. Were it not for the dust and the flies and the sickly, cloying smell of a cottage so unnaturally sealed over the summer, Josephine could easily have believed that Hester would return at any minute. The intimacy of these redundant, commonplace items moved her, and she felt again the lack of privacy in death that had so horrified her in her own home.

The rest of the room was well furnished, but sparse: a dresser and Wedgwood dinner service; a central table, missing the chairs she had seen earlier; and a heavy oak sideboard with an oil lamp and wireless set, the latter placed within easy reach of Hester's chair. A clock on the wall above it must have met with an accident at some point because the glass from its face was missing; Josephine set the hands to half past three, then wound it and was pleased to find it working. The clock had a light, amiable tick, not one of those ponderous sounds that seem to drain the life from a room, and only when it filled the air did she realise how silent the house had been. Her foot caught something under the sideboard and she bent down to look at an old wicker dog basket, covered with a blanket; there was a ball inside, chewed and squashed out of shape, and Josephine wondered what had happened to the dog. She looked round the room and the self-contained life it bore witness to: an animal's love, the voice of a stranger on the radio – all the company that Hester had wanted.

In the far corner of the parlour, an open doorway led through to a scullery and a brown velvet curtain covered the entrance to the staircase. There was another downstairs room, but Josephine went over to the windows first: the air in the cottage was stale and oppressive, and she wanted to let the outside world in again, to fill the house with the contentment she had felt in the garden. She opened each casement as far as fragile hinges would allow, much to the relief of the flies that tapped pointlessly against the glass; many had not been so lucky, and she brushed them off the window ledge with the edge of the curtain. A rich fragrance rose up from the flower beds below, and she was glad of the time of year: the bleakness of winter would have made a sad task unbearable.

When she walked into the room next door, she found the first real

traces of the person she had read about: the parlour could have belonged to any elderly woman, but this was unmistakably the home of
an actress. Production photographs and framed playbills covered the
walls, and Josephine's attention was drawn to the poster in the centre,
an advertisement for a week-long run of *Maria Marten* in Lincoln starring Hester and her husband. She was interested to see that the 1910
cast had included a young Tod Slaughter, and that Walter Paget had
also arranged the music; the upright piano at the end of the room was
probably his, she thought, and she wondered if Hester had played, too.
A modest bookcase along one wall had exceeded its limits long ago,
and the books spilled out onto the floor – play texts, mostly, interspersed with well-thumbed memoirs by Hester's contemporaries and a
few novels, read less avidly if their spines were anything to go by. There
were several editions of the Red Barn melodrama, some with acting
notes scribbled in the margins, and Josephine was touched when she
recognised her own play *Richard of Bordeaux* among the volumes. She
walked over to Hester's desk and picked up the address book that lay
open on a blotter; the desk stood under the window with the missing
pane and rain had stained some of the pages, but enough was still visible to show the circle of people that Hester and Walter had numbered
among their friends. Josephine was struck by the contrast between her
godmother's married and widowed lives, and she wondered which had
come more naturally to her – conviviality, or solitude? The handwriting, bold and flamboyant, suggested the former.

The drawers were full of letters and bills, stashed away without any
apparent order; only one of them was locked, and Josephine hoped
that she might find the rumoured memoir there when she eventually
located the key. In the mean time, she contented herself with a closer
look at what Hester had surely regarded as the most precious thing
her desk had to offer – a photograph of her husband. He was pictured
many times on the wall, but this image – with only his wife for an
audience – was relaxed and spontaneous. He was sitting on the bench
where Josephine had sat earlier, dressed in old gardening clothes, and,

from the immaturity of the flower beds, she guessed it had been taken when the cottage was still new to them. In the background, she could see a figure tending the climbing rose – perhaps a daily woman, hired to look after the cottage while they were away on tour – but nothing could detract from the true focus of the picture: the love and happiness on Walter's face. A vase of dead roses stood next to the frame and, as Josephine leaned forward to open the window, she caught a faint whiff of foul-smelling water; she picked up the vase and emptied it into the bushes, then put it back in place, ready to be refilled.

There was a cupboard in the corner of the room, but the clutter of the desk had made a coward of her and she decided it could wait; she wasn't ready yet to see the full extent of what Hester had asked her to do, and there was still another level to go. She lifted the latch on the staircase door and found that the unevenness of the floor prevented it from opening any wider than a few inches; no doubt there would be other quirks to get used to, changes in the cottage as it had shifted and settled over the years, and she squeezed through the gap and climbed the stairs, careful not to catch her head on a low beam as she came out into what must have been Hester's bedroom, the room where she had died. Someone had made a cursory attempt to tidy the sheets and restore some dignity to the bed, but the rest of the room was in chaos: clothes and books under the bedstead, shoes all over the floor, and piles of unopened post spilling out of a box in the corner. A section of the room had been partitioned off, probably to form a children's bedroom in the days when the cottage had housed a large family, and Josephine could see through the open doorway that there was still a bed inside, piled high with clothes, knick-knacks and a miscellany of boxes. Her heart sank, not just for herself and what she had agreed to do, but for the lack of care with which Hester had obviously lived; her professional life – the life she had shared – was preserved and valued, but everyday pleasures seemed to have brought her little comfort. How anyone could have slept in a room like this was beyond Josephine; it held no peace, no sense of stillness or retreat. She flung open the windows, caring little now for their fragility. There was an unpleasant smell in the room that came partly from its staleness and partly from her own imagination, fed by the awareness of death, and she wanted it gone. It occurred to her for the first time that she had no idea who had found Hester's body, or – with her solitary way of life – how long she had lain here undiscovered.

The layout upstairs followed the one below and Josephine hesitated at the door to the final room, suddenly uneasy about what she might find on the other side. The sadnesses of her godmother's life and death had been cumulative, filling her with a growing melancholy as she moved through the house, and she was reluctant to look at anything else that would damage her sense of Hester's spirit and vitality. She took a deep breath and lifted the latch. The room was empty except for a neatly made single bed and small dressing table, and its tidiness was as disconcerting to Josephine as the confusion next door: she had never thought of Hester as the type to keep a room ready for guests. It was cleaner than the rest of the house, perhaps because there was less to trap the dust: a silver hand-held mirror and a rose bowl on the dressing table were the only signs of use, and Josephine had the odd sensation of standing in a room that had been prepared for someone who had never arrived. The roses here were faded but still alive, and she collected a handful of fallen petals and crushed them between her fingers, breathing in the smell of summer as a welcome relief from the staleness of the cottage. Had someone got this room ready for her? She dismissed the idea immediately: no one had known she was coming, and even if they had, it was an unlikely gesture of hospitality from a village that had never been welcome here. The flowers were fresher than they should have been, but they were the only intimation that Hester's instructions about access had not been observed and she put the thought to the back of her mind, preferring to believe in a trick of nature.

In the far corner there was an open doorway to a second staircase and she realised with relief that it led to the study, emerging in what she had believed to be a cupboard. One of the windows gave a view of the woods and the path to the village, the other looked out over fields that had changed neither their shape nor their purpose for hundreds of years. She watched as a horse pulled a cart up the hill, making easy work of a punishing rise, and thought about those who had stood here before her, contemplating the very same scene. The barn that had given the cottage its name might be long gone, but it was easy to see how the crime had lived on; there were no barriers to the past in this landscape, and Josephine could understand how real Maria Marten must have seemed to Hester here, how effortlessly she might have imagined herself back in that time.

The room's dual aspect made it airier than the rest of the house, its emptiness was more peaceful, but Josephine knew that she could not sleep here. It wasn't so much the knowledge that Hester had died next door – in a building as old as this, it would be more remarkable if someone hadn't reached the end of their days within its walls – it was more a sense of intrusion, stronger here than anywhere else in the cottage. The instinct would have been hard to explain and even harder to rationalise, but it seemed to Josephine that Hester had never really been comfortable in this room and the feeling was infectious. She considered her options: choosing somewhere from Miss Peck's list meant either ingratiating herself in the village or finding some transport to go further afield, and she was tired and not in the mood for conversation. She also knew that the longer she avoided spending a night at Red Barn Cottage, the more significant its drawbacks would become in her mind. Better to start as she meant to go on. The study was the room she felt most at home in, where there was an open fireplace and a chaise longue. It would do, at least for now.

Back downstairs, she realised how much she took for granted in her own kitchen. It would be a miracle here if she could make a cup of tea before nightfall, let alone anything more substantial, and she cursed herself for not bringing any basic supplies with her; the village shop – if such a thing even existed – would have closed long ago. There was a bucket of coke standing ready by the range, and she used it to give herself at least the prospect of hot water; the water pump, she had noticed, was by the back door and she prayed that the Suffolk summer had not been sufficiently hot to dry the well, but she was in luck – when the water hit the bottom of the pail, it was clear and plentiful. One of the hotplate covers was missing from the range and the lid of the kettle was nowhere to be found, but she put the two together in good faith and hoped that the system would prove more efficient than it looked.

The scullery was dark, even with the back door ajar. Over the years, the climbing rose had been allowed to cover the window, making it impossible to open the casement or to see anyone approaching the cottage from the track to the road. Josephine rejected several lamps before finding one with some oil left in it, but she persevered in her search because the gloom was depressing. It would have to be used sparingly, because there were only stub ends in the candlesticks and she could not rely on being able to find replacements, but she did not intend to spend long in this part of the house and it would see her through a cursory investigation of the cupboards and, if she was lucky, the makings of some sort of meal; after that, she could retreat to the study with a fire for company and worry about everything else in the morning. As soon as the lamp was lit, she wondered if ignorance had perhaps not been better after all. She had not expected the floor to be clean – the stickiness and crunch of sugar underfoot had told her as much – but she was unprepared for the volume of ants and other insects that it seemed possible to squeeze into a Polstead square inch. In the absence of any other interest, nature had set about taking the cottage back, and nowhere more vigorously than in a damp patch on the outside wall, where a family of slugs seemed so at home that Josephine was tempted to ask them where they kept the tea. Shuddering, she forced herself to open the nearest cupboard door and was surprised to find it piled high with tins and packets. There was no order to the arrangement, and nor were the supplies limited to food items: tomato soup sat alongside weedkiller, corned beef next to furniture polish, and she eventually found the tea caddy hiding behind a tub of ant powder. She checked to make sure the tea was what she thought it was, and emptied the ant powder onto the floor.

The cups and plates from the dresser were dirty and stained, and she knew as soon as she looked at them that the first kettle of hot water would not be wasted on tea. As she piled the crockery into the sink ready to wash, she noticed the marks of age and use and smiled when she remembered what John MacDonald had said: if the kitchen sink *was* what Lucy Kyte wanted from the cottage, she was welcome to it. She chose an unambitious meal from the newer-looking tins, and allowed herself to be lured back out into the garden. It amazed her, as it did every year, that summer passed so quickly, slipping through her fingers into August long before she felt she had made the most of its beauty. The dense canopy of woodland was reassuring, though, its leaves still tightly stitched together, its green a youthful contrast to the hedgeless acres of corn. The persistent call of a wood pigeon seemed to deepen the silence as she opened the garden gate and walked out into the field to look back at the cottage from a distance. A thin pencil line of smoke rose leisurely from one of the chimneys now, and Josephine wondered why that small gesture of something restored should hearten her so. She had a long night in a strange house ahead of her; no bed to speak of, tinned ham for supper and a whole house to clean before she could even begin to make sense of Hester's past. If she had known the extent of what awaited her, she might never have got on the train; now she was here, she had rarely felt more content.

3

Josephine woke early to a morning full of sunshine, a bright, no-non-sense day that matched her mood. She had slept like the dead, despite the inadequacies of her makeshift bed, but the crick in her back and neck soon brought her to her senses: however reasonable her reser-vations about the bedrooms, she could not continue to behave like a nervous guest in her own home. While the kettle began its leisurely journey towards boiling, she went upstairs and stripped both beds, not allowing herself to look too closely at anything, then took the bundle of laundry outside. The washhouse was at the back of the cottage next to the lavatory, and the path to both was marked by a rope at waist height – a practical gesture for which Josephine had been grate-ful when she ventured out reluctantly the night before. She loaded the sheets into the copper and made several trips to the pump, vowing to be more lenient with Mrs McPherson the next time her laundry came back with something missing or damaged.

The water would take some time to heat – a country life, it seemed, involved a lot of waiting when you were new to it – and she took her tea out to the garden to see what had been missed the day before. The state of the land belied the years of work that had gone into making it beau-tiful, and she wondered if Hester had had any help, or if it had simply been a labour of love. On closer inspection, the vegetable patch was not as redundant as it had seemed: the potato plants had flowered and withered, signalling the time to dig, and there were good crops of both peas and beetroot – never her favourite food, but she supposed she would find a use for it. Most of the soft fruits had been lost to the birds but, from the various birdbaths and seed trays that she had seen dotted around, Josephine guessed that they would not have been grudged their victory. In the far corner, where the nettles were advancing from the shade of the woodland, she found a couple of collapsed henhouses and an old well, reclaimed by ivy and scrambling bindweed, its handsome flowers covering the brickwork with hundreds of small white parasols. For something so crucial to most of her daily comforts, the well was in a woeful state. She lifted the lid gingerly, afraid that the rotting wood might disintegrate in her hand, and peered inside; the rope was frayed and the bucket long gone, so she threw a stone down and hoped for the best; the splash came quickly and Josephine replaced the lid, confident that the water was plentiful for now and grateful to an unseen network of underground streams. There was a certain magic in the idea of cool, clear water running silently below the earth, rewarding the faith of generations even when the grass was brown and the soil dry and cracked from the sun; all the same, as she walked back to the cottage, she found herself calculating the cost of a new drainage system.

By the time the sheets were hung on the line, Josephine felt as though she had already done a full day's work and it was only half past ten. She used the rest of the hot water to sluice down the flagstones in the scullery, then made herself respectable and set off into the village, wondering how accurate Bert's half-mile would prove to be. Her path made its way between the wood and a fragrant hay meadow, still to be cut and rich in buttercups, scabious and thistles. The day was warm for its hour, and Josephine was content to walk in the shade of the trees and marvel at the beauty of the English countryside, a scene as carefully shaped by generations of craftsmen as any line of buildings or architectural triumph. She found it impossible to say why England moved her so – whether it was her roots here on her mother's side or the places she had been happy in, or some far less tangible emotion – but it had always been this way. Scotland was in her blood and she would defend it to her very last breath, but England gave her a sense of peace and belonging that needed no defence – and for that she blessed it.

Everything was still as the route led her past another pond and into a woodland thicket: there was no scurrying in the bushes, no flapping of wings from branch to branch, and the birds seemed too hot even to sing. Before very long, she caught sight of some chimneys through the trees and the path brought her out onto the village green, opposite Bert's garage. There was no sign of him, but two young girls – identical except for their clothes – were playing in the small yard at the front. 'Is your father about?' she asked, walking over to them.

'He's up at the Hall, fixing the Bentley again,' one of them said, and something in the exaggerated way she gestured with her arm told Josephine that this was the Lizzie of theatrical ambition. 'He won't be back until dinner-time.'

'Then perhaps you could give him a message for me?'

Lizzie nodded, but before Josephine could tell her what it was, a woman came out from the house. 'Can I help you?' she asked.

The voice was an octave higher, but the tone matched Bert's first words to her exactly. Josephine smiled and introduced herself. 'You must be Mrs Willis?'

The woman – an older version of her daughters and the source of their red hair and freckled skin – shook the hand that was offered to her but made no other show of friendship, and Josephine acknowledged the foolishness of assuming that affability ran in families; she had reckoned without the natural suspicions of the female sex. 'I wanted to thank your husband for his help yesterday,' she said. 'He gave me a lift to Red Barn Cottage.'

'Yes, he mentioned it.'

'He also said I should come and see you if I needed anything, and there's a broken window at the cottage. I wondered . . .'

'Bert's very busy at the moment.'

'Oh I didn't mean I wanted *him* to mend it. I just wondered if he could tell me who might. Or perhaps you know someone?' Josephine looked at the woman's stony face and felt herself begin to ramble. 'I'm still finding my feet and I have no idea who does what in the village, but I'd like to get the basics done while I'm here.'

'Are you selling it, then?'

She was tempted to remind Mrs Willis whose business that was, but stuck to the simple truth. 'I haven't decided.'

'Well, Deaves will sort you out. He's over in Stoke. Odd jobs aren't really Bert's sort of thing. He did enough of those for Miss Larkspur and precious little thanks he got for it.' To Josephine, a car seemed a reasonable acknowledgement of kindness; Bert's wife seemed to know what she was thinking. 'Oh I don't mean the car. What use is that to us? I mean her attitude to him and the kids before she died. Friendly with them for years and then nothing. It was as if they didn't exist. I don't mind people keeping themselves to themselves – the world might be a better place if a few more of us did that. But you can't give friendship and then take it back for no reason. They worshipped her, all three of them.'

'I'm sorry,' Josephine said, resenting the apology but feeling obliged to make it. 'I had no idea there was a problem. Your husband didn't say anything.'

'He wouldn't. Too soft by halves, my Bert.' There was a slight emphasis on the 'my', and Josephine wondered how much of Mrs Willis's anger on behalf of her family was actually a more personal resentment. She pulled the twins close to her, as though afraid of history repeating itself, then said again: 'It's Tom Deaves you want. He'll sort out anything that needs doing around the cottage.'

Josephine thanked her and walked back across the green, bewildered by such an unexpected confrontation and wondering – almost as a challenge to herself – whom she could offend now with a simple request for groceries. There was a small sweet shop on the corner, but nothing more substantial so she set off down the hill, wary of asking directions. She found what she was looking for at the top of a lane leading off the main street, but stopped before she got to it, distracted by a striking sixteenth-century farmhouse – the only building that fitted Bert's description of William Corder's house. It dominated the hill, looking out across the village pond and distant countryside, and it occurred to Josephine that such a commanding position would not have been quite so enviable once news of the murder got out. There was a small boy playing under an old cherry tree, but no other signs of modern life and the house must have changed very little in the last hundred years. She looked up at the dark windows, trying to imagine what they had seen: the pain of Corder's family – if he had had a family – the simmering resentments of class within the village which must have been intensified by the murder. She knew next to nothing about it, but what interested her was what interested her about any crime: how ordinary people had felt, caught up in the violence through no fault of their own, their lives changed for ever by a few minutes. Somehow, she didn't think she would find the answers in Hester's melodrama.

Sounds from the shop brought her back to the present day – the clang of a bell and soft murmur of voices; the hiss of rice poured onto scales and chime of coins in the till. Bracing herself as she went in, she found herself in a queue of three and the object of a barely disguised curiosity. The shop was, she was pleased to see, very well stocked, although it seemed to be arranged according to the same principles as Hester's cupboards. 'Won't keep you a moment, Miss Tey,' said the woman behind the counter, her familiarity suggesting that Josephine had been shopping there for years. The speed with which news had travelled unsettled her but she, of all people, shouldn't have been surprised: everything there was to know about Inverness passed through her father's high-street shop and she swore sometimes that he knew other people's business better than they did; there was no reason to think it would be any different here.

'Right – what can I get you?'

The other women had finished their shopping but showed no sign of leaving, so Josephine handed over her list. 'There's rather a lot, I'm afraid.'

'And you'd like it delivered?'

'Yes please, except for the fresh food. I'll take that now. When will the oil arrive? I ran out last night.'

'You spent the night in that cottage?'

40

Josephine looked at her. 'Of course,' she said, as though the thought of going elsewhere had never entered her head. 'Why ever not?'

The bystanders exchanged a glance and Josephine thought she saw one of them shudder, but the proprietress recovered quickly. 'Oh, just that you must be used to your home comforts,' she said, so convincingly that Josephine almost believed it was what she had meant. 'You'll be selling it, I expect.'

The determination to get her out of the village before she had even settled in was, she supposed, a natural reaction to outsiders and not reserved especially for her, but it was beginning to grate on Josephine and she said, a little waspishly, 'Not at the moment, no. There's a lot to sort out and I want to spend some time there.'

'Probably just as well. You'd be hard-pushed to find a buyer, stuck all the way out there on its own.'

For Josephine, that was beginning to be one of the cottage's most attractive features. 'My godmother loved it for its history,' she said. 'I'm sure she's not the only person who finds that interesting.'

'Yes, we saw you having a look at the old Corder place.'

'It's a handsome house,' Josephine said defensively, then stopped trying to hide her interest; if Hester had been brazen about it, why shouldn't she? 'Are there any Corders or Martens left in the village?'

The elder of the two customers gave her a filthy look. 'They'd hardly show their faces round here, would they?'

Quite why two families – and particularly the family of the victim – should be held responsible for a hundred-year-old crime was beyond Josephine, but she didn't argue. 'Well, you must be pleased to be opposite one of the attractions,' she said brightly, picking up her basket. 'I expect it's good for trade. Now – can you tell me how to get to Stoke?'

'It's a couple of miles out on the Mill Road, past the rectory,' the shopkeeper said, her words barely audible over the muttering in Josephine's left ear.

'Thank you, Miss . . . ?'

'Elsie Gladding. *Mrs* Elsie Gladding. And the oil will be round later.'

Josephine closed the door behind her, wondering if one of the legacies of Maria Marten's fate was an obsession with the marital state: the women of Polstead seemed very keen to lay claim to their husbands. Her brief visit to the shop had given her plenty to think about: she had declared her intention to spend time at Red Barn Cottage out of sheer defiance, but she realised now that it was true. If she worked hard, the cottage would be in good shape by the weekend and she could leave it ready to come back to in September, when she had had time to make arrangements at home. It would give her the peace and quiet she needed to get to grips with *Claverhouse*, as well as sorting through Hester's papers; she could even ask Marta to join her for a few days. Having made her decision, she smiled all the way down the hill, her pace quickened by the smell of bread baked that morning and the prospect of a decent lunch.

As she started down the track to the cottage, she saw someone leave the garden by the far gate and head out across the fields. It was a woman, but that was all Josephine could be sure of from a distance, and her calls went unheeded; by the time she reached the gate herself, the visitor was out of sight. She went round to the back, where she had left the door open to dry the scullery floor, and knew instantly that someone had been inside – not from any tangible signs, but from the subtle imprint in the air of a room that has recently been occupied. In the parlour, she found the proof of her suspicions: two parcels stacked neatly on the table, one addressed to her in Marta's handwriting, the other to Hester and postmarked London. She breathed a sigh of relief: it wasn't the most orthodox of postal methods and she resented the intrusion, but at least the caller had had no other motive. Although she had tried to put it from her mind, the prospect of an unannounced visit from Lucy Kyte was not something that Josephine welcomed and she hoped John MacDonald would be able to track the woman down before it happened.

The post was poignant: two names and only one address, another reminder of the changes that the cottage had lived through. She put

Hester's package to one side and tore the paper off her own, thinking how typical it was of Marta to find a way of welcoming her without intruding. The present was a book – a gift from Marta invariably belonged on a shelf or in a vase – and Josephine laughed when she saw the title: *First Home, First Class: The Modern Woman's Guide to Household Management*. Inside, she found The Modern Woman engaged in a series of domestic tasks, each of which she accomplished with irritating perfection by following the manual to the letter, and she took comfort from the thought that one encounter with Elsie Gladding, Mrs, would soon wipe the modern smirk off her modern face. She turned to the inscription on the flyleaf – 'Let me know when it's decent. I won't sleep with slugs, even for you.' – and pictured Marta's face on seeing the state of the scullery. Her message, as she no doubt knew, was a greater incentive to Josephine than any words of wisdom from the manual's anonymous author.

There was already enough post in the box upstairs, so she unwrapped the parcel meant for Hester, too. It was another book, but this one came from a dealer in London and there was nothing remotely modern about it. Intrigued, Josephine read the accompanying letter.

My dear Miss Larkspur,

Please accept my apologies for the delay in sending your 1811 edition of The Old English Baron *by Mrs Clara Reeve, but I have only recently returned to London from France. The validation which you requested – quite rightly, I might add – also proved more difficult to obtain than I first anticipated, but I enclose the book now with every assurance of its authenticity and I trust you will agree that it is well worth the wait. It is, as you are aware, a very special volume – one of the most precious I have come across – and it gives me great pleasure to know that it could not have ended up in better hands. As a small point of interest, its author was local to you – born in Ipswich – and the novel was originally published as* The Champion of Virtue. *There is an irony in that which I am sure you will appreciate when you consider the book's history!*

It has recently been my good fortune to acquire something which I think you will find even more fascinating than the present volume. When I am satisfied that the object is genuine, I will write to you with the details and perhaps you would care to drop by next time you are in town? It is always a joy to see you.

The letter was signed by a John Moore. Looking at the accompanying bill, Josephine found it easy to believe that his joy was genuine; she was astonished by how much Hester had been willing to pay for what seemed to her a perfectly ordinary book. It was a nice edition, illustrated with a series of elegant engravings, but the binding was scuffed and worn and the flyleaf – inscribed by a vicar whose name Josephine could not quite make out – suggested nothing more out of the ordinary than a Sunday school prize. Hester had valued it, though, and the delay in its dispatch mattered more than the bookseller could have known. It saddened Josephine to think that her godmother would never see something that she had obviously coveted. Although Gothic novels were hardly her cup of tea, she resolved to keep it to read. One day.

Tempting as it was to while away the day looking through Hester's book collection, Josephine resisted. There was work to be done upstairs which she wasn't looking forward to, and the sooner she made a start, the better. Other than setting aside some financial papers to leave with John MacDonald when she was back in Inverness, she made no attempt to sort through the mound of post or to rationalise the chaos under Hester's bed; instead, she put it all in a box to deal with next time, and shut it away in the small end room where it was at least out of sight. It took her the rest of the day to scrub the floorboards upstairs, clean the windows and make up a comfortable bed in Hester's old room. By the time she had finished, late into the evening, she was ready to fall into it.

4

The climbing rose put up a good fight, but eventually Josephine cleared enough of its branches away to free the scullery window. She picked up the debris, cursing as the thorns caught her hands, and was about to take it round to the back when she heard the click of the front gate. A woman – smartly dressed and around her own age – was peering through the study window, and there was a bicycle propped up against the hedge.

'Ah! You are here – splendid. Thought I'd had a wasted trip.' The woman advanced towards Josephine with her hand outstretched. 'Hilary Lampton. Vicar's wife, for my sins – quite literally, I sometimes think. I was hoping you might give me a few lines for the parish newsletter.' She must have seen Josephine's face fall because she added: 'I know. We're a dreadful breed but, if it helps, I wasn't born to it and I'm generally thought to fall rather short of the mark. We'll have some tea, shall we? I've left the children with their father so there's plenty of time. I love them dearly, of course I do, but it's so nice to pretend they're someone else's for a while.' All of this was said in a single breath, and she was inside the cottage before Josephine had a chance to argue. 'Gosh, it's changed since I was last here. You *have* been busy.'

Josephine looked round the only room she hadn't touched, and was distracted from expressing a polite interest in the vicar's children. 'Changed in what way?'

'Emptier. It's been a couple of years since I was here, I suppose. It was when Miss Larkspur got a part in that film – something for the bloody newsletter again. I don't remember exactly, but she had some lovely things – paintings, antique furniture, that sort of stuff. We all have different tastes, though, don't we? And there's much more space now.' The compliment was recompense for an imagined faux pas and Josephine opened her mouth to explain, but Hilary had moved on for both of them. 'Madeira,' she said, bouncing a cake onto the table. 'Don't worry – I didn't bake it myself. One of Stephen's parishioners sent it over. I've no idea which one. So many women in the village are desperate to look after him and I'm not sure he needs me at all – but it does mean there's always something to pop round with.' She looked doubtfully at the cake and moved it to a different angle. 'Bit bashed from the basket but I'm sure it'll taste all right.'

It took Josephine a moment or two to catch up with the way in which her peace had been shattered, and only when her guest sat down and beamed expectantly at her did she remember that she was supposed to be boiling the kettle. 'I see you've caught the bug,' Hilary said into the pause, picking up the copy of the melodrama that Josephine had got out to read. 'Funny how it does that to incomers. I was exactly the same when I moved here, but people who are born in the village don't give a hoot about the Red Barn murder.'

'So I've noticed. I made the mistake of asking about it in the shop.'

'Ah, you've met Elsie, then? Her bark's worse than her bite and she's a good sort, but three of her brothers were killed in France and the death of a whore has lost its power to shock.'

The words jarred and Josephine looked at the vicar's wife with a new interest; tea with someone who was willing to discuss the village and its history in such an open way might not be the ordeal she was expecting. 'Sugar?' she asked, and Hilary nodded.

'As far as Elsie's concerned, Maria Marten was a silly girl who got what was coming to her, and you won't find many dissenting voices. I suppose they're right, in a way. Why should her name be shouted from the stage – celebrated, even – when their dead only get a line on a plaque and a service once a year? The fact that it's a good story doesn't seem a very adequate answer, somehow, does it?' She turned the pages thoughtfully, then smiled. 'It *is* a good story, though.'

'Is it?'

'Good God, yes. It's marvellous. I shouldn't say this to a writer, but you couldn't make it up.' Hilary settled back into Hester's chair, her reason for coming all but forgotten. 'What *do* you know?'

Josephine repeated what she had been told. 'Innocent maiden, seduced by the village squire and killed in a barn in eighteen something.'

'Eighteen twenty-seven, yes. William Corder wasn't the squire, though. He was the son of one of the richer tenant farmers. The squire was at Polstead Hall, and Maria never had him. The closest she got was his brother-in-law, a chap called Matthews who lived in London. She had a son by him before she started seeing William.'

'And didn't she have a child by Corder's brother as well?'

'Yes. Thomas Corder was her first lover, but the child died.' She grinned. 'Doesn't look good on paper, does it? You've got to admire her spirit, though, and she aimed high – that's what I like about Maria. It's what I always tell the girls at Sunday School – know what you want and go for it.'

A murdered girl with illegitimate children by different fathers was an interesting role model for a vicar's wife, Josephine thought. She was beginning to see why Stephen's choice might be frowned upon in certain circles; personally, she thought Hilary Lampton was the best advert for the church she'd seen in years. 'What was so special about Maria?'

'Well, she was very pretty, in that fresh-faced, rather coy way. Have you seen Curtis's book?' Josephine shook her head. 'There's bound to be a copy here somewhere. James Curtis – he covered the case for *The Times* and published a book on it afterwards. There's a drawing of Maria in that. She was a real charmer, by all accounts. William might have been above her socially, but he was punching well over his weight in every other sense, and that's always dangerous in a man. Are you married, Josephine?'

She rapped the question out with a no-nonsense brusqueness and Josephine felt at liberty to answer in the same vein, without explanations or apologies. 'No.'

'I don't blame you. It can cramp your style.'

The comment was wistful rather than bitter, and Josephine wondered whether the regrets it implied stemmed from the role Hilary had married into or the marriage itself. She looked forward to meeting Stephen. 'How long have you been here?' she asked.

'Sixteen years,' Hilary said, so readily that Josephine half-expected her to count off the months and days as well. 'We met in London. I was involved in a charity in the East End, and Stephen was the pastor. He got the job up here soon after we married.'

'And your children?'

'Sixteen, ten and eight. All boys. Probably just as well. If we'd had a girl, I might have called her Maria out of sheer devilment.'

Josephine laughed. 'So what about the original Maria? Any other lovers before William?'

'No, he was her third but there was nothing very lucky about it. They walked out for a bit, moonlit trysts in the Red Barn, that sort of thing, and then the inevitable happened. Her family wanted Corder to make an honest woman of her, but he always had an excuse.'

'Yes, I can imagine.'

'To be fair, they were good excuses. His father died, so he had more responsibilities on the farm, then one brother drowned in the pond and two others caught TB and shuffled off as well. God knows what that must have been like for his mother – then the only son left gets himself hanged, selfish bastard. But I've jumped – where did I get to?'

'Maria was pregnant.'

'Oh yes. Well, they shipped her out to Sudbury to have the baby, but it died soon after she brought it back.'

'That must have solved a few problems,' Josephine said cynically. 'How did the child die?'

'Natural causes, I think, although there *were* rumours later when the whole thing came out.'

'Still, it must have taken the pressure off Corder to get her to the altar.'

'You'd think so, wouldn't you? But it didn't. Nobody else was going to touch Maria by then, so he was her family's last hope.' She drained her cup, and Josephine poured more tea. 'Stephen sees his fair share of modern-day Marias, you know, and nothing's really changed. The shame for the Martens in a village like this must have been unbearable.'

Josephine couldn't help thinking that things must have been blacker still for Maria. 'Did she actually *want* to marry him, I wonder?'

Hilary gave a sympathetic smile. 'I shouldn't think anybody stopped to ask. A woman in Maria's position doesn't have many options. Anyway, after a few more false promises, Corder finally agreed to take her to Ipswich and marry her there. He turned up at the Martens' cottage one morning with some men's clothes for Maria so that nobody would recognise her, and they went separately to the Red Barn.' Hilary paused, then finished dramatically in a hushed tone of which Hester would have been proud: 'Maria was never seen alive again.' Josephine tried not to look disappointed. She was pleased to hear a story that belonged to a village she was getting to know, but she still didn't quite understand why it had become so legendary. 'I know what you're thinking,' Hilary said, 'but it gets much more interesting once Maria is dead.'

'Go on.'

'William came back to the village a few days later, claiming some sort of delay with the marriage licence. He told Maria's family that she was staying in Ipswich until it could be sorted out, then spun a load of other reasons why they hadn't heard from her.'

'Such as?'

'Oh, she was too busy to write or had hurt her hand. That sort of thing.'

'Were they particularly stupid?' Josephine asked.

'I think it was more a case of life being easier with Maria out of the village. They chose not to ask too many questions, and whatever they really thought, William was confident enough to stay in Polstead until the harvest was in. Then he left as well.'

'Thinking he'd got away with it, I suppose.'

'For a while, yes – until they found Maria's body, buried in the barn. She'd been there for nearly a year.'

'Is it true that her mother told them where to look?'

'Her stepmother. Maria's mother died when she was a little girl and her father remarried. It came to her in a dream, apparently.'

'I bet it did,' Josephine said, beginning to see why the story was so popular.

'It's funny, isn't it? Nobody questioned that at the time. They tracked Corder down to London, and do you know what he'd done?'

It was a rhetorical question, but Josephine took a guess. 'Killed someone else?'

'No, quite the contrary. He'd advertised for a wife, married one of the respondents and started running a girls' school.'

'Good God!'

'Quite. Can you believe the nerve of the man?' Hilary cut another large slice of cake for each of them. 'It's not bad, this, is it? I must tell Stephen to thank whoever it was so we get another one. Anyway, the police brought Corder back here to attend the inquest. I'd love to have been a fly on the wall that night.'

'If Maria had been in the earth for a year, there were probably plenty of those already,' Josephine said. 'Did he confess?'

'Not until the eve of his execution. He put up his own defence – they had to in those days – but I gather the legal stuff on the other side was quite clever. They weren't sure how he'd killed her, so they charged him with every method they could think of just to make sure.'

'I'm not sure if that sounds clever or incompetent.'

'No, you've got a point. Still, he swung for it. I doubt Bury's ever seen anything like it. Thousands of people turned up, from all over the country. They sold the rope for a guinea an inch, apparently. His scalp's still on display in Moyse's Hall. You must go while you're here.'

Josephine remembered the name of the museum from Hester's will. 'Yes, I'll do that. There are some things of Hester's there that I'd like to see as well.' She smiled and pointed to the study, where piles of scrapbooks and theatre programmes could be seen through the open door. 'Not that I'm short of Hester's memorabilia here. I've barely scratched the surface.'

'Do you need a hand? I'm sure it's fascinating stuff.'

A vision passed through Josephine's mind of Hilary and a band of Stephen's loyal parishioners descending on the cottage to get things organised, and she said hurriedly: 'Thank you, but it's fine. There's no urgency and I'm actually quite enjoying myself.' She looked out of the window and changed the subject: 'Where *was* the Red Barn?'

'Oh, about a hundred yards from here,' Hilary said. She waved her hand in an indeterminate direction that left Josephine none the wiser.

'And did you say Corder's mother was still alive at the time?'

'Yes, although I imagine she wished she weren't. She didn't stay in the village for very long afterwards. You wouldn't, would you? Just came back to be buried.' She dabbed at the crumbs on her plate absent-mindedly. 'Have you been to the church yet?'

'I'm afraid I'm not really a churchgoer.'

'Oh, don't apologise for that. Quite frankly, the chapel's knocking us into a cocked hat at the moment. It's such a shame for Stephen – he writes lovely sermons, and they take him days. No, I just wondered if you'd seen the graveyard. The Corders are there, lined up in a row, and it's really quite impressive. I hate to say it, but there's often a bigger crowd outside than in.'

'Is Maria there, too?'

'Some of her.'

'I'm sorry?'

'I tell you, Josephine, that girl's been in and out of the ground more often than a farmer's shovel. They dug her up from the barn and hauled her into the Cock for the inquest, then it's up to the church as quick as you like, only to find they don't know enough about how she died, so up she comes again. They were even passing her skull round in court during the trial. Is it any wonder the press had a field day?' She was quiet for a moment, then spoke more seriously. 'It's her son I feel sorry for. I know he was only two when Maria was killed, but she was a good mother, by all accounts – husband or no husband. Kids take things in, don't they? He must have missed her.'

'What happened to him?'

Hilary shrugged. 'Who knows? That's one of the frustrating things about the story – no one bothers with the minor casualties. But yes, his mother's in the churchyard. Stephen can show you where her grave is. There's no stone left now – it was all chipped away by souvenir hunters. I can understand people taking bits of the barn and selling them, but I'd like to think a gravestone was off limits. No wonder your godmother wouldn't be seen dead there.'

It was said without any obvious irony, and Josephine stifled a smile. 'What happened to the woman Corder married?'

'She stood by him throughout the whole thing. Did I tell you she was carrying his child by then?'

'No.'

'There was a son, born a few months after the execution. She was religious, apparently – one of those genuinely good people.' She spoke with a sense of wonder, and Josephine couldn't help but think that someone in Hilary's position should sound more blasé about goodness. 'Anyway, talking of faith and duty, I must go and rescue Stephen from the children so he can get on with Sunday's sermon. He works far too hard. If he's not careful, he'll end up as archdeacon and then I really will have to leave him.' She stood and picked up her gloves, apparently oblivious to the newsletter's lack of copy. 'It's been lovely, though. We must do it again.'

They walked out into the garden together and Hilary paused by the gate, looking back at the cottage. 'I'm so pleased she didn't leave after all, aren't you? It would have been such a shame.'

'I'm sorry – I don't know what you mean.'

'Miss Larkspur. She was making plans for when the cottage got too much for her. She told Stephen that it would break her heart to leave, but she wasn't getting any younger. I think she intended to go back to London, but that might be my assumption.' The plan was perfectly sensible – its isolation alone would make Red Barn Cottage impossible for an older woman – and yet it surprised Josephine. She was trying to work out why as Hilary added: 'It's right somehow that she should die here. She was so much a part of the place. Now she can stay with her ghosts.'

Josephine smiled. 'Maria and William, you mean?'

'Oh I'm sure they're about somewhere, but I was thinking more of Mr Paget. Stephen said she always felt him very strongly here after he died. That was one of the reasons she didn't want to leave.' She retrieved her bicycle from the hedge and put her bag in its basket. 'It must be nice to have a ghost you're fond of. We're stuck with the Reverend Whitmore. He was vicar here during Maria's time and he's supposed to ride a headless horse down Rectory Hill or something. I've never seen him, but we were blessed with a run of particularly nervous maids for a while and we couldn't keep one for more than a month. I begged Stephen to exorcise him but he said it wasn't ethical. Now we've got Beattie, and she seems to be made of much sterner stuff, thank God.' She smiled. 'Another couple of weeks here, and you'll never be short of a story.'

'I'm beginning to realise that.' Josephine thought about what Hilary had told her. 'Did you and Stephen know Hester well?'

'Stephen more than me. Miss Larkspur was one of those women who values men, I suppose. Please don't take that the wrong way – I don't mean it in the Maria sense. She was gracious and charming to me, but she sparkled when Stephen – or any man – came into the room, and they loved her.' Josephine remembered the look on John MacDonald's face and knew exactly what Hilary meant. 'You must come and speak to him about her. He'd love to meet you. How about supper after evensong on Sunday?'

'I'll have left by then, I'm afraid. I'm going into Hadleigh tomorrow morning to get the train.'

'All right. Let me know when you're back and we'll make a date.'

It was refreshing for Josephine to meet someone who expected her to stay. 'I don't suppose you've heard of a Lucy Kyte, have you? I think she was a friend of Hester's, but I'm not sure if she was local to here or not.'

Hilary thought for a moment and shook her head. 'Sorry, no, but I'm hopeless with names. You could try the parish register if you've got enough hours in your life. Then at least you'd know if the name was local. Would that help?'

'Yes, I suppose so,' Josephine said, although she couldn't quite see how. 'One last question before you go: do you know if Hester was writing a memoir? I read something about it in the Inverness paper.'

'She was definitely working on something. I don't know what – she wouldn't tell me – but when I went round about the film, she promised to give me something else for the newsletter before too long.'

'And that was two years ago?'

'Give or take, yes.' She started to push her bike out into the lane, then thought better of it. 'There was one other curious thing – you've probably heard it already. Back in May, the church bell rang in the middle of the night.'

'Because someone had died?'

'That's just it. No one *had* died – or so we thought – and no one would admit to the ringing. Then a couple of days later, Bert found Miss Larkspur's body.'

'Bert Willis?'

'That's right. Have you met him?'

'Yes, but he didn't say anything about finding Hester's body.'

'He probably didn't want to upset you. Now, how are you getting to Hadleigh in the morning?'

Josephine shrugged. 'I hadn't thought. A taxi, I suppose.'

Hilary's laughter rang out through the afternoon. 'You'll be lucky. I'll run you in myself – I've got to do some shopping. Nine thirty suit you?'

She pushed her bicycle away up the track, leaving Josephine in peace with plenty to think about.

54

5

She woke suddenly, her head full of dreams. The images from her conversation with Hilary had, in sleep, metamorphosed into a more personal hell, a nightmare in which she found herself searching Hester's garden for a body while a stream of strangers told her there was nothing wrong. She lay in the darkness, waiting for the real and illusory worlds to fall back into place, but her relief at waking did not entirely dispel the grief and anger of the dream. There were tears on her face, but she needed no physical reminder of the despair she had felt as she clawed at the earth until her hands bled, banging the ground in frustration and screaming for someone to listen because the body she was looking for was Marta's.

When the panic subsided, she realised that the banging, at least, was real, and was coming from the boxroom next to hers: a dull, regular thud where the window, freed by her efforts with the rose, had swung loose and was knocking against the cottage wall. She fumbled for the torch on her bedside table and pushed the sheets aside, glad to feel the cool night air on her skin. It was hardly the moment she would have chosen to face the chaos of that room for the first time, but she could not leave without securing it. She pushed some boxes to one side and stepped past them, the light from her torch picking out random objects that seemed as disconnected and surreal as the dream she had just left. The small bed was buried under mounds and mounds of clothes, all smelling of mothballs, cigarette smoke and a heavy, sickly perfume, and she had to fight a wave of claustrophobia as she crawled over them to get to the window. The catch had broken, and when she pulled it gently to she noticed that the hinges moved precariously in rotten wood – something else to add to the list of repairs when she was next here. For now, she wound an old piece of material around the handle and stared out into the blackness, hoping to see just one light that would connect her to another human being. There was nothing. Only memory led her gaze in the direction of the road.

Wide awake now, she went downstairs and lit the oil lamp in the study, using its reflection in the window as a comforting shield against the darkness outside. A pile of scrapbooks had toppled over onto the floor, and she opened the nearest one, delighted by the photographs of Hester in a series of contrasting roles. The year was 1901, the theatre a very different place from the modern stage, but it was a world that she could just about remember, and it was captured perfectly here: soft gas lamps, so like natural light; backcloths painted in a slapdash style and tattered around the edges; fumes from the warm, yellow foot-lights, creating a veil in front of the actors, and making them remote and mysterious to the audience. The scrapbook finished with a pan-tomime, *Babes in the Wood*, and she caught her breath when she reached the final picture, taken backstage and labelled simply 'Christmas, In-verness'. Hester was dressed as Robin Hood, but she had removed the feathered hat and given it to the little girl in her lap, and Josephine did not need to see the reflection in the dressing-room mirror to know that her mother had taken the photograph. The memory that had nagged at her in John MacDonald's office began to take shape: the house lights fading to a glimmer as the leader of the orchestra drew soft, shivering music from his men; the curtain rolling up to reveal the actors' feet, then their knees, then their faces, and finally the whole scene – all so magical to a five-year-old. Afterwards, her mother had taken her hand and led her round to the stage door, and she could still recall the bustle and laughter of the dressing room, the excitement of being allowed into a world that was out of bounds to ordinary people. She felt it to this day, even though she had earned her right to be back-stage in any theatre, and she realised now that Hester's legacy to her was more than bricks and mortar.

Gently, she removed the photograph from the page and turned it over. Sure enough, there was her mother's handwriting, a mild admonishment to a friend to come home more often. She looked again at the happiness on Hester's face and the loving way in which she held her goddaughter, and knew her for the first time as more than a ghost. In her mind, she could hear Hester's laughter, the sweetness of her voice, but it was impossible to know after so many years if it was a genuine memory or an obliging trick of the imagination, conjured up to soften the longing for all she had missed – all those years when she could have got to know Hester properly, perhaps even shared the grief of her mother's death. She tucked the picture in Curtis's book, which she had found and packed for the train, saddened by the knowledge of moments gone – precious moments, and she not there to see them.

6

Glancing through the window of Stewart, Rule & Co., Josephine marvelled at the deception practised by any decent secretary. The ability to go unnoticed was an essential requirement amongst a certain type of professional woman, and Jane Peck – small, quiet, faded Jane Peck – had excellent credentials: very few people would have given her a second glance, but in the tidy, unambitious world of Stewart, Rule & Co. she was a giant, and Josephine's experience of the firm over the years had shown very clearly who kept it going.

The secretary looked up as she heard the door, and smiled at her visitor across a modest, organised desk. 'How lovely to see you, Miss Tey – and congratulations. I hear your new book is to be made into a film. Your father told me all about it while I was shopping the other day.'

Of course he did, Josephine thought, picturing the pride on her father's face as he piled fruit into the basket of a captive audience. Normally she would have been embarrassed, but Miss Peck loved theatre and had shown a genuine interest in her work over the years, and she was one of the few people in Inverness whose good wishes could be taken at face value. 'Thank you,' she said, 'although I've no idea if I'll still be pleased when I've seen it. My meeting with Mr Hitchcock wasn't without its surprises.' That was an understatement, but she saw little point in disturbing the calm routine of the office with anything more. 'I've brought some papers for Mr MacDonald to look through.'

Miss Peck took the envelope from her and placed it on the desk with the rest of the morning's post. 'He's busy with a client at the moment, but I'll give them to him as soon as he's free.'

'They're not urgent – just some bank books and financial bits and pieces from Miss Larkspur's cottage. He asked me to look out for them while I was there.'

In a rare display of curiosity, Miss Peck seized her moment. 'We've been longing to know how you got on,' she admitted. 'Do you mind if I ask how you found the cottage?'

'It's winning me over gradually,' Josephine said, happy to indulge a glimmer of human curiosity from someone whose discretion she had always believed to be flawless to the point of indecent. 'It's in need of some love and it's far more isolated than I expected, but I'm not sure that's a bad thing. I've only met a few of the locals, but I think we'll take a while to get used to each other.'

Miss Peck nodded, apparently knowing exactly what she meant. 'The best way to deal with any village is to go about your business and keep your head down,' she said. In Josephine's opinion, it was a strategy that needn't be confined to village life, but she kept her thoughts to herself. 'And what sort of state is the house in?' Miss Peck asked. 'Were you able to stay there?'

'Yes, although I was tempted to flee to something on your list for comfort. Let's just say I got through an awful lot of bleach and I've taken out shares in ant powder.'

The secretary laughed, and gestured to the envelope that Josephine had brought with her. 'Well, at least you've made good progress in sorting through Miss Larkspur's papers. That must be a great weight off your mind.'

'To be honest, I've barely scratched the surface. I swear there's enough material there for three lifetimes, not one.'

'It's a very kind thing that you do,' Miss Peck said, and her sudden seriousness took Josephine by surprise. 'A decent thing. Sorting through someone's effects after a death can be distressing. We all do it as a duty, but not many of us would volunteer.'

She spoke from the heart, and Josephine remembered that she had had her own bereavement in recent months, a brother to whom she had been devoted and whose care throughout a long illness had fallen to her, the unmarried daughter of the family. 'I was sorry to hear about your loss,' she said.

'Thank you, but it was expected.'

It was the standard response from someone whose grief was still too raw to cope with kindness; Josephine had used it herself for months after her mother's death. In Miss Peck's case, she suspected that the sorrow of the loss itself was beginning to blur with a more complex mourning for sacrifices that had been asked of her own life. Josephine could only imagine the pain of acknowledging those lost, unreclaimable years, no matter how freely they had been given – although in time there was a chance she would know exactly how that felt. 'It must be difficult,' she said gently. 'When you've cared for someone for a long time, it's hard to find yourself again.'

She wondered if she had overstepped the mark with someone she barely knew, but Jane Peck seemed grateful for the understanding. 'I was certainly glad to come back to work,' she admitted. 'Giving this job up during those final months, when Cameron needed me all the time, was like losing my last hold on a normal life. It was good of Mr MacDonald to let me come back.' She glanced affectionately at the closed office door. 'It certainly keeps me occupied.'

Josephine allowed Miss Peck her pride, and wished that she did not know from gossip in the town that the secretary needed more than something to do. A woman of her age – late fifties, Josephine guessed, although she could not remember a time when Jane Peck had looked any different – should not *have* to work, but financial security was just one of the casualties of illness. 'I'm sure the firm was only too pleased to have you back,' she said, hoping not to sound as patronising as she felt.

'It does feel as though we've never been apart, I must say, and that makes things easier. And I was pleased to see your father looking so well.'

There was an implied solidarity in the comment, a comparison of their respective situations that Josephine resented but could not entirely dismiss. The knowledge of how her life would change if her father's health deteriorated was something she tried to push from her mind, although it often visited her late at night, when sleep was elusive. Was that how people would look at her? she wondered. With the same well-intentioned pity she felt for Miss Peck? 'Yes, he's very well,' she said firmly, as if she could will it to continue indefinitely.

Her defensiveness was obvious and Miss Peck respected it by turning back to business. 'Anyway, what I was going to say was that if you change your mind and decide you've taken on too much after all, just let Mr MacDonald know and he'll pay someone out of the estate to clear the cottage.'

Josephine nodded. 'That's kind of you, but I'm afraid I'm already hooked. Apart from anything else, I've started to come across things that my mother sent to Hester, and I couldn't possibly let a stranger dispose of those.'

'No, of course not. I understand.' She thought for a moment, then added: 'An unlikely friendship, I always thought. They were so different. Sometimes that helps, though, doesn't it?'

'I suppose so,' Josephine said. One of the things she hated most about living in a small town was this shared history amongst families: in Inverness, people always seemed to know each other well enough to have an opinion, but never well enough for it to be accurate. As far as she could tell, her mother and Hester had shared a sense of fun and independence, a love for those closest to them, which made them obvious companions.

'Your mother must have missed her dreadfully when she left,' Miss Peck continued. 'Still, it was the right thing for Miss Larkspur, no doubt. It left her free to have a life of her own, and she certainly made the most of it.' The words were positive enough, but they carried a note of resentment that Josephine had often heard in the voices of women whose lives bound them to Inverness; she herself was a peculiar hybrid of captive and deserter, fitting comfortably into neither camp, and she was glad when the telephone gave her an excuse not to respond. She waited patiently while Miss Peck dealt with the call, thinking about the expectations that her mother and Hester must have had placed on them when they were young. Her own family had once entertained the notion that she might enter into an understanding with the local gunsmith's son, and she had had to disillusion them with a phrase that contained the words 'dead' and 'body'; it must have been so much worse for an earlier generation of women, who had not had the barbed encouragement of war to persuade them of their own worth. Hester had rebelled, but, as far as she knew, her mother had always been happy with the quieter life she had chosen in her home town. Perhaps Miss Peck had been right after all: it was their differences that made them close.

'Has Lucy Kyte turned up yet?' she asked as the secretary replaced the receiver.

Miss Peck hesitated. 'Not to my knowledge, no,' she said, and her tone implied that Josephine was putting her in a difficult position by asking about a part of Hester's will that did not concern her.

'I'm surprised she didn't make herself known at the funeral. Actually, there's something I've been meaning to ask you about that. Mr MacDonald said that you spoke to Tod Slaughter?'

'That's right. He was charming once I'd got used to how tall he is.'

Josephine smiled. 'Did he say anything about why Hester pulled out of the Maria Marten film?'

'No, but to be fair I didn't ask him. He made a very gracious speech about working with Miss Larkspur and Mr Paget at the Elephant and Castle, but when I spoke to him afterwards he spent most of the time telling me about his garden. Do you know him?' Josephine shook her head. 'Well, I rather got the impression he prefers plants to actors these days.'

'There are times when I'm inclined to agree with him.' She looked at Miss Peck, who seemed not to have heard the last comment. 'Is something wrong?'

'No, it's just that you've got me thinking now – about Lucy Kyte and the funeral.'

'Oh?'

'There *was* a woman at the church. Let me see – it was after the service, and I was in a group of people listening to Sybil Thorndike. She was saying what a versatile actress Miss Larkspur was, and how impressive she was when they were in *The Old Women* together in the early twenties. Did you see it?'

'No. I was working away at the time, and I didn't get to see much theatre.'

Miss Peck shuddered. 'It was a horrible little play – a whole evening of horrible little plays, if I remember rightly. There was a scene in it where a young girl had her eyes gouged out with a needle. Not my cup of tea, at all.'

'And the woman?' Josephine prompted.

'Oh yes. She came up to us and I thought it was Miss Thorndike she wanted to speak to, but then she started asking me about the cottage.'

'What did she want to know?'

'Oh, what was going to happen to it, who was going to live there now.' She saw the look on Josephine's face and was quick to reassure her. 'I didn't mention you, of course. I thought at the time that she was just one of Miss Larkspur's fans, come to pay her respects, but I suppose there could have been more to it.'

'What was she like?'

'Quite ordinary, really. About my age, perhaps a bit younger; dark-haired and slim, smartly dressed, but not extravagant. I wish I could remember her name, but I'm not sure that she even introduced herself.'

'It's probably not important,' Josephine said, getting up to go. 'I'm sure Lucy Kyte would have made herself known if she'd been there. This woman is far more likely to be a fan, as you say, or even someone from the village who was curious about her new neighbour.'

'Yes, I suppose so.' She smiled. 'Anyway, I'll tell Mr MacDonald your news and let him have these right away.'

'Thank you. I'm going back to Suffolk in a few days' time, so if there's anything else I think he should see, I'll bring it back with me.'

'Excellent. Enjoy it, and do get in touch if there's anything we can help with.'

Josephine thought about the long days of tidying and sorting that still lay ahead of her at Red Barn Cottage. 'Be careful what you offer,' she warned. 'I might just take you up on it.'

7

The first thing Josephine noticed when she arrived back at Red Barn Cottage was that someone had repaired the study window. She looked at the new pane of glass, unsettled by the idea of strangers coming and going in her absence, and wondered if it was churlish of her to feel that all Bert's acts of kindness were a little 'off'. It had to be Bert – his wife was the only person who knew it needed fixing – and she should have been grateful, but that in itself irritated. Perhaps the row with Hester had stemmed from the same thing: feeling ever more beholden to someone for unsolicited favours might easily have exasperated her godmother sufficiently to break off all contact. She would probably never find out, but whatever had gone on in the past, Josephine knew that if Bert's wife was aware of his latest good deed, her name would be mud in the Willis household.

She got the fire under way in the range and laid out some good intentions of her own on the table: a few carefully selected research books for the biography of Claverhouse. Set against old photo albums and boxes of Hester's correspondence, *The Scots Peerage*, *The Despot's Champion*, and learned volumes by Barrington, Morris and Sanford Terry looked even less inviting than they had at home, and she wondered how long it would be before one of them was opened. Hours of travelling had made her too restless to read, so she left the cottage and set out over the fields, eager to see how the countryside had changed without her.

It was one of those soft September evenings, where the distinction between summer and autumn is lost. The dark green of the woodland was broken by the first telltale threads of gold, and the harvest was almost complete: sheaves of corn stood abandoned, like the forgotten tents of a retreating army, and the industry of the day – an industry to which the whole cycle of the year was geared – had been replaced by stillness. Chance rather than purpose led Josephine towards Maria Marten's cottage, but, when she realised where she was, she lingered by an obliging gap in the trees, her interest in the case intensified by the somewhat lurid account she had read while back in Inverness. James Curtis had used all the tricks of his profession to lift the story to the status of legend, but neither the sensationalism nor the moralising could completely obscure what was, essentially, a very human tragedy, and Josephine looked in fascination at the house Maria had left one midday in May to walk to her death. The cottage was shabby and neglected, and it occurred to Josephine that the handful of pristine houses around the village green was hardly typical of Polstead or of the area in general; Suffolk was an agricultural county whose fortunes had declined with the industry, and she had noticed from the train today how few of its farm buildings looked prosperous or even well kept. Like Red Barn Cottage, the house stood as it was built, a typical labourer's dwelling with nothing to distinguish it except the woman who had once lived there; it was modest in size, four rooms or five at the most, and Josephine could imagine how claustrophobic it must have been for Maria, living not only with her parents, siblings and a son of her own, but with the weight of her family's disapproval and the shame of her situation. No wonder she had aimed high, to use Hilary's phrase.

The cottage was surrounded by an orchard and large gardens, which – according to Curtis – Maria had loved and tended. Feeling a little like one of the crowds who had flocked there after her body was discovered, hoping for a glimpse of her family or leaving money for her orphaned son, Josephine turned away and left the house to its past. She had been out longer than she had intended, and when she reached the brow of the hill and looked down on Red Barn Cottage it was bathed in evening sunlight. The scene reminded her that the murder site had got its name from a trick of the Suffolk light, a strange red glow that often fell on the barn at sunset. Needless to say, on that night in 1827 the effect was said to have been particularly intense, as if the violence inside the barn had stained the very fabric of the landscape; cloud and a light drizzle would hardly have done justice to the folklore. All the same, as Josephine looked in awe at the scorching sun, setting the fields on fire with a blaze of colour, she could easily believe that Nature had seen to the destruction of the Red Barn herself.

She walked on, absorbed in the beauty of the evening, and only when she was within a few yards of the cottage did she notice a familiar figure leaning nonchalantly against the gate, smoking a cigarette. 'You chose the right day to come back, Miss Tey. Lovely, isn't it?'

'Bert,' Josephine said, hoping for a tone that was neither too welcoming nor too hostile. 'How did you know I was here?'

'Your chimney. Elsie saw the smoke and happened to mention it.' She looked up at the undeniable signs of life from the range and realised that she might as well buy a flagpole and raise the standard as soon as she arrived. 'I've brought you these,' he explained, holding out a set of keys. 'There wasn't room in the garage, so I've tucked her just behind for now.'

Josephine opened the gate and walked over to her gift. It was an old Austin Chummy – open-topped, bright turquoise and very much a 'ladies' car', as Bert had said. Her heart sank. She would be conspicuous enough in any vehicle – at most, there could only be three or four cars in the village – but no one would miss her in this. 'I don't know what to say,' she murmured truthfully. 'It's really too kind of you.'

'I'm glad you're pleased. I wouldn't try getting back to Scotland in her, but she'll run you about all right down here.' He grinned. 'Most of the time, anyway.'

Josephine was touched by the genuine pleasure on his face at being able to give her something precious of Hester's. She looked again at the highly polished car, which had obviously received hours of attention, and entertained the thought that the problem lay with her. If she were honest, much of her antipathy towards Bert stemmed from that uncomfortable exchange with his wife, and he wasn't the only one who came and went as he pleased; it seemed to be the country way, and she shouldn't blame other people for her own cynicism, or expect them to behave differently because of it. 'Thank you,' she said, more sincerely this time. 'I appreciate it. The window, too. It's good of you to take the trouble.'

'Oh, don't worry about that. It only took me five minutes and it was the least I could do. Jenny told me she gave you a bit of grief over it.'

'Something like that, yes.'

'She didn't mean anything by it. She's just a bit overprotective about me and the kids.'

Josephine couldn't quite see why she posed such a threat to the Willis family, but she let it drop in favour of what she really wanted to know. 'Your wife seemed very resentful of Hester and the things you did for her.'

'She thought Miss Larkspur took it for granted.'

'And did she?' Thinking about what Hilary had said, Josephine would not have been surprised to hear that Hester had made the most of Bert's loyalty, or that she had relished the ability to create a spark of jealousy in another woman, even in her later years.

'It never seemed like that. I only ever did what I was happy to do.'

He spoke defensively, as if wary of reliving an old argument with a new adversary. Josephine hesitated before pushing him, but in the end her curiosity got the better of her. 'What did you and Hester fall out about, Bert?'

'Jenny told you that?' Josephine nodded. 'It was something and nothing, really – the sort of thing you look back on later and wonder why you let it happen. Miss Larkspur accused Lizzie and Vicky of stealing something from the cottage. She said she heard them downstairs in the house one morning, and later that day she discovered that an ornament was missing.'

'And they denied taking it?'

'Of course they did. They don't lie.' Josephine's face must have expressed a doubt in the absolute honesty of children, because he added: 'I know they were telling the truth.'

'What was it?'

'One of those pottery figures of William and Maria. Miss Larkspur loved all that stuff. She collected anything to do with the Red Barn. Beats me why people will pay a fortune to remember a murder. I could think of much better things to spend that sort of money on if I had it.'

Josephine was inclined to agree with him. 'I suppose it's a piece of history,' she said unconvincingly. 'And it meant a lot to Hester personally. She'd devoted so much of her life to the story.'

'I suppose so.'

His resentment of the item that had caused so much trouble was only natural, Josephine thought; such an accusation would have hurt more than his pride. 'I don't understand why Hester would say something like that, though.'

Bert shrugged. 'Oh, I don't know. She wasn't herself those last few months. Everything had got on top of her. The business with her eyes came from nowhere, and she wasn't coping with it as well as she thought she could.'

'What do you mean?'

'She made me promise not to tell anyone, but I don't suppose it matters now.' Bert took a handkerchief from his pocket and busied himself with a mark on the car's paintwork that was invisible to Josephine. 'Miss Larkspur was losing her sight.'

The admission came as a surprise to Josephine. 'She told you that?'

'Only because she had to. There were a few signs early on, I suppose – she'd put salt in my tea instead of sugar, and one day she insisted I stop and have a bit of dinner with her and there was a bar of soap in the bottom of the soup bowl.' He smiled, and Josephine was struck by the warmth that seemed to have existed between the two of them; never in a million years would she have imagined a friendship between an actress and a garage mechanic, but that probably just showed how little she knew about either. 'They were easy mistakes to make and I didn't think anything of it,' Bert continued. 'Then last Christmas I took her a photograph of Lizzie in her school nativity. She was thrilled to have it, but she kept talking about the wrong girl, pretending she could see the picture when she obviously couldn't. It's not as though Lizzie was hard to spot – she was the Virgin bloody Mary.'

Josephine smiled. 'That *is* about as big as roles come.'

'Anyway, I challenged her about it and she admitted that she'd been having trouble with her eyes, but she swore me to secrecy. She'd been to a doctor in London, apparently, and there was nothing they could do.'

'Nothing at all?'

'That's what she said.'

'So that's why she gave you the car.'

'Yes. She knew she wouldn't be able to drive it any more.' He patted the bonnet affectionately. 'They made quite a pair, those two.'

'I can imagine.' Things made more sense to Josephine now: Hester's withdrawal from the film, the piles of unopened post, the chaos of the scullery, and the clock with no glass, time gauged by touch rather than by sight. 'That's why she was thinking of leaving,' she said, more to herself than to Bert. 'She knew she wouldn't be able to cope.'

'Leaving the cottage? I didn't know that.'

It surprised Josephine that Hilary had known this and Bert had not. 'It makes sense, surely?'

'It seemed to me that she clung to it more than ever. She always told me that when she and Walter first moved here, they vowed they'd be carried out and I don't think that changed. She was obsessed by the place, and the more frail she became, the more she wanted what she knew.' That made sense, too; certainly, a great deal of Hester's will had been about the cottage, and that did not smack of someone who was ready to leave it. Perhaps Hilary had been mistaken, or had automatically assigned to Hester the intentions that she herself thought sensible. 'It might have been better if she *had* left,' Bert said quietly.

'Why?'

'It didn't do her any good being here on her own, while everything she loved faded. She couldn't read or write any more, and the beauty of the countryside – well, it was a memory to her by the end, not a reality, and memories fade, too, don't they? Whenever I came to visit her, she'd ask me to tell her what I could see, how the year was changing. You wouldn't think you could find two people more different, would you?' he asked, taking the words out of Josephine's mouth. 'But we shared that, at least – every inch of this place was precious. It was the cruellest thing that could have happened to her, losing her sight. I think she could have coped with anything else.' He looked directly at Josephine for the first time and she was moved by his sadness. 'In the end, she lost the will to live. I've said that so many times over the years, but I didn't really know what it meant until I saw it in Miss Larkspur. She stopped eating properly or taking any care in how she looked. She let the house go, and herself along with it. All the joy had gone out of life.' It was what Josephine had sensed the first time she had walked into the cottage, and she knew exactly what he meant. 'It's enough to drive anyone out of their mind.'

'Is that what you think happened?'

'I don't know what happened, Miss Tey. All I know is that she changed. She never needed much company – just the house and her memories. She lived in the past, and those of us who were still living and breathing never seemed quite as real to her somehow. But it was different towards the end. She stopped seeing anyone, even the few friends she did have, and she got rid of the girl who used to help her out round the house.'

'What girl?'

'Someone came in from Stoke to do a couple of mornings a week for her.'

'I don't suppose she was called Lucy?'

He shrugged. 'I can't remember what her name was. But Miss Larkspur didn't trust anyone by then, not even me. There were times when she wouldn't let me in. I'd hear her talking to herself, but she wouldn't come to the door. And the ornament was the last straw. After that, I stopped trying to help. I wish I hadn't, but I did. Jenny and I had made light of the row over the pottery with the girls, told them that Miss Larkspur had made a mistake, and I went round to the cottage to set her straight. That was the last time I saw her.'

Josephine remembered what Hilary had said about things disappearing from the front room; only Bert was here to testify to his own honesty and an elderly woman in Hester's position would have been very easy to exploit – but somehow she believed him. 'The last time you saw her alive, you mean.' He looked at her in surprise. 'You found her body, Bert. You never said.'

'It's not something I like to think about.'

There seemed more to his reluctance than a simple sorrow at Hester's death, or even guilt at having withdrawn his support when she needed help more than ever. Josephine stared at him, a man of an age to have fought, old enough certainly to have known grief in his own family, and wondered what was too painful to think about in the death of an elderly woman who had, by his own admission, found life too wretched to cope with. 'My solicitor told me she died in her bed. He implied it was peaceful. Is there something I don't know?'

'She wasn't in her bed. I put her there, but it's not where I found her.'

For a moment, Josephine was too surprised to speak. 'Why on earth did you move her?' she asked, trying to keep any note of judgement out of her voice.

'No woman would have wanted to be seen like that, especially not Miss Larkspur.'

'Like what?'

'You don't want to know.'

Whenever anyone said that to her, it was Josephine's instinct to disagree. In this case, she thought more carefully, knowing that – once she had pursued it – she would have to live in the cottage with whatever she discovered. On the other hand, she also knew that her imagination would readily supply anything she chose not to hear, and that seemed the greater evil. 'Please tell me, Bert. How did Hester die?'

He leaned against the car and looked back at the cottage, reliving the day in his mind. 'She was upstairs, in that tiny room at the end of the house, burrowed under a pile of old clothes.' Josephine closed her eyes and fought back a wave of nausea when she remembered her only visit to that room – the touch of those clothes against her skin, the heavy, cloying smell of them in the darkness. 'God knows how long she'd been there – a few days, I'd say. She was right in the corner of the mattress, curled up. It looked as if she'd pulled a load of stuff on top of her – clothes, newspapers, anything she could find.'

'To keep warm?'

'More like she was hiding from something. As if she'd crawled away to die, like an animal rather than a human being. I wouldn't have known she was there if it hadn't been for the . . . well, you know.'

He tailed off to spare her feelings, but his meaning was obvious; Josephine did not have to guess at how a body that had lain in a cottage for days in early summer might reveal itself. 'Why were you there?'

In her shock, it was the only thing she could think of to ask, and it sounded more accusatory than she had intended. Bert didn't answer straight away, and she wondered if she had offended him. 'The kids fetched me,' he said at last, his voice unnaturally even.

'Good God, please don't tell me they found her first?'

'No, not exactly. They just knew something was wrong when they went to the cottage. It was the anniversary of the murder, you see – the eighteenth of May.' Josephine didn't see at all, and Bert had to explain. 'Every year, the girls would go to the church with Miss Larkspur and put some roses from her garden on Maria Marten's grave. There's no stone there now – the last of it was chipped away in the 1890s, but Miss Larkspur remembered where it was from when she first came to the village. It put everyone's back up, seeing those flowers there every May as a reminder of what had happened, but Miss Larkspur didn't give a damn about that and there was no harm in it. Lizzie and Vicky couldn't get enough of the story the way she told it, and there's nothing wrong with learning a bit of respect as a kid, is there?' Josephine shook her head. 'So they went round like they'd normally do, not knowing things had changed. It wasn't their fault. Jenny and I had made light of the business with the pottery because we didn't want to upset them, and we hadn't really explained why they didn't see Miss Larkspur any more. We should have been more honest with them, but it was hard to know what to say. They knocked on the door and let themselves in like they always used to, but there was no one downstairs so they went up to the bedrooms.'

'But they didn't look round?'

'No, thank God. They swore to me that they'd only gone to the top of the stairs. But like I say, they knew something was wrong. There were flies everywhere, and places have an atmosphere when something like that happens – kids pick up on it as much as any of us. That was enough to stop them going any further. They ran straight home. They were both in tears when they got to me.'

'So you went to see what had happened?'

He nodded. 'It didn't take me long to find her. I knew I couldn't leave her there like that for anyone else to see. She never had any time for the local doctor and word soon would have got round. She'd have hated being humiliated like that with everyone talking about her, saying she'd gone soft in the head. No, I couldn't just leave her.' His voice was firm and definite, suggesting that he was still trying to convince himself that he had done the right thing; when he continued, Josephine noticed that he spoke matter-of-factly about what he had done, almost as if he were giving a statement, and never once hinted at his own feelings. She didn't blame him: the emotional impact of the experience was hard to imagine, and not something to be discussed with a stranger. 'There was nothing of her,' he said. 'She'd lost so much weight – I hadn't realised. I got her out as gently as I could and put her in her bed. She was in her night things anyway, so it looked right enough. Then I tidied up a bit and went for the doctor.' Josephine wondered why he hadn't done that straight away. It must have been obvious from what his children said that Hester had died, and it would have been more natural to fetch some proper help

74

– or perhaps that was simply her own cowardice talking. Privately, she could not decide if what Bert had done had been an act of extraordinary humanity or something rather less heroic. He was still talking, but she had been too wrapped up in her own thoughts to listen. 'I was just saying that I'd never have forgiven myself if the kids had seen everything,' he repeated. 'That's why Jenny's so angry. She's cross with herself, really, for allowing them to go there at all. We both are.'

'Does *she* know how you found Hester?' Josephine asked. The more Bert had talked, the more relieved he had seemed, and she sensed that this was a burden he had carried alone.

'No, not exactly.' He looked uncomfortable at having shared something with Josephine that had been withheld from his wife. 'I shouldn't have said as much to you, either. I'm sorry.'

'Don't apologise. I asked you to tell me.'

'Even so. You probably wish you hadn't.'

'It's not that. If I'm wishing anything, it's that someone had been here to help.' She thought about all the people that Hester had known in her life, the names in her address book, the people who had come to remember her in Covent Garden. 'Did she really have no one?' she asked. 'No visitors from London? No old friends who came to see her?'

'If she did, she never said anything to me. Before she lost her sight, she'd go down to London for a few days now and again, but I never saw anybody here. I think that all stopped when Walter died.' He looked at his watch and gave the car one last polish. 'I should go, unless you need some help moving that stuff in the garage?'

'No, thank you. The car can stay out here for now.' He seemed eager to leave and Josephine was in no mood to delay him. It was impossible to return to normal conversation after what had passed between them, and under different circumstances their hurried goodbyes might have amused her, like the embarrassment of lovers who regret their intimacy and can't wait to part. As he reached the gate, she remembered the fresh flowers in the guest room and wondered if Bert had been keeping them there as a mark of respect. 'Have you been inside the cottage since then?' she called after him.

'No,' he said, turning back to her. 'I fixed the window from the outside. And nothing personal, Miss Tey, but I'm not sure I'd want to go in again.'

She watched until he was out of sight, then went reluctantly back into the house and poured herself a drink. For a long time, she sat by the fire in the study, instinctively retreating to the part of the cottage that was furthest from where Hester had died. Surrounded by the evidence of her godmother's vitality, she found Bert's testimony of the last few months almost impossible to conceive – and all the more heartbreaking because of it. 'Soft in the head.' She remembered the phrase from her childhood; later, the reality of it in her grandmother's final years. Then, as now, the label did so little justice to the truth. Her grandmother had been much older than Hester – nearly ninety when she died – but she, too, had outlived her husband by several years. During that time, she had buried two daughters, the only girls in a family of seven children: Mary, her eldest, who had died of heart failure when she was little more than Josephine's age, leaving behind six children; and Josephine's own mother, killed by cancer just thirteen years later. Josephine remembered how frail and confused her grandmother had been at the funeral, destroyed by her grief for one daughter, sheltered from the death of another by a mind that could no longer cope.

But she had never been alone. When her own time came, she was living with her youngest son in Crown Street, next door to the house where she had raised her family, in touch with the children who remained. Josephine had visited occasionally during the last years of her grandmother's life, when she was back in Inverness and finding her feet again in the town she thought she had left for good. The small parlour at the front of the house was as cluttered in its way as this study of Hester's, although the memories were of a very different life: Jane Horne's audience had been her family, her stage a domestic one where she was loved rather than adored. It was diminished eventually to a single room which she never left, except in her mind; a small world, assembled in every sense from bits of the past, but it had been safe and she had been cared for. And she had never been alone. How must it have been for Hester, isolated not only from the life of the village but – through her loss of sight – from everything that had once been familiar, clinging to a house she loved but an old, contrary house that must have conspired with her blindness to make each day more difficult? How desperate was she to end her life in such a way, and how long had it taken her to die? Nothing left of her, Bert had said. Days without food and drink until she would have been too weak to change her mind, even if she had wanted to. Had she cried out towards the end, knowing there was no one to hear, or had the prospect of a reconciliation with Walter brought her comfort? Peace or fear in those last terrible hours, that was what Josephine would never know; she had been too afraid herself to ask Bert if the answer lay in the expression on Hester's face.

His revelations nagged at her conscience like a personal rebuke, although she knew in her heart that the one person from whom Hester might have accepted help was gone, another charge to lay at the feet of her mother's early death. It was Hester who had had to stand at her friend's grave, wishing that she could have done something. Once again, Josephine tried to picture her among the mourners, but she would not come when summoned, except as the pitiful wretch of Bert's testimony. Plenty of other images did, though. The coffin waiting in Crown Cottage, a house that Josephine had never lived in and didn't really know. She had left home by the time her parents bought it and she loved it now, but then it had been alien to her and she had longed for the small, ordinary house in Greenhill Terrace where she had grown up, and where she would not have felt like a guest at her own mother's bedside. Her father in a new suit which he would never wear again, fiddling constantly with his tie and worrying about the dress he had chosen to bury his wife in. Neighbours standing by the gate, kept at a distance by a request for privacy but stubbornly determined to pay their respects, pity and curiosity mingled on their faces. Her parents' friends telling her that she looked well, that England obviously suited her. It had been all she could do not to scream at them to stop, because she did not want to look well, or to be reminded of her absence.

The study was too quiet, the tears too close and too insistent to risk. Josephine stood up and made the fire safe, then took her glass upstairs. She had so looked forward to her first night back in this room, warm and welcoming now in the lamplight; she had imagined herself falling asleep over one of Hester's books, then waking in the morning to the sun on the fields and the soft smell of freshly cut hay. The door to the boxroom was firmly closed, just as she had left it, but it taunted her with the sadness it concealed and the nausea came again with the memory of crawling over clothes that had so recently covered Hester's body. Unable to be near it any longer, Josephine swallowed the rest of the whisky, ripped the sheets off the bed and went next door.

8

She slept in the guest room for the next three nights, but her dreams followed her there. During the day, she tried to stick to a routine: *Claverhouse* in the morning, then a walk to the village and Hester's papers in the afternoon, but she found herself slipping earlier into Hester's world each day, as if reading obsessively about her life would somehow blot out the awful knowledge of her death. Four times she put her hand on the door to the boxroom, and four times she withdrew it until, after a while, she took to using the other staircase and avoided that end of the upper storey completely. She wrote a letter to her father, and found herself inventing a normality for her stay as she would an adventure for a novel, stretching out the mundane, domestic details of her life at the cottage, and writing far more than she would normally write as a distraction from the real news and how she felt about it. At night, she drank to sleep, only to wake again in the difficult early hours, troubled by things she could do nothing about. Alone, and with no one to fool, she cried more often than she had in years.

In the end, she wrote to Marta and asked if she could come to the cottage earlier than planned. She kept the letter casual, not wanting to cast a shadow on the visit when they saw each other so rarely, and relied on the simple truth of longing to see her. The answer came by return of post: Marta would be with her on Wednesday, and Josephine no longer cared that the cottage would not be as miraculously transformed by then as she had hoped. They needed nothing more, really, than clean sheets, a warm fire and plenty to eat and drink, and she woke on Wednesday morning with a sense of relief that she would not have to spend another night alone. She had sent Marta directions and told her to come straight to the house via the Stoke road. One of the blessings of a house at the end of the village was that visitors did not have to submit to any rigorous inspection from Elsie Gladding and her friends, something that Hester must have appreciated during the days when she entertained at Red Barn Cottage. For now, Josephine felt that she was novelty enough for the people of Polstead; asking their curiosity to cope with Marta as well might put too much of a strain on everyone.

The day dragged by, and she waited for her lover with the impatience of a child on Christmas Eve, busying herself with cooking and cleaning; by late afternoon, when she finally heard Marta's car, the cottage had never looked finer. Josephine went outside, soothed by a day that had involved nothing but the sort of domesticity she had written to her father about, and waved as the Morris bumped slowly down the track. In spite of everything, she was excited at the prospect of sharing the cottage with someone she loved while it was still so new to her, and she desperately wanted Marta to like it. The car negotiated the final pothole and drew up outside, and Josephine leaned over to give Marta a hug.

'Well – it's nice to see you, too.' She pulled back and smiled at Josephine, pleased by the welcome. 'I'm sorry I'm so late. I got hopelessly lost and had to ask in the village. The publican was very helpful.'

'Yes, I imagine he was.' Josephine watched her get out of the car, and wondered if Marta's beauty would always silence her the way it did now. If Jenny Willis thought *she* was a threat to Bert's moral fibre, God help them all when she saw Marta. Perhaps it was wrong to be so frightened of anyone guessing the truth of their relationship: in a village where the men were historically susceptible to temptation, it might actually be a relief.

'He even offered to bring me out here himself. I'm not sure what his wife thought about that, but it was a kind offer.'

'Very kind,' Josephine said dryly. 'I'm glad you didn't take him up on it. Who did you say you were?'

'I didn't say I was anybody. You didn't warn me I was supposed to arrive in character.' She smiled mischievously. 'They'll get used to it. The first six months are the worst. When I first started to stay with Lydia, the daily woman walked in while I was playing the piano and I had very little on. I didn't know whether to apologise or brazen it out, so I just carried on while she banged the tea down, fuming with moral outrage. I honestly thought she was going to hand her notice in there and then, but do you know what she said on her way out of the room? "Those bottom notes sound a bit flat, Miss. You ought to get that looked at."'

The impression was finely judged, and Josephine laughed. 'Luckily I don't play the piano.'

'Then what is there to worry about? Come here.' Marta pulled her close, and Josephine felt a familiar mix of shyness, joy and desire. 'This is absolutely beautiful,' Marta said, looking round. 'From the landlady's reaction, I wasn't quite sure what I was going to find.'

'Why? What did she say?'

'That you'd be pleased to have some company, stuck out here on your own. I think her exact words were "in that godforsaken field". She pulled the rug off the back seat, and Josephine saw a haphazard collection of boxes and bottles, piled on top of a suitcase. 'Let me get this stuff out of the car and then you can show me round.' She unloaded a hamper and a case of wine. 'If it's anything like the villages I know, you'll be missing a few luxuries so I stopped off at Sudbury on the way.'

'Just as well the publican *didn't* bring you over. He'd think we were setting up in competition.' Josephine picked up the hamper and Marta caught her arm. 'What have you done to your hand?'

'Oh, just burnt it on some steam. The kettle's seen better days. In fact, all Hester's kitchen facilities leave a lot to be desired.'

'Fine by me if gin is easier than tea. I'm dying for a drink.'

When the luggage was inside, they walked round the cottage together and it did Josephine good to see it through Marta's eyes: filled with flowers from the garden, and with the evening sunlight streaming in through the windows, it was every bit as warm and welcoming as she had wanted it to be. For the first time, she was conscious of her own presence in what she still thought of as Hester's cottage, and, although they were simple things – her books laid out on the desk in the study, the preparations she had made for their evening meal – Josephine felt more at home than she had since she first got there.

'I've got you a house-warming present. Hang on a minute.' Marta found the box she was looking for and Josephine opened it curiously. 'I thought you might need some company occasionally, and this seemed more practical than a dog.' It was a portable gramophone and Josephine set it up on the table, delighted with the gift. Marta gestured apologetically to the large stack of records that came with it. 'While I was in the shop, I realised that I have absolutely no idea what sort of music you like, so I bought a selection. There are some play recordings there, too, just in case you're bored with that melodrama stuff you've been talking about.'

'You have no idea how welcome this is,' Josephine said. 'Thank you – I love it. Shall we have a look round the garden? It's beautiful at this time of the evening. We can have a drink outside.'

They sat on the bench and talked while the sun set. The music drifted out from the house, seemingly written for an evening such as this, and Josephine was pleased to see that the Suffolk light was playing its customary trick on the landscape, weaving a cloth of rich red and gold across the fields. 'You'll be building a bathroom on, obviously,' Marta said, looking doubtfully at the outhouse. 'I can't see that being much fun in the winter.'

Josephine laughed. 'Where's your sense of adventure? Anyway, I've got to decide if I'm keeping it before I get the builder in.'

'You're not in a hurry to give this up, surely? I can't imagine anything more peaceful. I'll move in if you don't want it.'

'Be my guest.'

'Careful. I might take that as an invitation.' Gently, Marta touched Josephine's cheek, just below her eyes. 'You look tired.'

'Do I? I was aiming at something rather more glamorous for you.'

'The two aren't mutually exclusive. You are all right?'

'Yes, I'm fine. I haven't been sleeping very well since I got here, that's all.'

'Aren't Hester's mattresses up to scratch either? We obviously need to go shopping.' The response was a feeble smile and Marta looked at her, concerned. 'What's wrong, Josephine?'

So Josephine told her, surprising herself with how much of the last few days she was willing to be open about, from the details of Hester's death to her own sadness and the other, more complex emotions about her family that it had revived. 'I'm sorry,' she admitted. 'I didn't mean to tell you all this the minute you got here.'

'Of course you must talk to me. I wondered why we moved so quickly through the bedrooms, and why you've obviously been sleeping – or not sleeping – in the single bed. I thought you were trying to tell me something.'

'Hardly. I haven't brought you all this way to sleep in separate rooms.'

'I'm glad to hear it.'

'It's ridiculous, though, isn't it? People die alone all the time and I didn't even know Hester, but I can't stop thinking about it.'

'Why is that ridiculous? You've been left an old house in a place you don't know, by a woman you barely met, in a will full of odd instructions that you can't make head or tail of. That in itself would be enough to fuck with your sanity, but then you find out that she died in a boxroom, estranged from the few friends she had, after what sounds like months of sadness and suffering.'

'I suppose when you put it like that . . .'

'There's no other way *to* put it. And apart from all that, when was the last time you were truly alone for any length of time?'

'I'm often alone at home.'

'No, you're not. You're on your own in an empty house, but that's not the same thing at all. You have routines and a town life and a woman coming in to clean, and you know your father will be home in the evening. Having a few hours to yourself is nothing like this.' She waved at the open countryside to prove her point. 'You've been brought face to face with yourself for the first time in years, and that's enough to send anyone screwy.'

'Thank you!'

Marta laughed, and held up a cigarette as a peace offering. 'I didn't mean that in quite the way it came out. I just meant that you only really ever learn who you are when you're alone. God knows I've found that out in the past, for better and for worse.' If Josephine had known a fraction of the grief and betrayal that Marta had experienced in her life, she doubted that she would ever have trusted herself with solitude again. They had known each other for little more than two years. Josephine had met Marta as the lover of a friend, had helped her through a terrible time in her life, and – against every impulse of loyalty, to Lydia and to a life free of commitment to anyone – had fallen in love. Marta rarely spoke of her pain, but the tragedy of that time – the death of two children, one executed for killing the other – was never far from Josephine's mind, a peculiar hybrid of barrier and bond between them. 'Look, I'm sure Hester didn't mean to cause you all this soul-searching,' Marta said, misreading her train of thought, 'but if she'd set out to ensure that you didn't sleep at night, she could hardly have made a better job of it.'

'That's true. Actually, my solicitor said that she was having second thoughts about leaving me the cottage.' Josephine told Marta about the phone call that Hester had made to John MacDonald, her evident distraction and the doubts that her goddaughter would even want the gift. 'By that stage, her sight was probably too poor to put *any* instructions in writing, so the will stayed as it was. But I can't help feeling that something might have happened here, something that tainted the cottage for Hester and made her afraid to be in her own home.' She thought for a moment. 'Yes, I suppose that's it. The thing that cries out to me about Hester's death is fear.'

Marta looked sceptical. 'I know it's all a bit strange and mysterious, but there *is* a simpler explanation for those last-minute doubts. Perhaps she was frightened of your knowing what she'd become. From what you've said to me, she was obviously quite something in her heyday and we all want to be remembered for our finest hour. She must have known that the state of the cottage would give her away. Perhaps all

that stuff about your deciding what was important was just an elaborate way of telling you to remember how she lived and all she achieved.'
She smiled provocatively at Josephine. 'Are you sure you're working on
the right biography? Couldn't the Scottish chap wait?'

'I've accepted money for the Scottish chap, God help me.'

'All the same, you should think about it. Hester's life interwoven
with the character she played and that murder you told me about.
Wouldn't that be an interesting book?'

'Yes, it would,' Josephine admitted, warming to the idea. 'I can only
imagine how that would go down round here, though. A celebration
of Maria Marten, on stage and in real life.'

'Well, maybe that's what Hester wanted – a tribute to them both. In
which case, she could hardly have left her secrets in better hands. And
it would be good for you, too – a way of working through the strangeness of all this and getting Hester out of your system.' She looked
curiously at Josephine. 'Why are you smiling at me like that?'

'Because I'm so pleased to see you.' She took the drink from Marta's
hand and drew her into a long, intense kiss. 'Thank you,' she said. 'Now
let's forget all about Hester and Maria, and go and eat.'

They took the long way round the garden to the house. 'I'm not surprised you're having trouble,' Marta said, bending down to smell the
roses. 'She's still here.'

'You sense that too?'

'Yes, very much. She's everywhere.'

'I thought it was just me. I didn't want to say anything for fear of
sounding like the vicar's wife. She dropped in with a Madeira cake and
left a stream of ghosts and spectres in her wake. Apparently, they've got
a headless horse at the rectory. I don't really feel I can compete with just
the odd faded memory and a nightmare or two.'

'They're far worse, if you ask me – you can choose not to believe
in the headless horse. No, I don't mean that Hester's hovering in that
room in a white sheet, unable to rest until you've sorted her paperwork.
But houses hold traces, don't they? Happy or sad. At least, I hope they

do. We must make a mark somehow while we're here, or what's the point? Hester hasn't given up the cottage yet, and she won't unless you help her.'

'What do you mean?'

'You need to make it yours, Josephine. If you want to keep it – and I think you do – you need to sort through Hester's stuff, get rid of what you don't want and fill it with things you do. Like I said, it's time we went shopping. Have a good time with the Scottish chap's cheque. Where's the nearest town with decent shops?'

'Bury St Edmunds, I suppose, or Ipswich.'

'Right. Choose one of them, and we'll go tomorrow.'

'If we went to Bury, we could visit the museum that Hester left some things to in her will.'

'What have I just said? You need a day off from Hester. We'll go to Ipswich.'

'I wasn't suggesting a pilgrimage,' Josephine said, laughing at Marta's impatience. 'I found some sets and props from the melodrama in the garage, and I wondered if the museum would like them to add to its Red Barn collection. They'll only gather dust if they stay here.'

'Excellent – Bury it is, then. I'm all in favour of anything that encourages Miss Larkspur to move over a bit.' She caught Josephine's hand by the door. 'Why don't you show me that room before we eat? You shouldn't let anything spoil this for you, and you might feel better about it if you faced up to it.'

It was the last thing Josephine wanted, although she appreciated what Marta was trying to do. 'I know what you mean and I'd love you to be here when I do it, but not now. It's not how I want to spend our first night.' She held Marta's hand against her own cheek and kissed her palm. 'If you feel short-changed on the tour of the bedroom, though, dinner can wait.'

Later, Josephine lay awake for a long time, watching Marta as she slept, freed now from the shyness she still felt whenever her gaze was returned. The candlelight flickered on Marta's face, emphasising her cheekbones and the lines at the corners of her eyes, giving her hair the radiant gold of sunlight on snow. The closeness they shared was something that Josephine had never wanted with anyone until now, man or woman, and the strength of her own feelings astonished her. Marta turned over in her sleep, and as her hand found Josephine's body next to her, she smiled; the response was entirely unconscious, an innate expression of happiness and trust, and it moved Josephine more deeply than any words could have done. 'I love you,' she murmured into Marta's hair, hoping that – even in sleep – Marta would know how much she meant it.

9

Bury St Edmunds had a peaceful, settled spirit that delighted Josephine from the moment they got there. As they drove towards the centre, she was astonished by how much of its original character it seemed to have preserved, not just in two great churches and some impressive monastic ruins, but in open squares and tiny lanes packed with houses from every age but the current one. The town had a quiet confidence and a beauty that came entirely from its sense of history: Josephine looked in admiration at the ruins of the Abbey, incorporated easily into everyday life with great pillars in domestic lawns and modern roofs built onto ancient flint walls, and it occurred to her that Bury could teach Polstead a thing or two about finding a peace with its past.

They parked on Angel Hill, a large square in front of the Abbey gate, and asked directions to the museum. 'I'm not sure I'm entirely cut out for rural isolation,' Josephine admitted, feeling instantly at home in the bustle of a country town. 'This is lovely.'

Marta nodded. 'It is nice. I bet they've even got electricity.'

Moyse's Hall was tucked neatly into the corner of the market square, a twelfth-century building whose walls seemed to offer more knowledge of the town's history than any number of deliberately fashioned exhibits ever could. 'Do you want to go shopping while I get this done?' Josephine asked, knowing how much the sort of artefacts on display would upset Marta.

'No, I'll come in with you. I'd like to see what Hester gave them and get a sense of who she was.'

'They're not the only things on display, Marta. There are exhibits from the real murder, too, details of the execution.'

'I know what you're trying to do and it's kind of you, but I don't need protecting, Josephine. I've become an expert in knowing what I can cope with and what I can't. Anyway, this was years ago. It's completely different.'

The only time Marta ever spoke to her like that was on this subject, and Josephine knew it was pointless to argue. She gave up and walked over to Moyse's Hall, wishing she had thought more carefully and insisted on going to Ipswich. There was a small admissions desk just inside the door, and she smiled at the woman on duty. 'I should have telephoned first,' she said apologetically, 'but I'm here about the items that Hester Larkspur gave to the museum.'

'Ah, yes. They're just behind you. All the Red Barn artefacts are together in that section.'

Josephine turned and saw that the murder occupied pride of place at the front of the museum. One of Hester's Maria Marten costumes was on a mannequin in the centre of the display, and it sat incongruously next to what she assumed was Corder's death mask, bringing the romance of the stage entertainment into stark contrast with the story's grim reality. She explained her purpose in more detail, and the woman seemed intrigued. 'You'll need to talk to Mr Andrews, the curator. If you don't mind waiting a moment, I'll see if he's free.'

'I don't want to interrupt him. It's rather a spur-of-the-moment visit, so I'm happy to make an appointment if necessary.'

'No, no – I'm sure he'll be only too pleased to meet you.'

She returned almost immediately, her optimism vindicated, and Marta and Josephine followed her up to the first floor. Josephine's surprise at the man who greeted them said more about her own prejudices than it did about the qualifications necessary to run a museum: experience had taught her to expect curators to be contemporary with at least some of the exhibits they watched over, but this one was barely more than thirty.

'How lovely of you to come,' he said, looking up from a case of gargoyles. 'I'm Henry Andrews, and this is my sister, Sybil.'

The woman he introduced sat by the window, a sketchbook on her lap. She waved, but did not get up for fear of knocking over the pots of brushes and paints that she had balanced precariously on the ledge in front of her. 'I hope you're not offering him anything too grisly,' she said, smiling. 'We've got enough body parts in this museum already and I don't think . . .'

The rest of what she said was lost in a barrage of hammering from outside, and Andrews showed them through to a tiny office where the windows were shut fast against the noise. 'They're building a cinema just behind us,' he explained wearily, 'and they've only just started. I think it's going to be a long year. Now – I understand you're Hester's niece.'

'Her goddaughter. We're not related and I never knew her, but she was my mother's closest friend.'

'I only met her a few times myself, but she was an amazing lady,' he said, with genuine warmth. 'Very knowledgeable about the history of the area, as incomers often are, and incredibly passionate about Maria Marten.'

Something in the way he said it made Josephine smile. 'Obsessed, you mean?'

He laughed. 'I didn't say that. Obsession is just a word people use to describe passion if they're not interested in the subject, but I know what you mean and I think it would be fair to say that very few people knew more about the Red Barn murder than Hester.' The familiarity with which he referred to her godmother interested Josephine, but it didn't surprise her; although not conventionally handsome, Henry Andrews had a warmth and charm that made him instantly attractive, and that – coupled with his interest in her favourite subject – would no doubt have appealed to Hester and disposed her to be generous. 'I'll never forget going to Polstead to collect the items she lent us,' he said, unprompted. 'She gave me a whole education in one afternoon – an education, and some very fine sherry.'

'When was that?'

'Three or four years ago, not long after I'd taken over here. I was born in Bury but I've spent a lot of my time in the Far East, and I didn't know much about the murder then. I wanted to make the museum more local, though, so Hester's offer to expand our collection of arte-facts was like a gift from heaven.'

'I bet you knew more about it by the time you left her,' Marta said.

'I did indeed. She gave me a guided tour of the village – Corder's house and Maria's, the churchyard, the site of the barn.'

'Where did she say it was?' Josephine asked, intrigued. 'No one I've met seems entirely sure.'

'About two-thirds of the way down the track to her cottage, as far as I can remember. She showed me some cherry trees which the people who lived there at the time had planted at that end of the house to shield themselves from the tragedy of it.'

'How on earth could she know that?' Josephine asked, bringing the trees to mind but unable to keep a sceptical note out of her voice.

He shrugged. 'The same way we seem to know lots of things about the Red Barn murder, I suppose: guesswork and a bit of wishful think-ing. Hester was very convincing in the stories she told, of course, but it makes perfect sense. There was a lot of talk in the press of how sinister the barn seemed after the murder, desecrated by souvenir hunters and left to rot – and of course it was haunted. The villagers wouldn't go near it at night, so I can't imagine it was the most comfortable feeling to lie in bed and see that silhouette against a darkening sky, all creaking timbers and screaming maidens.'

'No, I suppose not.' Josephine thought about the way in which the cottage still tenaciously hid that particular view, and wished she hadn't pursued the subject: the last thing she needed was another reason to fear the room that Hester had died in. 'How *did* it burn down?'

'Vandalism. There was a lot of unrest among farmers in the 1840s, and the barn was a casualty of those disturbances. But going back to Hester – the quality of her collection was extraordinary. Well, you know that – it's your collection now. I remember thinking while she was showing it to me that it was as close to living in that time as one could ever get, and that made it more than a story, somehow. The excitement of it was infectious, and it made me want to do that here. Have you seen the displays?'

'No, not yet.'

'Come and have a look.'

He led the way downstairs, Marta following less eagerly than Josephine. 'I'm with his sister on the body parts,' she whispered, pulling a face. 'If it turns out to be more fact than fiction, I'll meet you outside when you've finished.'

Josephine nodded. 'Why do you think it was so famous?' she asked, as they walked past Etruscan tombs, bits of Egyptology and endless proud photographs of colonels from the Suffolk Regiment, Bury being – like Inverness – a garrison town.

'Well, it's partly because not much else was happening at the time Maria's body was discovered – not until Burke and Hare later that year, anyway, so the coverage in both the broadsheets and the tabloids was remarkable. The supernatural element helped a lot, of course. Not many bodies had been dug up after a dream, and that gave all the melodramas an excuse to include Maria's ghost in the story. And people like your godmother have kept the story alive: audiences see the play or hear the ballad and they want to know more.'

A family with two overexcited young boys was poring over the displays at the front of the museum, and Andrews hung back until they had finished. As she approached the glass cases, the first thing Josephine noticed – by chance or by the prominence with which it was displayed – was a section of William Corder's scalp and ear, blackened and wrinkled now and scarcely recognisable as something that had ever belonged to a human being. Next to it was Curtis's account of the trial, and Henry opened the book so that Josephine and Marta could read the inscription. 'The binding of this book is the skin of the murderer William Corder,' it said, 'taken from his body and tanned by myself in the year 1828.' It was signed George Creed. 'He was the surgeon who dissected Corder's body,' Andrews explained. 'They say that bits of skin were passed around the town afterwards so that people could taste it to see if it was different from normal leather. There's a chunk of it in a Cambridge college, I believe.' He saw the expression on Marta's face, and sympathised. 'I know. If I'm honest, I feel much the same way but these two items bring more people into the museum than the rest of the collections put together, so I feel obliged to make the most of them. And I live in fear of being offered Corder's skeleton. That really would be a moral dilemma.'

Marta looked horrified. 'Haven't they buried him?' she asked.

'No. He's on display at the hospital here. They use him for anatomy classes, and I'm told the nurses sometimes take him to dances. At one point, he was in the entrance hall with a spring in his arm that made him point to a charity box whenever someone approached.'

'How dignified,' Marta said, when she realised that Andrews wasn't joking.

'He made about £50 a year, I think. I suppose today we'd call it prisoner rehabilitation.' He smiled, and added more seriously: 'Corder was a rarity, I'm pleased to say. They abolished dissection as a punishment four years after he hanged.'

'Thank God for that.'

Andrews began to remove a pair of pistols from another case. Marta squeezed Josephine's hand and wandered quietly off to another part of the museum. Josephine watched her, concerned about how she must feel and sorry that they had come here at all. 'These are the guns that Corder was supposed to have used that day. See – they removed the hammers before the trial so they couldn't be discharged by mistake in court.'

Josephine tried to concentrate on what Andrews was telling her, and looked at the pistols in surprise: they were only about six inches long, and seemed barely capable of harming anyone. 'He claimed Maria shot herself, didn't he?' she said, remembering the line of defence that Curtis had reported.

'At first, yes. But it was unclear how she had died – that's why they charged him with ten counts, so he couldn't get off on a technicality. It made legal history. But he denied stabbing her right to the end; he said the stab wounds were made afterwards, when they were prodding about the barn floor, looking for her body. That's feasible, because she was only nine inches or so below the surface. This is what they're supposed to have used. It was her father's.'

He pointed to a mole spud, and Josephine shuddered when she thought of how Thomas Marten must have felt when he uncovered his daughter's rotting body. The other items on display were less sensational, but somehow more evocative: a horn lantern, used to find the body; a snuffbox in the shape of a shoe, made out of wood from the Red Barn; and a pair of box irons belonging to Maria, the only thing that testified to her life rather than her death. 'There's not much about the real Maria here, is there?' she said. 'That's not a criticism. I just find it interesting that history tends to remember the murderer and not the victim, while the melodramas all seem to celebrate *her* name.'

'I know exactly what you mean.' He grinned at her, and Josephine sensed that she had given him the opportunity he was waiting for; when it came, his pitch was both charming and shameless. 'Of course, you could put that right if you would ever consider loaning the rest of Hester's collection to the museum. We'd take very good care of it, and it would rather redress the imbalance to have more of Maria's things on display.'

'To be honest, I haven't seen anything that looks remotely as though it might have belonged to anyone from that time, but there's still a lot of sorting out to be done.' Her heart sank when she thought of the box-room. 'What should I be looking for?'

'Maria's wooden clothes chest is the jewel in the crown,' Andrews said. 'It's about four feet by two, made of oak and lined with very faded silk. It's scuffed and marked and you wouldn't give it a second glance if you didn't know whose it was. But if you look closely, you can see where she's scratched her initials on the lid.'

'I found a chest in the garage. It holds the stage props I told your assistant about.'

'I doubt Hester would have put it in the garage,' Andrews said. 'It was her pride and joy, and she had it next to the fire when I saw it, but it always travelled with her when she and Walter were on tour. She kept her costumes in it for luck. Hers, but never his; she told me that nothing to do with Corder ever went near it.' Of all the theatrical superstitions Josephine had heard over the years, Hester's was one of the more original. 'Then there were lots of Maria's early letters to a friend, and her mirror . . .'

'A small silver hand mirror with roses round the glass?'

His face lit up. 'Yes, exactly.'

'That's still there. I did my make-up in it this morning.' It was the only mirror in the house. Until she found out about Hester's blindness, Josephine had been surprised by such an uncharacteristic lack of vanity in an actress. Before she had time to consider the strangeness of looking into the glass that Maria had used, Andrews was moving on through his inventory.

'Hester also had two Staffordshire figurines, one a Sherratt piece with William enticing Maria into the barn, and the other a group of murderer, victim and judge all standing together. There was an original iron bar from one of the doors to the Red Barn, and something made out of the wood, not unlike the snuffbox we've got already. I particularly liked the collection of painted backdrops she had from the early peepshows that travelled round in the 1840s. They were done by a chap called Jack Kelley, a drunken Irishman who lived in Leather Lane – one of them depicted Corder boiling an egg on the morning of his arrest. And last but not least, she had a small elm table that came from the Corder house. Actually, we had that on loan for a while but she asked for it back not long before she died. She said she missed it too much.'

'Where did she get it all?' Josephine asked, ignoring for now the more pertinent question of where it had all gone.

'There are dealers who specialise in that sort of thing, and there always have been. I suppose it goes back to the tradition of the hangman having the right to a murderer's clothes. It didn't take him long to realise that he could sell those for far more than he was paid to open a trap. Madame Tussaud paid handsomely, I believe. She used to buy clothes and accessories from real murders to display with the waxworks. In fact, I read somewhere that when they sold off the contents of Road House after the Constance Kent case, they kept back the victim's little cot in case it ended up in the Chamber of Horrors.'

'That's fascinating,' Josephine said. 'I had no idea.'

'Oh yes. It encouraged a lot of fraudsters, of course. Corder's head was allegedly exhibited by a showman at Bartholomew Fair, although as far as we're concerned it's still firmly on his shoulders in the hospital. I suppose Hester was following in a theatrical tradition with her collecting, too. Owners of the sort of theatre that *Maria Marten* played at used to snap these things up for props, so you might be lucky in your chest in the garage.' He must have realised he had Josephine completely enthralled by now, because he added mysteriously: 'Then there are the things that we know exist but have no idea where.'

'Like what?'

'Maria's hand is the most legendary, but there are also rumours that Creed bound a second copy of the trial.'

'You're surely not telling me that Hester had Maria Marten's hand tucked away somewhere?'

'No. She always denied buying any of the more gruesome relics, even the rope that hanged him – and several people own an inch or two of that.'

'Don't you believe her? You sound sceptical.'

'I'm always sceptical where collectors are concerned, probably because I'm one myself. We lie, and play things very close to our chests. But I did believe Hester. She was always more interested in the social history of the crime, in Maria as a woman.'

'And the things she owned were valuable?'

'Good God, yes. Murder relics have always been big business, even though people are divided about them. Some are disgusted by them, like your friend; others would go to great lengths to get hold of them.' He smiled at her. 'Where do you stand?'

'With most people, I suspect. In my heart, I know it's wrong and the inhumanity of it disgusts me – but I'm also fascinated by it. And as far as Hester's collection is concerned,' she added, telling him what he really wanted to know, 'I can see the appeal of owning something that Maria loved when she was alive, but I'm not sure I'd want anything from the place where she was killed, and pottery figures are just something else to dust. You're welcome to those if I come across them.'

'That's very kind, but I must warn you against being too generous. Those Staffordshire models alone are probably worth more than your cottage. Relics attract very large sums of money – if they can be authenticated, and Hester's always were.'

'Yes, I rather got the impression she was a stickler for that sort of detail.' She told him about the letter that had arrived with the rare book and the hoops through which the bookseller had obviously been made to jump to prove its value.

'That sounds about right. Did you say John Moore?'

'Yes. Do you know him?'

'No, but Corder's son was called John Moore. He took his mother's maiden name, for obvious reasons.'

'Unless the years have been miraculously kind, it must be a coincidence.'

'Yes, and it's a common enough name, but it will have amused Hester.'

Josephine cast a quick glance round the museum, but there was no sign of Marta. 'Thank you for everything you've told me,' she said, holding out her hand, 'and especially for taking those stage sets off my hands. I had no idea that trying to do the right thing for someone you never knew would be quite so difficult.'

'I'm sure there's a lot to think about, but they'll be greatly enjoyed here. Who knows? We might even put on a performance or two in Hester's honour.'

'I'll arrange for them to be sent over to you before I leave.'

'You're not here all the time?'

'No, and there are easier places to commute to Suffolk from than Scotland, but I'm sure it will work out eventually. And I'll be in touch if I find any of the other things you mentioned, but it seems that Hester got rid of an awful lot in the last couple of years.'

He looked doubtful but didn't argue, and Josephine walked out into the sunshine, glad to be free of the museum's shadows. She looked round for Marta and saw her coming out of a bookshop, looking pleased with herself. 'What have you got?' she asked.

'I'll show you later. Have you finished in the Black Museum?'

She spoke lightly, but Josephine knew that what she had seen had affected her, no matter how old the crime. 'I'm sorry for taking you there,' she said. 'I should have gone another time.'

'Don't be silly – it was my choice to go in. It's a damned good story and I can understand why it interests you, but all I can see in those cases is a woman who was desperate and a man out of his depth. Now – what shall we do first? Shopping or lunch?'

The change of subject was sudden and final. It bothered Josephine that Marta had an intuitive understanding as far as she was concerned, drawing her out and encouraging her to speak about her feelings as she had the day before, but she rarely allowed the gift to be reciprocated. It was the only imbalance in their relationship, but it seemed to Josephine an important one, and she had not yet found a way to fight it. 'Shopping, I think,' she said. 'I'm not sure I could face food just yet.'

'Good. There's a department store just down here.'

Plumpton's offered everything that Josephine wanted; within an hour, she and Marta had bought new linen, ordered curtains, chosen pans and a kettle for the kitchen, and argued over crockery as if they had years of domestic compromise behind them. 'I still think you should have gone for the Susie Cooper,' Marta said, as they struggled back to the car with all they could carry. 'Whoever's heard of Charlotte Rhead?'

'If I wanted brown and dingy, I'd use what I've got already,' Josephine insisted. 'But if it makes you happy, I'll buy you a nice beige cup of your own.'

After lunch, they walked through the Abbey Gardens, enchanted by its ruined beauty. A long stretch of green sloped down towards the river bank, and they sat for a while, watching families picnic in the sun. 'I can't go there, Josephine, and I never will,' Marta said, out of nowhere. 'I know you want me to talk about what happened, and I know you want to help, but it wouldn't help. It would destroy me even to say his name.' She was close to tears and Josephine longed to hold her, but she sat staring into the distance, her face impassive, her body tense and wary of the slightest touch. 'Is that all right?'

'Of course it's all right,' Josephine said quietly.

'I don't want you to feel that I'm shutting you out, but I can't let that be part of our life. Part of *my* life.'

She started to say something else, but Josephine put a hand on her cheek. 'Marta, look at me. It's all right. I understand.' She felt Marta's relief and it saddened her, because she knew she could never truly understand. Marta's son had killed her daughter, and paid the ultimate price. It was what had brought them together and what would always, to some extent, keep them apart.

10

The following day, Josephine spent a long and dusty morning in the garage, emerging at last with two large boxes of rubbish but no clue as to the fate of Maria's clothes chest. 'Any luck?' Marta asked.

'No, just props in a trunk with travel stamps all over it. I'm not sure Maria ever went as far as Karachi.'

'Don't you think it will all be in that room you're avoiding?'

'Perhaps, but I'm not ready for that yet.'

'I'll help you.'

'Not on such a lovely day. What have you been up to?'

'Waging war on the vegetable garden. I hope you like beetroot. Hester obviously did.'

'Not especially,' Josephine said, looking doubtfully at the mound by Marta's feet.

'No, I can't stand it either. Still, we could always take it to the church.'

'What?'

'The vicar's wife called while you were busy. She seems nice.'

'Not much like a vicar's wife, you mean.'

'Exactly. She told me not to disturb you, but she brought an invitation to the harvest service tonight. I said we'd go.'

'You are joking.'

Marta laughed at the horror in her voice. 'No, I thought it would be fun. It's the ideal opportunity to have a look at the rest of the village.'

'Isn't that the best possible reason *not* to go?'

'I'm dying to see them.'

'Yes, and I'm sure they're dying to have a look at us. Did you say we'd *definitely* be there?'

'I'm afraid so, although I did decline the communal supper afterwards. She was thrilled, Josephine – you can't possibly let her down. I rather got the impression you're the most exciting thing to have arrived here for some time.' She grinned, and held up the beetroot. 'One generous contribution to the harvest table, and the invitation to open next year's fête is yours for the asking.'

The evening in prospect had not grown on Josephine by the time the bells rang out over the fields to call the congregation to worship, and she followed Marta reluctantly to the car. Polstead church was set apart from the village, as if even St Mary wanted to distance herself from what had gone on there. It stood at the top of a hill leading up from the village pond, and was distinguished by an unusual medieval spire and by commanding views over the surrounding countryside – gentle, sloping fields on one side, and a deer park on the other, fronting an eighteenth-century manor house which Josephine assumed was Polstead Hall. 'Is Maria Marten buried here?' Marta asked, looking round the churchyard.

'Yes, but I don't know where. Hilary told me that the gravestone was chipped away over the years. It doesn't seem right that she should go unmarked, does it?'

'At least she gets some peace and quiet.'

'Lucky her,' Josephine muttered, already feeling the eyes of the village upon them from a stream of people filing into the church by the south door. 'Shall we have a look round out here first? Let the queue die down and slip quietly into the nearest pew? With a bit of luck, Hilary will be too busy to make a fuss of us.'

Marta smiled at her cowardice, but humoured her by breaking away from the path and heading off into the oldest part of the churchyard. It did not take them long to find the Corder graves: the family made its presence felt in six substantial stones, standing side by side and facing defiantly back towards Polstead Hall, as if daring anyone to mention the son whose body was elsewhere. None of the Marten graves seemed to be marked, and again Josephine found it strange that it was the victim's family who had been shamed out of history.

'Perhaps they're not buried here,' Marta suggested. 'They might have left the village – you'd be tempted, wouldn't you?'

'Yes, I suppose you would.' She looked back at the church, and added reluctantly: 'We should go in.' The flaws in her plan to remain inconspicuous became obvious as soon as they crossed the threshold. 'Ah, visitors,' announced the verger in a tone designed to discourage such an aberration, and everyone turned to look at them. Elsie Gladding whispered in his ear and Josephine caught the words 'cottage' and 'theatre', neither of which seemed to improve her standing in the community; if anything, the verger's frown deepened.

Undaunted, Marta beamed at him and held up the basket of vegetables. 'Where would you like us to put these?' she asked, and was directed grudgingly over to the harvest table. As they put their offering down with the rest, Josephine could feel the entire congregation's eyes on her and felt somehow as though she were stealing from the poor rather than making a donation. She looked at the impressive array of produce, and wondered if it was uncharitable of her to think that its outward message of generosity stemmed from a rather less Christian competitive streak among the givers.

'Josephine! You made it – how lovely.'

Hilary kissed her on both cheeks and shook Marta's hand warmly. 'You two met this morning, I believe,' Josephine said. 'I'm sorry I missed you. I was on a wild goose chase in the garage.'

'Don't worry – I felt much the same in the village, but it seems to have paid off. Not a bad turnout at all. Are you in the theatre, too, Miss Fox?'

'No, I work in film. I'm a scriptwriter.'

'Oh, even better.' Hilary clapped her hands together at the prospect of two interesting women for the price of one, and Josephine saw Marta stifle a smile. 'I must introduce you to Stephen.'

She went to great pains to point him out – somewhat redundantly,

Josephine thought, bearing in mind the occasion and what he was wearing, but she looked with interest at the Reverend Stephen Lampton. He was older than his wife by several years, and had a thoughtful, kind face and an air of unworldliness that must have made him easy prey to the more assertive of his female parishioners. He excused himself from two of them now in response to his wife's frantic gesturing, and came over to welcome them. 'Miss Tey – I'm delighted to meet you. Your godmother was a remarkable woman, and we miss her dearly.'

The words were a cliché, but the warmth with which they were delivered made anything more elaborate unnecessary, and Josephine had no doubt that he was speaking as a friend rather than a vicar. 'I hope we'll have a chance to talk about Hester,' she said, shaking his hand. 'When you're less busy, of course. I'm still finding out about her, and I get the impression there's a lot to learn.'

'Of course. You must come for dinner, both of you. But in the mean time, just let me say how much I enjoyed *Richard of Bordeaux*. I was thrilled when Hilary told me that you were taking on the cottage. It's nice to think that the theatrical tradition will continue.'

Josephine thanked him and led Marta firmly towards the back of the church, choosing a pew from which they could watch the congregation without themselves being the subject of too much attention. 'They haven't exactly gone to town on the decorations, have they?' Marta muttered, nodding to the five cooking apples and a tiny pot of corn that stood near the altar. 'Has it been a particularly bad year?'

Josephine smiled. 'At least it won't take long to be thankful for it,' she said, standing for the first hymn. After a somewhat flowery preamble, the organ launched unexpectedly into 'We Plough the Fields and Scatter', catching the congregation by surprise. It took everyone a few lines to catch up, and Josephine leaned over to Marta. 'Trust us to get stuck with a warbler,' she whispered, as the woman in the pew behind found her stride. Marta's snort earned them a glare from a couple on the other side of the aisle and a nervous smile from Hilary, and as they reached each chorus, Josephine marvelled at the number of syllables that the word 'love' could have in the wrong hands. The singer built to a crescendo and the hymn struggled to keep up, and Josephine could feel the muscles in her own throat straining in sympathy. She tried to control her laughter by imagining a face to go with the voice, but the tears ran helplessly down onto her hymn book, smudging the words that she did not trust herself to sing. Next to her, she could feel Marta's shoulders heaving but she dared not meet her eye.

After the brief respite of a psalm, Stephen Lampton took to the pulpit and Josephine smiled when she remembered what Hilary had said about his sermons. The words were certainly well considered, thought-provoking without being pompous, but what really stood out was the beauty of his voice; as far as Josephine was concerned, he could have spoken gibberish for the whole ten minutes and she would still have been riveted. When he had finished, she noticed several people passing a private verdict on his address and wondered how long the Reverend Lampton would have to preach in the parish before his performance went unjudged; sixteen years seemed an unnecessarily long trial period.

There followed a series of readings from parishioners, and Josephine could only imagine the amount of feathers that had been ruffled in the selection of readers. Some lines from Corinthians drifted out to her but she could see no one; only when she craned her neck did she realise that the man was too short to see over the lectern. It was an impressive effect, the words seeming to come genuinely from on high, and she wondered if Stephen had judged it carefully or simply struck lucky. As a choir of four began a surprisingly rousing rendition of 'Oh Lord, My God, When I in Awesome Wonder', Marta leaned over to her. 'That's the woman from the pub,' she said. 'I think her name's Marion.'

'Margaret.' The whisper came sharply from behind, and Josephine stifled another laugh. She recognised Margaret as one of the women who had been in the village shop on her first visit, and she looked at her now in admiration as she delivered the line 'when Christ shall come with shout of acclamation and take me home what joy shall fill my heart' with real conviction – although the longer the service went on, the more attractive the sentiment became. At last, the Lord's Prayer signalled that the end was in sight. Josephine looked round at the bowed heads and thought about the words and how easily they were spoken. She thought of Maria Marten, lying close by in an unmarked grave, and remembered the look of hatred on the faces when she had asked about descendants of the families: there had been no forgiveness there, even after a hundred years, and she doubted that things had been different in any past congregation.

Two of Stephen's women stood for the collection, and Josephine wondered if either of them had been responsible for the Madeira cake. There was a mass exodus during the final hymn, as people left to prepare the harvest supper, and Josephine took the opportunity to turn round casually and see how accurately she had pictured the warbler. She was too late: the pew was empty and the woman had gone, her identity for ever a mystery. As soon as it was decent, Josephine and Marta slipped from their own seats and headed for the door before Hilary could renew her exhortations to come to supper. The hollow church clock struck eight as they walked through the graveyard to the gate, choosing their steps carefully in the darkness. Marta took her hand and Josephine looked round anxiously. 'Don't worry,' Marta said. 'It's pitch-black out here. No one can see what we're doing and even if they could, I'm not sure we could disgrace ourselves any more tonight than we already have.'

'That's true. Thank God I'm not a churchgoer, if that makes any sense. I'll never be able to show my face in there again.'

'I told you it would be fun.'

'Yes, I suppose it was – in a twisted sort of way.'

They headed for the green to collect the car, guided only by the stars. As they rounded the pond, the flap of swans' wings against the water sounded unnaturally loud in the darkness, and Josephine held Marta back. 'Look – that's the Corder house.' The lamps were lit in every room, the curtains drawn back, as if the house were trying to prove to the rest of the village that it had nothing left to hide. As Josephine watched, a shadow passed the window upstairs – so fleeting, and in rooms so unchanged, that it was easy to believe it had nothing to do with the current occupants; that the house, too, was trapped in its own history, scarred by the past, and still living with a shame for which it had not yet been forgiven.

11

It was a morning of soft, thin cloud which – if the pattern of the last few days was to be followed – would clear by lunchtime into a warm, sunny afternoon. Josephine walked down Polstead Hill, sorry that Marta had chosen to stay at the cottage but glad of some time to think quietly about what she had learned over the last few days. In her heart, she did not think that the treasures Henry Andrews had described were still in the cottage, and she wondered what might have persuaded Hester to sell them. An operation, perhaps? Bert had said that nothing could be done for her eyes, but maybe she had learned something to the contrary; that, surely, would have been worth the sacrifice. It was odd, too, that Hester had not thought to mention such precious items by name in her will if their value was indeed greater than the cottage. Josephine wished now that she had looked at Hester's financial papers before handing them all over to her solicitor; they might at least have told her if Hester had received any large sums of money recently, and laid to rest her own fears that something more sinister lay behind the disappearance of those artefacts. Hester had obviously not made any secret of what she owned and that would have made her vulnerable, either to an opportunist from the village – she tried to keep this hypothetical and not picture Bert when the phrase came to mind – or to one of the more ruthless dealers in relics. From there, it was only a short step to imagining a darker scenario around Hester's death, and, for now, Josephine pushed the thought to the back of her mind.

The shop was busy with deliveries, and Elsie Gladding offered nothing more combative than a raised eyebrow at the idea that she might stock tinned asparagus. Outside, the clouds had cleared on cue, and the sun-touched houses looked as inviting now as they had on the day she first arrived, a subtle collage of white, pale ochre and chalky green. More striking still, though, was the gilding that no one had chosen: trees laden with burnished apples; rosehips, pyracantha and Virginia creeper, and it seemed appropriate to Josephine that red should be the predominant colour of nature in the village. She reached the bottom of the hill and turned left past the post office, towards Marten's Lane. As soon as she was out of the sun, the cold air against her face reminded her that it was autumn, and she felt the brittle crunch of acorns underfoot. Passing Maria's cottage, she wondered if the arrangement of its rooms reflected her own and tried again to work out what it was that unnerved her so about Hester's boxroom. Not a squeamishness about death, certainly; she had cared for the sick herself, and no one with her training in nursing was superstitious about the body's physical humiliations. No, her fear – and fear was what it was – stemmed almost entirely from a growing conviction that the room had known a sadness too great to be contained within a single generation. Judging by its uncared-for state, Hester had felt exactly the same way herself – which raised the question, why would she choose to die there?

The 'godforsaken field' looked anything but this morning, and Josephine paused at the top of the track, thinking about Red Barn Cottage and its reputation. Everyone grew up knowing a house like that. As children, she and her sisters had played near a derelict building in Daviot, and she could see it now in her mind's eye – a dark silhouette on the lonely bend of a narrow road, shadowed by melancholy elms and surrounded by hemlock and nettles. Encouraged by local stories and by the fertility of a child's imagination, she had filled that house with every conceivable horror, of this world and the next, and she wondered if Polstead's children would think of Red Barn Cottage in a similar way, if – in their memories – one legend would grow and tumble into the next: the house that saw the murder and the fire; the old woman who lived there, obsessed with the past until it drove her mad.

When she got back to the cottage, she found the table in the parlour looking like something from a church jumble sale. 'You were quick,'

Marta said, struggling downstairs with another box and swearing as the bump in the stone floor thwarted all her efforts to force it through the door. 'I thought I'd be able to get everything out before you got back.'

'I wondered why you were so keen to get rid of me.' Josephine looked at the growing pile of clutter, touched that Marta had wanted to help her through something she was dreading, but horrified at the Pandora's Box it had unleashed; once started, it would have to be finished, as Marta no doubt knew. 'But you're leaving tomorrow. We can't spend your last day on this.'

'It's not as bad as it looks,' Marta insisted, in spite of the evidence to the contrary. 'It won't take all day. Here – grab some of this to sort through in the garden while I finish the clothes and scrub the floor-boards.'

'You don't have to do this,' Josephine said, although she was more grateful than she would have known how to express. 'It should be my responsibility, not yours.'

Marta put the box down and held her close. 'That's why it's easier for me than it is for you. I don't want to leave here with this still hanging over you.' She grinned. 'Anyway, the sooner that room is cleared, the sooner I get a bathroom. It would be perfect.'

'No sign of Maria's clothes chest, I don't suppose? That would buy you a bathroom to die for.'

'I'm afraid not, but look on the bright side – there's no sign of her hand either.'

'What on earth would Maria Marten think if she knew how valuable her death had made her, I wonder.'

'Probably much the same as I do: that the whole world had gone mad.'

'Yes, I suppose so. I bet she'd happily have settled for a little more recognition while she was alive.'

'Quite. I did find this, though.' She showed Josephine a small collection of broken pottery that she had placed carefully on the sideboard.

'It was under the bed, already broken. I thought it might be one of those figures you mentioned, but it's not Staffordshire. As far as I can tell, it's an actress in character and it looks a bit like Hester. All the pieces are there, in case you ever have enough hours in your life to mend it.'

'Was this there as well?' Josephine asked, holding up a tiny key.

'Yes, between the floorboards.'

'It must be the key to the bureau drawer. I've been looking for that for ages. I thought I was going to have to force it.'

'Good, but you're not using it now.' She took it from Josephine's hand, laughing at the expression on her face. 'We're finishing this bloody room if it kills me. You can rummage through the bureau for as long as you like after I've left, but now I want you to go and sit in the sun and throw away as much of Hester's junk as you can bear to. I won't be long.'

Josephine picked up the suitcase nearest to her and did as she was told. It didn't take her long to realise that Hester had packed her entire Inverness life away into one modest piece of luggage, probably the very case that she had left home with. Intrigued, she glanced through a pile of photographs of the town as it was before she was born, recognising buildings and rituals more often than people. They were interesting, but most of them meant nothing to her, so – with the exception of one or two pictures that featured Hester or members of her own family – Josephine put them to one side to give to the Inverness Museum.

The bundles of letters were harder to pass off as someone else's problem. Josephine found herself sifting through the envelopes, instinctively looking for her mother's handwriting, and it did not take her long to find what she was looking for. Hester seemed to have kept even the most inconsequential correspondence from her friend, and, to Josephine's surprise, the suitcase also contained some letters that had passed the other way, parcelled up by Josephine's father and returned to Hester a year or so after his wife's death. It amused her to see that, as young girls, they had written to each other even while living side by side in Crown Street. She read at random – letters about school and other friends, about their families and life in the town, postcards from holidays, notes about books they had read, and, as they got older, thoughts of what they wanted to do with their lives, journeys they longed to take, boys they admired and others who admired them. In the briefest of snatches that Josephine read, their separate personalities shouted from the page: Hester's language, even as a child, was elaborate and dramatic, as though she were continually trying out different personas to see which one suited her best; her mother's tone was far more down to earth, but with a streak of dry humour that cut through Hester's wilder fancies without seeming to cause offence. Josephine picked up another envelope, the first she had found with a non-Inverness address; it had been sent to Hester in Newcastle, and was dated November, 1890.

My dearest Etta,

Well, you've gone, as I always knew you would one day. Restlessness is not something to be grown out of when it has been as carefully nurtured and encouraged as yours has, and I suppose I realised a long time ago that we would not live side by side for ever, watching our children grow up together like we did, growing old in the town we were born in.

You are right to go, no doubt, and you must have the courage of conviction in your decision. You owe it to Walter as well as to yourself not to allow the happiness you have found together to be poisoned by guilt. People love, or they don't love. That is the simplest fact of life, if sometimes the hardest to accept, and you cannot choose where your heart goes. A marriage where you did not love would never have suited you. It would only have brought more pain to everyone in the long run. Ronnie will forgive you eventually, and so will his family. You know how we are in this town, how we have always been – one grudge is soon forgotten for fear of missing the next.

I'm sorry we argued before you left, and for everything I said, but I was angry and sad, and I spoke out of selfishness. We have always had each other, and this town seems very different without you. But Etta, you were wrong, too, to say that I settle for too little. Perhaps there was a time when I dreamed of those adven-

*tures – escape and travel and all the things we talked about. But that's all it was
for me – a dream. Everything was always possible for you: there was no such
thing as fantasy, only lives you hadn't lived yet. Did you never know how much I
envied you for that? But please don't blame me now for needing different things.
We're not children any more.*

*Travel safely, my dear, difficult friend, and have the adventures for both of
us. I hope in my heart that you will find happiness wherever you are, and that
Walter will bring you the joy you deserve. One day, perhaps, I will see your name
outside a theatre and think: 'So she has found herself after all.' That would
make me very happy.*

Intrigued by what Hester might have left behind in Inverness,
Josephine looked for a reply but Marta interrupted her before she
could find one. 'Jesus, you can't move in this garden without tripping
over something.' She disentangled herself from a particularly determined bramble and sat down on the bench.

It was true, Josephine thought; the paths were littered with statues
and overgrown plants, and she wondered how Hester had coped.
'What's wrong?' she asked, watching Marta light a cigarette. The
cheerful determination of earlier had completely gone; she seemed out
of sorts, angry even, and Josephine took her hand, surprised to find it
like ice. 'Why are you so cold?'

'I don't think that room has been warm in a hundred years.' Marta
inhaled deeply, and lifted her face to the sun. 'There's something you
need to see up there. I was going to cover it up but you'll find it sooner
or later, so there's no point in my trying to pretend it's not there.'

'What is it?'

'Let me finish this and I'll come up with you.'

'No, I've let you do too much already. Stay here and get warm.'

Josephine climbed the stairs, her mind teeming with possibilities,
each less welcome than the last. The door to the room was wide open
and, now that Marta had freed it from most of its contents, it looked
bigger than she had originally thought. She stepped inside, and noticed

that the window was still fastened with the scarf she had used as a temporary fix, but outside the rose had grown back over the glass, more virulent than ever, and the sun struggled to get through. The room was above the scullery, Josephine told herself; of course it would be cold. Even so, the chill in the air was surprising, as noticeable against her face as the difference between sun and shadow, and she felt the same sense of sadness as she had when walking home, accompanied by the season's proof that another summer was lost to her. Marta had stripped the bed and bundled all the clothes into pillowcases, but she had been able to do nothing about the staining on the mattress, and an air of utter desolation hung over the room. As she stood there, Josephine had the curious sensation of intruding on someone's grief, as much a part of the building as the stone and the wood. It was, she thought, a room entirely without hope.

The smell that she had found so claustrophobic was barely noticeable now that the clothes were gone and the floor had been scrubbed with soap and water. Marta had pulled the bed away to get to the boards underneath, and Josephine could see that a wooden window seat had been built into the wall on that side of the room. It did not take her long to realise that it was this, and not the atmosphere in general, that Marta had found so disturbing. Immediately below the window, the word 'sorry' had been scratched again and again into the wood, the letters running into each other until they were barely legible. Too shocked to think properly, Josephine traced the marks with her fingers, feeling how deeply each had been scored into the oak, sensing the desperation with which they had been made. What in God's name had Hester done to drive her to a penitence like this? The only response to her question was silence, a silence which echoed the death that stood between Josephine and all she wanted to know.

'Perhaps it wasn't Hester,' Marta said from the doorway. 'Perhaps someone else did it.'

Josephine looked at the doubtful expression on her face. 'You don't believe that any more than I do.'

'No, I don't suppose I do, but it's hard to tell how old they are. What do you think it means?'

'I have absolutely no idea.'

'I don't have to go tomorrow, Josephine. I can't just leave you with this.'

'It's a nice thought, but you must go. You've got a script meeting on Monday, and you told me how important it was.'

'Then come with me. Spend a few days in London.'

Josephine was tempted, but she shook her head. 'I can't just run away like that, Marta. Anyway, Lydia will be there, and I don't want things to be more awkward than they are already.'

'It will be fine.'

Josephine smiled at her. 'That's what you always say, but one day you'll be wrong. And the worst is over now here, thanks to you. There's nothing left hidden and the room's clean and empty. All I need to do is shut the door on it. The clothes can be burnt and I'll get someone to take the mattress away. As far as I can see, those boxes downstairs are full of knick-knacks. I'll have a quick look through to make sure there's nothing important, and the rest can go to Hilary's next jumble sale. The theatre stuff in the study isn't a problem; it's actually a nice thing to look at when I can't stand Claverhouse any more, particularly if I *am* going to do something about that book, but there's no urgency. It can wait until I'm ready.'

'So you're not going to worry about Hester's death any more, and all the other questions that you can't answer?' Marta sounded unconvinced.

'I dare say they'll cross my mind, but I've got to put them in perspective, haven't I? Hester is gone. Whatever demons haunted her at the end of her life, I can't help her with them now, and I can't allow her to hand them down to me like an unwritten clause in her will. She's taken enough of our time already, when every hour we have together is precious. Let's make the most of it.'

She closed the door firmly to bring the conversation to an end.

They took some food and a bottle of wine and walked through the woodland until they found a sheltered spot on the edge of a field, away from the cottage and from thoughts of anyone else but each other. Josephine lay back in the grass, her hands behind her head, and Marta ran a forgotten ear of corn playfully over her lips. 'It makes a change, I suppose – me running out on you. You've got the hasty departure down to such a fine art.'

It wasn't an accusation, but it didn't need to be for Josephine to take it seriously; she had run away from their relationship so often in the past that Marta's continued love was nothing short of a miracle, but it was too important to her now to test again with cowardice or selfishness. 'I know,' she admitted, 'and that's why I'm so determined to make this cottage work. I want somewhere that isn't London or Inverness, somewhere just for us. No grand plans and elaborate arrangements – just you and I, whenever we can.'

She closed her eyes against the fierceness of the sun, and felt Marta's hand, still cool, brush her cheek. 'Are you sure you want to stay here tomorrow?' Marta asked.

For a moment, Josephine questioned her decision, but she knew her original instinct was the right one: she could not keep running away, and – although she had not admitted as much – she was determined to find at least some of those answers, if only to make sure that she and Marta could be truly at peace in the cottage. 'Yes,' she said. 'I'm positive. As long as *you're* sure you want to come back.'

12

Marta left late on Sunday afternoon, and Josephine was glad to have plenty to distract her from the emptiness she felt as soon as the car was out of sight. She went through the remaining boxes on the kitchen table and found what she had expected to find: shoes, scarves and handbags in varying degrees of use; souvenirs from the towns Hester and Walter had toured to; and ornaments that Hester had grown tired of but could not bring herself to discard. Josephine, free of any sentimental doubts when it came to bric-a-brac, took them all out to the garage, ready to give to Hilary or to another local charity. There was no sign of anything more precious.

The clothes and bedding from the boxroom filled three large bags, and she dragged them outside to the furthest corner of the garden, safely away from the thatch. Here and there, the field at the back of the house was dotted with a scarlet crown as pheasants picked about in the stubble, their vibrant beauty no longer so out of place now that the reds and yellows of autumn had begun to make their mark. The birds were her only audience as she poured petrol over the sheets and threw a match into the middle of the pile, then stood back to watch, surprised by how quickly the fire took hold. Gradually, she fed the rest of the clothes into the flames, hoping somehow to cleanse the pain of the room by burning it out of existence. The fire was ruthless in its work, and Josephine understood why the razing of the Red Barn had been so symbolic for people living through those times, no matter what its true origins were: it was a way to heal the shame and the sorrow of a whole community, and she could not imagine that there had been much of an effort to save it, even from farmers whose livelihood the fire threatened. For the first time, she thought seriously about Hester's final wishes for the cottage: Josephine, or complete oblivion. Clearly, there was something that she had only intended Josephine to see, perhaps something that only she would understand, and the most meaningful communication she had yet found was on the window seat in that room. Except, of course, Josephine had no idea what it meant. She thought about what she and Hester had in common – her family, Inverness, the theatre – and wondered if the explanation lay there rather than in the village and its tragic past.

The church bell rang clear across the fields, announcing the beginning of evensong. The air was chilly and the fire had lost its heat long ago, but still Josephine stayed outside, knowing that the atmosphere in the cottage would deaden her thoughts. She felt more strongly now than ever that at least some of the answers lay in Hester's bequest to Lucy Kyte; at first she had assumed it was a thank you, but the gift could just as easily have been an act of reparation, made out of remorse rather than gratitude. If so, who was she, and what had Hester done to her? Were those terrible words, scratched into the window seat, the thing she was to take from the cottage? Was that what would bring Lucy Kyte peace – the knowledge that Hester had suffered before her death, that she was sorry?

The sound of birds at roost grew louder in the half-light, their calls ricocheting against each other and gradually fading away, the very essence of an English autumn at dusk. Reluctantly, Josephine left the fire to burn itself out and went back into the cottage, the smell of smoke on her clothes. She lifted the lid on the gramophone for company, but – distracted by the sight of the key still on the sideboard – went through to the study to try the bureau instead. If Hester had left anything particular for her to discover, then surely this was where it would be. The drawer opened easily. Nervously, Josephine looked inside, suddenly aware of how desperately she wanted to find Hester's memoir, to hear about her life – confession or celebration – in her own words. Her godmother did not disappoint her. The locked compartment of the desk contained items of more obvious value – jewellery, a cash box –

but the most precious thing by far to Josephine's eyes was a manuscript, page after page of purple ink in the extravagant handwriting that was now familiar to her. She took it out eagerly and saw instantly that it was written in diary form, but the dates bewildered her and the life it described was certainly not Hester's.

Sunday 1 January, 1826

This is the sixth New Year's Day that I have spent in service with the Corders, and the first since the Master died. We have had no Christmas to speak of, and the house in all its mournin' stood apart from the village celebrations. Everyone is wonderin' how life will be with Thomas over us instead of his father, but there is still a good deal o' work to do in a house with four young men and I hope my Missis will keep me on. I am used to the place now and want no other, and I suppose that means I am happy.

Lit the fires and made breakfast, then chang'd into my best clothes and went with the Missis to church. Usual sermon from the Reverend Whitmore and not much of it to do with God as far as I could see, but the Missis seem'd to find comfort in it. Waited while she put holly on the Master's grave, but she sent me on without her. Met Maria by the pond on the way back to the house and she took me to task for not comin' out with her last night as I had promised. She thinks I can come and go as I please, and has no idea how my time belongs to the Missis. We squabbled but I was in too much of a hurry to stand in the cold and argue over a trifle. I knew she w'd forgive me. Maria's temper blows itself out like the fiercest of storms. Ever since we were children she has never been able to stay vex'd with me for long, nor I with her.

Sure enough, she came to the back door later with a scarlet ribbon for me, even though she is not suppos'd to come to the house. The Missis had gone out again so I made Maria tea and play'd with Thomas Henry for a while but William came into the kitchen while they were there. I told Maria to go but she gave him the prettiest of smiles and it was he who went in the end. That smile will get her into trouble again one day and I told her so, but she only laugh'd and said she w'd take her chances.

Clear'd away the supper and warm'd the Missis's bed. Went to her for evenin' prayers then lock'd up and to bed at 11.

So that was what Hester had been working on: not a true account of her own life, but a fictional interpretation of Maria's. Josephine could not decide whether to be elated or heartbroken. Once again, Hester had slipped through her fingers, but she could not deny that the idea was a splendid one, and the novelist in her could only admire Hester's choice of narrator: a woman who was both friend to Maria and servant to the Corders was uniquely placed to know the intimate life of both families, and to express the divided loyalties that must have torn the village apart. It was, she thought, exactly what she had longed for when she first stood outside the Corder house: an ordinary view of the crime that looked beyond its infamy to lives for ever stained by horror, grief and shame. Admittedly it was fiction, but Hester's knowledge of the case and her empathy with the woman she had played so often on stage were likely to make it as refreshingly different an account as it was possible to get, one that asked history to look again at Maria as something other than victim or whore.

She flicked through the manuscript, saddened to see that the handwriting had begun to deteriorate by the final pages, as Hester battled with failing eyesight to get the book finished. The victory had been hers, though; the last entry was barely legible, but the date told Josephine that Hester's story of her heroine's life and death was complete. Instinctively, she knew that this was what Hester had wanted her to find and had hoped she would value: it was a simple request for approval from one writer to another, and one with which Josephine was more than happy to comply. Not once did it occur to her to doubt the book's quality; somehow, she knew it would be good and the excitement of its discovery drove all other thoughts from her mind. More than anything, she wished that Marta had been there to share it.

It was tempting to stay up all night and devour the manuscript in a single sitting, but she resisted. The fascination of reading it for the first time would only come once, and she wanted to make the most of it. Now, she was too tired to think straight and too restless to sleep. She made herself an easy supper and settled down by the range with the gift that Marta had been so pleased to find in Bury – a recording of the Maria Marten melodrama, with Hester and Walter in the leading roles. It was the first time that Josephine had felt truly comfortable in this room, certainly the first time that she had dared to sit in Hester's chair, but she did not attempt to analyse whether her contentment came from a new sense of purpose or from the time she had spent with Marta: she was simply happy to embrace it. As Hester spoke her opening lines and Josephine heard her voice again, it was easy to believe that the cottage, too, was pleased to have something more tangible than a half-formed memory, to feel that something lost had returned. She felt the house's ghosts very strongly that night, but they were the ghosts we all know and can do nothing about – the times we want again, and can't have.

13

She dreamed again that night, the images vivid and disturbing. In that twisted nocturnal world, fire tore through the cottage, destroying every trace of Hester but leaving the building itself miraculously un-touched. She looked on helplessly while someone – the dream would not reveal who – walked about inside, adding the manuscript to the flames page by precious page. When she finally awoke, her relief was tempered by the smell of burning. It was just light enough for her to look at her watch without the help of a torch: half past five, neither night nor morning. She grabbed her dressing gown and hurried down-stairs to check the fires, but the grate in the study was as grey and lifeless as the dawn, and the range would need a lot of coaxing before breakfast. The smell was less detectable downstairs. She opened the back door and went a little way out into the garden, shivering as her bare feet touched the paving stones, but the bonfire had died quietly with no stray embers to find their way into the thatch as she had feared. The air was damp and still, the fields half-veiled in a lingering, delicate ground mist, and she was struck by the dark bulk of trees behind the cottage. Stripped by the hour of all the individual colours that softened and tamed it, the wood seemed alien and forbidding, a melancholy hint of the dark days to come and a reminder that the month had bor-rowed beyond its limits from another season.

Upstairs, the smell still lingered and she could only assume that it came from the pile of outdoor clothes that she had been too tired to do anything with the night before except leave in a heap on the floor. The door to the boxroom was open again, and it exasperated her to think that the only latch in the cottage to prove unreliable should be that one. She went to close it but found herself drawn in again, and discovered that the scent of smoke was strongest here, although she could see no reason for it. This morning, in the half-light, the scratches by the window seemed to have faded and it was much easier to believe in Marta's suggestion that their sorrow belonged to a different age. It mattered little, though; someone had suffered enough to make them, and the atmosphere of the room remained the same.

It took her a while to fall asleep again, and when she did, she slept heavily and woke later than usual. The sun shone nonchalantly through the window, and she felt a stab of excitement when she remembered the reading that awaited her downstairs. The manuscript was piled on the desk – smugly, she would have said, as if it knew that it had no competition for Josephine's attention among the more pressing research books and half-finished notes that flanked it. It was something of a slap in the face for Claverhouse to be eclipsed by an unmarried mother from an obscure English village, she thought; he would not have taken kindly to her early defection from his story in favour of a girl whose life had not even begun when his ended in a blaze of glory on the battlefields of Killiecrankie.

Hester's book – it had no title, Josephine noticed – was divided into three sections: the months of Maria's courtship with William; the year of the murder itself; and the aftermath of trial and execution, delayed but somehow inevitable – the most interesting part of the story, according to Hilary Lampton, although Josephine guessed that Hester's imagination would have relished the opportunity to recreate a living, breathing Maria. It was the warmest time of day, so she isolated the pages devoted to 1826 and took them outside to read with a cup of coffee. Just for a change, she chose the other end of the garden, which found the sun earlier in the day, and threw a rug down on the ground, welcoming the warmth of the red-brick wall against her back. She sipped her coffee, a strong dark blend from Marta's hamper, and started to read, skimming through the first entry to remind herself of how the book began, then moving on.

5 January

Slept too well and it was past six when I got up. Wash'd up in the scullery and clean'd all the knives, but the Missis found fault with them so I clean'd them all again. She is hard to please these days, when she has always been kind, but the Master's death has knock'd the life out of her and she is not herself. People in the village say she is lucky to have sons to take the worries of the farm from her shoulders, but havin' her children is not the same as havin' her husband and the worries of the farm are not the same as the worries of the heart. And they have all given her pain. William is her favourite and she will not admit it when he disappoints her, which he does often. He is kind enough, but weak, and that is worse, I think, than ill-tempered and strong. So I hold my tongue when she scolds me and try to please her by waitin' on her well.

7 January

Went for a walk with Maria up by Flaggy Pond after dinner was clear'd away. She has quarrelled again with her stepmother, who wants her to ask Thomas Henry's father for more money. Sometimes I do not know how she stays in that cottage with no room to breathe, and I am more grateful than ever for my tiny room, small and cold as it is, because it is mine and private for the few hours I am in it.

Samuel was busy carryin' straw from the barn for threshin', and he came over when he saw us and I wish'd I hadn't been so keen to leave the house and come out in my workin' clothes with my face all dirty. I am a drudge next to Maria, my hands black with lead from the grates so that scrubbin' will not clean them, and in frosty weather I dare not scrub them anyway for fear of makin' them more red and raw than they are already. W'd have liked to talk to him longer but had to get back to make supper and did not want him lookin' at me in my dirt. Wash'd up, wound the

clocks and put a saucer of beer down for the slugs, then to bed at
11 with my diary.

13 January

The sky was grey and heavy early on and it look'd like snow but then
the sun came out and everywhere thaw'd quickly. Cut sandwiches
and took them up to the men workin' the top field. Help'd Samuel
fill two cartloads of turnips to feed the cattle and it was nice to be
out in the air for a bit, even tho' it was cold. He talk'd about his little
girl, who has just had her third birthday, and we pass'd the time until
I had to go back. He is easy to talk to and seem'd glad of the company. He has been with the Corders longer than I have and he felt
the Master's death sorely. It was nice to see him smile.

Maria was out walkin' by the barn and came as far as the village
green with me. She is goin' to town next week with Mr Matthews
and his friends and she pester'd me to ask the Missis for an evenin'
off to go with her. I said I had no time ow'd me, which is a lie, but
I w'd rather not go. Such company is not for me. Maria teas'd me
and said I was dull and old afore my time and she is right, so I will
ask if I get the chance. Waited up for William before I c'd lock up.
It was gone midnight when he came in.

Josephine went indoors to fetch her copy of Curtis's book; she was still
only familiar with the principal names in the case, and wanted to get
every nuance out of Hester's writing. A quick glance through the account of the trial told her that Peter Matthews was the father of Maria's
second child, the boy who had lived and whom she named Thomas
Henry. Matthews was related to the Cooks of Polstead Hall, not resident in the village but a frequent visitor from London. His sister and
brother-in-law owned most of the village, including the land farmed
by the Corders. Hilary had been right: Maria's ambition was admirable
and, if Hester's account was accurate, Matthews's affection for Maria

did not seem to have waned after the birth of a bastard son. That in itself said much for her charms.

The next few entries were taken up with domesticity, an exhausting round of cooking, errands and cleaning things that Josephine didn't even know needed cleaning; it was an authentic insight into how hard the life of a servant was in those days, and it made Josephine ashamed of the fuss she made over the most basic of chores, but it was Maria who interested her and she skim-read until she found another entry that mentioned her.

17 January

The Missis went out and Maria spent the afternoon with me in the kitchen. I watch'd her as she held Thomas Henry in her lap, she so fond of him and he of her, and wish'd that other people c'd see her as she was then. However many mistakes she has made, she w'd not be parted from him for all the world, and she is right not to care what people say. I am happy for them, but had to shake myself from the foolishness that comes to me when I am idle and be glad that I am too busy most days to feel lonely.

21 January

Up early to sew at my new dress for tonight. It was a poor job, and I wish'd I had spent more nights sewin' and fewer scribblin' in my diary, but it hardly matters with nobody lookin' at me. Hurried through my work, left supper ready, and was early for once to meet Maria. We gossip'd in the coach all the way, and I forgot my nerves in the pleasure of being with her and wish'd that it c'd be just the two of us all evenin'.

Bury is a nice town and I was pleas'd to see it again. The coach took us past the gaol and dropp'd us in the market place and – it bein' Reckonin' day – there were plenty of people out in the streets with money in their pockets. The inns were spillin' out onto the pavements, and we had to push our way through the crowds to get to the hotel opposite the old Abbey Gate where we was to meet Mr Matthews and his friends. Maria can look and talk like a lady when she chooses, and she was surely as pretty as any other in the room. People were kindly enough, but I was too shy to talk much and they soon forgot me in all the laughin' and dancin', which pleas'd me. It is such a different world from what I am used to and I c'd never be as comfortable in it as Maria, nor truly myself. Mr Matthews and Maria were not so close tonight, although he is always courteous and attentive. She was quiet the whole journey back, and I c'd not lift her spirits. Went straight to bed, knowin' I w'd be up again in a couple of hours, but was too tired to sleep and wrote my diary instead. I shall be fit for nothin' tomorrow.

31 January
Rain in the night, then a damp, grey mornin' with a fog that w'd not lift. There is no weather more dreary, and we have our fair share of it here. Counted a score of aconites in the front garden, tho', and the ground is thick with daffodils, so there is hope of spring. Have hardly seen Maria since Bury.

She had only finished the first month, but already Josephine had a better sense of the real Maria than she had managed to glean from any of the factual accounts she had read, and she wondered at the power of fiction to bring history to life. Compared with her own faltering attempts to write accurately about Claverhouse's childhood, Hester's casual biographical sketches were vivid and convincing, and Josephine began to feel even less enthusiastic about the pact she had made with truth in her latest book. Briefly, she toyed with the idea of telling John Graham's story through the eyes of a soldier who had served with him, but such an approach was enough to bring on apoplexy among the more earnest historical reviewers as well as from the publisher who had commissioned the book. Reluctantly, she abandoned the idea and left the freedom it offered to Hester.

11 February

The sun came up in a rare blaze of gold and the sky was streak'd with colour. Swept the steps and shook the mats, glad to get plenty o' fresh air into my lungs and light into the house. This afternoon Thomas and William had words about William goin' off for days and not doin' his share around the farm. The Missis smooth'd things over and sided with William as usual. How she spoils him!

It is my birthday tomorrow, so I am waitin' up to see it in. I shall be 24 yrs old, and will have spent ½ my life in service and a ¼ of it in this house.

12 February

The Missis wish'd me happy returns and gave me leave to take myself off this afternoon, so I call'd round to see Maria. She left Thomas Henry with her sister and we went for a long walk through Dollop's Wood. The birds were full of song and we stood for a long time and listen'd to them, just as we used to when we were girls and had nowhere to be and nothin' to fret about. Maria seem'd more herself, and gave me a green silk handkerchief and a little silver brooch, nicer than anythin' I have ever owned. She told me that Mr Matthews had sent the money for Thomas Henry, like he does every month, and I said she sh'd not spend it so, but she laugh'd and said that 5 pounds was more than enough for the family, and she w'd rather spend it on me than hand it over to her stepmother.

Met Samuel outside the Cock Inn. I made a bet with him that he c'd not guess my age and won sixpence, so we all had beer. I put on the brooch and tied the handkerchief round my neck like a lady, and Samuel said they look'd nice on me, which I was pleas'd about because he once told me that I was plainly dress'd, without an ounce of pride in me. He meant it nicely but a girl does not always want to feel plain and humble, even if she is.

13 February

Open'd the shutters to a dreary day. Got the Missis's clothes ready for her goin' to Stoke this afternoon. It was still rainin' as she left and I carried the umbrella over her to the front gate and help'd her into the carriage. No sooner had it pull'd away than Maria was at the back door, wantin' me to help her make a Valentine. I was glad to see her brighter than she has been of late. I said how pleas'd I was that she and Mr Matthews were gettin' on again, but she smil'd and said that the Valentine was not for him. She w'd not tell me who she means to give it to, which vex'd me because it is the first secret we have had that I can remember, tho' I tried not to seem bother'd by it. She dar'd me to make one for Samuel, and because I was vex'd with her I did. I shall not send it.

Hester's anonymous diarist was beginning to intrigue Josephine. She had the right balance of common sense and humour to comment perceptively but without judgement on Maria's hopes and dreams, and enough spirit and vulnerability to be interesting in her own right. As she read on, Josephine found herself looking less often for Maria's name, and caught up instead in the life of the narrator.

14 February

Got up and put the Valentine on the kitchen fire first thing in case I got the better of myself. It is only harmless fun but I do not want to become fond of Samuel and start hopin' for things I sh'd not be hopin' for. He likes my company, I think, but he w'd not want me for a sweetheart.

22 February

Up at 6 and birds singin' by ½ past. Clean'd Master William's room before dinner and found the Valentine Maria made hidden in a book, but heard him comin' down the landin' before I c'd look inside. To bed at 11 with my diary, but cannot concentrate for worryin' about Maria and the trouble she will get herself into.

6 March

The Missis away for two weeks to stay with her daughter at Sproughton, and the chance of a good spring clean at last! Set to clearin' all rubbish out of the understairs cupboard, which I never have time to do with the Missis to look after. Thought I heard Maria callin' from the kitchen, and went to tell her I was too busy to stop and w'd see her later, but soon saw it was not me she was after. She smil'd at me and put a finger to her lips and fol-low'd William up the back stairs and I was glad that he had not seen me. I cannot stop thinkin' of the trouble Maria got into with Thomas, and what the Missis will do if she finds out. Did not see Maria leave. William went out later with his brothers. Left the door on the latch for them.

9 March

Thomas and John out early to help with the lambin', so only two breakfasts to make. William says nothin' but he watches me now whenever I am in the room as tho' darin' me to speak of his secret. Maria has been here every day.

Alone in the house for the rest of the mornin' and enjoy'd hav-in' the chance to finish one job without the Missis movin' me on to another. Samuel turn'd up at the back door and ask'd if I w'd look after little Molly for the afternoon as his sister had been taken ill and he has no one else. I know what it w'd mean for him to lose a day's wages and with the Missis away there is no harm in it. We muddled along together and she seem'd content enough to sit on the table and play with the spoons while I did my bakin' and chattered away about nothin'. I enjoy'd havin' her and it was nice to stop thinkin' about Maria, so I told Samuel he could bring her tomorrow if his sister is no better.

14 March

Pick'd some primroses, the first of the year, and Molly help'd me put them in bowls for the house. I am gettin' us'd to havin' her and she is no trouble, sunny and gentle like her father, altho' she has a streak of mischief which is as it sh'd be at her age. God knows I sh'd not wish ill health on anybody, but I shall be sorry to lose her when poor Hannah is well again.

Maria came over with Thomas Henry this afternoon but William was not back from Stoke and I had her to myself at last. Tried to talk to her but she can see no wrong in what she is doin' and she chang'd the subject whenever I reminded her of that poor baby lyin' in the churchyard and all the trouble she had playin' the same game with Master Thomas. Then William came back and Maria went upstairs with him and left me to look after TH as well. There is only a few months between him and Molly, so I put them together on the floor in front of the range, and they play'd nicely enough until Maria went home.

16 March

Hannah was well enough to have Molly again, which was just as well as I had to get the house ready for the Missis to come back at the w'kend, altho' I w'd be lyin' if I said I did not miss her chatter while I work'd. William ask'd me to clean his ridin' boots again at dinner time and fidgeted while I did it. I know he is worried that I will say somethin' to his mother about him and Maria. When I had finished, he said it would be best if his mother was not worried by anythin' when she is still gettin' over his father's death. I nodded and went on with my work as if I did not get his meanin', and thought less of him for using the Missis's grief to excuse his shame. If Maria knew how little he cares for her against his good name, she w'd see through the charm he uses to her face, but there is no tellin' her that when she is all caught up in the adventure of it. She is her own worst enemy, Maria, and there is nothin' to be done except wait for her to come to her senses and mop up the tears when she is done.

Samuel gave me a little trinket box that he made himself to thank me for lookin' after Molly. He sh'd not have bother'd but I am glad he did.

3 *April*

Took some bakin' to Samuel after dinner. The cottage has gone down a bit since his wife died. He works too hard to have time for housework and is likely too proud to let his sister help him much other than lookin' after Molly. I offer'd to do a bit of tidyin' for him but he said it was too lovely a day to waste on scrubbin' and anyway he w'd rather talk to me, so we sat by the pond while Molly chas'd the moorhens who are so tame they go nearly up to the cottage door. It is a lovely peaceful spot, out of the village, with only nature nearby and nothin' to keep you from your thoughts. I can see why he loves it as he does.

Josephine had been sure that Hester would build her own home into the story somehow, and she looked forward to seeing what role Red Barn Cottage would play in the narrator's life as the diary moved on. 'Nothing to keep you from your thoughts.' The phrase was a simple one, but it so perfectly described the trick that the house played on its inhabitants; even in her own short tenure, Josephine had come to regard it as a mixed blessing, and she wondered what the manuscript might go on to reveal about Hester's relationship with the cottage as she transferred her personal experience to the character she had created.

She put a stone on the pages to stop them blowing away and got up to stretch her legs. While here, she had paid very little attention to the pond at the bottom of her garden, noticing it only when she crossed the wooden footbridge to head into the village. She walked over to it now and smiled when she saw the moorhen's vermilion beak. Disturbed by her approach, the bird scuttled over the water, half-flying and half-running, leaving a troubled trail behind as its toes splashed the surface; its loud, metallic call echoed through the trees as it had from the pages, and Josephine realised that her pleasure in the manuscript was twofold: a fascination with the narrative itself, and a delight in the continuity between Maria Marten's time and her own. She left the bird in peace and made some more coffee, then returned to the story, which – with the benefit of hindsight – began to take a darker turn.

> Saw William and Maria goin' across the field to the barn later on. Samuel said they were often there, and my face must have given me away because he said I sh'd not fret about it – one would surely tire of the other soon enough, and he is probably right. If anythin' is certain, it is that people will always give one thing up if somethin' better comes along. I watch'd the barn on and off, but they did not come out again all the while I was there. It was dusk when I left, and Samuel walk'd me back to the house, Molly asleep in his arms.

> *12 April*
> Went over to Mr Payne's to pay the Missis's bill and fetch some supplies for the week. Caught him gossipin' with Mrs Stowe about Maria. They stopp'd when they saw me but not before I heard her tellin' him about the moonlit walks to the barn she has seen from her cottage. C'd not resist tellin' her she was wrong, which was stupid because it made her think more of it and I was angry with myself for makin' things worse.

Things hadn't changed much, Josephine thought dryly. She wondered if Elsie Gladding was by any chance a descendant of Mr Payne, or if the trait belonged to a profession rather than a family.

Tuesday 18 April

The Missis went to Stoke this afternoon, so slipp'd out to see Maria and found her in the garden, which she has made one of the finest in the village. She was pleas'd to see me and show off what she had been doin'. The potatoes were showin' already, and the roses will be a picture. In all the years I have known Maria, I never like her better than when she is here, doin' somethin' she loves and has a gift for. It is the only time she is content.

I told her what Mrs Stowe had bin sayin' but she only shrugg'd and said Mrs Stowe was sour and jealous and she had never lik'd her anyway. I said she wasn't the only one and it w'd not be long before Maria's father found out what was goin' on. She laugh'd then and told me they know already, that William is welcome at the cottage and how else did I ever think they were goin' to get her and her bastard child out from under their feet? It upset me to hear her talk so because I know how much she loves Thomas Henry. She made me feel stupid for not thinkin' about her situation, so I told her that if she thought a Corder w'd ever marry someone like her she was a fool. She said I knew nothin' about it and anyway she w'd rather be a fool than a drudge and scorn'd me for havin' no ambition 'cept to be a married skivvy rather than a maiden one. We said terrible things before I left, which I do not want to repeat here or think about. She made me so angry that I wanted to pick her up and shake her, and I do not see how things are to be mended between us.

19 April

Slept little, and even my dreams were angry. I cannot stop thinkin' about what Maria said, and my work was badly done all day. We have grown up together, she and I, and neither of us has a better friend, but we are so different, and we hope for different things. It w'd be nice to be warm, I suppose, and always comfortable, and for people to be agreeable and to see more places and do more things, but there w'd be no pleasure for me in the life Maria craves. Or rather, the life she is forc'd to look to because of what has gone before. I c'd not marry above me – not for money nor even for love – and be a lady with everyone lookin' at what I did and what I said and how I dress'd, and all of them havin' somethin' to say about it. There is no freedom in that, whether you are born to it or no, and altho' I am tied to this house and my time belongs to someone else, I am me.

It was remarkable how little a certain type of friendship changed through different times and different circumstances. There was a special bond between women who had grown up together, a bond that might fade with the years but that was never entirely replaced by anything else. The sentiments expressed in the diary were not so different from the letters that had passed between Hester and Josephine's mother, and she wondered if Hester had based the entries – consciously or otherwise – on their squabbles and reconciliations. The rift continued for some time, and the next few months concentrated almost entirely on the narrator's work and growing closeness to Samuel; other than a brief sighting with Corder at a summer fair, Maria was not mentioned in the diary again until the autumn. By then, she needed a friend more than ever:

8 September
Maria is with child again. She came to the back door in tears and I knew right away what she had come to tell me, but the Missis was about and I had to get Maria out of the house quickly before anyone saw her in such a state. Fetch'd my basket and gather'd blackberries for a pie, which gave me an excuse to talk to her outside. Not that there was much I c'd do, 'cept hug her and promise her that it w'd be all right when God knows it will not. How can it be? Maria has not told William yet but he will never marry her. He has not got the courage to go against his mother, and she w'd cut him off sooner than see him marry so low. Maria will not admit it, but I

know she is afraid that William will abandon her, and another bastard in the house will go against her with her parents.

To bed at 11, but every creak on the landin' disturbs me. The Missis must never find my diary. This is the first time I have ever had somethin' to hide. I wonder if that means I have led a blameless life, or a dull one?

11 September

Walk'd to the fields wi' some breakfast for the hay men. We have had fine warm days, even for the time of year, and if the weather holds they are sure to get the harvest in early, which will be a blessin'. Goin' out like this of a mornin' has meant I can see more of Maria. She has had to tell her parents – her stepmother has had too many children herself not to guess Maria's trouble – and she says they are pressin' William to marry her every time he goes to the cottage. It is as much as he can do to be civil to them, but he fears what they will say about him in the village. He comes back to the house in a sore temper, but at least he has not denied that the child is his. He has kept it from the Missis, and I am happy to oblige him by doin' the same, for her sake and Maria's if not for his. There is talk in the streets, but the Missis has grown frail of late and is barely seen about 'cept in church. Samuel is workin' all hours on the harvest and I have seen very little of him.

24 September

All to church this mornin' to give thanks for the harvest. William went with his mother and never left her side for fear she w'd speak too long to someone. It hurt me to see how touch'd she was by his attentions when I knew they were for his own ends. They visited the master's grave, and it is wicked of me to say if it is not true, but I c'd not help thinkin' that she wishes she was in the ground with him, and w'd be there for certain if she knew what ½ the village knows.

Went to the Cock later with Samuel and the other harvestmen, and if the amount of ale down'd is any measure, God will surely know how thankful we are. Samuel took my hand and we walk'd back to his cottage in the moonlight. He told me that the Missis had given him more work, and said he w'd be Bailiff before long. Then he laugh'd and kiss'd me and we sat there for a long time.

8 October

Summer has gone, but the sun pays no regard to the calendar and shines as she will. The Missis poorly wi' the flu, so pick'd some dahlias from the garden and put them in her room to cheer her, and she said how nicely I had done them. Plump'd her pillows and got her comfortable, and notic'd how pale her skin is against mine. She has seen no summer. She watch'd me, as tho' there is somethin' she wants to say to me, but perhaps I imagin'd it. Tried not to linger all the same, in case she finds the courage to ask me somethin' I do not want to answer.

19 October

Wet and windy night, and the rain has broken down all the plants in the garden so it is a sorry sight. Missis is much better but her illness has left her carin' little about her food, so slipp'd out to fetch somethin' to tempt her. Saw Maria with William up by Bell Hill. He has begun to go about the village with her now, as if he means to stand by her, and I know she is darin' to hope for marriage. People still talk behind her back but they are less certain of themselves and I have notic'd they speak with envy now, not scorn. If he loves her and does right by her, no one will be more glad than I to be proved wrong, and it is the child what has made the difference. She has often talk'd of wantin' a little brother or sister for Thomas Henry. She is such a good mother and no child of hers w'd want for anythin' if only she were supported as she sh'd be. I have never seen her so happy as she is now, with a man on her arm and the little one inside her, and I wonder if we do not want the same things after all.

21 October

Maria brought me some roses from her garden to give to Samuel. It is the anniversary of his wife's death, and it was kind of her to think of it. They are blood-red with the sweetest scent and every flower is perfect. I took them over to him this afternoon and stay'd wi' Molly while he went to the grave because he says it is no place for children. That is not how he wants her to know her mother. He was gone a long time and I thought I sh'd not be there and felt awkward, but he seem'd happier when he got back and ask'd me to stop and have tea wi' them. He kept some o' the roses in the cottage and when I left he put one on my coat and told me that flowers sh'd be for the livin'. I can smell it now. It makes me think o' the people I love.

31 October

All Hallows' Eve. A windy day, with the air full o' dust and scurryin' leaves. Missis back to normal, so the bell rang at ten for the orders. Walk'd over to see Samuel this evenin'. We sat by the fire and Molly pester'd me for a story. I remember'd how I loved ghost stories at her age, and how nice it is to be frighten'd when you are warm and safe and with people you love, so I told the ones I knew and she ask'd for more. Then I was sorry, because Samuel's dead are real and not the stuff of stories, especially at this time of the year, but he did not take it wrong and told some himself which were better than mine.

10 November

Sh'd have gone into Layham this afternoon to collect somethin' for the Missis, but Master John was taken sick and I stay'd at home to look after him. He has been troubled with a cold these last few weeks and the Missis has been frettin' about him but it takes a lot to bring him to his bed. He grows thin and weak, and his coughin' shakes the house late into the night.

13 November

Went to fetch the doctor first thing as Master John was much worse. He is short of breath and has pains in his chest, and is pale one minute and flush'd the next. The doctor ordered quiet and rest and cod liver oil, and I did not like the look on his face. How much work there is with illness in the house!

23 November

James is takin' like his brother now, and the doctor has order'd him to bed so the Missis now has her oldest and youngest boys to fret about. It is not for a servant to have favourites, but I am fonder of James than of the others. He is a sweet-natured boy, gentle and kind, and it w'd grieve me if anythin' happened to him. He acts brave and does not take sympathy for his illness, but he likes me to read to him when I have time. Have not seen Samuel, nor Maria. The house turns in on itself with so much work and worry and there is no time for the world outside.

28 November

The Missis has hir'd another girl from the village to take some work off me while I look after James and John. Her name is Sally, and she is pleasant enough, I suppose, altho' it takes more of my time to show her how things are done than it w'd to do them my-self. Still, the Missis meant well and I dare say we shall rub along. Thomas and William are out all day doin' the work o' 4, and we are all prayin' that the Missis will not fall ill. She is not strong enough to bear it at her age.

How much kinder it would have been if illness *had* taken Mrs Corder when it threatened the household. Josephine pictured the row of Corder graves in the churchyard, a mother's name the last to be added to the family, one son for ever missing from the line. It was hard to imagine the bleakness of that time on a day like this, but the diary did a good job of creating a very different Polstead, where sadness threatened with the darker days of winter and fortunes turned with the weather. Josephine looked up at the sky, glad that she had come to know the village at this time of year, that the beauty of this particular season would be fixed in her mind throughout the months to come. Hester's words seemed heartfelt, and Josephine had no doubt that she would see another, less hospitable side to Red Barn Cottage if she chose to spend time here during the bouts of rain and mud and bitter cold that stretched ahead.

4 December

The first snow of winter, and so cold I c'd almost see the trees shiverin' from my window. The room is icy and the draughts come through gaps in the window frame so wide that it scarcely matters if they are open or shut. At least Sally is in with me now, so there is the warmth of another body at night. It is the most useful thing she has done since she got here.

12 December

Sally has left. The Missis caught her takin' stuff from the pantry and told me to see her out o' the house. December is a wretch'd month to be out o' place in and I felt sorry, but she sh'd know better. It is not like the Corders to forgive. I help'd her pack her things and gave her a shillin' of me own. She left then, but she did not take the Missis's temper with her, more's the pity.

22 December

It is the anniversary of the Master's death, and we have all been fearin' more sorrow to come before the year is out, but Master

John rallied a little and the doctor seemed pleased with him. Pray God that James will follow. The first snowdrop is out in the garden.

The misplaced note of optimism marked the last entry of the year, and Josephine put the pages down reluctantly. A warm, cheerful light had lingered into the afternoon and she was tempted to carry on reading, but her sense of duty got the better of her and she went inside. Hester's book would have to wait until she had done some more work on her own; it was shameful for a woman of her age to need incentives to get on with something she supposedly enjoyed, but a few entries of the diary would be a nice reward when she had earned it.

She made herself a sandwich and took it through to the study. A peacock butterfly fluttered against the window, its wings raggedy and faded, and she let it out into the sunshine to enjoy its last few days, then settled down at her desk, determined to remind herself of how it felt to write a thousand words in a single sitting. After three stilted paragraphs, during which she had struggled to explain Claverhouse's military training to a bewildered mythical reader, she was distracted by the sound of a bicycle and the lunchtime post. There were two letters: one was a polite enquiry about publication dates from her publisher, marked urgent and forwarded with an apologetic note from her father; the other was not for her, but the envelope had a London postmark and she had seen the handwriting before. She had intended to write to John Moore to let him know of Hester's death, but it had slipped her mind; now, when she read the bookseller's latest letter, she was glad that it had.

My dear Miss Larkspur,

I trust this finds you well, and very much hope that the last volume I sent met with your approval.

As I mentioned in my note, something genuinely unique has recently come into my possession and I am now in a position to offer it for sale. I would rather

show it to you personally, but let me say for now that it harks back to Maria
Marten's time and is, in its own way, as fascinating as Curtis's account of the
circumstances surrounding her murder. Without wishing to sound too presump-
tuous, I am certain it is something which you would be pleased to own.

I would be extremely grateful if you could find time to view the item here at
Leather Lane – or, if it is not convenient for you to travel to London at the mo-
ment, I will of course be more than happy to bring it to you. It is more than a
year since we last met, and I look forward to seeing you. I must ask, though, if you
would contact me at your earliest convenience; the item in question has a very
special interest for collectors such as yourself, and – as much as I hope that its
home lies with you – I cannot hold it indefinitely.

Yours very sincerely,
John Moore

The pitch was expertly delivered, despite being couched in such courteous terms: nobody with a passion like Hester's would have been able
to resist the bait, and even Josephine was intrigued. She looked at the
letters side by side and played with the idea of killing two birds with
one stone. Clearly she needed to devote herself more seriously to the
research for *Claverhouse*, and it made sense to go to London now, while
she was south of the border, and spend some time in the libraries there.
And if her memory served her well, Leather Lane was easily walkable
from the British Museum; she could deliver the news of Hester's death
in person, and find out what John Moore was so pleased about. Best of
all, she would be able to see Marta again, sooner than either of them
had dared to hope. Her decision made, she cast a sheepish glance at
Bonnie Dundee and walked into the village to telephone her club.

14

The Underground train pulled into Chancery Lane with a protest of brakes and Josephine was relieved to get out. The Tube always depressed her, and she could never quite work out if its atmosphere made people dull and listless, or if they were already like that when they got on and had simply been gathered together in a common space. But today it had served its purpose, allowing her to stay longer at the British Museum and still get to Leather Lane before John Moore would think of closing for the day. She climbed the steps to the street and came out at the corner of Gray's Inn Road and Holborn, where two stone pillars in the road marked the City's former boundary to the west. It was not a part of town that Josephine knew particularly well, which was silly because the beautiful old courts that lay hidden and unchanged between Holborn and the river appealed to her sense of history and of peace. Even here, on the main thoroughfare, the commercial needs of the present day could not entirely eclipse the past. As she walked, she looked in admiration at a sixteenth-century frontage whose closely set timbers and mullioned windows – each row projecting a little farther over the street than the one below – proclaimed its period as faithfully as any document, and she vowed to get to know the area better.

Leather Lane was a narrow street on the left, linking Holborn to Clerkenwell Road, and Josephine wondered how it had got its name. Gamages, the department store, took up the entire corner block, but its windows – filled with household goods and a glittering array of toys – were the last hint of shopping on a general scale that the road had to offer. Further down, the shops were more specialised in what they sold – jewellery, clock repairs, a bootmaker – but there was a faded individuality about them that, if anything, made them more intriguing. She found what she was looking for about halfway along the street, just before Leather Lane Market. John Moore's premises were so subtly announced that it would have been easy to miss them. Sandwiched between a pawnbroker and a public house, the tall, narrow building looked more like a dirty, neglected office or private residence. There were no elaborate window displays and no boxes of books lined up along the pavement to tempt people over the threshold. Only the words 'John Moore & Son, Bookseller' on a discreet brass plaque by the door gave any indication of what went on inside, and Josephine guessed that spur-of-the-moment customers were few and far between. The obscure location and the tone of John Moore's correspondence suggested that most of his trade came from clients like Hester, directed by word of mouth to his door for their own specific tastes and nurtured over a period of time.

Above the plaque, there was a white ivory doorbell circled with discoloured brass, but the door was open and Josephine did not bother to ring. Inside, the business was far less modest about its purpose: the front of the shop was filled with boxes of books that spilled out onto the floor, and it was impossible to say if they were new acquisitions that had yet to be sorted or if the effect was deliberate, a version of the market barrows that teased browsers with the hope of a bargain. Elsewhere, the shop was more conventionally arranged, not dissimilar to those she had just left in the streets around the British Museum, where everything was ordered, tidy and catalogued. The bookshelves were organised in such a way as to offer plenty of scope for undisturbed browsing, although Josephine suspected that very little escaped the sharp eye of the proprietor. John Moore – it seemed a safe assumption; she doubted the establishment employed a large staff – was an elderly man, in his late sixties at least, and she wondered how long the firm had existed and whether he was father or son. He was a striking man, even from a distance, with greying sandy hair, a heavy brow and a pronounced squint which a pair of small round glasses seemed to do very little for, and Josephine could not help thinking that if Uriah Heep had been thirty years older, this was what he would have looked like. His right arm, she noticed, hung uselessly down by his side, and she guessed it was a defect of birth rather than a war wound – he was surely too old to have fought. He acknowledged her arrival with a nod, but was too engrossed in conversation with another man to ask what she wanted, and she was grateful for the chance to look round without having to explain herself. The men sat opposite each other across a long, leather-topped desk, and their manner was more redolent of a consultation than a commercial transaction; had they been divorced from their surroundings, she would have said that they were lawyer and client or doctor and patient rather than bookseller and customer. Incongruously, the wall behind the desk was covered almost entirely with a painting of the Battle of Waterloo.

It didn't take her long to realise that the bookshop was devoted exclusively to the history of crime. Even the more general subject areas – literature, theatre, cinema – consisted of Victorian novels that centred on a murder or mystery, and films and plays that brought notorious killers to life. The largest section by far, though, dealt with true crimes, and Josephine was astonished by how much time had been spent in chronicling the misery of others; there were hundreds and hundreds of individual volumes, many covering cases she had never even heard of, and the collection as a whole would have put any police library to shame. The books were organised by the particular murder they described rather than by author, and she cast her eye along the shelves: Burke and Hare, Crippen, Florence Maybrick, Madeleine Smith, John Thurtell and Henry Wainwright were just a few of the more familiar names whose deeds seemed to have been widely celebrated in print, and those not famous enough to warrant their own section had been charmingly gathered together under headings like 'Poison', 'Railway Murders' and 'Infanticide'.

The Red Barn murder had a shelf to itself, packed for the most part with different editions of Curtis and one or two of the anonymous fictional accounts that had been published shortly after the crime. Josephine recognised many of the spines from Hester's bookcase, but she picked up something she hadn't seen before – a pamphlet called *Maria Marten's Dream Book*. She looked at the date and was interested to see that it had been published as recently as the year before: more than a hundred years on, there was obviously still an appetite for new insights into the crime, and she had no doubt that Hester's book – if she could get it published – would be widely read. On closer inspection, the pamphlet she had found was only tenuously connected to what had happened in Polstead: the author – whoever he or she was – had simply used Mrs Marten's visions of her stepdaughter's body as a justification for a book on the interpretation of dreams. Amused, Josephine looked up those that had troubled her recently and learned that seeing a fire meant luck, but being burned was a warning of trouble, and that dreaming of a burial was generally the sign of a birth. It was hardly Freud, but she decided to buy it anyway.

She wandered further down the aisle, in time to see John Moore leave his desk and disappear into a room marked 'private'. Daylight seemed to want nothing to do with the back of the shop, and the walls here were lit with lamps whose warmth belied the nature of the material. The final rows of books were interspersed with artwork, if that wasn't a contradiction in terms for such a morbid display. There were framed front pages from the *Illustrated Police News* and a few original examples of the broadsheets printed by James Catnach, but Josephine's eyes were drawn instantly to a hangman's noose, mounted in a wooden case shaped like an upside-down coffin; there was a label underneath the rope to tell her which poor devil it had dispatched, but she could not bring herself to go anywhere near it. Most startling of all, a life-size wax model of a woman dressed in black silk stood in the corner of the room, so realistic that it would have been easy to believe she was a customer left over from another age. Josephine walked over to her, intrigued and repelled at the same time. The woman was staged and carefully lit, and had a peculiarly sinister face, with dark, slightly oblique eyes and a sullen mouth;

even if she had not been given pride of place in a room such as this, Josephine would have said that her expression was secretive and threatening, malevolent even. There was something about the waxen face, the stillness of the glance, that made Josephine feel as if she were actually staring at a corpse and she wanted to turn away, but the bookseller had returned and she was reluctant to show her distaste. Out of the corner of her eye, she saw him hand over an odd-shaped parcel which clearly did not contain a book. The other man left the shop with his purchase – although purchase was perhaps the wrong word because no money seemed to have changed hands – and Josephine was conscious that she now had the bookseller's full attention.

'Kate Webster,' he said, nodding to the waxwork. 'Irish maidservant. Bludgeoned her mistress to death in Richmond in 1879, and was immortalised by Madame Tussaud a few months later.' His accent was pure East End, his voice light and surprisingly young. 'Are you familiar with the Webster case?'

Josephine shook her head. 'No, I've never heard of her. Looking at this, though, it's the maidservant part that surprises me, not the bludgeoning.'

'Quite. I'm not sure she was constitutionally suited to the profession.' He smiled, and she could not resist the temptation to look for a resemblance to William Corder in his face, but his age made it impossible; in any case, all the images of Corder she had seen had been drawn after the news of his arrest, when people were more interested in seeing the face of a murderer than a true likeness. 'She'd been given notice, and on the day before she was due to leave, she waited for her mistress to come back from church and set about her,' Moore explained with relish. 'Actually, I said bludgeoned to death but it's not certain that Mrs Thomas was dead when Webster started to mutilate and dismember her. She left her boiling in the copper while she went to the pub. The next day, she went round the neighbours offering best dripping for sale.'

The case was so extreme and so sensational that Josephine was surprised she had never heard of it. It made shooting or strangling someone in a barn seem lacklustre by comparison. 'Is that how Webster was caught?' she asked.

'Not immediately, no. Mrs Thomas was something of a recluse and wasn't much missed. Then Webster made some mistakes – dumped the rest of the body in a box in the Thames, dressed in Thomas's clothes and told people she had inherited a cottage from an aunt, even passed herself off as the victim to sell furniture and other bits and pieces from the house. She fled to Ireland, but the police soon caught up with her. The middle classes were much more careful in their choice of servant after that.'

'I'm sure they were.' The story struck a chord with Josephine's concerns about Hester's missing treasures, and she wondered what else John Moore might sell that was not so readily on display. 'How on earth do you get hold of things like this?' she asked.

'Oh, the Chamber of Horrors is never short of new recruits, and the old guard like Kate here eventually outstay their welcome.'

That told her nothing, but it was the only answer she was going to get. 'And there are people who actually want to live with something like this?'

'Some of my clients have, shall we say, a more rounded interest in crime. But most of them stick to books and illustrations.'

'And paintings, I see.' She gestured to the enormous canvas behind the desk. 'I know Napoleon gets a bad press, but I'm not entirely sure he's earned his place in here.'

He laughed. 'Ah – that's not for sale. It belongs to the building, and I'm sentimentally attached to it. It was painted by a chap called Jack Kelley who used to lodge in a room upstairs.'

Josephine remembered the name from Moyse's Hall. 'The artist who painted for the peepshows?'

'That's right.' Moore looked at her with a new respect. 'He'd be amused to hear himself dignified with the term artist, though. In reality, he was a drunk who was handy with a paintbrush, and could turn his hand to anything if the price was right. Three and six for an ordinary picture, seven and six for a battle scene like this.'

'I don't suppose you have any of the backdrops he did for the Red Barn murder, do you?'

'I'm afraid not. I've read a lot about them, but I've never actually seen one.' He looked at the book in her hand. 'Is Maria Marten your main interest?'

'Yes, in a manner of speaking.' She held out her hand and introduced herself. 'You are John Moore?' He nodded, curious now. 'At the risk of sounding suspiciously like an Irish maidservant, I've recently inherited a cottage from one of your clients. Hester Larkspur was my godmother. You wrote to her recently, and I wanted to let you know that she had died.'

'Miss Larkspur? I had no idea.' To his credit, he looked genuinely sad. 'I'm so sorry to hear that. Miss Larkspur was one of my most knowledgeable customers, and one of the most colourful.'

'How long had she been coming to you?'

'Oh, for many years now.' He sat down at his desk and offered her the seat opposite. 'I thought it was strange that I hadn't heard from her. She was always so excited when she received a new book, and I'd invariably get a letter from her within a few days. I'd expected an instant reaction to *The Old English Baron*. She'd been hoping for something like that for years.'

'Why? What was so special about it?'

'It once belonged to Maria Marten.' He must have seen the look on her face, because he added: 'Yes, I know it's hard to believe. Miss Larkspur had similar reservations, but I was able to confirm its authenticity, I'm happy to say.'

'How?'

'When her mother died, Maria was sent to work for a parson in Layham and it's his inscription on the flyleaf. That's the first clue. Then, if you look very closely, there are little notes in the margins at various points in the book. They match the samples we have of Maria Marten's handwriting. It was those that Miss Larkspur asked me to check.'

'When was that?'

'Months ago now. I was busy abroad earlier this year, and I couldn't deal with it until I got back. I wish now that I'd done it sooner.'

'I must pay you for it.'

'Only if you're sure. I'm very happy to take it back – there's always a market for anything to do with the Red Barn.' He paused, as if wondering how to phrase an indelicate question. 'In fact, when you told me who you were, I thought that might be why you were here – to sell Hester's collection.'

His efforts to keep a note of hope out of his voice were not entirely successful, and Josephine felt naive for believing that his sadness over Hester's death was anything but financial. 'No, not at the moment,' she said. On her way here, she had rehearsed stories of her closeness to Hester, guessing that it would not serve her well to admit that they had been strangers, and borrowing from other people's anecdotes to make her story authentic. Now, she realised she would need to offer John Moore a greater incentive than sentiment to get what she wanted. 'This is all very new to me and there's still a lot to sort out,' she said, 'but I can't possibly keep everything. It's quite a collection, as I'm sure you know. I'll be in touch.' She got her chequebook out of her bag to pay for the book. 'In the mean time, you said you had something else for her.'

'Yes. It's a great shame. I would have liked her to see it, but it will have to go to another buyer.'

He obviously had no intention of telling her more, and Josephine wondered if that was because he assumed she wouldn't want it or because he did not want to sell it to her. Either way, she couldn't bear to leave without at least finding out what all the fuss was about. 'What is it?' she asked, her voice warm but casual.

Moore's eyes went from the chequebook to her clothes and her bag, and she knew he was calculating that money would not be an issue. 'You're interested in adding to Miss Larkspur's collection?'

'I'm interested in buying the right things at the right price, and theatre and crime are my two biggest passions. My godmother and I were very alike in that respect.' It was truth of a sort, and she saw that she had John Moore's interest. 'Hester got me interested in Maria Marten, but I've always been fascinated by Burke and Hare, too. Native loyalty, I suppose.' She had deliberately chosen the largest section in the shop, and it worked: a new world of opportunity opened up in John Moore's eyes. 'I understand that you have a loyalty to your existing clients,' she added, deciding that it was time to play him at his own game, 'but I'll consider anything that's genuinely unique. If it's authenticated, of course.'

'Of course.' He smiled cautiously and stood up. 'There's no harm in showing you, I don't suppose, as you've been kind enough to come all this way.'

She waited while he went into the back room and returned a few minutes later with a small suitcase. 'This is it,' he said, opening the catches one by one and turning the case round to face her. 'It's quite the most original discovery to have come to light in years, certainly in all the time I've been dealing with the Red Barn murder.' He allowed her the pleasure of opening the lid for herself. The case was filled with tiny booklets, made from individual sheets of paper folded and cut. The pages were held together with pieces of ribbon or neatly stitched along the spine, and every inch of paper was covered in ink. 'It's a diary, obviously,' Moore said. 'It starts in 1821, and belonged to a servant girl who worked for the Corders. She was also a friend of Maria's, and that's what makes it special. An insider's view of the Red Barn murder is, as I'm sure you'll agree, a very desirable commodity.'

Too astonished to speak, Josephine picked one of the bunches from the top of the pile and stared in fascination at the meticulous handwriting, straight out of a copy book, and the scratchy ink marks and blotches that spoke of the effort involved in what seemed such a simple task. There was no order to the makeshift diaries and the one she had selected was from 1823, dated only once on the front page. She sifted carefully through the rest until she found 1826, aware that Moore was staring at her, keen for a reaction. The entries were longer, the words abbreviated, and there was no hint of the standardised spelling and punctuation that marked the version she had read, but she recognised enough of the text to know that what Hester had been working on was not a fiction but an edited transcript of a real diary. No wonder she had been so excited about it; the feeling was infectious, and Josephine started to speak without thinking. 'But this was Hester's . . .' She stopped herself just in time. There was no proof here of any wrongdoing, and she could not even begin to work out in her own mind what it might mean; the important thing was to get the diary safely off the premises, and she would not achieve that by causing trouble.

'Yes?' Moore said, watching her face intently.

'This was Hester's dream,' she said instead. 'Something so ordinary, and yet so revealing. Where did you get it?'

He shook his head, as though she had disappointed him. 'I'm sure you understand I can't break a confidence of that sort.'

She knew instantly that it had been the wrong question. One glance at the library-bound newspapers and official documents on the shelves had told her that much of the shop's stock was stolen or at least of dubious origin. She didn't think for a moment that Moore was the thief, and he certainly wasn't stupid enough to sell something back to Hester that in all probability she had owned already, but she doubted that he would care about legality or ask questions about provenance, and he survived by demanding the same moral ambivalence from his customers. 'Of course,' she said, her tone suggesting that his had been the derisory comment. 'What I meant was – are you sure it's genuine?'

'Oh yes. Or to be more accurate, I'm sure it's genuinely from that period. The materials are easily datable, and so is the language. It could be a fabrication from the time, of course. Novelists fell on the Red Barn murder like bees to a honeypot, but nothing like this has ever appeared in print and it has the ring of truth about it.'

'Have you read it all?'

'No. I haven't had time, and anyway, it adds something to the purchase for the buyer to feel that he is the only person to read this other than the girl who wrote it. There's nothing like that sense of being first to discover something.'

What it added to the purchase was likely to be a zero, Josephine thought, and decided to take the initiative. 'How much is it?' she asked.

'My price to Miss Larkspur was fifty pounds . . .'

'That sounds fair,' Josephine said, unscrewing the top from her pen.

'. . . but that was based on the long relationship that we shared. I have other, less valued, clients who would happily pay double that . . .'

'All right, a hundred pounds.'

'. . . perhaps more. It might be best if we said . . .'

'Mr Moore, I will give you one hundred and fifty pounds for the diary, *The Old English Baron* and this book on Maria Marten. Next time I'm in London, I will bring you a list of items that I'm happy to sell from Hester's collection, and you will have first refusal on them all. Do we have a deal?'

He smiled, and offered his left hand. 'It's a pleasure doing business with you, Miss Tey. I can see why your godmother passed you the baton.' She wrote the cheque before he could change his mind, and tried not to seem in too much of a hurry to leave the shop. 'And Miss Tey?' he called, when she was almost at the door.

'Yes?'

'Is it *just* books you're interested in? If I come across other . . . curios, shall I let you know?'

Josephine had a vision of all Hester's belongings offered back to her for sale, complemented by one or two of the less savoury items she had refused, but it was one way of getting to the bottom of what had happened to them. 'Please do,' she said, trying to sound more enthusiastic than she felt. 'You can contact me at Red Barn Cottage.'

She walked out into the street and didn't slacken her pace until she was back in Holborn, shoulder to shoulder with the normality of a rush-hour crowd. Her mind was racing with questions and with the thrill of what she now owned, but she had no idea what to do about any of it. What she had read of the diary took on a new resonance now that she knew it was rooted in truth, and she could not wait to read on through the murder and its aftermath – but her excitement was tempered with unease. There was no doubt in Josephine's mind that Hester had owned the diary and that her intention had been to publish an edited version; she was also sure that nothing would have persuaded her to part with the real thing, even if she had completed her work on it. Nearly everything of any great value had been removed from Red Barn Cottage, either before or after Hester's death, and there was a more frightening possibility which Josephine had no choice now but to face: that Hester had died because of what she owned. The idea seemed remote and fanciful in the heart of the city, but she knew that it would take hold of her imagination the moment she was alone in the cottage again, and the prospect chilled her. She needed to talk to someone who could tell her if her suspicions were ridiculous and if not, what to do about them, and the only person who could do that was Archie. As she had a friend at Scotland Yard, she might as well use him; if she was lucky, he would be at the end of his day and free to have dinner.

The Underground would be crowded by now, and Josephine was reluctant to take something so precious onto a packed train. She wasn't in the mood to fight for a taxi and the Embankment was in easy walking distance, so she cut through Fetter Lane and headed down the Strand, too preoccupied with her thoughts to delight in a London evening as she would normally have done. In no time at all, the red-brick splendour of New Scotland Yard was in front of her, dominating the river with its baronial architecture until it was outshone by Parliament a little further west. She had been here on numerous occasions to see Archie, and usually felt intimidated by the businesslike efficiency that ran throughout the building; today, though, her purpose was more than a social call and she felt less guilty about approaching the front desk to ask if Detective Chief Inspector Archie Penrose might be available to speak to her.

'I'm sorry, Ma'am, but the Chief Inspector is away on a job at the moment. Is it a personal call, or could someone else help?'

'Will he be back tomorrow?'

'I couldn't say, Ma'am. I'm sorry.'

There was a real art to being so obligingly unhelpful, Josephine thought; whoever had assigned this charming young constable to the enquiries desk had chosen well. 'Is Sergeant Fallowfield away as well?' she asked, disappointed not to see Archie but willing to settle for his colleague.

The constable perked up at the chance to offer something more positive. 'No, Ma'am. He's on duty upstairs. Who shall I say is here?'

Josephine gave her name and waited for Bill to come down. When he arrived, she was touched by how pleased he seemed to see her, and the feeling was mutual. She had known Bill Fallowfield for nearly twenty years, ever since Archie had joined the police. In all that time, they had rarely spent more than an hour in each other's company, but had settled into an easy if unlikely friendship, based on shared interests – Bill was an avid reader of detective fiction – and their affection for Archie. There were not many people whom Josephine liked to impress, but Bill's good opinion mattered greatly to her. He ushered her into a side room, somehow managing to open the door for her while carrying two cups of tea. 'Arriving or leaving, Miss?' he asked with a twinkle, nodding towards the suitcase.

'Neither, Bill. It's rather a long story. I was hoping to talk to Archie about it, but I understand he's away.'

'That's right, Miss.' He paused, and she wondered why he looked so shifty. 'Actually, he's in Suffolk.'

'In Suffolk? Why on earth didn't he tell me? I had a letter from him last week, but he didn't mention it.'

'No. It was all a bit last-minute. He's been gone a few days.'

'Whereabouts in Suffolk? He might at least have called in.'

'I'm not sure, exactly.'

She laughed at his pained expression. Deception did not sit well with Archie's sergeant, even when it was a professional obligation. 'You're a terrible liar, Bill, but I won't push my luck. Can you at least tell me if it's worth my while to hang on in London for a day or two?'

'Nothing's really been decided yet, Miss.' He brightened a little. 'I could give him a message, though. Only if he telephones in, obviously.'

'Obviously.' Josephine scribbled a note and handed it to Bill with a wry smile. 'Perhaps you could pass that on to him if he happens to let his address slip when he calls.'

'Of course, Miss.' He tucked the note into his inside pocket, and Josephine knew that it would be with Archie within twenty-four hours, whether he 'telephoned in' or not. 'How are you finding life in my neck of the woods, anyway?' he asked.

She had forgotten that Bill came from Suffolk; in her eyes, he was more of a Londoner than most people born to the city would ever be. 'I'm getting used to it,' she said.

'Polstead, isn't it?'

'That's right.'

'Nice place. Shame about the murder, though. They haven't really got over it, have they?'

Josephine could not have put it better herself. 'To be honest, I haven't really seen much of the village. The cottage is a little way out, and I've spent most of my time there. It needs a lot of work.'

'Those cottages always do. Takes me back a bit. Five of us in a bedroom, and my mum and dad and the baby in the next. All the houses were like that.'

'How old were you when you left?'

'Fifteen, but I spent five years before that wondering how to get away.'

'You weren't happy there?'

'It wasn't so much a question of happy or unhappy. I loved my family, but my father worked on the land and there was a war between farmers and their men in those days. The farmers took all they could, all the life and strength those men had, and there was no arguing if you wanted to keep your home. I never heard my father complain once – it's just the way it was.' He smiled. 'My mother was a different story, mind you. She was the one who knew how bad the wages were because it was her job to make them last.'

'It must have been hard for her when you left.'

'Yes, that's why I stuck it for a bit. My father got eight shillings a week for me in the fields, long days and four hours off on a Sunday. I didn't mind the work, but there was no respect. Village people in my day were worked to death, Miss Tey. My dad wasn't much older than I am now when he died. That's no age, is it? But the life made him ancient. I can see his face now, the lines on it from working under that fierce sun. I wanted something different, and deep down my parents wanted that too. They never once grudged me a better life, and I'm grateful to them for that. And I was damned glad to get away.'

It was a far cry from the idyllic country life that most people believed in if they didn't know better. Josephine pictured the countryside around her cottage, the gentle farmland and golden fields, and marvelled at how easy it was to be deceived by its beauty. 'Where did you go?' she asked.

'I walked to Ipswich and got a train to Colchester, kissed the bible at the barracks there and took my shilling. Do you know, Miss, I put on a stone in my first month with the regiment? That's how hard that farm work was. An army training was easy by comparison.'

'Do you ever go back, Bill?'

'Not much. Not after my mother died, anyway. I've got a sister and a couple of brothers there still and we keep in touch, but I don't think of it as home.'

'Promise me you'll let me know if you do, though. Or, of course, if you happen to be there in the next few days . . .'

She gave him a meaningful look, which he acknowledged with a grin. 'I'll let the Chief know you're after him, Miss.'

'Good. Thank you, Bill.' She said goodbye and walked out into the early evening sunset. London's personality was as affected by the seasons as the countryside around the cottage, she thought. Her favourite time of year in the city had always been spring; it arrived with a thrilling softness, a lightness and gaiety that contrasted with the age of the buildings – and it was a London springtime that had brought her Marta, and would now be for ever precious. But an autumn evening by the river had its own charms. The waning sun blended beautifully with the man-made colours of Scotland Yard, and Josephine wondered if the architect had had an evening such as this in mind when the building was conceived.

She took a taxi back to her club in Cavendish Square and asked the receptionist to put the precious suitcase in the safe overnight. Her failure to find Archie had left her restless and unsure of what to do next. She telephoned Marta at her home in Holly Place, but her mood was not improved by finding Lydia there instead and learning that Marta was 'still at Shamley Green with the bloody Hitchcocks'. She excused herself from Lydia's dinner invitation, checked again with reception that by some miracle Archie had not left a message for her there, and went to bed early, ready to take the first train back to Suffolk in the morning.

15

It was half past four when Josephine arrived back at the cottage, relieved that Hester's car – or Chummy, as she was now known – had got
her to Hadleigh station and back in one piece; it was hardly the most
ambitious of maiden voyages, but at least if she bumped into Bert she
could tell him truthfully that his gift had been used. She set the precious suitcase down in the porch while she looked for her key, feeling
very strongly that she was returning something to Red Barn Cottage
that belonged there, something that was part of its history years before Hester. With the door ajar, her hand still resting on the latch, she
turned to look back at the space where the barn had been, barely fifty
yards from where she stood. The slope was covered with grass and
thistles now, an ordinary square of an ordinary English field; no one
would guess the violence of its past, or that its secrets continued to
define the atmosphere of the village, even to this day. The horizon was
peculiarly empty, the air deathly still, as if the peace of the late afternoon were daring her to prove the lie. Even the house seemed to be
waiting to see what she would do next.

While it was still light, she busied herself with the chores that would
allow her to read the diary uninterrupted later: building fires and making dinner; filling the oil lamps and making sure there was enough
water for the night ahead. When she was ready, she found her glasses
and emptied the suitcase carefully out onto the floor of the study.
Hester's manuscript, which had seemed so fresh and so exciting when
she first discovered it, looked bland and featureless next to its inspiration. The booklets were made up of individual sheets of paper, folded
and cut into four, and small enough to tuck into the pocket of an apron. She found the earliest one and looked through it, scarcely able

to believe she was holding something that had been created by Maria Marten's closest friend and written in the Corder house, as excited by the physical reality of the diary as she was by the testimony it contained. The diarist – whoever she was – had initially used her books to record the weather and a list of daily duties. At first, her phrases were stilted, the language self-conscious, as if she had been embarrassed to keep a diary at all; then, as she grew in confidence, the entries began to adopt the voice that Josephine had come to know through Hester's transcript, and the diary became fuller and less formulaic – something to which its author could trust the ordinary and extraordinary events of her life, where she could share the secrets of her heart.

Josephine found the book for 1826 and placed the two versions of the diary side by side to see what sort of editing Hester had done. Much of the domestic work had been cut out, she noticed, and Hester had standardised some of the spelling for a modern reader whilst remaining faithful to the language and speech rhythms of the original. More often than not, the diarist wrote things down phonetically, a habit that told Josephine almost as much about how she must have spoken as a recording of her voice would have done. She had her own shortened version of words, too – not a code exactly, but a means of writing quickly at the end of a long day. What struck Josephine most, though, was the scale of the undertaking: there were hundreds of pages, often scrambled out of order, and as well as the challenge of the writing itself, some of the leaves were faded or discoloured and blotched with ink. Hester must have spent years on this, finishing – thank God – before her eyes let her down. In fact, such close work, done in the sort of light that Josephine was struggling with now, had probably played a significant part in Hester's loss of sight.

For speed and the pace of the story, Josephine decided to continue with Hester's transcript in the first instance and refer back to the original if there was anything she wanted to check. The only sounds to break the stillness were the gentle ticking of the clock from next door and the occasional cracking of a beam as the house settled – a strange, brittle sound, she always thought; a sigh of relief, almost, that another day had been safely negotiated. Otherwise, the cottage was silent, offering her every possible encouragement to get on with a story that was in part its own.

Monday 1 January, 1827

A new year, and I shall try to do better with my diary, altho' there has not been much I w'd want to keep a record of these last few weeks. James is lookin' much better, and is in good spirits. Master John got up for his dinner for the first time. Walk'd by Flaggy Pond with Samuel this afternoon. The woods are a tangle of branches and thorns like in the fairy stories Molly likes me to read to her. We were talkin' and laughin', and I did not notice how far we had walk'd. I shall be footsore tomorrow, no doubt.

Josephine guessed that work had got the better of such good intentions: the next few entries were sparse, and many days missed out altogether. When they picked up again, she noticed that there was a change in the writing as the crisis of William and Maria built; now the writer hardly ever mentioned her work, even in the original, but used the diary to record the atmosphere in the Corder house and her anxiety for her friend.

23 January

I hardly know how to write about today. Master Thomas went out after dinner and took a short cut across the pond, but the ice c'd not hold him. The first we knew of it was the hollerin' and shoutin' outside, then William went out to help and John, too, altho' he is not well enough, but Thomas was ½ way across and they c'd not reach him. I stay'd behind wi' the Missis and James, and c'd do nothin' but watch their hopes fade. It was dark when they brought his body back to the house. He was 25 today, altho' it is silly to find more cruelty in the loss because it is his birthday. We had brac'd ourselves for sorrow with James or John. Now this has come so unexpected, just as they are farin' better. The Missis took to her bed. She is sorry, no doubt, for the times she and Thomas were at odds, and I w'd not wish those thoughts on anyone. Her daughter has come to be with her.

Slipp'd out late to tell Maria. Thomas was her first and she cared for him, and they had a child together, altho' that was the end of them. Stay'd a long time as the news upset her and made her think of that poor little one whose father has now gone to be with her. She ask'd after William and I told her he was consolin' his mother. He and Maria have been arguin' over money but she will forgive him in his grief, I know. As I was leavin', Maria's stepmother ask'd me to give their condolences to Mrs Corder, but there are some things best left unsaid. Cannot sleep now for thinkin' of how cold he must have been in that water.

24 January

Glad when the light came after such a long night. We are a house of grief again, so I put me in my black and did my usual work. The Missis is heartbroken, but her anger at Thomas for wastin' his life is stronger even than her sorrow. William is busy with his brother's death, and a servant is useless at a time o' mournin' when meals are not needed and no one cares if the brass is polish'd or no, so there was time to see Maria. She ask'd me to go with her to put snowdrops on Matilda's grave. The Reverend stared as tho' we had no right to be in the churchyard, and Maria turn'd to leave because her shame is plain to see now, but I made her stay and stared back while she put the flowers on her dead baby's grave. It is not Whitmore's place to say who can be in a place of God, and it makes me angry when people do not understand how she feels. She fears this child will go the same way, as it is of the same blood. It w'd kill her to lose another.

29 January

We buried poor Thomas next to his father. John and James were too ill to leave the house, and William was the only son by his mother's side. Maria had sense enough to stay away, but I saw her standin' at the end of her lane as we follow'd the coffin past the pond that brought us there and up the hill to the church. It is at times like this that she feels her distance from William. For all her hopes, when I see how far Matilda lies from her father, even in death, I do not see how that separation is ever to be overcome.

The next few entries showed William in a surprisingly good light, taking charge of the farm and working hard after his brother's death, but Josephine could not help thinking about Maria, and how isolated and frightened she must have been.

19 March

Maria left today for Sudbury. William has book'd lodgings for her to have the child there, and they left together. She did not want to go and has been low for the last month, but she promis'd to write and let me know how she is. William came back this evenin' in high spirits. I expect he is glad to have Maria out o' the way.

26 March

Letter from Maria this mornin', askin' if I will go and see her. The Missis said I c'd have Thursday off as long as I leave the meals ready and do not fall behind wi' my work. She w'd never have given it to me if she knew where I was goin' or what is bein' kept from her, and I feel poor for deceivin' her.

She came into the kitchen later, which she never does, and caught me with Molly. She ask'd who the child was, so I told her and apologised, but she sat down and took Molly on her knee for ½ an hour while I work'd. When she left, she said she hop'd to see her again, and it was the most content I have seen her since the Master went. I suppose she expected this house to be ringin' with grandchildren, but we are a far cry from that at present and the one she has got comin' she will never know about if William has his way.

29 March

Took the coach to Sudbury and arriv'd at midday. Maria is stayin' in Plough Lane, and her rooms and the woman lookin' after her are nice enough. She was glad to see me, but seem'd in poor spirits and I c'd tell she had been cryin'. I thought William was neglectin' her, knowin' how busy he is wi' the farm, but she says he has been kind, payin' for her lodgings and the best doctors, comin' to see her twice a week and bringin' her nice things. Still, I have hardly seen her so low and it is more than the baby gettin' her down. She misses Thomas Henry and worries he will forget her, and said once or twice that her family will have hardly notic'd she has gone. And she does not smile as she us'd to when she talks about William. She feels trapp'd and is makin' the best of it, but that is not love.

Got back late to a dark house and William waitin' for me at the top of the stairs. He knew where I'd been and ask'd how Maria was. I told him she w'd be pleas'd to be home. He nodded and let me go to my bed.

Josephine shivered, although the room was not cold. The incident was simply expressed, and she could not help but embellish it with her own imagination – the shadows of the Corder house, the silence of grief and the smell of sickness, William waiting silently in the darkness to safeguard his secret. For the first time, Josephine sensed that this girl – paid by the Corders to do as she was told, seemingly without a family to look out for her – was as vulnerable in her way as Maria.

3 April

Master James took a turn for the worse and we were up ½ the

night with him. He is wastin' away, and his face is so pale and hollow that I can hardly look at him. All night he was troubled by a cough which comes in waves and leaves him pantin' and exhausted. It frightens me to be with him and I was glad when daylight came. The Missis is despair one minute and hope the next, and there is no tellin' which it will be.

Fetch'd the doctor first thing and saw Mrs Martin down Water Lane with George and Thomas Henry. A stranger w'd o' thought they were both her boys, and I was glad I had not seen them last week when I was tryin' to comfort Maria.

7 April

Some good news at last! Maria has had a son, a little brother for TH, and she is well and recoverin'. William disappear'd, on farm business so he said, and when he came back I look'd for a sign of pride or joy in his face, but there was nothin'. God only knows how things will be when Maria brings the baby home.

17 April

Maria is back, so call'd to see her between clearin' the dinner and gettin' the supper. Pick'd some bluebells and cowslips on the way, and I swear they were the only bright things in that cottage. The baby is a poor little thing, sickly-lookin' and small tho' he went his full time, and Maria cannot take to him as she w'd like. Mrs Martin has him most o' the time. Maria is tired and at her wits' end wi' the endless back and forth between William and her parents about marriage, as if it is of no matter. And perhaps it is not. Something has died in Maria, and she seems not to care now what happens to her. She is lost, and I do not know how to help her.

25 April

William sent me to the Martins wi' some money this mornin'. It is the first time he has ask'd me to go between them, and I was glad of the excuse to leave the house. I have tried to see Maria most days to lift her spirits, but it is hard to get out sometimes, with John and James so sick. She was upstairs wi' the baby, as she does not want anyone to know she is back. I hate to see her there – it goes against her nature to hide away, and she has never liked to stop inside. The garden is lookin' poor for missin' her. She told me William has agreed to marriage at last, altho' he says he cannot set a date while everythin' in his family is unsettled, wi' more grief ahead for his mother. He cannot dally too long as far as Maria is concern'd. She is sick of love, and has sense enough to know that bein' tied to him by law will never make her a proper wife, one he can be proud of to his family. She w'd refuse him, I think, but for her father. She has lost her own will. It is a wicked thing to wish for, but I hope William's weakness will save them both.

As she read on, it seemed to Josephine that the relentless wearing down of Maria's spirit was as tragic in its own way as her murder, and she could not begin to imagine how bleak and hopeless her future must have seemed. How many women did this diary speak for? she wondered. Women who did not go on to be as notorious as Maria, but whose fate was a slower, longer death – trapped in a loveless marriage if they were lucky, for ever tainted by scandal if they were not. It always amazed her that the shame of illegitimacy was not diluted by its ordinariness, even now; it touched every family, including her own, but inclined none to understanding. Her father's younger sister had been a domestic servant and had fallen pregnant at twenty – to the man of the house, Josephine assumed, although no one had ever told her that and she soon learned not to ask. It had happened long before she was born but, throughout her childhood, her cousin was still known within the family as Mary's bastard, and neither mother nor son had truly forgiven each other for the lives they could never have: marriage and a head held high on one side; certainty and belonging on the other. The two women were separated by sixty years, but shame was the same whatever age it lived in.

30 April

William came back in the early hours, and had words wi' the Missis later. Went to see Maria between my chores, but knew somethin' was wrong the minute I stepp'd in the cottage. Mr Martin sat starin' into the fire and even his wife was lost for words. She told me the child had died in the night, but that is all she w'd say. Went up to Maria, and saw that tiny body in a makeshift box, as far out o' sight as can be in the little end room where Thomas Henry usually sleeps. I cannot recall seein' anythin' more wretch'd, or lift myself out o' this sadness for a soul who was not lov'd nor wanted for a single moment of his short life.

Maria w'd not get out o' bed and barely spoke to me, and the blankness in her face frightens me more than all the tears and despair o' the last few days. Downstairs, the Martins were arguin' over where to bury the child, and it seems he is not even to have a proper Christian funeral. Stay'd with Maria for a long time, even tho' it w'd get me into trouble and even tho' she did not want me there. Ask'd her if William knew, and he does. Her parents are worried that he will not have to marry her now, and I chided myself for bein' silly enough to mistake their troubl'd looks for grief.

2 May

Samuel call'd at the back door after market. He is worried about me, he says, and it is true I have been short and distant, so promis'd to walk over Thistley Lay with him later. A beautiful evenin', it was, with the cherry trees a mass of pink and white and the laburnum in full bloom, but I c'd not enjoy it. Samuel was kind and did his best to cheer me and I wanted nothin' more than to tell him why I am sad, but it is not my secret and I know my silence hurt him.

Sat late into the night with Master John. Heard Maria cryin' in

166

William's room on my way up to bed and listen'd to make sure she was alone before goin' to her. William brought her up the back stairs earlier, and was off buryin' the baby. Her parents think they have taken him to Sudbury where he was born, so she must stay in the house long enough to give truth to the lie. Stay'd with her until I heard the back door close, then came to bed, my dress soak'd in her tears.

A sadness crept up on Josephine as quietly and as gradually as the coming on of the night. She got up to pour a drink and stood at the window, looking out into the blackness. Somewhere nearby, at the edge of the wood, a vixen howled, but she could see nothing outside – no stars, no lights, no movement. She drew the curtain across the void, hoping to shut out the sense of oblivion that she felt so strongly, but it lingered with her in the room, created as much by the unsettling world of the diary as it was by the physical remoteness of the cottage. She half-wished that she was reading the manuscript in London, where she would not have felt so isolated by both place and time, but she had come too far to stop now.

13 May
Maria sent little George with a note this mornin', askin' me to meet her by Flaggy Pond. William has said that Constable Baalham is threatenin' to take her up for bastard children, and she wanted to know if it was true. I have heard nothin' in the village, but I have been about less than usual so it may be. She is frighten'd ½ to death at the thought of goin' to prison and leavin' Thomas Henry, but William has said he will take her to Ipswich tomorrow and marry her there, and she has agreed. She is here with him now. I c'd hear them arguin' as I pass'd his door.

14 May
No sign o' Maria this mornin'. William took his breakfast with his

mother, so I nipp'd upstairs but the room was empty. Kept waitin' for him to leave the house after that but he stay'd and help'd with his brothers. Poor James is nearin' the end, and perhaps that is why they have not gone. God knows I have no time for William and the way he has treated Maria, but it is heartless of the Martins to plague him when his brother lies dyin' and his mother needs him. Not all parents are as keen to rid themselves of a child, and I c'd happily shake Mrs Martin – for this will be her doin'. Maria's father only does as he is told.

16 May

Maria is beside herself because William says they cannot take Thomas Henry with them when they go to marry. He is to stay behind for the present, and she must be parted from the only thing in the world she loves. She fears that William will never let her fetch her son and that TH will forget her, and cries with rage at the thought of Mrs Martin takin' her place with her son just as she has with her father – but she still has the threat of arrest hangin' over her. To my mind, there is precious little difference 'tween the two sorts o' prison open to her, so I told her to get her father to talk to the constable – but she said she c'd not trust her parents to tell her the truth as they are desperate for her to marry. There is nothin' more to be said. They are goin' to Ipswich to-morrow, and she is to be ready.

17 May

C'd hardly bring myself to wait on William this mornin'. I c'd brook losin' Maria if she were happy, but he is takin' her away against her will and it is not only Thomas Henry who will miss her. He went out after breakfast. I watch'd him walk across the back fields to the Martins' cottage, and felt more alone than I have ever been. I have always had Maria to talk to and laugh with, and even tho' things have been difficult and out o' the ordinary for months, she was still here. I do not know what I will do without my friend.

Clean'd the scullery so the Missis w'd not see me cryin', but William was back ½ an hour later and stay'd for the rest o' the day. No notion what is happenin', and if the doubt unsettles me, what can it be doin' to Maria?

18 May

A lovely day, but I c'd not enjoy it. She is gone. William came upstairs this mornin' while I was cleanin' his room and told me to put some of James's clothes in a bag. I thought they were takin' him somewhere for his health, but William took the bag and left the house at a ¼ to twelve. With all the comins and goins of the last week, I had begun to hope the worst w'd never happen and was content in my work for a while, but this time William did not come back. So Maria is gone, and I do not know when I will see her again.

The simplicity of the entry was particularly poignant, Josephine thought. By the time the words were set down, Maria was dead. Her friend's ignorance of what had really happened was heartbreaking, and Josephine would have given anything to be able to reach back through the years and let her know the truth. In her mind's eye, she pictured Maria saying goodbye to her young son and walking across the fields, dressed in William's dying brother's clothes, and wondered how the diarist would feel when she knew she had unwittingly colluded in his plan. In all the melodramas, whether on stage or screen, Maria was killed at night in the middle of a storm, but the reality was so much more powerful: an early summer's day, when the year promised so much and the sun was at its highest – that was no time to be wrenched from the world.

19 May

Sat up wi' James to the best of my strength tonight. There is no surer way of comin' face to face wi' your own life than watchin' over someone in the last hours of theirs. Every memory came back to me twice as strong in the quiet and the dark. Then I thought about Maria, and wondered where she and William were, and if she is more at peace with herself now her fate is settled. Most of all, I hope she had the chance to talk to Thomas Henry before she left, not that he is old enough to understand. I cannot think what William has told the Missis, but she has not question'd his goin'. I do not know why he wanted James's clothes, not that the poor soul has any more need of 'em. He slept at last and I came to my bed. Maria's mirror was on the pillow, left from when she was here. I held it up to the candlelight, wishing it c'd show me what I wanted to know, but all I saw was my own face.

When she was a child, Josephine's grandmother had often held a mirror up in front of her, telling her that if she looked hard she would see her future in its glass. Josephine had never believed in it, or in any of the similar superstitions attached to mirrors, and yet – since she had found out to whom it once belonged – she had not been able to look at her face in the glass upstairs.

20 May

William came back this mornin', strollin' into the parlour and whistlin' as tho' there was nowhere else he sh'd be. I was cleanin' the grate at the time, wi' the Missis watchin' me, and the surprise must have shown on my face because he took his mother out o' the room before I c'd say anythin'. Went round to the Martins later, but Maria is not there. Her stepmother told me that William had call'd first thing to say she is with the sister of a school friend of his in Ipswich. The marriage licence cannot be got for another month, and he has given Maria money to tide her over. He did not give them an address, but Maria will surely write soon.

22 May

Master James died this mornin', and I clos'd the shutters. A beautiful day has no place in a house as curs'd as this. The Missis sat with him for a long time afterwards, and William paced up and down outside. The burdens of the family are beginnin' to tell on him. Wi' James gone and John so poorly, he is the hope of his mother and the farm, and the thought of tellin' her who he has tied himself to must prey on his mind. If he intends to keep his promise, which I w'd not trust him to do. Maria w'd not be the first girl to be kept out o' sight by a rich man's pocket, and she will not be the last.

So tired tonight. James is out o' the sufferin at last, but I c'd weep for his sweet face and kind ways, and his goin' so young.

24 May

Clean'd William's room, and found a pair of leather gloves and Maria's best shoes. I expect he is savin' them for the weddin'.

28 May

Polish'd William's boots, then brush'd my black frock and did my black straw bonnet up with a bit o' crape. The air was heavy and thundery, and the church bell toll'd too loud and clear as we follow'd the cart that took James to his buryin'. The Missis is thin and pale and wrung out wi' cryin. I notic'd her lookin' at the Master's stone and the space where her own name will go, and I doubt she ever thought there w'd be two more stones beside his grave before her time comes.

Saw William talkin' to Mrs Martin in the churchyard, but c'd not hear what they were sayin'. He was carryin' Maria's green umbrella, and it reminded me o' the times we used to go about together and how we w'd laugh – and I wish'd more than ever that I had her here to talk to. I cannot remember the last time anyone laugh'd in this house, or when I have felt less like doin' so.

171

1 June

Took William's ridin' boots for mendin', and was stopp'd at the bottom of the hill by Mrs Martin, who wanted to know what William is doin' and where he goes and if he talks about Maria. Told her it was not my place to bring that business into the Missis's house and that William was out most o' the time seein' to the farm. Might have added that it was a fine time for her to start bein' concern'd about Maria, but held my tongue.

All the men are workin' from daylight to dark at cutten the grass in the lower fields. Took bread and cheese up to Samuel in Hare Field and we drank beer in the sun and smil'd at the cows standin' in the stream out o' the heat. The corn looks well and he says it will ripen early if we are bless'd with a month that finishes as it has started. Told him about Mrs Martin. He said that Maria has gone away before without any harm comin' to her, and I was not to worry.

14 June

Wi' the men out all day, there are plenty of yard jobs to get on with, as well as my usual work and nursin' poor John. He is not long for this world. This watchin' and waitin' is like a terrible dream night after night, knowin' what the end will be. It is a wonder the Missis is not mad wi' the grief of losin' so much in so short a time.

I have tried to do as Samuel said and not think about Maria, but it is nearly a month since she went away. I ask'd William for an address where I might write to her. He said he c'd do better than give me the address, for he was goin' to Maria on Saturday and w'd take the letter himself. I have written it, tho' I c'd not put in all I wanted to say for fear of him readin' it – but at least Maria will know I am thinkin' of her.

17 June

William back from Ipswich at ½ past five. Waited for the Missis to go to bed so he might give me the letter from Maria. Still nothin' by the time I came down from evenin' prayers, so I ask'd him how Maria was, thinkin' that might remind him he had somethin' for me. He told me she has hurt her hand and cannot write, but was pleas'd to hear from me and hopes she will see me soon. It was better than nothin', but a message is not the same as her own hand and I am no wiser now than I was before I wrote to her.

The excuses that Josephine had thought ridiculous during her conversation with Hilary sounded much more plausible when read in the context of day-to-day life. It was easy to be wise after the event, but why should anyone in that village have suspected the worst at this stage, particularly those who depended on the Corders for their livelihood? The diarist was already in an impossible position and Josephine suspected that it would only get worse for her.

25 June

William off takin' ewes to market and the Missis corner'd me while I was in the dinin' room and ask'd me what had happen'd to my friend Maria, because she had heard of her goin' from the village. For the first time, I was glad that I c'd truthfully say I have not heard from Maria since she left. I hope she does not keep askin'.

6 July

I heard talk o' Maria in the post office and c'd say nothin' to defend her. Why does she not write to me? Can she forget me so easily now she has better in her sights? Or is she so used to people wantin' her out o' the way that she tars me wi' the same brush as William and her family? Either way, it does not say much for our friendship. Everyone seems to know somethin'. Maria is in France, she is workin' up north, she has jilted William, she is wi'

child again. This village will make anythin' up to suit, but I am
her friend and I sh'd know. This frettin' must stop. If I dwell too
long on it, I will begin to hate Maria for her silence, which is a
wicked thing to admit and somethin' I can only say here, where it
will never be read.

15 July

Master John was took from us today. Sat with him a while as the
Missis ask'd, and remember'd him as he was when he was well and
full o' life and tried to kiss me in the kitchen – then look'd so hurt
when I box'd his ears that I let him try again. It seems so long ago.
I w'd like to think this is the last piece of sufferin' for the Missis,
but I fear she has a different pain ahead of her. The Martins are
set on makin' William do right by Maria, and he is surely runnin'
out o' reasons to delay.

18 July

Samuel took me to the Cherry Fair tonight. It was full o' colour,
as it always is, wi' drinkin' booths, gingerbread stalls and
sideshows, and plenty o' brandy to go round. How Maria used
to love it! We went every year together, and I can hear her now,
laughin' at the learned pigs and fortune-tellin' ponies, mockin'
the patter of the showmen. I cannot be angry with her any more.
We have not been apart like this since we were children, and I
miss her, but that is not her fault.

20 July

It rained all the way to the churchyard today, all the way through
the service and all the way back. Most o' the village came out and
those who were not mourners stood bare-headed as we walk'd
past – showin' their respect for the Missis's grief and the tragedy
that has been her shadow these last few months. Stood back from
the grave while they put him in the ground, thinkin' how cold

and drear it all was, and a line from an old rhyme w'd not go away. 'We laid 'em along by the churchyard wall, and all in a row we buried them all.' Please God this is an end to the sorrow.

12 *August*

William has started seekin' me out in the house or yard to bring me some bit o' news from Maria that he has just remembered. He behaves as tho we are sharin' a secret and I suppose there is no one else he can speak to, but there is no pleasure for me in his words because I only long to hear from Maria. He found me in the scullery and said Maria has bought a new pink dress and he has given her a saucy summer bonnet to go with it. I can only think she is tryin' hard to please him, because it is a colour she has always hated and c'd never bear to wear.

13 *August*

Scrubbin' the hall floor on my hands and knees, when William came downstairs in a hurry and stepp'd over me as tho I was not there. My temper got the better of me for how he thought he c'd treat girls like me and Maria, and I call'd down the hallway after him and ask'd him if he was ever goin' to marry her. He took his hand out o' his pocket and I thought he was goin' to strike me, but he was holdin' a gold ring. He told me Maria w'd be his wife in a month. I must have shown me doubts, for he said that he c'd not do it before, what with his brothers' deaths and bringin' in the harvest, because there were very few reliable men – and that is true. Samuel has been workin' all the hours God sends. Then he said I w'd see Maria very soon because he was bringin' her back for Michaelmas, and she and I w'd be able to have a good long talk, and after that I w'd see her every day. Told Samuel what had happen'd and he teas'd me and said I w'd not be so eager to see Maria once she had been my mistress for a few days, but he was pleas'd for me and we pass'd a cheerful evenin'. Six weeks is not long to wait.

175

18 August

Up at 4 to help get the barn ready for the harvest home. The men set the tables while we women decorated the yard wi' greenery and coloured ribbons – a picture it look'd, when we were done. At 6 o'clock people were makin' their way over the fields from all directions. It is a sight I have always loved, the whole village happy and with a common purpose for once – a church o' sorts, you might say. William took the top table and carv'd the meats, and everyone ate well, knowin' the barn was full for another year wi' not a foot o' bare earth to be seen.

Molly was not best pleas'd when Samuel took her home to bed, so he said she c'd watch from her window a while. William raised a toast to the men, and there were three cheers for him and for the harvest, and he stay'd till the drink run dry and every last man had gone to his bed. Wish'd Maria c'd have been there, but how she will love it next year.

It was a scene that any journalist would have killed for, Josephine thought – but they would never have been able to write it. The power of the image lay in its lack of self-consciousness, and in the horror and grief that the author would feel when she found out what had happened to her friend.

27 August

William furious 'cause two sheep are lost from the top fields. He will not rest until he finds them and he left all hot and bother'd to see the constable. Clean'd his room while he was out, as I did not want to get under his feet with him in such a temper. Found a letter ½ written under his blotter, and look'd in case it was to Maria and show'd her address. It was to Mr Matthews, and it said that Maria has been stayin' with a distant relation of William's, which was not exactly what he told her family nor me but perhaps she has moved on. He wrote that she will be his bride as soon as he has settled his family affairs, and until then she prefers to stay with his kindred. Mr Matthews might be fool enough to believe that, but I am not. Maria w'd never choose to be with strangers over her son, and I wish now that I had never look'd at the letter. I am more worried than ever about her, but I do not know what to do except wait and hope.

William's deceit was beginning to catch up with him, and Josephine wondered how much longer he would stay in the village; it would have been much wiser to decide on a lie and stick to it.

Outside, she thought she heard the latch on the front gate. She looked at her watch. Half past twelve. Far too late for visitors, but she listened anyway for a knock at the door. There was nothing and she resumed her reading, but the noise came again, more definite this time. She stood up, unable to concentrate, and took a lamp over to the front door to look outside. The light shone dimly onto the path. The gate was open, blown back and forth by a rising wind that blew uninterrupted across the fields in front of the cottage, and she heard the latch clatter again as the wood hit its post. Relieved, she went out to fasten it, but when she reached the hedge she could hear footsteps along the wooden bridge that crossed the pond. They were moving away from her, off into the woods, and the sound faded so quickly that she questioned whether or not they had been real. She went a few yards down the track and called out, but the only answer was the scream of some small creature set upon in the shadows, and she was too frightened to venture any further. The mystery and seclusion of the woods were even more forbidding than the open darkness of the fields, and she retreated to the cottage before anything else could conspire with her imagination. A gust of wind took the door out of her hand and blew it firmly shut behind her, as if the cottage had decided that what went on inside its walls was no one else's business, and Josephine was happy to defer to it. She stood in the kitchen, listening to the rose tapping against the glass through the open scullery door; as a child, she had loved nothing better than to lie in bed at night and listen to the wind and rain outside, but she was not a child now and an unquestioning trust in her own safety was no longer a luxury that she enjoyed. Unnerved, she closed the scullery door so that nothing from that end of the house could encroach upon her thoughts, and went back to the study, grateful for the packet of cigarettes that Marta had left behind.

4 September

How I used to love this time o' night, when the house was quiet and it was just me and my thoughts. Now they are no comfort. What is terrible enough to keep Maria away, stronger even than her love for that little boy? Is she expectin' William's child again and frighten'd of what might happen to her? Is she shut away somewhere, out of her wits wi' grief? Is that why the Martins have let her go so easily – a shame even greater than the last?

William complains of bein' feverish, and fears he is goin' the same way as his brothers. God forgive me for what I feel in my heart about that, but I am not asham'd of it. Perhaps if he were dead, Maria c'd be home where she belongs wi' the people who w'd love her and look after her.

8 September

William has gone. He left today to go to the sea for his health, and Pryke took him to Colchester to catch the coach. I carried his bags out to the cart, hopin' to have a chance to ask him if he is goin' to Maria, but he w'd not look at me. Now there is just me and the Missis, and I feel as tho' my last hope of seein' Maria has left wi' William.

29 September

Michaelmas. This was suppos'd to be a happy day, and I am angry wi' myself for believin' that William w'd ever bring Maria back here. I was a fool to listen to his promises. He must be laughin' at us both, wherever he is. I take his letters up to the Missis when they come, and they never bear the same mark twice. She reads them quickly – never more than a single sheet – and I can tell by her face that they bring no real news.

25 October

The village is full o' rumours again today. Pryke told someone about the last talk he had wi' William, and he said that he had not seen Maria since May. I do not know what to think. Lies have always come easy to William, but why would he say that when it goes against all he has led us to believe?

Went to see Mrs Martin this afternoon to tell her what I had heard, but she said it was idle tittle-tattle. She said she had a letter which proved different and my heart lifted until I saw it was from William and not Maria. He says that Maria is now his wife, and she sends a kiss to Thomas Henry and asks that her clothes be given to her sister as she has new ones. Mrs Martin look'd at me as tho' the words proved me to be a fool, but they have only worried me more. Maria loves her clothes far more than her sister. They have been at odds since their mother's death, and the finest new clothes w'd not persuade Maria to have Nan dress'd up in what is rightly hers. I know somethin' is wrong, but if Maria's family will not listen to me, who will?

The diary continued in the same vein for the next few weeks, a mixture of frustration and anger and despair as the writer noticed more contradictions in the stories of what had happened to her friend. By the end of the year, Josephine saw that she had begun to give up hope.

20 December

The snow has been comin' down hard for two days, and the village is cut off from the world. There are deep drifts everywhere, and Samuel help'd the shepherd dig the sheep out and make a path for them to the yards.

It is strange to have so much light at night with the moon shinin' on the snow, and yet for the days to be dark and dull in the house wi' drifts up against the windows. Everywhere looks so different, and it is easy to let my imagination get the better of me. A dreadful fear has taken me over these last few weeks. When I am quiet and alone like this I cannot hide from it. I have thought up so many reasons for Maria's silence, but I am afraid that none of them is as terrible as the truth I do not know. I am done with hopin' and prayin', because I feel certain in these dark moments that I will never see my friend again.

26 December

Went to see Samuel after dinner and it took me a long time to get to the cottage wi' the paths deep in mud after the snow and I need not have bother'd to look nice. Molly c'd not wait to show me the little decorations she had made for me and the room was warm and pretty with holly and a cloth on the table. It was all so cheerful and homely that I c'd have cried wi' happiness.

We had the food that I took wi' me, all proper Christmas fare, and Samuel gave me some honey wine that Hannah had sent. Later, when Molly was asleep, he ask'd me why I have been so sad of late, and I do not know if it was the wine or his kindness but I found myself tellin' him all I fear'd most about Maria. He put his arms around me and said it is not good for me to be on my own in that house with all the darkness and w'd I not rather be here in the firelight with him and Molly? I did not answer him at first for fear of not understandin' what he was askin', but he kept on talkin', sayin' that William bein' away has given him more to do on the farm and the Missis is good to him and pays him a fair wage, and Molly loves me as her own mother and that he w'd like to love me as a husband and be with me all my days, if I c'd ever think of Red Barn Cottage as my home. And I knew then that I already do.

How I long to be tellin' Maria my news rather than writin' it down. I know she w'd hug me and laugh and tease Samuel for takin' so long to ask. But I will not feel guilty for being happy, not after all this time.

How short-lived that happiness would be, Josephine thought sadly; there was still so much horror and tragedy to come. She was tired now, but she could not think of putting the diary down until she had finished it, and neither did she want to lie awake upstairs in the darkness, listening for sounds outside. She went through to the kitchen to make some tea and closed her eyes while she waited for the kettle to boil, picturing the scene she had just read taking place in this very room. If the marriage went ahead, the writer would come to live at Red Barn Cottage, and she wondered if Hester had actually found the diaries somewhere on the premises; she had always assumed them to be another shady purchase with no questions asked, but perhaps not; perhaps Hester really had been the first person to read them other than their author, in which case her discovery was so much richer. She took her tea through to the study and picked up the final year.

Tuesday 1 January, 1828
God willin', this is the last new book I shall begin. The Missis cannot go on as she is in this big house all alone, and when her daughter fetches her away and she is settled with her family, I will be Samuel Kyte's wife.

Josephine looked at the page in astonishment and read the lines again. The further she got with the diary, the more frustrated she had become with its anonymity; she had longed to know the author's name, but never in a million years would she have guessed at Kyte. Excited now, she rifled through the booklets on the floor until she found the diary for 1828, and double-checked that the name was exactly as it had appeared in the original. It was, and she tried to put her tiredness to one side and think clearly about what that might mean. Was the Lucy Kyte in Hester's will a descendant of the woman who had written the diary, or the writer herself? Had Hester actually made a bequest to a dead woman? There was no way of knowing at the moment, and Josephine read on, hoping to find another clue.

I must say goodbye to my little books when I am wed. There will be no need to dwell on my own thoughts for company when I have a family, and I know there is nothin' I w'd wish to hide from Samuel. But I will keep these pages to read when I am old.

12 February

Samuel brought me snowdrops for my birthday, enough to fill my tiny room. I do not know if they are the last flower of winter or the first of spring, but today they are a beginnin'.

Tom Martin was in the Cock tonight, talkin' about his wife. He says she is not sleepin' and has not been herself since their Maria went away, and now Mr Matthews has stopped sendin' money for Thomas Henry she has taken a turn for the worse. Maria's sister says her stepmother is goin' out o' her mind, wi' visions of Maria at night, knockin' on the door and cryin' for help. I suppose it w'd suit her if Mrs Martin was put away – with Maria gone, she w'd be free to rule the household at last. But if anythin' upsets Mrs Martin's sleep, it will be her conscience. A proper mother w'd have stopped Maria goin' with William when she was so low after the baby. If she is sufferin' for that now, I am glad.

18 April

Tom Martin came to the house and ask'd to speak to the Missis. I heard him ask leave to go to the barn and look for clothes that he thought Maria might have left there on the day she went away.

182

He did not mention William. The Missis said Pryke w'd take him to the barn tomorrow. Later, I begged Samuel to take me but he said only William and Pryke have a key. He promis'd to watch for them tomorrow and told me not to worry, but there is more to this than lost clothes. I shall not sleep tonight.

19 April

Saw Pryke go off this mornin' to meet Tom Martin. The Missis watch'd him from the window, and we both waited for news. It was Samuel who came back to the house. He was a few minutes wi' the Missis, then he came to me and I knew by his face that they had found her. He c'd not speak at first, but I begged him to tell me and he knew that if he did not I w'd go up there and find a way to see the truth myself.

They found her in one of the bays, not a foot down in the earth. She was tied up in a sack, her poor body bent double and a handkerchief around her neck. I scream'd at Samuel to stop, to tell me that it was not Maria, but they are sure. They have found earrings and shoes and a pair of combs. Her family say they are Maria's. Nothin' more is left of her to know.

She is still there, lock'd in the barn. They are waitin' for the coroner to come from Bury. She is found and her misery known, but she must wait another night in that place. Tomorrow, the men of the village will stand over her body and look and point and talk about her as tho they care. It is Maria who will be judged, and Thomas Henry will never truly know his mother. If she is re-member'd at all, it will be as the poor murder'd girl or the whore. Where is William? How c'd he live on here and smile and lie so easy, passin' that barn every day, all the time knowin' she was in-side? And I have been happy in that cottage, laughin' and talkin' with Samuel, never knowin' that she was so close, and so alone.

Tonight, Samuel walk'd with me up to Barn Field. The flowers I left for her look'd sad in the fadin' light. He says we do not know what happened and I must not judge for the Missis's sake, but I know. She is dead, and I have bow'd and scrap'd to the man who killed her. I c'd have wash'd her blood from his clothes, and the thought of him makes me sick to my stomach.

Maria. She is here now, in front of me, her face black and swollen, and she stares at me, unforgivin' because I have let her down. I can still hear her voice in the silence, and she is tellin' me that if I had been in trouble, she would have found a way to save me.

Josephine rubbed her eyes and stared into the light of the lamp, but the image would not go away. She remembered how she had felt after dreaming of Marta's death, but this was not a nightmare that Maria's friend could ever wake from. '*Nothing more is left of her to know.*' She imagined those words spoken about someone she loved, someone she had grown up with, and felt their pain as if it were her own. For a moment, the sense of loss inhabited her so strongly that it frightened her, and she had to put the pages down.

When she was ready to go on, she brought another candle forward to give herself more light. Its flame enlivened the delicate greys and browns of the photographs on the wall where she was sitting, and she looked at Hester's face in one of the many stage shots of *Maria Marten*. How must she have felt when she read the diary for the first time and learned that – for all its heightened drama and excessive thrills – the play could not touch the truth for sadness and horror?

20 April

I heard the cart as it was beginnin' to get light. From my window, I c'd see the men makin' their way slowly across the fields towards the barn. The procession was ghostly in the mornin' mist, and I wish'd I c'd wipe their purpose from my mind as easily as I c'd imagine the sight of them to be a dream.

I left the house and waited on the edge of the village for them to bring Maria back. They were gone a long time. Word had spread overnight and a crowd gather'd on the green and along the path to the Martins' cottage. For once, the village held its tongue, and the silence when the cart came back was broken only by the sound of the wheels on the stones and the heavy footsteps of the men who walk'd behind it. Their faces told me what they had seen, but all I can think of now is Maria on that cart, cover'd in a sheet, as slight as a bundle of rags. How can that be the friend I loved? Her father walk'd with her all the way. As they lifted her body from the cart and into the Cock for the inquest, I thought his grief would break him but he found the strength to go inside.

I went back to the house to wait for news. The Missis ask'd me what was happenin' and I told her what I had seen, but she said nothin'. At 6 o'clock, while I was clearin' away a supper that had never been wanted, the church bell began to toll. It was late for a funeral, but they c'd not wait to get Maria back in the ground. To lay her to rest properly in the mornin' light is more than our shame will allow. Samuel was one of the six who carried the coffin and the Martins walk'd behind, with Thomas Henry cryin' in his grandfather's arms. Mrs Martin star'd at the Corder house as we pass'd it. She look'd back at me as if I was to blame. There will be some who think the money the Missis pays me to serve her family is stronger than my love for Maria. It is only a matter of time before the village takes sides. But I will not be given lessons in loyalty by Anne Martin, and I hope my face told her so.

As we climb'd the hill to the church, I look'd back and saw hundreds of people followin', far more than had known Maria while she was alive. Why did she have to die to matter? I caught myself wishing for her sake and mine that she c'd have been happy wi' less, but why sh'd she not have dreams?

They buried her near the wall at the back of the churchyard, in sight of the Hall and away from the Corder graves. Reverend Whitmore has never had such a congregation, and he seem'd very pleased with himself, but all his talk about the power of spirit c'd not comfort me after the sight of that cart this mornin'. I stood under the sycamores, the wind rustlin' their branches and mixin' with the sobs of family and strangers, and forgive me, Maria, but I c'd not cry. Time will come when I turn to you as I always have and you will not be there, and I will weep for the loss of you, but until he is found and punish'd my anger serves you better than my tears.

23 April

All the talk in the village is of Mrs Martin's dreams and how Maria was found. She is makin' quite a name for herself, and does not like to be outdone by a dead Maria any more than she did by a livin' one. Went to their cottage this afternoon to take some treats to Thomas Henry. He was playin' under the cherry trees and I pick'd him up and told him how his mother loved this garden, but Mrs Martin snatch'd him away and snapp'd at me not to upset him by talkin' about Maria. Started to answer her back, but I c'd see that our shoutin' was troublin' him so held my tongue.

I swear to you, Maria, I will make sure your son knows who you are. He will never forget you as long as I live, and when he is old enough, I will read him this diary so that he knows what your life and your death have meant to someone who loves you.

24 April

William is married. The newspapers say he has been found in Brentford, at a school where he lives with his wife. All the time he was writin' to the Martins and spinnin' lies about bein' happy with Maria, he was courtin' another woman and Maria was rottin' in the dirt of a barn.

A letter came for the Missis today from Colchester. It was in William's hand. She lock'd her door to read it, and I c'd hear her cryin'. When I clean'd her room, I found it in the grate and I know why she has lost her strength. In all his talk of shame and disgrace, there was no denial of what he is charg'd with. They are bringin' him back here for the inquest, and he asks that she receive his wife and her brother. Their name is Moore. I hope the Missis turns them away. I will not serve tea to the woman who wears Maria's ring.

25 April

No one sleeps in this house any more. I wonder if the Missis will ever rest again. It has been like livin' with a ghost since Maria was found. She fades more each day and does not notice when I speak to her. Her face is pale, the sorrow of each of her men written as clear there as it is on the stones that mark their graves. I can hear her now, movin' around next door, a ghost too tired to disturb the livin'.

There have been people in the village all day. They stand outside the house, revellin' in our scandal. Some have even come to the door and only turn'd back when Samuel threaten'd the dogs, but it will take more than dogs to protect her. She is at their mercy, and her shame will break her where her grief could not. They brought him back in the early hours of the mornin'. I heard the chaise just after 2, the horses strugglin' up the hill. Her footsteps went to the window and she stay'd there long after the sound of the hooves had died away. God forgive me, but I want William to suffer for her pain as well as for Maria's.

I was call'd to the inquest this morning, and Samuel came with me. There was hardly room to breathe inside the inn. They kept William upstairs while the evidence was given. The man who made the arrest said that William denied knowin' Maria, but he had Maria's reticule among his things. I was with her when she bought it on one of our visits to Bury, and I c'd not breathe when I saw it, rememberin' how happy she was that day. Her stepmother was shown her clothes, torn and cover'd with soil. She cried as she was examin'd, cried for her 'poor Maria', and it was all I could do to hold my tongue.

Then they called my name and all eyes turn'd to me. The coroner ask'd me what I had seen when I clean'd William's room the week after Stoke Fair. I told him about the box wi' the shoes and gloves and he ask'd me to describe them. Then I was dismiss'd. I tried not to listen as a surgeon describ'd Maria's body, but there was no escape from the horror of it. He spoke of the eye and the cheek and the heart as if they had never sparkl'd or glow'd or lov'd, as if Maria was an object and only matters to the law because she is dead. When the surgeon had finished, they brought William down. He saw me and smil'd – that smile that always charm'd Maria – and all I c'd feel was hate. I look'd at his hands and remember'd what the surgeon had said – her bones fractured, her neck strangled. I c'd not stay to hear any more.

Went back to the house and scrubb'd William's room. I will not touch anything that he has touch'd. Did not see the Missis. Her meal had not been eaten, and when I knock'd at her door she did not answer. To my shame, I was glad. I c'd not think of any words that w'd bring her comfort.

As far as Josephine could recall, James Curtis had given a full account of that inquest in his book and she took it down from the shelf to consult. Sure enough, all the witness testimonies were reported in full and she scanned them eagerly to see who had given the evidence about William's room. It only took her a few seconds to find the name she was looking for, and she slapped the desk in triumph. Lucy Baalham. The maiden name of Lucy Kyte. The village constable had been called Baalham, too, she remembered, and wondered if they were related, or if it was a common Suffolk name.

It proved nothing, of course. This Lucy Kyte had probably had children and grandchildren who were named after her, and it might easily be a living, breathing relative who was to take whatever would bring her peace from the cottage, but somehow Josephine doubted it. She remembered what Bert had said about Hester living in the past, about her ghosts being more real to her than her neighbours, and she knew in her heart that Hester's legacy was to Maria's friend, whose diary she knew so well. The revelation raised as many questions as it answered, but she set them to one side until she had finished the story. Lucy's story, as she now knew it to be.

8 May

His wife came today. I wanted to hate her for Maria's sake, but there is no evil in her. She speaks well and she is pretty, tho' if Maria was in the room, you w'd not notice her. And I c'd not help feelin' that Maria was in the room, that she had come out from the shadows of the back corridors to look at her rival. And I felt her pain when I saw that William's wife is carryin' his child.

A child, Maria. How will you rest, knowin' that there will still be somethin' of William on this earth? And she will have her child to love, when yours was taken from you and buried where you c'd never find him, when William stole out at night with his shame in a box and got rid of it as if it was nothin' to him.

18 May

It is a year to the day since Maria went to the barn. I cannot stop thinkin' about what I was doin' at the time she died. Was I cookin' the dinner or cleanin' the parlour or scrubbin' the stairs? I sh'd have known she was dead.

Hundreds of people have been to the barn since Maria was found, wantin' to see where she died. They are takin' it down piece by piece for keep-sakes and soon there will be nothin' left. I w'd take an axe to it myself if I c'd bear to go near it. I have not been to Red Barn Cottage since they found Maria. I cannot be easy there, seein' that place from the windows, thinkin' about that day.

It was a cruel trick of fate that had brought Lucy to a new home so close to where her friend had died, Josephine thought, but there would have been nothing she could do about it. It would have been a tied cottage, linked to Samuel's position on the farm, and there would have been no question of moving, even if Samuel had understood how hard it was for her. She must have been cheering inside when someone set light to it, although its horror would not have been so easy to erase.

19 May

Voices woke me in the night and I saw two men walkin' past the house wi' spades and ropes. I watch'd their lanterns up to the church, and I knew what they were doin'. There has been talk, altho' I did not want to believe it.

When I got to the churchyard, they had put burnin' torches by Maria's grave. There were three men I did not know and the parish clerk. I stood by the Gospel Oak and watch'd, not able to bear what was happenin'. I open'd my mouth to shout, but the sound died in my throat. There was nothin' I could do. There is evil at work and Maria will never rest.

They lifted her coffin out and plac'd it by the side of the grave. They forc'd the lid off and pull'd at her body with handkerchiefs over their mouths, and one of them took somethin' from her coffin and put it in a sack. When they had seen all they wanted, they left the dead to themselves. I waited until they had gone and put Maria's flowers back on her grave. Then I lay down on the earth and wept for her until it was light.

15 July

Seven days in a row it has rain'd from dawn to dusk. The rivers burst their banks, and the meadows are deep in water. Samuel came to see me at dinner time. The pond has flooded and the cottage, too, so I went to help. Tried not to think about the barn but all the time it was in my mind. I had to draw the curtains over the window. Molly thought it was a fine old game, all the moppin' and buckets and rain, and she tired herself out by teatime. Took her up to bed because Samuel said she was missin' me. Her window looks to the barn, and I remember'd her face there on the night of the harvest, watchin' us, before Maria was found and we knew what we were dancin' on. I sat in the window and told her stories until she fell asleep, then watch'd as the barn faded into the darkness. If it rains for forty days and forty more, that place will never be cleans'd.

The atmosphere in that room now could not have been more different from the scene that Lucy described, where all the horrors were kept at bay on the other side of the window, and Josephine wondered if the sadness had actually found its way into the cottage long before Hester's time.

16 July

At last, the rain has stopp'd. Folk began arrivin' for the fair, and I watch'd them comin' over the fields, laughin' and talkin'. Since they found Maria, we are full o' strangers. I wish they w'd stay away.

A man has been askin' questions in the Cock and Phoebe Stowe says he is a newspaper man from London. She says there is to be a book about Maria's murder, and this man Curtis has come to find out more about the village where Maria and William liv'd. Samuel pointed him out to me on the green so that I w'd know him if he came to the house. He has sandy red hair and looks kind, but I suppose it is his job to make himself popular among us. Samuel said we sh'd not speak to him, because gossip is not fair when William has not been tried yet, but I w'd like this man to know who Maria was if he is goin' to write about her, and I do not feel like bein' fair.

17 July

Pryke came first thing to tell the Missis that some showmen were makin' an amusement of the murder. She sent him up to the green with a warnin' to them not to play foul with her son's name.

It is the busiest fair we have ever had, but no one is here for the cherries, nor even the brandy. Me and Samuel walk'd among the stalls, and every way we turn'd, the ballad-mongers sang of William and Maria. By the Cock, there was a tent with a painted wooden sign outside, 'The Late Murder of Maria Martin'. Samuel tried to stop me but I shook him off and paid my penny. It was crowded inside, but I push'd my way to the front and star'd at the wax models – a butcher'd woman lyin' on a door, wi' the coroner and jury lookin' on. Maria, the day after she was found. It was a terrible sight and I c'd tell from the look on Samuel's face that it was truthful. The crowd laugh'd and cheer'd, and I c'd stand it no longer. Without thinkin' I took one of the burnin' torches from the side of the stage and set it to the curtain. The flames took hold and a woman near me scream'd, then someone threw a pail of water. Samuel dragg'd me away before the showman c'd catch me. The crowd laugh'd, and the anger and shame are still with me. I miss Maria. She is the only one who w'd know how I feel.

24 July

Maria's birthday. She w'd have been 27. There is a row in the village over a stone for her. Some have offer'd money so her grave might be mark'd after William is brought to justice, but the Revd Whitmore has said that it will never happen as long as he has power to stop it. He says that a stone will remind folk of how she died. Does he think we will forget even if her grave is only mark'd by grass? He lets them plunder the dead in his graveyard, but worries that a stone might upset the livin'.

Went to meet Mr Curtis again today, and he ask'd me more about Maria. He writes while I am talkin', strange marks that make no sense to me. He tells me it is somethin' that newspaper men use to make a true record of what is told to them, and he show'd me what some of the marks mean so that I can use them in my diary. It is nice to talk about Maria in a normal way, to remember her as she was before all this happen'd, when she was just my friend.

Engrossed in the story, Josephine had allowed the fire to burn low in the grate and she put more logs on, holding an old newspaper in front to coax the flames into life again. It had begun to rain outside, and the water down the chimney made the wood spit and crackle spitefully in the grate. She settled back down, determined to finish the diary before sleep got the better of her, but she had not got far before she was disturbed again. This time, the footsteps were inside, climbing the far stairs slowly, step by step, as if too weary to reach the top. Panic gripped her, but she listened intently as the noise drifted away, and decided that she must be mistaken; the steps were not muffled, as they would have been on the shabbily carpeted stairs she knew, but hollow, as if on bare wood. The sound must have come from somewhere else.

She took a lamp through to the kitchen and hesitated, trying to work out what was different about the room. The stair curtain was pulled back, just as she had left it, but the door that had always stuck against the bump in the floor was now completely open and moved freely back and forth when she tested it. The stairs were in shadows, and she wished she had left a lamp burning in her bedroom so that she would not have to climb into the darkness. She paused again, listening, but there was nothing – no creaking of floorboards overhead to confirm her worst fears, no rattling windows to explain away what she had heard. Frightened now, she followed the beam of her lamp up to the first floor, but her bedroom was reassuringly familiar, the other rooms empty and undisturbed. There was no one else in the cottage, and she cursed Lucy Kyte for playing havoc with her imagination, and herself for allowing it to happen.

The boxroom smelt of sickness. In spite of Marta's cleaning, the heavy, cloying odour had returned, stronger even than before. She took the lamp over to the window and put it down on the window seat, drawn against her better judgement to the words scarred into the wood. The letters seemed deeper than ever, and there were more than she remembered. The room, too, seemed more oppressive tonight, but how much of what she felt here was Hester's cumulative darkness, and how much Lucy's? How much – if she stayed in the cottage and allowed it to happen – would be her own? The lamplight in the window threw a likeness back at her, but the face she saw was pale and drawn, transformed by a sadness she had never seen before, a reflection barely recognisable as her own.

She turned away, took the blanket from her bed and went downstairs. The stub of her candle was guttering on the table, and some of the wax had run like tears onto the pages. The manuscript had been put down hurriedly and she found herself reading the section about the floods again before she realised that the pages were out of order. Still unsettled, she found it harder to concentrate now.

29 July

Mr Curtis came to say goodbye. He leaves on the Bury coach in the mornin' ready for the trial. He has promis'd to bring me a copy of his book as soon as it is publish'd. I told him that the only promise I want from him is to do justice to Maria, and he smil'd. I will miss his smiles and his kindness and his voice. He has given me back the Maria I knew, and I am grateful to him for it.

1 August

The Missis told me that I am to go to the trial and give evidence – for William, not for Maria. I am to speak up for the family that pays me, and not for the friend who knew every secret of my heart. I w'd rather die than betray her like this, but I cannot see a way out of it.

7 August

My lodgings are in Sparhawk Street, and the Missis has had to pay a guinea for a single bed. The inns and public houses are full, and Bury men must be smilin' for the good fortune the trial has brought them. There is not room for everyone. Folk are sleepin' in doorways and on pavements, carin' little for their comfort as long as they are here. There are puppet shows everywhere and men on street corners sellin' drawings. William and Maria's fame grows by the day, while the rest of us are strugglin' to make sense of what has happen'd. Maria cannot be spoken of now without William, nor he without her. There was a time when that was all Maria wish'd for.

Samuel came early to collect me. It was only a short walk to the court, but it took an hour to get there. The old churchyard at the front of the building was full of people. They fill'd the gaps between the graves, and I was glad to get inside. Just after eight, the gaol cart came and the crowd ran forward. There was a fight to make a path through and I saw people hurt in the crush. William jump'd down from the cart. He wore a fine new coat and blue trousers, white neckerchief and silk stockings, and I felt sick and frighten'd when I saw him.

We were not let into the court, but kept in a side room until our turn came. I was glad to have Samuel with me. The Missis's bailiff is call'd for the prosecution, and look'd as troubl'd with the side he is on as I am. Mr Matthews was there. I heard him ask after Thomas Henry, but there was little talk among us. We waited, as frighten'd as if we were the ones on trial, and time went slowly. There was a fierce storm and the sound of rain on the umbrellas outside fill'd our little room.

They call'd Maria's stepmother first, and her fear as she was taken into the courtroom was plain. I pitied her, but her face told me there is to be no change of feelin' between us. I am judged by what I am, not who, and I am servant to the Corder family. I am here to speak for William, and that is what will be recorded. No one will know how my heart screams against it. The day pass'd, and I was not call'd. Samuel walk'd me back to my lodgin's and I must do the same tomorrow.

8 August

I was call'd at eleven and led into the court. I saw they had a model of the barn, which made me shudder. And then the people, cramm'd into the seats, all starin' at me. I tried not to look at them or William, but the court was so quiet that I c'd hear heavy sighs comin' from where he sat. Then I saw Mr Curtis, sittin' with some other men. He smil'd at me, and I was glad to see him. William's man ask'd me if I had seen pistols in his room. I said yes. I told them William had left his mother's house two weeks before Old Michaelmas Day. Then he ask'd if William had ever behav'd badly towards me. I wanted him to ask about Maria, not me, so I c'd tell him how poorly she had been treated. But I had to tell the truth and say that William had always been kind to me. That was all. I was told to stand down.

They let me stay in the court after that. William's doctor was call'd next, then Samuel, but he had to wait because of the noise outside. I look'd up to a trapdoor in the ceilin' which had been open'd to allow air into the room. It was full o' faces, as folk were climbin' on the roof for a glimpse of William.

Mrs Martin was call'd back, and Maria's clothes were put in front of her – the handkerchief that she had worn round her neck, the earrings taken from her body, a fragment of her bonnet ribbon and the bosom of her chemise. Filthy, rotten and dragg'd from the dirt, kept in boxes for men to pore over and shown to the court like a sideshow. Samuel took my hand. It was so hot and pails of water were brought into the court for the crowd, but the stench of death rose from those clothes and fill'd the air. Maria's stepmother had to be help'd from the stand, and tears ran down Thomas Martin's face as his daughter's misery was laid out before him.

I must set down what happen'd next for the sake of my sanity. One of the surgeons held up a skull as he talk'd about wounds to Maria's face, and I knew that the skull which now turn'd its dreadful stare on us had once been my friend. The surgeon walk'd towards the jury, Maria's skull in one hand, William's sword in the other. I scream'd, and all eyes turn'd to me. That is the last I remember. Samuel told me later what the verdict was, and that William will hang on Monday, but I know what I have seen today will haunt me for the rest of my life.

Josephine could not even begin to imagine the effect that such a scene must have had on Lucy, and on Maria's family. It was straight out of the most lurid of melodramas, even if it was carried out in the name of science and justice, and she was shocked by the lack of dignity shown to Maria's remains. She remembered what Henry Andrews had told her about the market for relics, and wondered if the skull had ever been reinterred, or if it sat in a darkened room somewhere, the most prized piece in somebody's private collection.

11 August
I thought that sleep w'd not come when I went to my bed last night, but when I woke it was after seven. I c'd not help wonderin' about him. Had he slept through his last night on this earth, or did he cling to his final hours? I hope he has suffer'd from know-in' the moment of his own death. Maria was spar'd that, at least.

Went to rouse the Missis, but her room was empty. Search'd the house, afraid of what her grief might have driven her to, but she was nowhere to be found. Then I saw her from the window, walkin' slowly up the hill, her bible in her hand, her head held high. The village was quieter than usual – a lot o' folk had gone to

Bury – but the few that were about star'd without shame. Some dar'd to speak to her, but she look'd straight ahead as if she had not heard. She walk'd past me, too, as she came back in. The world only had room for her and her wretched son. She has not spoken to him since his sentence.

I c'd not do my work, and sat at my window. Just before 12, the sun came out. The church clock began to strike the hour, follow'd by the clock in the hall and the clock in the parlour, and I imagin'd the roar of the crowds buildin' outside the gaol. I thought I c'd actually hear them, but the cries were of a mother lettin' her son go from the world, in more pain now than ever she was when she brought him into it.

I went to her. There is only one grief, it seems, and the sorrow that stood between us has brought us together in the end. I have no idea how long we clung to each other, but when I left her the sun was much lower in the sky.

Josephine put the pages down gently, and cried – not for the Corders, but for Marta. It was the first time that her own life had truly broken through into her thoughts all night, and the collision of the two worlds felt strange and unsettling. They had hardly known each other when Marta's son went to the gallows, and yet she longed to have been with her, to have taken on some of her pain as Lucy had done for Mrs Corder. Even now, she had no idea what Marta had done during the final moments of her son's life, how she had coped with being alive in the hours and days that followed, how she ever faced another morning with that grief always at her shoulder. No matter how much they loved each other, or how strong Josephine's instinct was for understanding and solace, she could not do for Marta what a servant had done for her mistress. Their distance hurt her, and it was a long time before she went back to her reading. When she picked up the final pages, the blackness outside had turned to grey, signalling the end of a long night.

12 August

The newspaper says it took him eight minutes to die. He confess'd on Sunday night. His wife kept faith with him until the end. It is a love he did not deserve. Mr Curtis's paper printed William's last letter to her, written on a page from a book of sermons that she gave him. They say she is ill in Bury. Perhaps William's second child will be as unlucky as his first.

They took his body on a cart to the Shire Hall and show'd it to the people, naked except for his trousers, shoes and stockings, the skin cut from his chest, eyes and mouth half-open, his neck showin' the marks of a shameful death. I wish I had known. I w'd have walked to Bury to see his body por'd over as Maria's has been. Thousands queued for a last sight of him, they say, but readin' about it is not the same as seein' it for myself. I have such violence inside me. It sh'd be enough that justice has been done, but it is not.

13 August

Nan Martin caught me by the pond today and accus'd me of betrayin' her sister at the trial. I open'd my mouth to argue but the words stuck in my throat because I know in my heart that she is right. I treated Samuel badly because of it. He pick'd a fight with Nan's man, tellin' him that no one is more loyal to Maria than I am, and I was cross because I do not want him to defend me. He was only tryin' to help and I told him I was sorry, but we are a village at war at the moment. William is dead and the crowds have mov'd on. Left to ourselves, we turn on each other.

It was not Nan's insults that upset me. It was lookin' at her and knowin' that she is replacin' Maria – in the Martin house, and in the village. Thousands of folk think they have seen Maria's picture these last few months, but they have not. The portraits that were sold in Bury, the ones in the newspapers, were drawn from Nan's likeness, not Maria's. No one drew Maria when she was alive. Now she is dead, even her face is a lie.

For some reason, Josephine found this as sad as any of the more shocking entries that Lucy had written; it seemed to sum up so eloquently the way that the real Maria had been forgotten even by those who knew her – replaced for posterity by someone who had never really lived, her image changed by history as easily as the spelling of her name had been. She turned to the picture in Curtis's book. Maria shared the page with Corder and Thomas Henry, a twisted parody of the perfect family group. Josephine looked at the small, doll-like face, the bright eyes and pretty rose-bud lips, the perfect curls framed by a bonnet that had never been hers, and she felt cheated. She longed for the diary to tell her what Maria had truly looked like, but of course Lucy needed no written descriptions to bring her friend's face to mind, and the pages – which had been so revealing otherwise – remained stubbornly silent.

26 August

Mrs Martin stopp'd me outside the forge and ask'd me if I w'd like to go to the cottage and see Thomas Henry. She needs any friend she can get. For every person who believes in her dreams, there are half a dozen who whisper behind her back that she knows more about Maria's death than she says. I do not know the truth of it, but I am willin' to forget our differences for the sake of that little boy.

The cottage has suffer'd like the rest of us. I w'd never say that Mrs Martin does not keep a tidy house, but the rooms smell of sadness. Thomas Henry's face lit up when he saw me. It made me want to cry, but he has seen enough tears this last year, so I took him out into the sunshine. It did us both good. When we went back, his grandmother said I sh'd see him more often and take him to play with Molly, and I was pleas'd. Nothin' would make me happier than to see them friends.

As I was leavin', Mrs Martin put some of Maria's books into my hand, remindin' me of how we had always lov'd a story. It is nice to have them, with her notes inside, and a flower or letter tuck'd between the pages. I smil'd when I saw *The Old English Baron*. I c'd hear her voice, readin' it aloud to me as we sat on the grass over Thistley Lay. The taller a tale, the more Maria lov'd it. Then I remember'd the part where a woman guides her husband to their daughter's body through a dream, and now I cannot sleep for wonderin'.

In her excitement over the diary, Josephine had completely forgotten about the book she had bought with it, and made a mental note to look through it later, when she had finished Lucy's story. The thought of seeing Maria Marten's handwriting, and gleaning what she could of her personality from it, almost made up for the lack of an accurate drawing.

8 September

The Missis is goin'. I have known since the day he died that she w'd not be able to bear another winter here, and she will be away by the end of the year. She is to stay with family, and the house and farm will be relet. I will not be sorry to leave it. I long to shake off its shadows and be a proper wife to Samuel and lovin' mother to Molly. I only wish that we c'd make our home somewhere far from here, not in the cottage so close to where Maria died, and where I will always be haunted by what happen'd to her.

12 September

One of the Suffolk papers has open'd a fund for the other Mary Corder. She is broken, it says, ruin'd in mind and body. Her school lost its pupils and she sold everythin' she had for his defence. Now she is poor, reduc'd to the very last shillin', with no hope of feedin' and clothin' her child when it is born. I thought she w'd come back here, but she has not spoken with the Missis, or look'd to her for money.

The harvest is in. It has been a poor year, Samuel says, and the barn is barely two thirds full. There has been no music, no dancin', no reason to be thankful. The last grain has been taken from Corder land. When it has gone, there will be nothin' left of them here but dust.

25 October

The Missis call'd me after breakfast and told me to get a room ready for William's widow. She is to come here to have the child. A birth under this roof after so many deaths, but I cannot be happy for it. Maria was sent away from all who lov'd her to bring his first child into the world, and now, after all that has happen'd, his second will breathe its first under his mother's roof. I am not to speak of it in the village.

3 November

She came after dark in a coach from Lavenham, where she has been stayin'. The child will not be long in comin' and I put her straight to bed. The Missis has told me to give her every care, but she w'd not see her tonight. She is doin' what she thinks is right, but there is no joy for her in the new life to come, and I think she fears that she will see her son in his child, and be reminded of more than she can bear.

16 November

William has a son. The Missis w'd not see the child and wanted only to know if he was well. He is a sickly little creature, and his mother prays for him. She has called him John, but he is not to take the Corder name for fear that it will go against him. As soon as they are strong enough, they are to leave the village, and the Missis soon after them.

21 November

The child is thrivin' now, and his mother sees only William in him. She cries with joy and grief, and I am sad for her. Everythin' that William has touch'd he has destroy'd.

2 December

The Missis left Polstead for the last time yesterday. It has been a busy week, and if it was not for the sadness of the work, I w'd have been glad. But packin' away a life of such loneliness all but broke my heart, and I am glad it is done. She wanted company on the journey and we took the mornin' coach. It was a bright winter's day and the village look'd its finest, but as the carriage rattled down the Hadleigh road, she did not once look back. She has ask'd me to tend the graves of her husband and children if I feel able to, and if it will not cause me grief wi' the village, but I think the churchyard is the only thing she regrets leavin' behind. It holds so much of her.

We rested overnight in Lavenham – the Missis will not set foot in Bury – and she talk'd to me as she has never talk'd before. She told me of the happiness of her marriage, and ask'd me about Samuel. She said he is a good man and we must cherish each other. She said she c'd have borne her sorrow better if she had still had her husband's love.

4 December

It is just before midnight, and I have wound the clocks and lock'd the doors for the last time. The house is silent, holdin' its ghosts, and I feel as though I am a stranger in these rooms now that my reason for bein' here has gone. The new tenant comes in a few days. His name is Tabor, and he has a family – daughters, they say. I hope he will be happier here than those who have made way for him.

Tomorrow, I go to stay with Hannah until Samuel and I are wed. There is so much to do. Molly is to be maid and I have promis'd her the prettiest dress a girl can wear – or the best my needlework will allow. She grows more excited by the hour, and my heart is full of joy when I see what my life with Samuel will be. I have forgotten what it is to wake and think only of ordinary things.

Samuel came to the house this evenin' and ask'd me to go to Red Barn Cottage with him. I had not been for weeks, but it is to be my home and I must grow to love it. At the end that looks to the barn, he has planted an orchard. Half a dozen cherry trees, with flowers in between. It is his weddin' present to me, and against the cottage itself he has set a climbin' rose. The trees are young at the moment, he says, but they will grow, and the rose has come from Maria's garden. He wants me to have somethin' that will remind me of her, somethin' beautiful. One day, he says, I will look out of the window and see only joy.

It was the end of the manuscript. Josephine looked through the diaries on the floor to see if its finishing there was Hester's choice or Lucy's, but there was nothing later than 1828 and she was bitterly disappointed: she longed to know what had happened to Lucy as she moved out from the shadow of Maria's death and took charge of her own life, but the pages had served their purpose and what happened later could only ever be guesswork.

She walked out into the dawn while the world of the diary still shrouded her from the present, and smelt the rose that had been Maria's, touched the ageing wood of cherry trees that had been planted out of love. Samuel's efforts to stem his wife's grief struck a chord with her, and she wondered how successful they had been, and if Lucy had ever managed to live here happily. In her mind's eye, which had been so dominant throughout the night, particularly as she grew more tired, Josephine saw Lucy Kyte as she tended the flowers. The image – and she had no idea how it could be so definite or so familiar – was of a young woman, dark-haired and ordinary-looking, but with a pleasant face. She watched as Lucy walked round the garden, stopping here and there to pull a weed or pick some herbs; after a few minutes, she went into the house and Josephine waited for her face to appear at the window upstairs. Lucy did not disappoint her. She stood looking out over the fields, and Josephine longed to know what she saw. Eventually, the woman turned and disappeared back into the room.

The night was over, and Josephine felt Lucy drifting away from her, vanishing irretrievably now that the diary had been read and a new day grasped greedily at the horizon. A sense of loss and desolation descended like a veil over her, inexplicable and yet impossible to ignore. She hesitated before going back inside, unsure of what she had just seen and reluctant to allow the cottage to close in on her again before she had had a chance to clear her head. She was tired now, exhausted, but the last thing she wanted to do was to go upstairs and sleep. If the long night had taught her anything, it was that she would only ever be a lodger here. The past was stronger than she was; how could it not be after all that had happened? It lived on in the cottage, regardless of whose present it was intruding upon – and if she was to stay here and be happy, she would have to accept that in the way that Hester had done for so many years. To Josephine's surprise, the idea held no fear for her.

She thought about Hester's bequest, to her and to Lucy, and wondered how to reconcile the two. What could she do to give Lucy the peace she needed? Was it as simple as publishing the diary and telling Maria's story at last, or was that only part of Lucy's sadness? It was hard enough to make things right with your own past, let alone someone else's, but Josephine knew she had to try – for Lucy's sake, as well as for Hester's. She made some coffee and changed quickly, then set out down Marten's Lane with a new sense of purpose. She had spent the night with the dead; perhaps it was time to see what more they could tell her.

16

The path to the church was lined with autumn crocuses. Their purple flowers looked oddly out of joint with the bleak, colourless dawn – too early or too late for the season to which they truly belonged, the butt of one of nature's jokes. Josephine walked up the wooded slope, pulling her coat close around her against the chill. The year seemed to have turned overnight, and her breath made patterns in front of her face. Above her head, the rustle of branches sounded like distant rain, although the day's only achievement so far was a damp, depressing mist that showed little sign of lifting. The trees closed in around her, refusing her a view of the church until she was almost upon it, and she noticed how each tree trunk bore the marks of a lifetime's experience. She hoped that Lucy's grave – if she could find it – would be equally revealing of a long life, well lived.

There was no lychgate to the churchyard, no ceremonial entrance through which to welcome the living or the dead. Only a crooked red-brick wall and a simple five-bar gate enclosed the sacred ground, as if the church were proud to serve a rural community. A few branches overhung the wall, scattering beech nuts onto the outer graves, but otherwise the churchyard was open and exposed to the weather. Never had Josephine seen a landscape so devoid of colour. The mist had conspired with the stone to drain the life from everything, leaving behind a blanket of grey, broken only by the shock of a single red rose on a nearby grave. In the stillness and the silence, she could almost believe that she was looking at an old photograph.

She left the path and struck out across the grass to the oldest part of the graveyard. Her shoes were soaked in seconds, and she wished she had thought to change into Hester's old galoshes, but her mind had been on other things. There was no way of knowing from the diary how long Lucy and Samuel had lived, or whether Lucy had gone on to have children of her own, but if she started with their contemporaries, she would be sure not to miss anything. She passed the Corder graves, and made her way along the back wall to the famous Gospel Oak that she had read so much about. It was easy to see why the tree was so revered. There was an ancient dignity about it that made the church feel like a young pretender, and its vast trunk – spectacularly split now, and streaked with the rain of ages – held a quiet strength. Some of the larger boughs sagged to ground level, others were angled and twisted, giving the tree a craggy and eccentric individuality, and Josephine thought of Lucy, watching her friend's exhumation from its shelter. Maria must be buried somewhere very near here. It made sense to hope that the Kytes were not too far away.

The gravestones leaned wearily in this part of the churchyard, hankering after the rest they signified for others. Josephine wandered between the rows, looking at the names on each stone or, where the letters were worn or covered in moss, tracing them with her fingers to find out whose death was marked there. Eventually, she found what she was looking for. Her heart leapt when she saw the Kyte name; she had not for a moment doubted the diary, but the letters carved in stone stood as confirmation of something almost too precious to be true. It did not take her long to realise that the story was still incomplete, though. Samuel was buried at her feet, a few yards from the boundary wall. He had died in 1843, and he shared his stone with two women: Ruth, whose dates suggested that she had been his first wife, and Molly, whom Josephine was shocked to discover had died a few months before her father, when she was just nineteen. Samuel's sister Hannah was buried nearby, but there was no sign of Lucy, nothing even to suggest that she might have had a place here, and Josephine wondered if the marriage had actually gone ahead. The plans had seemed so certain in the diary, but the only proof she had was Hester's use of the name, and she could have jumped to the wrong conclusion about that. Or perhaps

Lucy had married again when Samuel died – she would have been in her early forties then and of an age to do so, or even to take another job in service and move away from the village. With Molly dying so young, there would have been nothing left here for Lucy but yet more grief.

The parish records might solve the mystery, but that was no comfort to Josephine's impatience. Frustrated, she walked through the rest of the churchyard looking for Baalham graves on the off-chance that Lucy had been buried with her birth family, but – although it was obviously a common Suffolk name – the only Lucy Baalham she could find was far too young to be the one she wanted, and she soon found herself at the bottom of the hill, near the church's war memorial. Polstead had not lost any of its men until 1916, she noticed, but perhaps that was because they had not been spared from the land for the first two years of the war; after that, the parish seemed to have made its fair share of sacrifices – enough, as Hilary had suggested, to put the death of a whore into perspective, although Josephine hoped that if more people had read what she had read, Maria might be remembered with a little more compassion. Nearby, under bare mounds of earth, lay the recent dead. She looked back towards the village, watched curiously by the sheep in the adjacent field; very few houses were visible from here, but she caught her breath when she saw how magnificent the Corder house looked on the horizon. It seemed both ironic and fitting that the finest view of it should be found in the graveyard.

'Miss Tey?'

Surprised, Josephine turned to see Stephen Lampton standing at the edge of the path. It was not unreasonable of him to frequent his own church at this time of the morning – there should be no such thing as an ungodly hour for a vicar – but she had not expected to have to explain herself to anyone, and she struggled to find something to say beyond an initial greeting. Either he found nothing strange in her visit or was too polite to say so, because he put her at her ease immediately. 'It's nice to see you again. I'm sorry we couldn't speak for longer the other night.' There was a twinkle in his eye as he added: 'I looked for you after the service, but you must have beaten me to the door.'

Josephine blushed, remembering how quickly she and Marta had left the church. 'I had an early start,' she lied, 'and I could see you were busy. It was a very good turnout.'

Her tone implied better than expected, but Stephen seemed to take the comment in good heart. 'Not bad, I suppose. Even some of the chapel folk will slum it with us for a harvest festival or a Christmas Day service, and it's standing room only for Armistice Day.' He smiled. 'You seem to have caught me out, though.'

'Have I?'

'Yes. I probably shouldn't admit it, but I feel most at home in St Mary's at times like this, when the church is peaceful and I don't have to worry about who's doing the flower arranging. I've never really thought that God cared much about that sort of thing, but it seems I'm in the minority on that here. Rotas must be adhered to. It's a sort of unspoken eleventh commandment, and it rather eclipses the other ten.'

Josephine laughed. 'Hilary did mention that you had a keen band of volunteers.'

'Oh, there's never a shortage of people to decorate the altar and polish the brasses. I've got more bakers than I can find fêtes for, and they're queuing down the street with embroidered kneelers – but ask anyone to come and worship here, and that's a very different story.'

It was hard to tell from Stephen's tone if he was bitter about his lot, or resigned to it. 'I imagine that's frustrating,' Josephine said, curious either way to know why he would stay.

'Sometimes, but I can see their point. When we first got here, men were quite literally being worked to death on the land. Things are a little better now, but it's still a hard life and who am I to criticise people for not finding a moment to call their own, or for choosing to spend it somewhere else if they do? Questions of who they are, to each other and to God, take second place – and probably rightly so.' His words echoed what Bill Fallowfield had said about his own youth. 'They bring their flowers and look after their dead, but I sometimes feel that the church is simply the building next to the graves.' There was sadness rather than arrogance in the way he spoke of his parishioners as a race apart, and Josephine realised that his efforts to belong here and to live up to the expectations of his role were as uncertain as his wife's. 'And how about you? What brings you here at this time of the morning?'

'I was looking for a grave,' she said, wondering how much else to tell him. 'I've been sorting through some of my godmother's papers, and I'm afraid I've rather got caught up in the history of the place. She mentions a family who used to live in Red Barn Cottage, and I wondered what had happened to them.'

'And did you find out?'

'Yes and no. The husband and daughter are buried over there, but there's no sign of the woman I was looking for.'

'What was her name?'

'Kyte. Lucy Kyte. Her maiden name was Baalham. I wondered if I might have a look at the parish registers to see if she married again?'

'Yes, of course. What period are we talking about?'

'She was a contemporary of Maria.'

'Ah, they're back at the rectory. I've been looking at them myself recently. Call in any time – I know Hilary would love to see you.'

'Thank you, I will.' She turned to go, then asked as an afterthought: 'Do you know exactly where Maria was buried?'

'I know what I've been told. Let me show you.' He followed the path round to the south porch, then struck out in a diagonal line towards the boundary wall, stopping about ten yards from Samuel's grave. 'She's here, as far as I can remember. That's what Hester told me, anyway. She said she'd tried to get the stone reinstated, but popular opinion was very much against her.'

Josephine recalled Lucy's description of Maria's funeral, and pictured the crowds of strangers packed into the quiet churchyard. 'It's hard to believe that something which happened so long ago can still rouse such strong resentment, isn't it?'

'Do you think so?' Stephen looked at her, genuinely interested in what she had to say, and it occurred to Josephine that his voice was by no means the only attractive thing about him. Suddenly, she felt very conscious of her lack of make-up and the tiredness around her eyes, and she understood perfectly why Hilary never had to bake her own cakes. 'I'm afraid I find it depressingly easy. We live in a world that loves children, except the ones born out of wedlock: it's never forgiven, and certainly never forgotten, and I don't just mean here. The last parish I worked in was just as bad, and it destroys people – the mother and the child.'

He spoke with a passion that seemed personal, and Josephine wondered if someone he cared for had felt the sting of illegitimacy. 'It must have been quite a shock for both of you, coming here from London.'

'Things never turn out quite as you expect, do they?' The comment had a wistful quality that reminded Josephine of something Hilary had said about her life, and it occurred to her that there was a lot of making the best of things involved in the Lamptons' marriage. 'I remember my predecessor telling me that I'd have to take things gently with people here, but I didn't realise that he meant for the indefinite future. I've been doing that for sixteen years now, and I still don't know them.'

'That's not a very encouraging thing for a newcomer to hear.'

'Ah – it only matters if you *want* to be accepted, and I'm afraid I do.' Not many people in his position would have admitted that to a stranger, and Josephine admired him for it. 'If you're anything like your godmother, though, you won't let that bother you.'

Josephine smiled. 'You knew Hester well, didn't you?'

Stephen thought carefully before answering. 'I knew the person Hester wanted me to know, if that makes any sense. I don't mean that there was anything false about her, or that she was pretending to be something she wasn't, but I always felt that it was . . .'

He tailed off, wondering how to explain what he meant. 'Thus far and no further?' Josephine suggested, quoting John MacDonald.

'Yes. That's exactly it. I suspect very few people got beyond that –

perhaps only Walter. But the person I did know I liked very much. She was warm and compassionate and very funny, and she had a particular view of the world that was never dull. And we both missed London – that was why we enjoyed each other's company, I think. It's certainly what we talked about – the city and the theatre and the people. We were like Englishmen abroad, gravitating towards someone else who remembered the same things.' It was the first time that Josephine had heard anything to suggest that her godmother was not entirely settled in Suffolk, and it interested her that Hester could so naturally be different things to different people: a woman of the world to Stephen Lampton, a countrywoman at heart to Bert Willis. She sympathised with the apparent contradictions because she was like that herself: if someone from Inverness met one of her London friends, they would probably fail to recognise her as the same person; the only difference was that she tried to run the two lives concurrently, while Hester had left one behind. 'I know what you're thinking,' Stephen added, 'and you're right. It *is* an extreme reaction for somewhere that's only two hours away on a train.'

'Not at all. It isn't about distance, is it? It's about a way of life. Sometimes a change can be a blessing, and sometimes not.'

He nodded, pleased that she understood. 'Don't get me wrong – Hester loved it here, otherwise she would never have stayed. When she and Walter bought that cottage, it was a dream come true, a symbol of everything they'd worked for and shared, part of who they were. But she had no sense of purpose here after he was gone, and I could understand that. Another day was just another day. That became less true as time went by. I suppose she got used to it, and learned to accept it.'

Or found a new purpose, Josephine thought, picturing the transcript of Lucy's diary and all the work it must have entailed. 'Was Hester thinking of going back to London?' she asked.

'She mentioned it once or twice in the long term. I think it was a question of practicality more than anything else. She started to say that her years were catching up with her, although I can't say I ever thought of her as old.'

'Not even towards the end of her life?'

'Not really, but bear in mind that we didn't meet very often. She'd come to us for dinner two or three times a year, and I'd occasionally see her in the village or drop in to the cottage. The last time I called, she had a visitor already so she didn't invite me in, and I have to admit – when she died, I was surprised and saddened by how long it had been since we talked properly. I regret that now. And you're right – when I went to pay my final respects, I was shocked by the change in her.'

'You went to the cottage after she died?'

'Yes. Bert Willis and his wife called me in. It was Bert who found her in bed.'

Josephine didn't correct him. 'Yes, I know. Bert's wife was there as well?'

'Yes. Bert was quite upset. I think she was worried about him.'

So much for Hester's final instructions, Josephine thought: Red Barn Cottage was beginning to sound like Finchley Central after her death. 'Did you notice anything different about the house?'

'Only that it was a mess. It didn't seem right to look too closely. Hester was always a proud woman.'

'Did she ever confide in you?'

He looked at her curiously, and Josephine knew that it was only a matter of time before she had to justify her questions to him. 'About what?'

'I don't know really. Anything that was on her mind, any worries or fears that she might have had. Obviously I wouldn't want you to break any professional confidences.'

'Oh, don't worry about that. If Hester had told me anything, it would have been as a friend, not as a vicar. She never needed any counselling on matters of faith. Her beliefs were quite straightforward, but very certain.'

'So *did* she tell you anything?'

'Not in so many words, no. The only thing I can think of was that she gave me the name and address of her solicitor in case anything happened to her. It came completely out of the blue and I thought it was a little strange at the time, but in hindsight it made sense and I'm glad that she did. Hester must have known she was likely to die alone. Sadly, that proved to be true, but at least I knew who to contact for her final wishes and we were able to look after her decently and make sure they were carried out.' He shivered, as much from the thought as from the chill that hung over the graveyard. 'Shall we talk somewhere more comfortable? Why don't you come back to the rectory and have some breakfast with us? I'll dig out the parish register for you, and if there's anything else you'd like to ask me about Hester, then please do.'

Josephine was about to refuse, but she suddenly realised how much she would welcome some company. She was still shaken by everything that had happened overnight, and a warm dining room and some easy banter with Hilary sounded considerably more enticing than returning to Red Barn Cottage with God knows who roaming about upstairs. 'Thank you. That would be lovely, and if it's not too much trouble, I wonder if I might use your telephone as well? There's a call I need to make, and I'd rather not do it at the post office.'

'Of course.' Instead of going back via the road, Stephen led Josephine across the fields to the rectory and they were there in a matter of minutes. It was a fine-looking house, a fifteenth-century building enhanced during the Georgian era and much less forbidding than its austere iron gates and high walls had led her to believe. The hallway was a classic example of good taste defeated by day-to-day living, and Josephine guessed that it set the tone for the rest of the house: a set of three miniatures on the wall by the door was obscured by an overburdened coat rack; gloves, loose change and a bewildering number of scribbled notes and memos swamped the elegant Sheraton telephone table; and the striking effect of a classical statue was considerably undermined by the old leather football that had become lodged between it and the wall. Even so, it was comfortable and inviting, and a reminder of everyday living was exactly what Josephine needed. For the first time, she realised how isolated her days had become. A smell of bacon wafted enticingly out from the kitchen, and upstairs she could hear Hilary telling the boys to do something; even at a raised volume, there was a note of weariness in her voice that suggested very little hope of a positive outcome, at least for the next five years.

Hilary appeared on the landing a few seconds later, and beamed when she saw she had a guest. 'Josephine! What a nice surprise! Where on earth did Stephen find you at this time of day?'

'In the graveyard. I was looking for Lucy Kyte.' Hilary seemed confused, and Josephine brought her up to date. 'I was wrong about her being a friend of Hester's. She was contemporary with Maria Marten and she lived in Red Barn Cottage – at least, I think she did. That was Hester's interest in her.'

'And?'

'No luck, I'm afraid. Her husband's there, and her stepdaughter, but there's no sign of Lucy.'

'A mystery – how intriguing. That must be right up your street.'

'I've brought Miss Tey back to look through the registers and have some breakfast,' Stephen said.

'Only if that's no trouble.'

'It's no trouble at all. Stephen hasn't eaten yet and it'll give Beattie a chance to practise on another pan of bacon. She's marvellous at most things, but judging that fine line between crispy and buggered seems entirely beyond her. Take your coat off and I'll make some coffee while we're waiting. You look as though you could do with some.' She took Josephine's coat and balanced it precariously on the others, piled one on top of the other until it was only an act of faith that a hook had ever existed. 'Are you all right? You look exhausted.'

'I'm fine, but I've been up all night working and I would kill for a cup of coffee. Can I make a telephone call first, though?'

'Of course,' Stephen said. 'Come with me – I'll take you somewhere more private.'

He showed Josephine into his study and shut the door discreetly on his way out. It was a peaceful room, if thoroughly masculine in its tastes, with a fine view across sloping lawns and parkland back to the church. While the trees clung stubbornly to their leaves, the distinctive spire was only just visible in the distance, and the church was more easily located by the pattern of gravestones on the hillside. There was no other house in sight, and Josephine tried and failed to think of another village in which both church and rectory were so utterly divorced from the heart of the parish they served.

Showing rather less discretion than her host, she allowed her eyes to wander along the bookshelves before going over to the telephone. It was a motley collection, more academic than she would have expected to find in most rural parsonages, but she also recognised some of the spines from the now-familiar histories of the Red Barn murder, and wondered if the ownership of those books was a sure-fire way of telling the house of an incomer from that of someone born in Polstead; she still found the lack of interest amongst local people hard to understand.

A grandfather clock struck the hour in the hallway and reminded Josephine of what she was supposed to be doing. She picked up the receiver, hoping that she was not too early to find anyone at the office, and was in luck on the third ring. 'Stewart, Rule & Co. How may I help you?'

Miss Peck's voice – as clipped and as economical as ever – sounded oddly out of place in the garrulous disorder of Stephen's study, but Josephine made an attempt to respond in kind. 'It's Josephine Tey. I'd like a word with Mr MacDonald, if he's available?'

'I'm afraid Mr MacDonald won't be in until lunchtime, Miss Tey. Can I ask him to ring you then?'

'That's kind, but I'm not at home.'

'Are you still in Suffolk?' The question was innocent enough, but the slight disapproval implicit in its tone irritated Josephine immediately. Quite why she felt the need to explain herself to her solicitor's secretary was beyond her, but she did it all the same. 'Yes. I'm still sorting through Miss Larkspur's things, and I have one or two questions. I wondered if Mr MacDonald had had a chance to look through the papers I left for him.'

'Yes, he did it straight away.' The pause made it clear that anything else would have been unthinkable in an office run by Jane Peck. 'I sent a letter out to Crown Cottage on Monday, but of course you won't have seen it yet. Just a minute . . .' Josephine opened her mouth with a more specific request, but the thud of the receiver on the desk told her that she was wasting her breath. She pictured Miss Peck in the ordered office, going immediately to the correct drawer to find the correct file with the correct letter that she had carefully typed according to John MacDonald's dictation, and wished that efficiency in other people did not grate on her quite as much as it did. 'Yes, here it is,' the secretary said, returning to the telephone. 'The balance owing to you once all funeral expenses are dealt with and all debts settled is £32, 15s and 6d. There is also a list of stocks and shares which I can read to you now if . . .'

'No, no,' Josephine cut in quickly, horrified to think that Miss Peck could assume that she was chasing Hester's money. 'That's not what I was phoning about at all. I wanted to ask Mr MacDonald if he had come across anything unusual when he was going through Miss Larkspur's financial papers.'

The question had been vague, even to Josephine's ears, and it got the treatment it deserved. 'Unusual?'

'Yes. Any . . .' She faltered under the enquiring scowl of the voice at the other end, and started again. 'I wondered if he had found any large sums of money coming into or going out of Miss Larkspur's accounts, any transactions that seemed a little . . . well, a little irregular.' Miss Peck's silence seemed to underline to Josephine that Hester's accounts while she was alive had been Hester's business and hers alone, so she tried a more confiding approach. 'Miss Peck, from what people have told me since I've been here, my godmother had an enviable collection of memorabilia and antiques pertaining to the village and its history,' she explained. 'I've had a chance to sort through most of the cottage now, and many of the things that Hester owned seem to have vanished. It's quite possible that she sold them before her death, which is why I wanted to ask Mr MacDonald if there was any sign of that in her financial affairs before taking the matter any further. The sums involved would be quite substantial.'

She had been prepared to share her anxiety over Hester's death if necessary, but when Miss Peck spoke again, her attitude had changed completely. 'I see. How terrible – for you, and for Miss Larkspur. Mr MacDonald didn't give any indication that things weren't perfectly in order, but of course he might have preferred to talk to you privately about his concerns if he had any. I'll certainly make sure that he looks into it as soon as he gets in this afternoon.'

'Thank you.'

'Not at all. How would it be best for him to get in touch with you?'

'I'll telephone again tomorrow. Will that be convenient?'

'Just a moment.' Josephine heard the pages of a diary being turned, and her tiredness began to get the better of her patience. 'Yes, he'll be here all day, so feel free to call whenever suits you.' She was about to ring off, but Miss Peck added: 'I was sorry to hear about your father. It must have been quite a shock for him and a terrible worry for you.'

'I beg your pardon?'

'Your father had a fall down by the river when he was out fishing with Mr Finlayson.' She paused. 'Surely you knew?'

Josephine considered trying to bluff her way through the conversation, but her concern for her father outweighed her need to keep up appearances in front of Miss Peck. 'No, I had no idea. Is he all right?'

'Yes, I think so. A sprained wrist, apparently, and I believe he was quite badly shaken, but other than that he was lucky. It could have been much worse.'

'When did this happen?'

'At the weekend. I called into the shop on Monday and Annie was rushed off her feet because he wasn't well enough to come in.'

'Why on earth didn't he let me know?' Josephine's guilt made her re-act unreasonably; it wasn't Miss Peck's fault that her father had had an accident while she was four hundred miles away, although she resented the self-righteous note in the other woman's voice.

'He probably didn't want to worry you. I shouldn't have said any-thing, but I was sure you'd know.'

'No, I didn't.' She swallowed her pride and added: 'Thank you for telling me. I'll telephone him now. Oh – one other thing. Will you tell Mr MacDonald that I've found Lucy Kyte?'

'Oh?' There was a long pause at the other end, and Josephine wondered if it was childish of her to enjoy her own sense of one-up-manship. 'Would you like me to give him some details of how to get in touch with her?' Miss Peck asked, recovering quickly.

'No, it can wait until I speak to him. She's not in any hurry.' She rang off without a goodbye, and asked the operator for Inverness 195, only to be told by her daily woman that her father had insisted on going to the shop, even though he really wasn't well enough; there followed a list of other things that clearly could not be dealt with in her absence, and in the end she just gave in. 'I'll be home by the end of the week,' she said when Morag finally drew breath. 'Please tell my father I called. I'll try him again tomorrow.' It was a timely reminder, she told herself as she replaced the receiver. What on earth was she thinking of, hiding away down here when she had responsibilities elsewhere, caught up in every-one's life but her own and obsessed now with not one dead woman but two? It was madness, and she needed to put it in perspective before she had something more serious than a sprained wrist to worry about.

Beattie seemed to have mastered the bacon at last, and a hearty breakfast put Josephine in better spirits. In any case, it was impossible to be downbeat in Hilary's company. The issue of Lucy Kyte was dis-cussed enthusiastically from every angle, and Josephine shared a few of the facts without explaining how she knew them or mentioning the diary; it was dishonest, and she regretted having to hold things back, but she wasn't ready to share Hester's precious secret with anyone yet, and certainly not before she had spoken to Archie. 'Go and look at the register,' Hilary said, nudging Stephen excitedly as soon as he put his knife and fork down. 'Let's see what we can find out.'

He left the room and returned a few minutes later with an enormous ledger, which he placed in front of Josephine, open at the right page. 'Here's the marriage,' he said, pointing to an entry for 26 December, 1828. 'There were two babies as well, but they both died. One was a month old, the other only a week.'

Josephine looked sadly at the entries for Lucy's little girls, Maria and Daisy, and wondered if there had been any surviving children. 'They're buried in the churchyard?'

'Yes, but their graves aren't marked. Babies' often weren't. Molly's death is recorded here,' he said, turning several pages, 'and Samuel's shortly afterwards.' There was no indication in the book of how they had died, and the lack of information frustrated Josephine. 'I can't find any mention of another marriage for Lucy – not in this parish, anyway, and she's not buried in the churchyard. She must have moved away, just as you thought.' He saw Josephine's disappointment, and added: 'In those days, if people left a village, they didn't go far. It might be worth your trying the records in Stoke and Boxford if you have time.'

She thanked him, and he left her and Hilary to talk. 'So – how is the cottage shaping up?' Hilary asked, pushing the toast rack across the table. 'Are you settling in?'

'Something like that. I suppose you could say we're still circling round each other, and I'm not entirely sure I've got the upper hand yet.'

Hilary raised her eyes. 'It gets easier once you stop fighting back. We made a pact, Stephen and I, when we first moved here. He'd worry about the church and I'd get to grips with the house, and I'm still not entirely sure about my side of the bargain. At least you haven't got children to worry about. Has your friend gone back to London?'

'Yes. On Sunday.'

'It must have been nice to have her here.'

Josephine reached for the marmalade and diligently spread some on her toast. She had no idea what Hilary knew or thought she knew about her relationship with Marta, or even if she cared, but it felt safer to change the subject back to the cottage. 'Do you know a good builder? There's a room upstairs in the cottage that I can't get on with, and I know I'll never use it if it stays as it is. And I don't need more than two bedrooms,' she added casually.

'You want Deaves over in Stoke. He practically lived here with us when we first moved in, and he's very reliable. Well, it's his son now, but you'd never know the difference.'

It was the same name that Jenny Willis had given her. 'He doesn't just do odd jobs, then?'

'Oh no. He can turn his hand to anything. Building or funerals – they do both.'

Beattie came in to clear the plates, and it reminded Josephine of something else she had been meaning to ask. 'Hester had a girl who worked for her for a while – you don't happen to know her name, do you? I think she lives in Stoke.'

'You mean Rose,' Hilary said through gritted teeth. 'Rose Boreham.'

Josephine laughed. 'Why do you say it like that?'

'I shouldn't say this, and it's petty of me even to think it when she's no longer with us, but I'll never forgive Hester for that. Rose was the best girl we'd had since we got here, an absolute bloody godsend and a breath of fresh air, and Hester came to dinner one night and stole her from under our noses. I was absolutely livid. Even Stephen frowned.' She smiled at her own indignation. 'Mind you, it was a damned neat manoeuvre. If I hadn't been on the receiving end of it, I'd have taken my hat off to her.'

'I think you can be forgiven your pettiness. She sounds worth fighting for. I have the opposite problem with mine in Inverness – I can't seem to get rid of her. Is Rose still in Stoke?'

'Yes. Her parents run a pub there – the Black Horse. She asked to come back when Hester let her go, but we'd got Beattie by then and it didn't seem fair.'

'Why did Hester let her go?'

'Rose wouldn't say, but I could tell she was cross about it. She's a girl who doesn't suit disappointment. If you want to talk to her, I can run you over now. You're halfway there already.'

'Thank you, but no. If she's as lively as you say she is, I think I need some sleep first.'

'What are you working on?' Hilary asked.

'A biography of Claverhouse.' It wasn't a lie, but only because of the way the question had been phrased and Josephine felt guilty for implying a diligence that she could not in truth claim. She saw Hilary's eyes glaze over at the name, and gave her the truncated version of the soldier's life. 'In fact, I'd better get back to him now.'

'Get some sleep first,' Hilary said, walking her to the door. 'Very few living men are worth staying up all night for, let alone a dead one.' She passed Josephine her coat and kissed her goodbye. 'It's been lovely to see you again. You know where we are if there's anything you need.'

17

The cottage seemed dreary and depressing when Josephine got back, partly because the heavy skies refused to let in the streams of light that she had come to love, and partly because of her own mood. Her brief conversation with Jane Peck had rankled more than she cared to admit. All the way back from the rectory, she had imagined what was going on in Inverness. Her absence would be the talk of that bloody little town, and she didn't need to be there to know what they were saying: she'd been away down south when her mother needed her, and here was history repeating itself; she always was a selfish little madam, putting her own life first, thinking she was too good for them with her plays and her books and her London friends – nothing like her father, who'd do anything for anyone, you only had to ask; in fact, now they thought about it, there always had been something a little queer about her – a bit too aloof, nothing much to like. She knew exactly what they were like because she had seen them do it to others, and she knew, too, that all the gossip in the world would not bother her unless, in her heart, she believed them to be right. Her father was seventy-three, for God's sake; something like this was bound to happen, and she had been fooling herself to think that she could ever make the cottage work, so far away from all she was tied to. More than ever, she missed Marta, but there was no time now to spend in London and the uncertainty of when they would see each other, combined with the memory of Lydia's voice on the telephone, brought back all the doubts that threatened their love. In the space of a couple of hours, Josephine felt her life tighten around her, and no matter how many times she told herself that it was her tiredness talking, the future filled her with a despair that would not go away.

She threw on some old clothes and spent the rest of the day in the garden, determined to work until she dropped to guarantee some sleep when she finally went to bed. The spade stood against the wall where Marta had left it, and Josephine dug over the rest of the vegetable patch, trying not to think of how precious and full of hope those few days together had been. The fields around the cottage were busier than ever as the farming year began again; ploughing was well under way, and in the meadow where the barn once stood, a handful of men cut back the hedges along Marten's Lane, marking their progress with a series of tiny bonfires that passed their flames along the edge of the field like medieval beacons. She was glad of the undemanding company, and sorry when dusk began to fall and the men drifted home to their firesides. The onset of darkness was less dramatic in a day that had never truly been light, and Josephine went reluctantly back inside. She lit a lamp in every room but the one she hated, then put some Benny Carter on the gramophone and made an elaborate supper, more to give herself something to do than because she was hungry. While it was cooking, she opened her suitcase on the bed in the spare room and began to fill it, ready to go home. She packed as much as she could, leaving only the clothes she would need for the next couple of days, and tried to decide what to do about the diary; there was no choice really but to take it with her – it was far too valuable to leave in the cottage, and she still didn't know anyone here well enough to entrust it to them while she was away. After supper, she settled down in front of the fire with a pile of her mother's letters. She wanted nothing more of Lucy or even Hester at the moment; she had too much darkness of her own to invite theirs in as well. Her resentment had faded as the day went on, leaving only the guilt and a complex longing for something familiar – for the home that pulled simultaneously at her conscience, and at her heart.

Exhaustion soon got the better of her, and she returned to the dead in her dreams – not in the quiet, contained Polstead churchyard this time, but among the vast, sprawling darkness of Tomnahurich Hill where for centuries the people of Inverness had laid their dead to rest.

She was walking up and down a long avenue of graves, looking for her mother's simple headstone, but it wasn't where she expected it to be. Her search grew more frantic, and she blamed herself for refusing to go with her father each weekend as he took flowers to his wife: if she had visited more often, she would know where to look now, when it seemed so important that she find it. In the distance, framed by a sliver of blue from the Moray Firth, she could see a funeral party gathered around a grave. Out of respect, she tried to stay away, but whichever path she took brought her closer and closer to the mourners. The crowd seemed to grow by the second, as if the whole town had come to pay tribute, and when she was almost upon them, the faces that she knew turned towards her. Her grandparents were there, and friends she had lost during the war, but it was Hester who beckoned her forward. One by one they moved aside to let her through, and she looked down in horror and disbelief at the brass plate that bore her father's name. Her mother stood with her hand on the coffin, wearing the dress she was buried in, pale and wasted from her illness but reminding Josephine of the final promise she had made, and broken. Josephine tried to explain that she didn't know, that her father had been well when she left him, that he had told her to go, but her words were lost in the babble of voices from the crowd, and she broke down in tears of sorrow and shame.

The sobs were violent and raw, and they woke her. A pile of letters had fallen from her lap into the grate, one perilously close to the fire, and she caught it just as it began to smoulder. Wide awake now, she wiped the tears away, but the image of her mother's face continued to haunt her – that, and the knowledge that what she had felt in the dream, along with the shock and the grief and the guilt, was relief. When she heard a noise upstairs – a soft thud that came from the guest room directly above her – it was almost a welcome distraction. She went up to see what it was, too numbed by tiredness now to fear any tricks that the cottage cared to play, and found her suitcase upturned on the floor, its contents sprawled at her feet. It must have slipped off the bed, and she bent down to repack it. As she fastened the case to avoid it happening again, a movement caught her eye through the open doorway between the two rooms, and she watched as the door to the boxroom swung softly back, revealing the dark recesses beyond. That was all – a door slipping from its latch as it had done many times before, and yet Josephine was seized by a sudden, overwhelming dread. She stood rooted to the spot, staring hard into the shadows, all sense of time now lost to her. After what might have been seconds or hours, she moved slowly forward, if only to prove to herself that she could, listening all the time for a sound other than her footsteps. She took the lamp from her bedside table and shone it into the blackness, but there was nothing – no one – there. The room was exactly as it always was – cold and desolate, guilty of nothing more than suggestion. The draught coming through the window seemed worse than usual, and she put the lamp down for a moment to tighten the fastening, which had still not been properly fixed. After the figure she had seen in the early morning, the ordinariness of her own reflection in the glass was welcome. She leaned forward to look down into the garden, resting her hands on the window seat. To her horror, the wood was warm, as if someone had just been sitting there.

Josephine grabbed the lamp and half-ran from the room, slamming the door behind her and tearing the belt from a coat to wind around the latch. She sat on the bed, her heart racing, and stared at the closed door, daring it to defy her, but nothing else happened. The house was calm and quiet, and as it lulled her with its peace, she began to find other reasons for what had disturbed her: the heat from the range, perhaps, or cold hands that made anything she touched seem warmer than it really was. None of them made much sense, and in the end, she blamed everything on her state of mind and a lack of sleep. She looked at her watch. It was still only ten o'clock, and she could not bear another restless night. In her bedside drawer, there was a sleeping draught that Marta had left in case she needed it. She had been sceptical at the time, as she was of any drug that dulled her senses. Tonight was different, though; she would take her oblivion wherever she could find it.

18

Archie's telegram arrived the next morning, and made Josephine's mind up for her. He was in Felixstowe – the clipped nature of the medium added to the mystery of why – and suggested they meet there for lunch the following day if that suited her. It did. She needed to talk to him more than ever, but had given up hope of being able to see him before she went back up north; now, she could use today to call on Rose Boreham, drive to Felixstowe tomorrow, and still keep her promise to Morag to be home by the end of the week. Energised by a new sense of purpose – and by eight hours of dreamless sleep, courtesy of Marta's miracle powder – Josephine walked briskly into the village to send Archie his reply; while at the post office, she telephoned her father again and managed to catch him before he left for the shop. He seemed bemused by her concern, dismissing his injury as 'a wee bit of a bruise', and told her to come home when she was good and ready; there were, apparently, enough women making a fuss over nothing already. His gruffness reassured her about his health, but not about her reputation, and she promised to see him on Friday. There was no answer from Stewart, Rule & Co., which was a shame because she was more than ready for Jane Peck, but she could always call later from Stoke. As she walked back to the cottage, yesterday's despair seemed a long way away, the product of tiredness and an overwrought imagination, and she was pleased to put it behind her.

The morning air was cold, but sweet with the scent of autumn. Rather than test Chummy's temperament by driving her out on consecutive days, Josephine decided to get Hester's old bike out of the garage and cycle to Stoke instead. She set out, her tyres crackling over fallen acorns in the road, and was pleased with the choice she had made. The October day had dragged a rich, warm yellow from the sun, and small flocks of fluffy white cloud blew about the sky, making it a pleasure to be out in the open with time to notice the beauty of the season. Hedgerows on either side were covered with hundreds of tiny webs, and blackbirds busied themselves in stripping fruit from the brambles. In fact, all of nature seemed to be preparing itself for the long, dark months ahead.

The road was kind to her, rising and falling gently all the way until a clutch of houses told her that she had reached the outskirts of the village. She dismounted near the top of Scotland Street, careful not to step in a trickle of blood that ran down the side of the road from the backyard of a butcher's shop, giving the impression that Sweeney Todd had abandoned Fleet Street and retired to rural Suffolk. It was a grisly introduction to an otherwise beautiful village whose streets were lined with medieval houses, unspoilt and full of character. Stoke was considerably bigger than Polstead, boasting several shops and pubs as well as a truly magnificent church. She remembered seeing its pinnacle from the graveyard yesterday, dominating the horizon with a quiet dignity. Up close, there was nothing quiet about it at all: the mighty brick, stone and flint tower stood tall and proud as the glory of the village, and Josephine had little doubt that when the bells rang from here, the whole county would know about it.

The sign for the Black Horse was further down the main street. It was too early for the pub to be open, so she left her bicycle by the village hall and did some shopping. The general stores, next to the rectory, seemed to stock everything under the sun, including a top-up of sleeping powders – just to have in, she told herself – and Josephine bought as many supplies as the bicycle basket would carry. She added a chop from the butcher's for dinner, then spent half an hour in the bookshop next door, buying presents for Marta and Archie. In the end, she chose two volumes by Virginia Woolf: a signed collection of short stories for Marta, including one called 'A Haunted House'; and a first edition of *Mrs Dalloway* for Archie, who – she knew – would be desperately missing London. She could never quite see the point of Woolf herself, but the devotion was strong enough in both of her friends to suggest that the problem lay with her.

The church clock struck midday, and Josephine made her way back to the Black Horse – a long, timber-framed building, dating back to the fifteenth or sixteenth century, and originally made up of two separate cottages. The sign rose up from an old boundary stone at the front, which declared that the pub was technically in the parish of Polstead; apart from that, it looked more like a house than a commercial enterprise, and the only other clue to what happened inside was a faint smell of beer from the pavement. The north-facing rooms at the front were cool and dark, but they had an austere homeliness about them, with polished brick floors and scrubbed tables. The Borehams obviously kept a popular house: she was by no means the first person across the threshold that day and, as she waited her turn at the bar, she noticed that a table in the room next door was laid out with pies, hams and cheeses, ready for a luncheon party.

'What can I get you?'

The woman behind the bar was dressed entirely in black, and Josephine wondered if the food was actually for a funeral. She ordered a glass of beer and handed over the money. 'Mrs Boreham?' she asked, relying on the fact that the woman was the right age to be Rose's mother.

'That's right. Who wants to know?'

'My name is Josephine Tey. I've come over from Polstead today, from Red Barn Cottage. Hester Larkspur was my godmother, and I've taken the place on.' Mrs Boreham's expression made a subtle shift from suspicious to downright hostile, and Josephine knew that she had found someone else whom Hester had managed to alienate. 'I was hoping to have a word with your daughter,' she added, less confidently now.

'Why? What are you going to tell me she's done now?'

Josephine was taken aback by the aggressiveness of the question. 'I wasn't going to tell you she's done anything. That's certainly not why I'm here.' Mrs Boreham's eyes hardened still further, and Josephine guessed that her accent wasn't helping; it placed her in the same camp as Hester the minute she opened her mouth.

'Forgive the lack of hospitality, Miss Tey, but the last time I heard a voice like yours it was telling me a load of lies about my own daughter.'

'I know, and I'm sorry,' she bluffed, not having the faintest clue what the woman was talking about, but ready to play along if it got her what she wanted. She couldn't help thinking that it would be easier to get an audience with the Pope than to snatch five minutes with Rose Boreham, but she bit her tongue and used the scant information she had gleaned from Hilary to weave what she hoped would be a placatory story. 'I understand there was some unpleasantness between your daughter and my godmother which led to Rose losing not one position, but two,' she said, relying on 'unpleasantness' to be suitably vague. 'I'm here to apologise, and to try to make it right with her if I can.'

God only knew how that was to be achieved, but her conciliatory tone seemed to have set her on the right track. 'Rose is busy at the moment,' her mother said, still difficult, but less hostile. 'We've got the men from the shoot in for lunch any minute.'

'That's fine. I'm happy to wait. Do you serve food?'

Mrs Boreham gave her a look that explained very eloquently what she thought of women who had all the time in the world, but the victory was Josephine's. 'I can do you a sandwich,' the landlady admitted grudgingly, 'and I'll send Rose over when the men are settled.'

Josephine took her drink over to a table in the corner and busied herself with making a list of questions for Archie. After a few minutes, the beaters filed into the next room and the noise in the pub went up a level. Through the open door, she watched the sought-after Rose pass hot toddies round amongst the men, giving as good as she got with the banter and innuendo that came her way. She was a pretty girl, with wavy dark hair, a heart-shaped face and full lips, but her appeal was less in the features themselves than in what Rose did with them – how easily she laughed or feigned surprise, the blend of innocence and worldliness that she could persuade them to convey. She had a natural spirit that a village pub – even at its most raucous – seemed to struggle to contain, and Josephine understood immediately why Hester would be charmed by her. The message had obviously got through: every now and again she stole a curious glance at her visitor, whilst somehow making it clear that she would come over when she was ready and not a minute sooner. She disappeared into the back and Josephine – her list finished – was just about to give Virginia Woolf another chance when a plate of cheese and pickle sandwiches was banged down in front of her. Rose took the chair opposite without waiting to be asked. 'Mum said you were after me,' she began, establishing from the outset that she was there under sufferance. 'What do you want?'

Josephine realised – a little late, admittedly – that she had no real answer to that question, and certainly nothing as direct to offer in return. 'Look, Rose,' she said, deciding to see where honesty got her, 'I have no idea what went on between you and my godmother. I didn't know Hester Larkspur, and we only met properly when I was a very small child, far too young to remember anything about her. Until she died, I didn't even know that she was an actress. I certainly wasn't expecting her to leave me anything in her will. All that should have gone to my mother, who was Hester's closest friend, but my mother is dead and now I find myself in a strange cottage, hundreds of miles away from my family, where nothing makes sense to me. Quite frankly . . . well, quite frankly I need some help. Can we start again?'

Rose wasn't going to forgive and forget that easily, but she softened a little and a smile played on her lips. 'You've met her, then?'

'Met whom?'

'Lucy.'

Josephine had never had any intention of discussing Lucy with Rose – either the diary, or the unexplained presence in the cottage – and she was shocked to have the rug pulled from under her. 'What do you know about Lucy?' she asked cautiously.

'Only what Miss Larkspur told me,' Rose said, and the fact that Hester had told her anything indicated to Josephine how well the two of them had got along. 'Who she was and when she lived in the cottage, that sort of thing. I never saw her myself, though, except in the photograph. I always hoped I would one day, if she got to know me and trust me, but it never happened.' She shrugged. 'Some people are more open to that sort of thing, aren't they? I must be about as psychic as a plank, because I could never see anything at the vicarage, either. You obviously take after Miss Larkspur. You're lucky. What's Lucy been up to?'

Josephine could not quite believe that they were discussing a dead woman as if she were just another girl from down the road who might turn up at any moment. It was hard to decide if Rose's calm acceptance of the situation was reassuring or disturbing, and she sidestepped the question with one of her own. 'What did you mean about seeing Lucy in a photograph?'

'It was the one of Mr Paget that Miss Larkspur kept on her desk. There's a woman in the background with Maria's rose, and that's her.' Josephine brought the picture to mind, and realised that the face she had seen at the window was indeed the same as the face in the photograph; that was why it had seemed familiar. She tried to recall how often she had looked at the image, and whether it was planted firmly enough in her mind for her to imprint it elsewhere, but in hindsight it was impossible to be sure. 'I always thought it was another daily woman,' Rose said, 'but Miss Larkspur told me I was the first help she'd had.' She glared at Josephine, misinterpreting her confusion. 'If you're not going to believe me, I'm wasting my time sitting here.'

She got up to leave, but Josephine grabbed her arm, conscious that Mrs Boreham was watching intently from the bar. 'No, Rose – please stay. It's not that I don't believe you. I'm just having trouble coming to terms with what's been going on.' She smiled. 'Until now, I thought I was cut from the same plank as you. Nothing like this has ever happened to me before.'

The girl took her seat again. 'That's what Miss Larkspur told me. She said it was the cottage that did it.'

233

'I'm sure she was right. Did she talk to you about what happened, the things she saw?'

'She said that Lucy was always around – she'd hear her coming up and downstairs sometimes, or things would move about the cottage for no reason. It always sounded a bit creepy to me, but Miss Larkspur liked having her there, said Lucy kept her company and it was better than being on her own. I'd hear her talking to her sometimes, to her and to Walter.'

'But nothing more sinister than that? Did she ever mention that room off her bedroom?'

'She hated that room. Filled it with junk, and never let me clean it. She said it had always been sad, even when they first moved in. You could smell the pain, she said.'

So the boxroom had been desolate even before Hester's death, Josephine thought. That answered one question, but it did not solve the mystery of why she had chosen to die in a room she hated. 'Did Hester ever *see* Lucy?' she asked.

'Oh yes,' Rose said, as if it were the most natural question in the world. 'Often in the garden, apparently, or standing by her bed. Sometimes she'd see her out in the field where the barn used to be. Once she told me that she would occasionally hear the sound of a fire and people shouting and screaming, said it was like being there when the barn burned down.'

'And you believed her, even though you never saw Lucy yourself?'

'Of course. It stands to reason that the poor cow wasn't going to rest in peace after everything that happened.'

Josephine felt as though the reins of the conversation had slipped her grasp some time ago, and she decided just to let Rose have her head. 'What do you mean?' she asked, picking up her sandwich.

For the first time, Rose hesitated. 'Miss Larkspur swore me to secrecy, but I don't suppose it matters now, and you'll know about it anyway now you're living there. I mean all the stuff that Lucy wrote in her diary. I don't know how she did it, moving into that cottage so close to where her best friend was butchered. I couldn't have done it, but I don't suppose she had any choice. What else was she going to do, on her own with no job and tainted by working for the Corders?'

There was no doubt that Rose had read the diary, Josephine thought, and if Hester had talked about it all the time, Rose would also know its value. Would she be stupid enough to admit all this, though, if it was she who had stolen it and sold it to John Moore? 'When did Hester tell you about the diary?' she asked.

'When I'd been with her about six months. I was moaning about cleaning the fires one day, and she laughed and told me that girls had never had it so good. She'd often tease me like that.' She smiled, and Josephine could tell that whatever happened later, she had loved working for Hester. 'That's when she read me some of the diary – and she was right, too. I don't know how many hours Lucy had in her day with all the work she had to do. After that, she'd read bits to me all the time. I couldn't wait.'

'Did she say where she got the diary?'

'She found it in the cottage when they were having some work done. The house was a wreck when they bought it. It was empty for years – there were sheep in the kitchen when they moved in – and Mr Paget got the farmer to sell it to them because of its history. Miss Larkspur said he must have seen them coming but they didn't care. It was part of the story for them, and worth every penny. She said that Lucy was there from the start, and it was as if she wanted the diary to be found. Miss Larkspur had worked on it for years. She said it was what got her through losing her Walter, and she felt that Lucy had saved her somehow. Stopped her from going mad with grief and doing something stupid.' So that was the kindness mentioned in the will, Josephine thought. 'She wanted to pay Lucy back by telling her story. Then a couple of months before she died, she asked me to help her with it. She made it out to be a treat for me – and it was a treat – but I knew it was really because she couldn't read it herself any more.'

'She told you she was losing her eyesight?'

'Not as such, but it was obvious. She was a lot less fussy about the dust, for a start, and she looked different. Small things – her jewellery didn't quite match or her hair was wrong at the front, but you notice those when you're a woman, don't you? Especially when someone's always been so particular. She knew I'd guessed, but neither of us ever mentioned it. We just went on as normal, and I helped her as much as I could without her knowing I was doing it. We're all entitled to a bit of pride.' It sounded as though Hester had come to rely heavily on Rose; like Bert, she had been in a position of trust, and like Bert she could easily have abused it. Josephine looked at the girl in front of her: she was wilful, cheeky and no doubt wily enough to have twisted a vulnerable old woman round her little finger, but Hester had obviously seen something special in her, and Josephine – without any good cause – trusted her godmother's judgement. 'So we had a system – I'd read the diary out loud, and Miss Larkspur would write down what she wanted to use. She said that Lucy would turn in her grave if she knew.'

'Why?'

'Because I'm on the wrong side. We're related to the Corders,' Rose explained when she saw Josephine's blank expression. 'William's sister married a Boreham – great-great-great-uncle Jeremiah to be precise. He was a miller. Miss Larkspur used to tease me about that as well, but you can't help who you're born to.'

'Did Hester know what happened to Lucy later, after the diary finishes?'

'No. It was enough for her to have Maria's story, I think.'

'What was she going to do when she'd finished transcribing it?'

'She wanted to get it published. Will you do that now for her?'

Rose's assumption was obviously that the diary had passed straight to Josephine without ever leaving the cottage; unless she was an exceptionally accomplished liar, that was another mark in favour of her innocence. 'Yes, if I can. When was the last time you saw the diary?'

The strangeness of the question didn't go unnoticed. 'The last day I worked at Red Barn Cottage,' Rose said warily. 'Why? Has something happened to it?' She looked at Josephine, suddenly unsure of who she was talking to and worried that she might have been tricked into saying too much.

'No, it's safely where it's always been,' Josephine said, choosing to miss out the interlude in Leather Lane. 'But have you told anyone else about it? Anyone at all?'

Rose shook her head. 'No. I haven't even told my mum and dad. Like I said, Miss Larkspur swore me to secrecy.'

'I know, but you could be forgiven for reneging on that sort of loyalty when you and Hester fell out.' Rose said nothing, but the way she shook her head told Josephine what she thought of that sort of pettiness. 'So what happened?' she asked gently. 'What went so wrong that you had to stop working there?'

'I don't know.'

'You must have some idea.'

The girl's face clouded over, but she remained adamant that her dismissal was a mystery to her. 'All I know is that things were never the same after that woman came to see her.'

'Hester had a visitor?'

'Yes. She didn't see many people once her eyesight started going. She couldn't travel to London any more, and even going to the vicarage or doing her own shopping about the village got too much for her. It made her bad-tempered sometimes, and the thought of people knowing and feeling sorry for her was the last thing she wanted, so she stopped encouraging people to call. There was a bloke from the village who'd do things for her like I did, without making a big deal of it, but that was about it.'

'Bert Willis, you mean?'

'That's right. But one morning I got there and she told me that she'd had an unexpected visitor the day before. She made light of it, like it had been a nice surprise, but I could tell it had bothered her. She was distracted all day.'

'So you didn't meet this person?'

237

'No.'

'Did Hester tell you who it was?'

'Only that she'd come up from London – from her old life, she said. They hadn't seen each other for years.' Josephine thought about the woman whom Miss Peck had met at Hester's funeral, the one who had been asking what would happen to the cottage; was it the same person, she wondered, and if so, who could it be? The only woman from Hester's old life whom she knew about was the theatrical dresser who had been mentioned in her will. Nichols – that was it. Dilys Nichols. She tried the name out on Rose, but the girl just shook her head. 'I'm sorry. I don't think she told me the woman's name. Like I said – she didn't make a big fuss about it.'

'Did the woman ever come back?'

'If she did, Miss Larkspur didn't tell me about it. But she was never herself again after that. She seemed agitated all the time, as if she had something on her mind. We'd always had such fun. Even after her eyes started to go, she was still interested in things, still full of life, but all that stopped. She lost weight, too, as though she wasn't bothering to look after herself any more.'

'Did you ask her what was wrong?'

'Yes, eventually. It took me a while to pluck up the courage, because she hated any fuss, but one day she said something very odd – she said that even Lucy had turned against her, and I asked her then if there was anything I could do. She didn't answer for ages, then she took my hand and told me that everything beautiful had a cost. That's all she said.' The rowdiness was building next door, and Josephine saw Mrs Boreham trying to catch her daughter's eye, but Rose was intent on her story. 'Then the following Monday I got there at the usual time and she wouldn't let me in. She told me I'd let her down, and she wouldn't be needing me any more. I tried to get her to come out and explain what I'd done to upset her, but she wouldn't. My mum went up there the next day. Furious, she was – she still hadn't forgiven me for chucking in the vicarage to go there, but it didn't do any good. Miss Larkspur said the same things to her, and worse besides. I never did find out what I'd done wrong.'

Josephine believed her, and felt desperately sorry for the girl. Injustice was such a strong emotion, and so scarring, especially at Rose's age; nobody ever forgot the first time they learned that the world was not designed for fairness, and she well understood the potent mix of rage, helplessness and resentment that Rose must have felt since that day, not to mention the shame and disappointment of losing a position she had obviously loved. There was nothing that could be done to calm that rage, either; it just had to burn itself out, but she tried at least to show she understood. 'Rose, my godmother wasn't herself when she died. Something made her turn her back on people who cared about her. She did the same thing to Bert. I don't know what happened, but I'm trying to find out and if I do, I promise I'll come and explain.'

'She'd lost her mind, hadn't she? That's what was wrong.'

'Why do you say that?'

Rose looked over to the bar and scowled at her mother, mouthing an 'I'm busy' in response to an unspoken question, and Josephine hid a smile: whatever had happened with Hester, she couldn't help but feel that Rose's days in service were numbered. 'I went back to Red Barn Cottage to try one more time,' she said. 'After I got over the shock, I wanted to have it out with her. Mrs Lampton wouldn't take me back at the vicarage, and I wanted to tell Miss Larkspur that she couldn't treat people like that.' She smiled at her own bravado. 'Well, that's what I told myself, anyway. What I really wanted was to find that she couldn't cope without me, and to be welcomed back with open arms. She didn't answer the door, so I let myself in. I knew she'd be there – she never went out. There was no one downstairs, so I called up to her but she didn't answer. I was worried then, in case she was ill or had hurt herself somehow, so I went up. She must have heard me on the stairs, because she started screaming long before I got to the top. She was on the floor in the corner of her bedroom, huddled under a blanket.' Rose paused, struggling with the scene in her mind, and Josephine waited for her to go on. 'She looked terrible. Far too thin, and there were burn marks on her hand from the fire or the hot plate or something. She wasn't in a state to look after herself. I went over to her, telling her it was me and saying I wanted to help her, but she didn't know who I was. She kept screaming, and I've never heard anyone make a noise like that. She was like an animal, when they're frightened and they don't know you're trying to help. There was no reasoning with her. And it was the same thing, over and over again. "Leave me alone or tell me what you want." This might sound daft, but I think she thought I was Lucy.'

'You mean she thought Lucy was tormenting her?'

'Yes. She said her name a couple of times. And I did feel it then, Miss – a presence in that cottage. It was the first time I'd ever sensed anything like that there, and it wasn't nice. I left Miss Larkspur then. I know I should have stayed to help, but I was frightened and I just wanted to get out.' She looked at Josephine. 'Is that what's happened to you? You've felt that too?'

Josephine was too shocked and saddened by the image of Hester to answer immediately, and Rose had to repeat the question. 'I have felt something,' she admitted, 'and I've seen and heard things I don't understand, but I couldn't honestly say that it was hostile. It frightens me, because I've never experienced anything like that in my life, but I've never got the impression that Lucy – if that's who it is – means me any harm. It's sadness rather than anger.' Rose's description of Hester's fear rang true with the way that Bert had found her body, although there was still no explanation for Hester's being in that room: if her mind was telling her that Lucy was trying to hurt her – and Josephine was particular in how she phrased the question to herself; she was not prepared yet to subscribe to the notion of vengeful spirits, if only for her own sanity – why would she retreat to the room most affected by Lucy's presence? 'Did you notice anything strange about the cottage that day?' she asked.

'Benjy wasn't there.'

'Benjy?'

'Benjamin Barker, Hester's dog. She named him after the man Sweeney Todd was based on. An old collie he was. They worshipped each other.'

Josephine remembered the basket, but no one else had mentioned a dog and until now she had assumed that he was long gone, and that Hester had kept his things out of sentiment. 'Anything else? Were any of Hester's things missing?'

Rose thought about it. 'Yes, now you mention it. Some of the pottery had gone from downstairs. You remember things you have to dust, don't you? I assumed she'd broken it. The sort of state she was in, anything could have happened.'

'What about the other things – Maria's chest?'

The girl smiled, in spite of her sadness. She had dark blue eyes, almost violet, and laughter lines creased back from their corners, unusual in someone so young; Rose must have packed a lot of laughing into her eighteen or nineteen years, Josephine thought. 'That old thing? That was no more Maria's chest than one of our beer barrels. Mr Paget bought that for Miss Larkspur from a dealer. He paid a fortune for it, and she never had the heart to tell him it was a fake.'

Josephine was sceptical. 'I gather it was very precious to her.'

'Yes, it was – because he bought it for her. She'd never disabuse anyone who jumped to the wrong conclusion, mind you – but if you look carefully, it's got a maker's mark on the bottom, a firm that didn't even exist when Maria died. But it was still there that day – by the range in the kitchen, where she always kept it.'

The thought of Hester proudly showing Henry Andrews what he thought he most coveted made Josephine smile, but the smile soon faded. Rose's account angered her beyond belief: whatever Hester had thought was going on, and whatever ghosts Red Barn Cottage held, she had no doubt now that a very human agency had systematically terrified and exploited Hester during her final days, and she was more determined than ever to find out who. 'And the diary?' she asked, trying not to betray how she felt.

Rose shrugged. 'I didn't see it, but it was always in the study and I didn't go in there.' She was quiet for a moment, then said: 'I let her down, didn't I? I should have done something about it, but I was scared and angry. Then a few days later, I heard she was dead.'

'You didn't let her down, Rose. She was beyond your help by then. Concentrate on all the months that you were there for her.'

Rose smiled, but the textbook reassurances did not convince her, and Josephine would have thought less of her if they had. 'She didn't mind that I wanted more than this, you see,' she said. 'Mum and Dad always take it so personally, and you can't have any ambition in this village. You're either with them or against them, and wanting to do something different with your life is like an act of bloody war.' She looked embarrassed at the outburst, but Josephine laughed. 'That's why I admired Miss Larkspur so much – she took it for granted that a girl could do anything. I suppose she was unusual in that.'

'Unusual, yes, but not unique.' Josephine smiled and pushed her empty plate to one side. 'I've kept you long enough, Rose, but thank you. I've got to go back to Scotland in a couple of days, but I'll probably be back here in November. Why don't you come and have tea with me at the cottage? I still haven't made up my mind about what to do with it yet, but if I keep it on, I'll need someone to look after it for me.' Just in time, she took Rose's pride into account. 'If you have time, and it's something you'd consider.' Rose nodded and stood up. 'Now – can you tell me where I might find a builder called Deaves? There's some work I need doing at the cottage. I can live with the ghosts, but the outdoor toilet is getting me down.'

'Thought you hadn't made your mind up?'

Josephine smiled and conceded defeat. 'It doesn't hurt to see what the options are, does it?'

'No, it doesn't.' She gave Josephine the directions she wanted, and held out her hand. 'I'll see you in November, Miss.'

19

Felixstowe was only thirty miles away, but Josephine left an hour earlier than she needed to, swayed by Bert's assessment of Chummy's reliability. She reprised her journey to Stoke, the map open and marked on the seat next to her, and headed out to the coast, relishing the twin prospects of some time with Archie and a spot of sea air: one of them, surely, would help her clear her head. She had gone over and over her meeting with Rose Boreham, and whilst it had helped her to get the house's history into perspective, it had brought her concerns over the more recent past sharply back into focus. When she had walked back into the cottage, all she could see was Hester's pain, and it filled her with a sense of rage and horror that was far greater than anything a ghost could invoke. Any injustices that Lucy had suffered were dead and buried, but Hester's were recent enough to be acknowledged and paid for, even if they could never be set right. When her godmother had sat down with John MacDonald to write her will, she could not possibly have foreseen the real challenges that would face Josephine after her death; even so, Josephine was determined not to let her down, and while her sense of purpose was strong, she was able to keep her grief at a distance.

She didn't know this particular stretch of the Suffolk coastline, but her first impressions were of a charming seaside town with a bustling high street and handsome villas. At the top of Bath Hill, she slowed Chummy to a stop to enjoy her first glimpse of the sea: dirty, slate-grey and dull under a heavy band of cloud, yet still powerful and invigorating. The hill declined steadily into Undercliff Road East, and she soon found the Fludyers Arms Hotel where Archie had suggested they meet. Accustomed as she was now to old thatched cottages and low timbered buildings, she looked on the modern, plain-speaking brick façade as a refreshing change; it was like any number of the larger public houses to be found on the outskirts of London, and it reminded her that one of the things she was coming to love most about Suffolk was its variety.

The only other cars in the street were parked outside the hotel, so she drew up in front of the restaurant next door, feeling as though she were driving a toy in comparison with the smart black Buick a few yards up the road. She was early, having underestimated what Chummy was capable of, and she didn't want to go in before the appointed time in case Archie was busy and felt obliged to entertain her, so she sat in the car for a while, marvelling at a silence that was disturbed only by the rhythmic sound of the sea breaking on a deserted beach. It had started to rain, and the drops stirred the surface of old puddles in the road, making a mockery of the beach huts that stood hopeful and redundant nearby, a remnant of sunnier days. There was something faded and melancholy about a seaside town out of season, she thought: it seemed to stand for all the summers that were lost, for a childhood that was now a distant memory.

The rain stopped as quickly as it had begun, and she walked over to the Fludyers Arms, bowing her head against the bitter air and pulling her fur tighter around her. As she reached the hotel, a man with a camera got out of the second car – considerably less impressive than the Buick – and took a photograph of her as she climbed the steps to the entrance; she looked back at him, bewildered, but he showed no sign of apology or explanation, so she shrugged and went inside.

The hotel's restaurant was at the front of the building and she asked for a table in the corner, where she and Archie would be able to talk in private. Through the archway into the hall, she saw him come downstairs and pause to talk to another guest in reception, and she wondered what duties had brought him here. The other man was about forty and dressed in an understated dark suit, and Archie could match him for height but certainly not for build; he didn't look like a policeman, and they seemed to speak as equals, and Josephine enjoyed a rare opportunity to watch Detective Chief Inspector Archie Penrose at work – serious and dedicated, unconscious of being observed. She had known Archie since the war and although their bond had occasionally been threatened by the no man's land between friendship and love, it remained the most constant and uncomplicated relationship in Josephine's life – in his, too, she hoped. She cherished it, and realised now how relieved she was to see him, and how unsettled she had been for those few days when she had not been able to speak to him.

His face lit up when he noticed her. 'You look lovely,' he said, bending to kiss her, then lowered his voice: 'Sorry about the venue. It's hardly a romantic country inn with a roaring fire.'

'Don't apologise – I like it. It's quite nice to be somewhere younger than I am for a change. I'm beginning to find history intimidating.' He smiled, intrigued, and she added: 'I thought we could sit here. It's out of the way, and we won't be interrupted.'

'Mm.' He looked doubtfully at the table, then went over to speak to the waiter. The next thing Josephine knew, a couple was moved discreetly from the centre of the window and given two large brandies by way of recompense, and she and Archie were ushered into their seats. She stared at him in amazement, but he simply shrugged and gave a sheepish grin. 'It's a shame to come all the way to the seaside and not have a sea view,' was all he could manage by way of explanation.

She looked out at the bleak October day, and noticed that the man with the camera was still sitting in his car. 'Do you know who that is?' she asked. 'He took a photograph of me on the way in.'

'I've no idea,' Archie said, but she could have sworn that he was trying to hide a smile. 'I'm sorry I missed you in London. Bill said you were keen to speak to me. What's been going on?'

Josephine began to explain, but she hadn't got far when she realised that she might as well have been talking to herself. Archie stared out at the beach, distracted, and when she stopped speaking, he barely seemed to notice the difference. 'Are you sure you've got time for this?' she asked, worried that she was keeping him from his work.

'What? Oh yes, of course. Sorry. Shall we order?' Josephine hadn't even picked up the menu, but Archie was obviously hungry or in a hurry, so she gave it a perfunctory glance and chose a game pie. Archie ordered the same, and smiled apologetically at her. 'It really is lovely to see you. How's the cottage?'

'Complicated.' She hadn't progressed much further with her explan-ation when another man appeared in the doorway, this time obviously a plain-clothes policeman.

'Excuse me a minute.' Archie got up and spoke earnestly with his colleague for a few minutes, while Josephine looked on, exasperated. She was giving up hope of getting his attention at all, and began to wish that she had never come; it was obviously awkward for him, and, in hindsight, it would have been far better to go home to Scotland and speak to Archie on the telephone when he was back in London and able to concentrate.

'Sorry,' he said, sitting down at the table, and Josephine honestly thought she would have to slap him if he apologised again. 'There's been a change of plan with things here. Where were we?'

Exactly where we started, Josephine thought ungraciously, but she tried to hide her impatience. He seemed pressed for time, so she dis-pensed with any lengthy descriptions of Polstead and the cottage and cut to what she really wanted to talk about. 'Have you heard of the Red Barn murder?'

'It rings a bell, but I couldn't tell you why.'

She outlined it succinctly, and Archie nodded. 'Yes, I remember now – Bill talks about it. Wasn't there something unusual about the trial that set some sort of legal precedent?'

'They charged him with everything,' Josephine said dismissively; of all the different aspects to the case, she found Corder's guilt and how it was proved the least fascinating. Two men sat down at a table nearby and chatted up the waitress in an American accent; one of them smiled at Josephine and she looked quickly away, uncomfortable with their obvious interest. 'And have I told you that Hester made a career out of playing Maria Marten?'

'Yes, you mentioned it in your letter.' Their food arrived and Archie picked at his, although the pie was exceptionally good. He still seemed fascinated by the beach, but all she could see was a couple out walking. 'So is the cottage near where it happened?' he asked.

'Archie, I've just told you that,' Josephine exclaimed impatiently. 'Look, why don't you go off and do what you need to do, and I'll just wait here until you're free? Or it can wait for another time,' she added reluctantly.

'No. Bill said it was important. I'm listening, honestly.' She began again, but stopped as the couple on the beach turned and headed back towards the hotel. The man with the camera got out of the car, and Archie pushed his chair back. 'Wait here. I'll try not to be long.'

By now, Josephine had lost the will to live and she simply nodded as he left the restaurant, followed by the shifty Americans from the next table. The giant she had seen in reception appeared from nowhere, and she watched, suddenly interested, as he and Archie flanked the couple protectively, making it impossible for anyone else to get close, and walked them quickly past the hotel. The woman was striking, dark and very slim, with clothes that were classy but unobtrusive; her companion was a couple of inches shorter, a slight figure in an overcoat with a shock of thick, fair hair, and there was something in his walk that . . . Josephine put her fork down and stared in astonishment. They were whisked out of sight before she had a chance to look again, and she waited impatiently for an explanation. 'For God's sake, Archie,' she whispered as soon as he returned, 'wasn't that . . . ?'

'The King, yes.'

'Who's that with him?'

Archie grinned. 'I can't say, I'm afraid, but obviously someone who looks very much like you.'

'Are the rumours true, then?' She stared out of the window, as if her questions could bring the couple back to give an answer. 'What on earth are they doing in Felixstowe?'

He was saved from having to respond by the arrival of his colleague. 'He's gone, sir,' the policeman said discreetly.

'And . . . ?'

'She's back at the house. Ladbrook's gone with her.'

'Excellent. Thank you, Storrier.' He left, and Archie winked at Josephine.

'Those men with cameras were from the press, weren't they? Please tell me I'm not going to be all over the papers.'

'If you are, it'll only be across the pond. Our lot are holding off – gentleman's agreement, and all that – so Inverness will never know.' He laughed at the expression on her face. 'The Americans have suddenly become great experts on our constitution and our divorce laws; they just need to go the extra mile and photograph the right woman. Thinking about it, it might be worth your putting an order in for the *Boston Globe* when you get back home.'

'You might at least have given me a hint so that I could get a better look at them,' Josephine said huffily, genuinely irked by what she had missed.

'Sorry, but now I really *am* all yours.' He looked at the cold lunch that sat neglected on the table between them. 'Shall we go somewhere else? I could do with a change of scene, and there's a theatre along the front with a very good tearoom.'

'All right. A damned good tea is the least you can do if you're using me as a decoy for the King's mistress.'

'I can't argue with that.' They walked arm in arm along the beach, and cut through some pleasant municipal gardens to get to the Spa Pavilion. This time, Archie let Josephine choose the table and sat with his back to the sea so that she could be sure of his full attention. True to his word, he ordered every sandwich and cake on the menu, and settled back in his seat. 'Right – your godmother and the Red Barn murder. Start again.'

She did as she was asked, beginning with the peculiar terms of the will and her first impressions of the cottage, then describing the ephemera she had found that revealed Hester's interest in Maria Marten. 'Everything was going well, and I was quite enjoying myself – and then Bert came round one evening to bring me her car.'

'Bert?'

'He's the garage man. He's lived in the village all his life – fearsome wife, couple of children, and a friend of Hester's. The only true local she had anything to do with as far as I can see. He helped her out with jobs around the house and looked after her car, and she gave it to him when she found out she was losing her sight. He wanted me to have it, because he said it was a ladies' car.'

'The turquoise Austin?'

'That's right.' She glared at him defiantly. 'Don't smirk like that. We're getting along just fine, Chummy and I. It's a female thing, but there's nothing wrong with that.' He raised his eyebrows, but didn't argue. 'Anyway, I'd found out already that it was Bert who discovered Hester's body, and I asked him about it.'

'Why?'

'Because *he* hadn't mentioned it, and I thought that was odd. There's a room in the cottage . . .' Josephine hesitated, suddenly shy of telling Archie everything that she feared about that room; he would think she was irrational, and she didn't want to look stupid in front of him or to detract from the real business of Hester's death. 'It's off the main bedroom, and Hester used it to store her junk. Actually, it's deeply unpleasant, but that's where Bert found her body, buried under a pile of old clothes as if she'd crawled away to die. As if she was frightened, and had tried to hide.'

'And that's what's concerning you?'

'It was the first thing, yes. It seemed an unlikely thing for her to do.'

Archie looked sceptical. He waited while a girl served their tea, then said: 'That sort of death is more common than you might think among elderly people. I've seen women – sometimes men, but usually women – who have crawled into wardrobes or the corner of a pantry, who've pulled books and furniture down on top of them, or covered themselves in newspapers. Sometimes the house is in such disorder that it looks like a break-in. They're often undressed when they're found. Was Hester . . . ?'

'She was in her nightclothes, yes.'

'Mm. No one quite knows why it happens. The cause of death is usually hypothermia, but we can't tell if the cold affects their mind and causes confusion, or if senility leads them to behave in that way and they die from the cold because of it. Presumably the doctor was called in?'

'Yes.'

'And what does the death certificate say?'

'I don't know, but the thing is – Bert moved her body.'

'He did what?' Archie frowned at her in disbelief. 'Why on earth would he do that?'

'For her dignity, he said. He told me she would never have wanted anyone to see her like that.'

'Very convenient. He could tell you anything with an excuse like that – or not tell you something you should know. Do you trust this Bert?'

'I don't know. He seems genuine, and I believe he really cared for Hester. And he didn't have to tell me *anything*, did he? How would I have found out? He's the only person who knows what happened.' She thought for a moment, trying to decide how she really felt about Bert. 'He fell out with Hester towards the end of her life; she said his kids had stolen something from the cottage – but she was behaving strangely by then, so who knows what really happened?'

'I had no idea it was Hester's death you were so worried about. Your note mentioned stolen goods, but are you saying that someone killed her?'

'Yes, I suppose I am – but I've got absolutely no evidence for that, and it's all tied up with stolen goods. Let me tell you about the diary.'

She did so, conscious of how good it felt to talk to someone whom she could trust with anything, someone who wasn't connected in any way to Hester or to the village.

'And Hester was going to publish it?' Archie asked, when she had finished her account of the bookseller in Leather Lane. 'It would be the most authentic account, I suppose – there'd be a lot of interest in it.'

'Not only that. It was written by a friend of Maria's and it treats her as a real person – not a victim, and not a whore. None of the other accounts tell it from Maria's perspective, not even Curtis. History is always more interested in the murderer.'

'That's true.' He nodded, and she could tell that her enthusiasm was infectious. 'It sounds unique.'

'It is. I've brought you a sample to look at.' She took the bundle of pages out of her bag and watched as he examined it, as fascinated by the diary as she was.

'Where did Hester get it?'

'Rose said she found it in the cottage when she moved in.'

'You should have brought a cast list. Who's Rose?'

Josephine smiled, and offered him another sandwich. 'Rose Boreham. She's the girl who charred for Hester. She lives in the next village – her parents run a pub there. I went to see her yesterday.'

'If she charred for Hester, she'd know about everything in the cottage. Was she interested in the Red Barn murder?'

'Yes, but I trust her, Archie.'

He gave her a look, but said nothing. 'So there's no actual proof of ownership of the diary, other than Hester's transcript and this girl's word?'

Josephine was deflated. 'Isn't that enough? John Moore readily admits he bought it from someone, and it certainly wasn't Hester.'

'He won't tell you who, of course.'

'No. That's where I thought you might be able to help me.' She reached for a cream horn and spoke nonchalantly. 'I know how heavy you can be – I've seen you strong-arm for royalty.'

'I'm never going to live that down, am I? But of course I can do that. I'll have a word back at the office and see if John Moore is known to us as someone who buys stolen relics. A lot of that goes on, and I'm ashamed to say that it's often our lot who encourage it. Sometimes things go missing from the archives, and you find out that a constable nearing retirement has decided to make things a bit more comfortable in his final years. If Moore has got a record already, that would make it much easier to put some pressure on him to reveal his sources.'

'Thank you.'

'I meant what I said about ownership, though. To prove it was stolen, you have to prove it was rightfully Hester's.' She was about to argue through a mouthful of pastry, but he pre-empted her. 'Assuming that can be done, though, who are the candidates for the middleman? Bert and his family, Rose Boreham – who else knew what was in that cottage?'

'Well, there's the mysterious woman from London,' Josephine said, warming to her theme; if the village spinster cap fitted, she might as well wear it. 'Two people have mentioned her. Rose said she came to call on Hester unexpectedly . . .'

'She tells a good story, our Rose.'

'. . . and my solicitor's secretary met her at Hester's funeral. At least, I assume it was the same person. How many shadowy, dark-haired women can there be?'

'What does your solicitor say about all this, by the way?'

'I haven't had a chance to talk to him properly yet.' Absorbed in her conversation with Rose, she had forgotten to telephone as planned from Stoke, but it could wait until next week now, when she would be able to speak to John MacDonald in person – and ask him about Dilys Nichols. 'But everything's in order with her estate as far as he's concerned.'

'All right. So – the woman from London.' He listened, increasingly concerned as Josephine described Rose's traumatic last meeting with Hester, and the elderly woman's sudden, unexplained decline. 'Listen,

Josephine – are you sure you should be getting involved in all this? If someone gets wind of the fact that you're asking questions, you could be making yourself very vulnerable. I hate the thought of you stuck out in the middle of nowhere, all on your own. Can't Marta come and stay while this is going on?'

'She's been for a few days but I don't need a minder, Archie.' He looked doubtful, and she tried to reassure him. 'Anyway, I'm off back to Scotland tomorrow and I don't know when I'll have time to come back. I've been neglecting things at home, and this bloody biography won't write itself, no matter how long I leave it on its own in peace and quiet.'

Archie smiled, but he wasn't convinced. 'Will you at least promise not to do anything else until I've had a chance to ask around for you? I'll get Bill to pay John Moore a visit straight away – it's the sort of job he loves, especially if he knows he's doing it for you. And I'll make subtle enquiries into a death certificate.'

She laughed. '*Is* there a subtle way of making enquiries into a death certificate?'

'No, I suppose not. But please, Josephine – be careful whom you trust. Don't invite anyone into your home, not even this girl Rose. I know you like her, but you know absolutely nothing about her or any-one else in that village. Any one of them could be spinning you lies.'

Rose was hardly another Kate Webster, Josephine thought, pictur-ing the infamous waxwork in her mind, but Archie meant well and she knew he was right. 'All right, I promise to be careful and I appreciate the help. Thank you.'

She could see him turning the information she had given him over in his mind, and knew he would continue to think about it long after she had gone. 'You were telling me who else might have been aware of Hester's collection,' he reminded her.

'Well, anyone from the village could have been inside the cottage at one time or another,' she admitted unhelpfully. 'They seem to come and go as they please. The vicar and his wife knew Hester quite well.'

'And are they interested in the murder? Or particularly hard-up, of course.'

'Definitely not hard-up,' she said, remembering how well the rectory had been furnished, and already familiar with Hilary's penchant for haute couture. She hesitated, thinking about the collection of books on Stephen's shelves and the parish registers that he had been consulting at home. 'They're interested in the case, I suppose, but only in the same way that I am. Oh, and there's the curator of the local museum. Hester charmed him over sherry one day, and made him salivate into his glass for what she'd collected.' She told him about the visit she and Marta had made to Moyse's Hall.

'So presumably he'd be very keen to have the things there?'

'Yes, but not at any cost. Apart from the fact that he seemed trustworthy, he'd give himself away the minute he put them on show.'

'He could say Hester gave them to him.'

'He could, yes, but he didn't. He made no secret of how valuable they'd be to him – he was all but panting for the chest that isn't the chest – but he also told me how valuable they could be to *me*, and cautioned me against letting them go easily. Of course, neither of us knew for sure then that I hadn't got them in the first place.'

'Yes, I see – but that *is* a problem, you know: anyone could say that Hester had given them the things, particularly if she wasn't quite herself, and there's no proof to the contrary. Is there no mention at all of them in the will?'

'Not individually, no. It was a blanket description of everything.'

'That's a shame – we could have argued they were legally yours if so. As things stand, even if I find out who sold the diary to John Moore, that's no proof of theft, and even further away from any bearing on Hester's death.' He saw her disappointment. 'I'm sorry not to be more positive.'

'No, you're right. I know it's a wild goose chase, but I just feel I need to do *something* – to know in my own mind what happened.' He seemed to understand, as she had known he would. 'And the nicest thing of all is to know I'm not on my own with it any more. Thank you.'

'It must have tainted the cottage for you,' he said, accepting more tea. 'Will you keep it?'

'If I can get to the bottom of all this, then yes. I don't know how much time I can realistically spend there when it's so far away, but in a funny sort of way the distance is also what it has in its favour. It would be nice to have a change of scene when I need it, a different life. Peace and quiet, time to think.'

Archie nodded, pleased for her. 'Of course, if you go ahead and publish this diary, that'll be an end to the peace and quiet. Red Barn Cottage will be a magnet for tourists – they'll be traipsing across that field again, just like the old days. I can't imagine that the village will thank you for raking it all up again, just when they thought they'd got the lid on it.'

Josephine hadn't considered that. 'I feel I owe it to Lucy, though. That might be the thing which brings her peace.'

'Is she restless now, then?' he asked, intrigued by her partiality. She looked at him guardedly, but he didn't seem to be mocking her. 'Seriously, Josephine – is the cottage haunted by more than Hester's death?'

So she told him everything – the way the room had affected her and the pain she sensed there, the unexplained noises and the words scratched into the window seat, the figure in the garden and the face at the window. 'Of course, I'd been up all night reading the diary, so I was exhausted. And to be honest, going back to my mother's early life has really got to me,' she admitted. 'It's as though I've had to come to terms with losing her all over again. It's made me oversensitive, I suppose – not really myself.'

'You don't have to make excuses to me.'

'Don't I?'

He shook his head. 'Not at all. I don't think you'd have to justify yourself to anyone who's been in the trenches. Sassoon wrote about an army of ghosts. He meant it metaphorically, but I saw the real thing.

Most of us did. None of the more elaborate visions for me, I'm afraid – no squadrons of silent cavalry or figures in white tending the wounded, but I saw people I'd lost.' It wasn't a confession or even an admission, just a simple statement; Josephine thought about all the people who had talked with similar matter-of-factness about the dead – Rose, Hilary, Hester, even Bert – but she had not expected it from someone who spent most of his life in a rational world where everything had to be proved, and she realised now that she had underestimated Archie. 'One day, when things were particularly bad, I poured my heart out to a chap from the same regiment,' he said. 'I didn't know him very well, so he seemed a safe pair of ears, more anonymous somehow. I only found out later that it couldn't possibly have been him. He was somewhere else completely, and he died that morning, round about the time I was talking to him.' There was a similar legend about Claverhouse, Josephine remembered: he had appeared to a friend at precisely the moment of his death on the battlefield. 'Like you, I was under stress and I suppose my senses were heightened – and I felt a strong connection with people I'd lost, but I've never been able to explain it away. I've never wanted to. We all need something to believe in, and it was never going to be God for me after that. *You* don't doubt what you saw, do you?'

'No, I don't.'

'Neither do I. And it's more surprising, surely, if people *don't* leave traces behind. Why would that sort of pain go away? Or joy, of course – I believe that hangs around, too. And whether ghosts really exist, or whether we carry them with us – does that actually matter? All it's really saying is that the past is important.'

Josephine nodded, thinking about what he had said. 'They're real all right. I've got a photograph of Lucy Kyte.'

She told him what Rose had said about the picture on Hester's desk, and he threw back his head and laughed. 'Now that I *do* draw the line at. Dead people don't pose for the camera.'

'She's not posing,' Josephine said defensively, feeling gullible now for believing everything she was told about Lucy. 'She's just in the background. And her dress looks old-fashioned.'

'How much has a servant's uniform changed in two hundred years, especially in a country village? I think Hester was having a laugh with your Rose.'

Josephine smiled, embarrassed. 'Yes, you're probably right. Or Rose was having a laugh with me.' It was getting late and, in spite of all their bravado, she did not want to arrive back at the cottage in darkness. 'I'd better go,' she said, 'and I've kept you long enough. But thank you, Archie. You have no idea how much I appreciate it.'

'You're welcome.' He looked at his watch. 'I'll give Bill a call from the hotel now, and see what he can find out. You said you were going back to Scotland?'

'That's right. Tomorrow.'

'Then I'll telephone you there as soon as I have some news for you.'

'How's Bridget?' she asked, as he walked her back to the car. 'Have you seen much of her lately?' By chance, Archie had bumped into someone from his past during a holiday at Portmeirion that summer, an artist called Bridget Foley with whom he had had an affair during the war.

'Not really. She's been busy getting ready for an exhibition, and then all this kicked off, so we haven't had a chance. But we'll see each other when I'm back in London, I hope.'

'How much longer are you here for?'

'Just a few days, then I have an appointment in Ipswich and it's back home.' He paused, obviously feeling awkward about something. 'You won't say anything about what happened earlier, will you?'

She laughed. 'Of course I won't.'

'Sorry, but I had to ask.'

'There is one condition, though. When it's all out in the open, *I* get to tell Ronnie and Lettice.' Archie's cousins, Ronnie and Lettice Motley, were stage and costume designers and two of Josephine's closest friends. Lettice, in particular, was renowned for keeping her ear so close to the ground that she risked damaging her jewellery, and Josephine relished the chance of trumping whatever gossip they had to offer when the time came.

'All right, it's a deal.'

Chummy was waiting patiently outside the restaurant, and Archie showed considerable restraint in resisting another comment. 'I nearly forgot – I've got you a present,' Josephine said. She reached behind the passenger seat and handed him a book wrapped in brown paper.

'Don't tell me – it's an early copy of *Claverhouse*.'

She raised her eyes to the heavens. 'If only.'

He unwrapped the parcel and smiled when he saw the jacket. '*Mrs Dalloway* – how lovely. Thank you, Josephine.'

'I know you've got it already, but you won't have brought it with you and I thought a vicarious walk around Westminster while you're here might do you good.'

He smiled. 'Only you would have thought of that. It's ridiculous, I suppose, but I do miss London.'

'It's not ridiculous at all – especially when there's someone there you want to see.'

She saw him flush a little, and hoped that Bridget understood how much he was beginning to care about her. 'Well, we both know how that feels,' he admitted. 'So you can borrow this when I've finished with it.'

'I'm far too busy to read, Archie. You keep it.'

He laughed, and was about to extol the novel's virtues when they were both distracted by a small group of people coming out of a driveway nearby. One of them was the woman whom Josephine had seen earlier with the King. She stopped when she saw Archie, and put a hand on his arm. 'Thank you for coming to our rescue earlier, Chief Inspector,' she said, in a soft American accent. Josephine tried to remain nonchalant as she looked at her, and was struck by her pale, smooth skin and wide mouth – an intelligent face rather than a beautiful one. 'We appreciate it.'

The woman rejoined her friends and Josephine watched them go, amazed that someone whose name would surely be on everyone's lips before long could pass unnoticed in the street; whoever this woman was, she had turned the head that mattered; for now, though, she might as well have been invisible.

20

It was late November when Josephine returned to Suffolk. The year had moved on without her, and the changes to the garden and surrounding fields were all the more pronounced for their delay. The long summer had finally moved on, and the landscape around the cottage defined itself in a subtle arrangement of greys, drained of all colour by heavy-hanging mists. There was no sign now of the clear, flutelike birdsong that had kept her company earlier in the year, but only the harsh, melancholy cry of rooks; from her bedroom window she could see them playing and bickering in the bare trees, their privacy snatched by the winter months. The village lanes were full of carts taking farmyard litter to be spread on the earth, and the men worked hard in the fields, seizing what time they could from the encroaching November darkness. Josephine caught the drift of their voices through the mist, heard the stamping of horses' feet in the lane outside, and felt more strongly than ever the urgency of the farming life to which the cottage had belonged for most of its life. When she walked into the village, she was struck by the smallest of changes in the hedgerows and gardens, and her familiarity with the landscape surprised and pleased her. It gave her a sense of belonging.

A month away had helped to clear her mind and banish some of the doubts she had felt when last here. She had dragged Claverhouse kicking and screaming into his middle years, and – although her progress owed more to pride and bloody-mindedness than to any sort of genuine inspiration – she had been able to look Margaret MacDougall firmly in the eye whenever she used the library and report truthfully that the book was on schedule. One night at home had been enough to reassure her that her father was telling the truth about his accident:

the most serious repercussion seemed to be a missed fishing trip while he waited for his wrist to heal, and – other than a resentment towards the salmon that continued to swim freely in his absence – his spirits remained high. He was interested in Josephine's news – at least, in the edited version he received – and encouraging of her plans for the cottage, but he also managed to convey in the nicest possible way that his life would continue in much the same vein whether she was there or not. Her exchange with Jane Peck still smarted, but she put it down to idle gossip and to the familiar mix of spite and self-righteousness that a number of Inverness women carried with them – as vital an accessory in the town as gloves or a handbag, and just as easily acquired. When she visited her solicitor, the subject of her father was carefully avoided, and – having learned that Hester's accounts were all in order as far as John MacDonald could tell – she parted with Miss Peck on civil, if not friendly, terms.

Her communications with Archie were less reassuring. As far as Scotland Yard was concerned, John Moore had done nothing more serious than peddle materials of a questionable taste. He had no criminal record and nothing on the premises that was known to be stolen, although he freely admitted buying his 'stock' in good faith and asking for very little information with regard to its provenance. The onus, as he had pointed out to Archie's disgruntled sergeant, was on the police to prove him guilty of an offence, which he challenged them to do. As far as the diary was concerned, he had paid cash to a woman who came in off the street; no names had been mentioned, and he had not seen her before or since; when pressed for a description, his memory was conveniently vague, and not even the full Sergeant Fallowfield treatment could come up with anything more specific than ordinary-looking and not dissimilar to the woman who had bought it – a double blow to Josephine which even Archie's careful paraphrasing could not soften. Hester's death certificate had proved equally unforthcoming: the doctor had recorded 'senile decay' as the cause of death, with neglect a contributing factor, and this was – apparently – consistent with the scenario that Archie had outlined to her. He apologised for not having anything more positive to report, and promised to circulate a list of the other items that were missing from Hester's collection, but she knew he had done his best with an impossible task: the chances of recovering anything once it was lost to such an underground industry were very slim indeed.

Frustrated by the brick walls that met her at every turn, Josephine resorted to the one idea she had left: she found Tod Slaughter's address in *Who's Who* and wrote to the actor, asking if they could meet to talk about the years he had spent on stage with her godmother. It was a long shot, but Slaughter would know as much as anyone about Hester's 'old life', and could probably identify the woman at the funeral. She received a charming reply just before she left Scotland, affectionate to both Hester and Walter and complimentary of Josephine's own work; Slaughter would, he said, be only too happy to do as she asked, and suggested tea after a matinee at the Little Theatre, where he was currently in rep. They settled on a date at the end of the month, when she was hoping to be in London to see Marta, and she smiled as she replaced the receiver; the actor's manner was as extravagant in real life as it was on the screen, and she looked forward very much to meeting him.

In the mean time, she returned to Polstead with a new resolve to look to the future. The cottage needed to be secured and made more comfortable, and there was no question of what her priorities would be. Mr Deaves – junior *or* senior; he was of an age that could have been either – scratched his head in bewilderment as she listed the changes she wanted made to the boxroom: a new window put in and the window seat replaced entirely, the fireplace opened up and made fit for use, a bath and sink installed, and all the necessary plumbing dealt with. At a loss to see why she would go to such trouble for the sake of the smallest room in the house, the builder launched into a lengthy explanation about drainage and septic tanks, but she cut him off with a promise of continued work into the spring – and confirmation that she did, in fact, have more money than sense. His reluctance to carry out the work in the winter months was reflected in the size of his estimate, but Josephine called his bluff and instructed him to start work as soon as possible. In the end, they agreed that the room – and consequently the fortunes of Deaves and Son – would be transformed by Christmas. It was her one concession to the outside world: mindful of Archie's warning, she sent Rose a friendly note to postpone their meeting, and saw Hilary only briefly when she collected some bric-a-brac for the next church jumble sale.

The rain arrived on her third night, biblical in its persistence and ushering in days of storm and shadow. Josephine lived a hermitlike existence, packing things safely into boxes to make way for the builders, sorting out her mother's letters and the Inverness photographs to take back to Scotland with her, while the wind whistled down the chimney and tore at the new curtains, and the cherry trees in the garden strained against its strength. The rain was relentless. Within hours, the thatch was sodden, as dark as slate, and she worked to the sound of water cascading from rain barrels that had never been designed to cope with such an onslaught. In the scullery, where she kept an umbrella to go to the outhouse, a permanent pool of water sat on the herringbone tiles, and she struggled to dry the coal sufficiently to keep the range alight. On the fourth day, the level of the pond rose perilously, then overflowed its banks, and Josephine feared for the cottage, remembering the flooding that Lucy had mentioned in her diary. The lower fields held the water, making it impossible to access the village that way, and – on the few occasions that she braved the weather for supplies – she found Marten's Lane almost impassable, too, and came back covered in mud, her boots trailing leaves across the floor. Her evening fires were slow and petulant. In the lamplight, the wind-blown bushes outside the window threw moving shadows onto the study wall, giving the photographs of Hester a troubled, restless look that preyed heavily on Josephine's conscience.

At last, the storms relented and peace returned. Josephine went outside to assess the damage, glad to be able to lift her head and look around without the sting of rain against her face. The wind had beaten down the plants and the garden was full of fallen leaves and other debris that cried out for a bonfire, but it would be far too wet to burn anything for some time. Apart from that, her land seemed to have escaped unscathed and the weather had only intensified the bleakness of what was there already: November was the most depressing time for any garden, Josephine thought; everything was static, held in time in a way that was peculiarly appropriate here, and no matter how hard she looked, the smallest sign of growth and renewal eluded her. It occurred to her as she walked around that flowers died as variously as they bloomed – the graceful fall of a rose petal, the harsh withering of the hollyhock on its stem – and she longed for the spring, when Hester's garden would surprise her with more gifts than she could imagine. It was a sizeable piece of land, and she and Marta would have their work cut out to bring it round, but it was something that they would both enjoy – the shaping of seasons to set a pattern for the future, a quiet promise of shared years to come that meant more, somehow, than any spoken declaration.

An ash tree had fallen across the pond, and the surface of the water was now a mangle of moss and twisted branches. Josephine walked over to the gate to have a look, relieved that the flooding had not reached the garage and orchard as it had threatened to do. Something caught her eye among the branches – a dark shape floating on the water, close to the trunk of the fallen tree, and she could see that it was the body of an animal. She went closer, hoping that something would tell her she was looking at a fox or even a badger, but foxes did not wear collars and she had never seen a badger with a rope around its neck. The rope was frayed, and it was impossible to tell whether it had once been a makeshift leash or something more sinister, but she knew in her heart that the body was Hester's dog, and he had obviously been in the water for some time. Josephine had no idea how to retrieve him. She only knew that she must manage it somehow, and bury the dog properly in the earth that had been his. With a heavy heart, she fetched a spade from the garage and found one of the old sheets that had covered Hester's stage sets. She decided to dig the hole first, then worry about how to move the body, and she chose a patch of ground close to the old iron bench, where the dog must have sat in the sun with his mistress, but even that part of the task seemed beyond her. The soil was soaked through and unbelievably heavy, and she was exhausted before she had dug a foot down. There was only an hour or so of proper daylight left; at this rate, she would never get the job done in time, but it seemed irrationally important that Hester's beloved collie should not spend a night in the open air, exposed to predators, and it was all she could do not to weep with anger and frustration.

'Miss Tey? Is there something I can help you with?'

'Bert! Thank God.' Josephine was so pleased to see him in her garden that she didn't care why he was there. 'It's Hester's dog – at least I think it is. His body was in the pond, and the rain has brought it to the surface. I can't . . .'

'In the pond?' Bert repeated, interrupting her. 'What the hell was he doing in there?'

'I don't know, but I can't get him out on my own and he's got to be buried before it gets too dark to see what we're doing.'

He put a hand on her shoulder, and spoke in a gentle voice. 'Leave him to me. I'll take care of it. You go into the house and make yourself a cup of tea.'

For once, Josephine didn't argue about a woman's place: she had no wish to make a point by insisting on helping with Benjamin's body. Instead, she went inside and watched from the window as Bert made short work of finishing the grave; he disappeared with the sheet, then returned ten minutes later, soaked to the waist and carrying a bundle in his arms. As he placed the dog carefully in the ground, Josephine was struck by the combination of strength and sensitivity in his manner; no wonder Hester had appreciated his friendship during the years following Walter's death. He picked up the spade, but she remembered something and hurried out to stop him. 'Bert – wait a minute.' She went into the garage and fetched the ball and blanket that she had found on her first day at the cottage. 'I didn't have the heart to get rid of them,' she explained, and put them on top of the dog's pitiful body. She waited quietly while Bert filled the grave in, then asked: 'What do you think happened to him?'

He shook his head. 'I don't know, Miss. It's just another thing that isn't quite right.'

Josephine could not have put it better herself. 'Did Hester keep him on a leash like that?'

'Not as far as I know. Mind you, I never saw much of him. She had to shut him in the next room when I called round. He hated visitors.' The expression on his face suggested that he knew what she was thinking, and that he shared her concern. 'I don't suppose we'll ever know what happened now.'

It was hard to tell if he was talking about the dog or about the end of Hester's life in general, but she felt his sadness keenly. 'No, probably not. But thank you, Bert. I don't know how I would have managed that on my own.'

'It's no trouble. Happy to help when I can.'

'Would you like some tea?'

'I won't, thank you, Miss, if you don't mind. I'd best be getting back to the house and change out of these wet clothes.'

'Yes, of course.'

'Nice to see you back, though. And you've got the place looking lovely – really shipshape. Anyone would think you were staying.'

Josephine smiled, and let him go. Only later, when her gratitude for what he had done had subsided a little, did it occur to her to question Bert's parting comment. He hadn't been over the threshold since she moved in, and she always kept the curtains drawn while she was away; the cottage might look shipshape – but unless he had been inside without telling her, how could he possibly have known that?

21

'*What a beautiful throat for a razor!*'

The poster outside the Little Theatre showed Tod Slaughter in his most famous role, the Demon Barber of Fleet Street, and announced that the King of Blood and Thunder was back on stage for a limited season. 'It's a shame they're not doing *Maria Marten* this week,' Josephine said. 'I'd love to see it on stage.'

Marta threw her a cynical smile. '*Maria Marten, Sweeney Todd* – do you honestly think there's much difference? I'll say this for Mr Slaughter – he's excellent value for money. At least six performances for the price of one. Or do I mean that the other way round?'

A group of friends peeled off from the Saturday afternoon shoppers in John Street to climb the steps to the theatre's foyer, and Josephine fell in behind them. 'You can scoff now, but you know you'll enjoy it once it starts.'

'Of course I will – it's not the play I'm here for.' Marta nudged her, and pointed to a crowd by the sweet kiosk. 'Obviously I'm in the minority there.' Several theatregoers had gone to the trouble of wearing mock Victorian garb in the spirit of the production – at least, Josephine assumed it was mock rather than an unconscious hangover from the music hall era – and all seemed ready to enjoy themselves. Slaughter's fans knew exactly what they were getting, and the idea that they might be disappointed had never crossed their minds; the faint air of challenge and scepticism that always radiated from a West End audience was entirely absent here, and for Josephine – whose own plays had enjoyed varying levels of popularity and criticism – it was a refreshing change.

The Little Theatre had been converted from a derelict banking hall between the Strand and the Thames, and it maintained a feeling of solidity in the face of uncertainty that seemed appropriate to its new life. Bombed during the war, the interiors had been carefully reconstructed along the original lines and the auditorium still lived up to its name, seating only a modest three hundred or so. The venue was unusual in that there were no seats or boxes at the side, only rows of chairs in straight lines – more like a church hall with delusions of grandeur than a conventional theatre, but steeply raked to ensure a good view of the stage all round. The room's simple, classical lines were emphasised by fresh, clean decor: walls of Wedgwood blue with white medallions, and no heavy drapes or rich colours except for a deep red stage curtain which stopped the overall effect from being too austere.

'This is nice,' Marta said, when they had found their row. Thanks to Slaughter's recent successes on screen, the entire run was a sell-out, but he had insisted on giving them his house seats, pleased that Josephine wanted to see the performance. 'Have you been here before?'

Josephine shook her head. 'No, never. Hester played here in the early twenties, though, so it's nice to see it.' She opened a box of chocolate gingers and passed it over. 'She was in one of the Grand Guignol seasons here.'

'As in the Paris idea? All horror, blood and sex?'

'Something like that – a whole evening of horrible little plays, as someone described it to me recently. Actually, it's probably not an exaggeration. I looked it up when I found out Hester was in it, and apparently they had nurses on standby in case it got too much for the audience.'

'She was quite a girl, your Hester, wasn't she?'

'Yes, she was. I believe she gouged Sybil Thorndike's eyes out in one of the plays.'

'Lydia's been wanting to do that for years.' Marta glanced through the programme and found a paragraph on the history of the theatre. 'This is interesting. The woman who started it – Gertrude Kingston?' Josephine shrugged. 'No, I've never heard of her either. It says here that she was a suffragette, and she insisted on withholding the name of a playwright until after the first night so that female authors stood a chance with the critics.'

'Now that *is* a bloody good idea. If everywhere did that, I might never have had to call myself Gordon.'

'Oh, I don't know,' Marta said with a wink. 'I quite like it.'

The house lights dimmed before Josephine could think of a suitable response. When the curtain went up, she was surprised to see that the stage itself was actually bigger than many West End theatres', and it rather dwarfed Slaughter's sets. The scenery was crude stuff – a few second-hand flats, an old backcloth, a lick of paint and a moderate lighting set – and it took her back instantly to the theatre of her childhood and to the pantomime she had seen Hester in. The whole thing had probably been done for less than twenty pounds, but it was exactly what was needed: pieces of frayed cloth, suspended from the roof and carelessly touching the walls of an interior set, did well enough for a ceiling and equally well for a sky; and a vaguely painted backdrop of buildings would be easily transformed next week from Sweeney Todd's London to Burke and Hare's Edinburgh. The audience seemed perfectly happy to help the play along with its imagination, and in any case it was the performers who mattered: from the moment Slaughter stepped on stage, wearing his barber's apron and a villainous grin, the peeling paint and crumpled curtains were forgotten. 'Not a single customer today,' he announced to the audience, his delivery timed to squeeze every nuance out of the phrase. 'I pine for something exciting to happen, so I'll just put a *beautiful* edge on my *beautiful* razor in case someone comes in.' An evil, throaty chuckle rolled out across the footlights, the first of many that afternoon, and Slaughter moved about the stage with a dancing, sinister step, graceful and precise for a man of his size. Everything about his performance was exaggerated, a reminder that melodrama had its origins in mime, but it held the attention of an audience that was considerably less reserved than the ones Josephine was used to, and it occurred to her that – as delicious as his performance

269

in the film of *Maria Marten* had been – live theatre was where he really came into his own. He was the consummate showman, always working the crowd: if someone called out a wisecrack, Slaughter fixed the culprit with a wicked stare, stroking his razor across his hand and purring 'Oh, I'd love to polish you off!' – and every time the trademark catchphrase was a cue for booing and cheering in equal measure.

'At least we won't have to bother with a pantomime this year,' Marta muttered as they got up for the interval, but she had hissed and clapped with the best of them and Josephine knew she was enjoying herself. 'Let's go and get a drink.' Their aisle seats gave them a head start to the tearoom. Like the rest of the theatre, it was tastefully decorated with pale yellow walls, Japanese prints and an Angelica Kauffman painting salvaged from the original ceiling, but the effect was confused by the temporary conversion of the room into Mrs Lovett's Pie Shop. A table at the far end promised pies 'to last you to Aldgate pump and back', and Marta shook her head in admiration. 'No one can accuse them of taking themselves too seriously,' she said. 'I bet the regulars who come here every week have had the shock of their lives.'

'Mm. Especially if they're vegetarian. What's it to be? Pork or chicken and ham?'

'Assuming that *is* what's in them, why don't we try one of each?' They found a table in the corner, and Marta ordered tea. 'Before you say anything, I give in – he's very, very good. Much better than I expected.'

'Thank God. There's nothing worse than going backstage after a performance and having to lie. "Darling, you were wonderful!" doesn't trip easily off my tongue, even when it's true.'

'That's a shocking admission. You'll never be a proper playwright. But I was thinking about the Hollywood lot when I was watching him, and he's just as convincing as Karloff or Lugosi. All right, so he milks it for all it's worth, but you do genuinely believe he could dispatch someone without breaking a sweat, and that's what you want from a villain.'

'And the actual plays are brave, too, when you cut through the stereotypes. They might be period pieces to us, but they were dealing in their own time with crime and class and gender, and I suppose that was quite progressive.'

Marta looked doubtful. 'I'm not sure about that. The next time I pinch your cheek and say "upon my soul, you're a delightful little baggage", you'll have to remind me of how liberated we're being.'

Josephine laughed. 'I wasn't trying to claim it as a feminist classic. I just meant that the scenarios must have seemed far more shocking to a contemporary audience than they do to us.' Before she could explain herself further, Tod Slaughter himself appeared in the bar, still in his bloodstained apron, and called everyone back in for the second half. The barber's crimes escalated as the play romped through to its conclusion, and Josephine watched in admiration as the audience was drawn along by the power of the company and by good, honest dialogue; if anyone had come to sneer at a second-rate drama, they were wrong-footed. Marta was right about Slaughter's villainous credentials: the laughter dwindled in the second half, and he played his character's growing insanity completely straight, never once allowing himself to lapse into burlesque. There was an integrity to the performance that equalled anything Josephine had seen on stage at the New or the Garrick, as if the actor really believed in good and evil, in a morality that had a thousand years of history behind it. Melodrama was not unlike detective fiction in that sense, she thought: a dream world with dream justice, ordered as it *should* be, not as it was, and peopled with characters who behaved exactly as they were expected to and got what they deserved. Hester had lived most of her life in that world, and Josephine wished with all her heart that the illusion had not been shattered before her death.

'You'd better go and find the stage door,' Marta said, as the company took the last of four curtain calls.

'Aren't you coming?'

'Would you mind if I gave it a miss? Between Lydia and the Hitchcocks, I see more than enough of actors and dressing rooms.'

'Of course I don't mind.'

'Unless you think Mr Slaughter is a crazed killer with a passion for murder relics, and all this is actually an elaborate double bluff?'

'That hadn't occurred to me and I'll bear it in mind, but I think I'll be safe enough in a busy theatre. What will you do?'

'Go for a walk by the river, I think, and watch the lights come on from Westminster Bridge. Then I'll wait for you in the bar. Don't hurry, though – there's plenty of time before dinner.'

They fought their way through the crowds in the foyer and parted in John Street. At the stage door, Josephine was a met by a woman of around sixty, no longer in costume but easily recognisable as the Demon Barber's partner in crime, Mrs Lovett. 'I'm Jenny Lynn,' she said, holding out her hand. 'Tod's wife. Come with me – he's just wiping the blood off, but he's looking forward to meeting you.'

Josephine followed her along a labyrinthine sequence of corridors and stairs. 'That was quite some performance,' she said. 'Are you in every production?'

'Most of them. He's killed me twice a night now for thirty years, and it doesn't seem to matter if I'm a beggar or a duchess – I'm never breathing by the end of the play.' She smiled, suddenly seeming much younger. 'There were times during the early days when I was every corpse in Burke and Hare. Fortunately the company's a bit bigger now.' Judging by the scene-shifting that was going on overhead, the dressing room area was directly under the stage, and the thickness of the walls suggested that they were standing in the old bank's original strongrooms. 'Tod's over there. I've made you some tea – unless you'd like something stronger after the matinee?'

'No, thank you. Tea would be lovely.'

'Good. You've got nothing to worry about. We keep chickens when we're not on tour, and he's far too soft even to polish *them* off, so you'll be quite safe.' She squeezed Josephine's arm, as if welcoming a distant member of the family back into the fold. 'He was so pleased to hear from you, you know. Hester was very important to him – to both of us, actually. That's how we met – working for her and Walter. Go and make his day.'

Touched, Josephine looked across the green room to where Mr Murder sat surrounded by his company, enthralling them all with another tall tale. He tore himself away as soon as he noticed her, and kissed her hand. 'Miss Tey – how delightful. Thank you so much for coming.' From his welcome, it would have been easy to believe that it was she doing him the favour – the old-fashioned gallantry of a different generation – and a number of the cast looked at her curiously. 'Did you like the show?'

'Yes, very much.' Close up, the actor's face was beginning to sag a little, but the twisted stage smile was now a broad one, and eyes that had been filled with madness were friendly and intelligent. The question was more than polite conversation; he seemed genuinely interested in her opinion, and Josephine was happy to give the answer he was hoping for. 'I can't actually remember when I enjoyed a performance quite as much.'

'I'm so glad. It's good old stuff, isn't it? I know it's fashionable these days to sit around on stage, smoking cigarettes and being witty, but I prefer to save that for my club. Give me the shadow of the noose and the scream in the dark any day – the good old plum-duff.'

His fondness was sincere. There was none of the resentment or false modesty that Josephine had seen in actors who were doing something that they felt was beneath them, and she liked him instantly. 'A lot of people are with you on that,' she said. 'You've sent a crowd home very happy today, and I imagine they'll keep coming as long as you're happy to entertain them. There's something timeless about it.' It was true, she thought; the heroes in her plays – Richard II, Mary Queen of Scots – had been given a contemporary relevance that had proved extremely popular, but she doubted that they would still draw an audience in thirty years' time; the plays about Sweeney Todd, however, or Jack the Ripper and William Corder, had outlived the moment in which they were written, and continued to flourish in a very different age – anti-heroes, almost, for each new generation.

'I'm pleased you said that – they're age-old truths,' Slaughter agreed, 'and keeping them alive after the war is the thing I'm proudest of. I cut my teeth on those stories forty years ago, and I still love them – when something catches you young, it usually holds on. I'll tell you a story,' he added, and Josephine suspected it would be the first of many; if she wasn't careful, Marta would still be on Westminster Bridge when the sun came up. 'We had Edgar Wallace in when I was at the Elephant, and you'll appreciate this, being a thriller writer. I kept a box for him but he wouldn't sit in it, and we had to shift four people out of the front row of the gallery for his party. At the end of the night, he got up on stage and told the audience that the first pennies he'd earned as a boy selling newspapers were spent on a gallery seat at the Elephant and Castle. That was where he learned to write – and look what it's given us. They call them thrillers now, but it's the same glorious stuff that I learned all those years ago from your godmother. She was a splendid woman, and I'm so sorry you never knew her – but let's see if we can do something about that, shall we?'

He opened a door for her – not dressing room number one, as she had expected, but an office and living room combined, which made it clear that he saw himself as an old-school actor-manager rather than a star. The room was busily furnished, and it took her a moment to establish that the things she was looking at – ornately framed portraits, a heavy oak settle and a fine collection of Toby jugs – were personal treasures and not props, objects designed to make the couple feel more at home during the long hours spent at the theatre. Tea was laid out on a central table, and she took the seat offered to her, feeling as though she had just walked into the pages of *Nicholas Nickleby*. 'I've brought you these,' she said, taking a small bundle of photographs out of her bag. 'I thought you might like to have some pictures of your early days with Hester and Walter.'

He took them from her, delighted with the gift. 'My goodness, these take me back.' He looked through the sepia images, smiling in disbe-lief at his younger self. 'The pantomime shots were taken in Inverness – did you know that? *Babes in the Wood*, I believe it was.'

'That's right.' She told him about the photograph she had found of herself as a child on Hester's knee. 'I realised then how much I owe her.'

'She'd be pleased with that. It was never easy for her to perform there after everything that happened. Tell me – are they as sniffy about the theatre now as they were in Hester's day, or have they warmed to your success?'

Josephine gave him a knowing smile and accepted a cigarette. 'I'd say tepid at best.'

'Oh well, that's not bad. Hester told me there was a civil war in the family when she announced she wanted to go on the stage.'

'Really? I didn't know that.'

'Her parents had decided that she was going to be a teacher. They never stopped to wonder if she was capable of teaching anybody any-thing, but the only other thing she could do was cook, and that smacked of service, God forbid.'

'My grandparents were exactly the same, except – as far as I know – my mother was happy to teach, and sorry when she had to give it up. Was Hester supposed to teach anything in particular?'

'Piano. All girls played the piano then, whether they could or not. Every house groaned under the protestations of the Collard and Col-lard.' Josephine smiled, remembering the upright that stood in the study at Red Barn Cottage to this day: it was indeed a Collard and Collard. 'The piano was her destiny. Or the pianoforte, as my dear grandmother insisted on calling it to her dying day. Hester hated it.'

'Did she? She still had one when she died.'

'That will have been Walter's. He was a wonderful musician. He ar-ranged all the songs for the shows, and Hester loved to listen to him – except when he played Gilbert and Sullivan. If they'd had a row – which they often did – he'd play a medley from *H.M.S. Pinafore* and train his dog to lie on the loud pedal.'

Josephine laughed, picturing the scene in her mind. 'So what happened? Hester obviously got her own way about becoming an actress.'

'She took lessons in private at first. No one found out – they all thought she was still intending to take money under false pretences by teaching an instrument she could never hope to learn, but it was only a matter of time before she got a part. Cornelia Carlyle in *East Lynne*, I think it was – a maiden lady of a certain age. No one could accuse *that* director of typecasting: Hester was such a pretty young thing. These days, it's about looking the part whether you can act it or not, but then there was a fetish for never letting people play their own age.' He was right, but Josephine hadn't come here for a discourse on modern theatre and she moved him on as subtly as she could. 'There was a hell of a row,' he continued. 'As far as Hester's family was concerned, actresses were no better than prostitutes; they both painted their faces, especially Hester for that first part – she always said she looked like a close-up of Clapham Junction, there were so many lines. But they really did believe that actresses were fallen women, you know – they must have thought she'd found her vocation in Maria, bless her. Then there was all the money that had gone to waste on piano lessons, when she'd chosen to sleep on the Embankment and die in the gutter. It's easy to see where she got her sense of drama from, isn't it?'

'I hadn't realised that it was such a struggle,' Josephine said. 'I knew there was trouble over Walter, but not over the theatre in general.'

'Walter was all part of it, I suppose. Hester was simply proving them right by running off with her leading man. A flagrant disregard of loyalty and morality, they called it – but you will never see a couple more loyal and more devoted than those two.'

'When did you meet them?'

'In 1901, at the Assembly Halls in Durham. I was sixteen, and they hired me for a pound and a shilling a week to play walk-on parts, open the show with a song and make myself generally useful. There were no contracts and no written agreements – just a handshake and a promise, and I've never regretted that. It's how I work to this day.'

'What was it like, being on tour at that time?' Josephine had vowed to stick to questions about Hester, but she had been sucked in as always by the romance of theatre, and she allowed herself a brief diversion.

'Magic, pure magic. Utterly exhausting, but we were far too excited to notice. We played halls and corn exchanges, mostly in towns that didn't have their own theatre, and we took everything with us, including the stage. The staff – if I can use such a grand term for a crew of four – built the whole thing up from scratch.'

'I've seen some of the sets,' Josephine said. 'They were in Hester's garage when I first went to the cottage.'

'Then you'll know how makeshift and how splendid they were. We built the stage on trestles, and often had to run the gas to the stage from the other side of the building, but I promise you something – that curtain was never late. And I was being paid to see the whole country – seventy-odd towns in five months.' He shook his head in wonder. 'I'll never forget how I felt when I walked onto the station platform and saw the notice on the carriage window: "Reserved for the Walter Paget Company". And I had a right to be there. It was freedom, especially at that age, and a very fine life. It still is.'

Josephine remembered her conversation with Jane Peck, and how the secretary had said that Slaughter seemed to prefer his garden to acting these days, but he didn't strike her as a man who was jaded with the stage; he sounded like the man who had listed his hobby as 'work' in *Who's Who*; perhaps it was just the sadness of the occasion that had made him seem tired of the profession. 'What was Hester like to work with?' she asked.

'Unforgettable. It was Walter's company, but she was the lifeblood of it, a real force of nature. I was terrified of her until she'd licked me into shape. She was a martinet about language and pronunciation, and I still had a trace of my Geordie accent back then. It infuriated Hester. Every rehearsal she'd shout at me if I lapsed. She did it in a performance once. Her voice rang out through the house, and I was so embarrassed.

277

I never did it again, so I suppose her parents got their way after all – she *was* a marvellous teacher.'

'And as an actress?'

'Oh, she loved the limelight – literally. She insisted that the spots followed her all over the stage, and she'd curse the crew if they didn't do as they were told. I can hear her now: "Put the lights on me, you fool! They've never seen a dress like this in Ulverston before!"'

It was a great story, and Josephine could tell that Slaughter was enjoying himself as much as she was. 'It sounds as though Hester was just honest enough to say what all actresses are thinking,' she said.

'Yes, you're right there, but she was good enough to get away with it. She was a great comic actress – I've still never seen a finer Beatrice to this day. But she spent most of her years tearing every passion to tatters, and she was good at that, too. She became a real barnstormer – it was in her blood, and audiences loved her for it. The Elephant was a rough old theatre, but she could charm the birds out of the trees and the money out of a miser's pocket, and she knew how to play to a crowd.'

'So that's where you get it from.'

'Oh, I'll always be a novice compared to Hester. She had two speeches on tour, one for an opening night and one for closing.' He got to his feet, turning the anecdote into a full performance and giving a passable rendition of the Inverness accent. '"Ladies and gentlemen," she'd say, "thank you for the splendid reception you have given us to-night. It has been like renewing an acquaintance with old friends, but nowhere do I feel I have so many *good* friends as here at . . ."' He shrugged. 'Wigan, Rhyl, Morpeth . . . wherever we happened to be. Cue loud applause, usually led by one of the stage crew who'd nipped round to the stalls. Then she'd run through what we were doing that week. On Saturday night, she would shed tears on behalf of us all at the thought of leaving Wigan or Rhyl or Morpeth, then brighten when she remembered she was booked to return the following year. She'd always finish with "And now ladies and gentlemen, I will not say goodbye, only

278

auf wiedersehen until we meet again." Obviously that became *au revoir* after 1914, but I'd left by then.'

He sat down again, and Josephine poured more him more tea. 'You took on Richmond and Croydon Hippodromes before the war, didn't you?'

Slaughter twinkled at her. 'You've done your homework. Yes, I did. It was too good an opportunity to miss, and Hester and Walter insisted I go – but it was as though a milestone had gone, as though I'd lost something that would never come again. I didn't know back then that I'd be able to recreate the spirit of all that with Jenny, and with Hester's blessing. I've been very lucky.' And worked very hard, Josephine thought; it was a completely different world from the theatre she was used to, with different obstacles and different pressures, and she had an enormous respect for those who had made a go of it. 'And do you know, Josephine – you don't mind if I call you Josephine? – Hester and Walter came to every new production that I did at those theatres. They were so loyal. They'd sit in the middle of the front row, and as soon as the lights went down, she'd lean over to him and squeeze his hand and whisper: "Oh Walter! I do so love a play, don't you?" And she was right – there's nothing like it. I'm grateful to the films – not every actor is fortunate enough to have that to fall back on now that so many of the houses we toured to have become cinemas – but it's the theatre I love.'

'It must have devastated Hester to give it up.'

'Yes. When Walter died she lost the two great loves of her life – there was never going to be one without the other. I'll never forget that night, or the look on her face when she knew he was gone. You know he died on stage, playing Corder?'

Josephine nodded. 'You were there?'

'Yes. I'd come back to work at the Elephant with them for a bit. Hester asked me to when she realised that it was getting to be too much for Walter, running the whole thing on his own as well as two performances a night. They both hoped I'd take the place on eventually, which I did – but it was supposed to be after Walter's retirement, not his death.' He stared at the floor, thinking back, and Josephine could see him reliving the night. 'He died during the murder scene, ironically enough. Maria's last laugh, Hester said afterwards – the only time I ever heard bitterness in her voice. His heart just gave out. You'd never believe the life could go out of someone so quickly. It was chaos for a while. There were people trying to revive him and pandemonium in the audience, but Hester just stood there in the middle of the stage. She knew there was nothing to be done – she felt it the moment he died – and I've never seen anyone so alone. Crowds everywhere, but they didn't exist for her. And I feared for her then, Josephine. I honestly didn't think she'd get through it.'

'I imagine the fact that she did was partly down to you. It must have helped to have friends who truly understood what that double loss meant to her.'

'That's hard to say, really. Yes, she had lots of friends in the theatre, but Walter was her soulmate and when you find that with someone, other people are on a different level, aren't they?'

It was another way of saying thus far and no further, Josephine thought. 'There was another friend mentioned in her will,' she said casually. 'Dilys Nichols?'

'Ah, yes. Dilys was her dresser. She worshipped Hester and was incredibly loyal to her. I'm not surprised that Hester would remember that.'

'Hester left her all her furs.'

Slaughter threw back his head and roared. 'That's marvellous. Dilys is in a nursing home – has been for years – and she'll love that, lording it over the rest of them in Miss Larkspur's furs.'

Another dead end, Josephine thought. It might have been a good idea in theory but, as entertaining as the afternoon had been, these stories of Hester's 'old life' had thrown no light whatsoever on her death. Before she could raise the subject of the funeral and who was there, Slaughter said: 'It was such a shame that she couldn't manage the film of *Maria Marten*.'

'How did you even persuade her to consider it?'

'With fine dining and a case of Tio Pepe, I seem to remember. It cost me a fortune, but it was worth every penny to hear her say yes. She was always a fool for Maria. There was a kinship there, and God knows that girl's had few enough friends over the years.' 'Kinship' was an interesting word to use, and Josephine asked him what he meant. 'I suppose they were both outsiders, in a way – isolated from their own communities by the choices they made. Hester always said that no one ever considered Maria as a real woman, and that was always how she played her. She'd have done the same with old Mrs Marten.'

For a moment, Josephine considered telling the actor about Lucy Kyte and the diary, but time was pressing and she still had things she wanted to ask. 'Hester's eyesight stopped her taking the role, though?'

'Yes. It took a lot of courage for her to admit that she wasn't up to it. She would have been splendid, too, and I'd have loved to work with her again. She'd certainly have given Milton Rosmer a run for his money: Hester and a director – now that *would* have been interesting! In some ways it was a blessing, though – she'd have hated what they did to the story. *Her* story, as she'd come to think of it. It was cut to half the length for cinema. All the supernatural stuff was taken out – Mrs Marten's dreams and Maria's ghost – and we weren't even allowed to show the hanging.'

'Really?' Josephine asked, fascinated by what was deemed too shocking – or too incredible – for a film audience.

'Yes. We shot the procession and the gallows scene, but they would only give the film a certificate if it was cut. It was the same with *Sweeney*. We couldn't show an actual murder; all I do is wave a razor and cackle.' He did it for her, rubbing his hands and slipping effortlessly into the voice and the face. 'Bloody censors. I really would like to polish *them* off. Mind you, Hester would probably have got round that. Do you know the story of how *The Old Women* was put on?' Josephine recognised the name of the Grand Guignol play that she had mentioned to Marta, but that was all she knew and she shook her head. This time,

Slaughter's chuckle was genuine. 'It was thanks to Hester that it went on at all. She was friendly with a vicar in Suffolk. Stephen something.'

'Stephen Lampton. He's still there.'

'Really? Nice chap, as I recall. But the play was the most shocking thing that had been put on, even in Paris. The Lord Chamberlain would never have passed it. But Hester thought of a way round it. Stephen had a hall licensed in Polstead for stage plays in the parish, so she sent the script to him, with the reading fee and the draft of a letter he was to send to His Lordship, saying he wanted to produce the play in the village hall to raise money for a new scout hut. The licence was issued by return of post, and the play went on there in the very next bill.'

'Is that really true?'

'Absolutely. All hell broke loose when the play was reviewed in the press, and it caused a huge sensation. It's a wonder the theatre wasn't closed down. It didn't do them any good in the end, of course. The Lord Chamberlain was on their backs all the time after that, and it was the end of the whole thing, but it was a small triumph for free speech – which I gather your vicar is all in favour of. And Hester – well, I should think she's still laughing, wherever she is.'

It amused Josephine to think of the serious-minded vicar involved in a conspiracy to pull the wool over the Lord Chamberlain's eyes. Slaughter was about to tell her something else, but they were interrupted by a tentative knock at the door and one of the younger members of the cast put his head round. 'Sorry, Mr Slaughter, but is there any chance of that loan we talked about?'

The actor raised his eyes to the heavens in mock weariness, and took a ten-shilling note out of his pocket. 'They'll be the death of me,' he said good-naturedly to Josephine when the lad had gone, and she was struck again by the paternal kindness he showed towards his company.

'Did you visit Hester at the cottage very often?' she asked.

Slaughter lit another cigarette. 'Yes, I did. It was so exciting to be where it all happened, and Hester's young people, as she called us, were always welcome. It was peaceful, too, especially during the war. I was in the Royal Flying Corps, but I'd often spend my leave in Suffolk. You could get away from everything there. It was a tiny pocket of fantasy. She had a gift for that, Hester – for creating a world where none of the distressing inconveniences of life could touch her, not even war. Less so, Walter. He wanted to fight, but he was too old and his heart was bad, even then. But Hester was an escapist: if something was too painful, she simply shut it out. I often thought that was why she was so good at creating fantasy for others – she did it for herself, to keep her own demons at bay.'

'What sort of demons? If she and Walter were so happy—'

'Oh they were,' Slaughter interrupted her. 'But there was a part of Hester that always regretted not having a family. Walter never wanted children. It wouldn't have fitted with their lifestyle, and Hester sacrificed that side of herself to be with him – but it *was* a sacrifice and there were times when it affected her more than she ever admitted to him. She had a friend back in Inverness – it must have been your mother, I suppose – whom she envied deeply for that settled family life.'

Josephine thought back to the letter she had read. 'There were times when my mother envied Hester her freedom and her adventures, too,' she said.

'Yes, I'm sure there were. But Hester could never quite escape the guilt of her life with Walter,' Slaughter explained. 'When he died the way he did – on stage, doing what had brought them together – Hester saw that as some kind of retribution, I think, an inevitable consequence of how their relationship had started. The trouble you mentioned earlier.'

'I don't know much about that,' Josephine admitted, remembering what Hester had told Rose Boreham: 'Everything beautiful has a cost.' 'What happened?'

'She broke off an engagement with a local man in Inverness.'

'But that was years before Walter's death. Surely she wasn't still feeling guilty about it then?'

'It reared its ugly head again – in this very theatre, in fact. Quite a scene, there was, and it brought back all the old ill feeling. We were

backstage after the first night of *The Old Women*. I wasn't in the play myself, but Hester had invited Jenny and me, and we were all in the green
room having a drink to celebrate. The performance had been quite a
triumph and Hester was magnificent in it – it was a great night for her,
until this woman turned up out of the blue. Don't ask me how she got
past the stage doorman, but she started screaming at Hester, accusing
her of ruining her life and saying the most diabolical things. I'll never
forget it – all that poison pouring out in a voice as beautiful as yours.
You sound so much like Hester, you know. Not even years of ranting
in third-rate theatres could destroy that voice of hers. If I close my eyes
and listen to you now, it's as though she's in the room again.'

At any other time, Josephine would have been delighted with the
compliment, but she was trying to make sense of what Slaughter had
told her. She should have realised that Hester's old life meant her home
town; in her heart, Hester had been an actress until her dying day and
she would never have described the theatre in that way. 'So Hester
knew this woman from Inverness,' she clarified, just to be sure.

'Yes. I can't remember her name – I'm not sure I ever knew it – but
she was the jilted fiancé's sister. It turned out that he'd had a stroke a few
years earlier, and – in the absence of a wife – his care had fallen to his
sister. She blamed Hester, of course; in her eyes, Hester was responsible for everything that was wrong with her life. It should have been
Hester tied to the sickbed, not her, and she was determined to have her
say. I'm not sure what she thought it was going to achieve, but it was
a marvellous performance; if she hadn't been so unpleasant, I'd have
offered her a job on tour.' It was a joke, but Josephine was too preoccupied to acknowledge it; her thoughts were racing, but the conclusion
they had brought her to made no sense. She opened her mouth to ask if
Slaughter had ever seen the woman again, but he pre-empted her. 'And
do you know what? She had the damned cheek to turn up at Hester's
funeral. She tried to talk to me – I don't suppose she realised I'd been
there when she made such a disgraceful show of herself – and I'm afraid
I had to be quite rude to her.'

'What did she look like?' Josephine asked, although she knew what he was going to say. 'At the funeral, I mean – not back in the twenties.' There were no surprises in his answer: it was a perfect description of Jane Peck.

22

Marta was in the bar, but her smile faded as soon as she saw the look on Josephine's face. 'What on earth's the matter?' she asked. 'You're as white as a sheet. Oh Christ, I wasn't right was I? You didn't walk into Tod Slaughter's dressing room and see a load of Hester's stuff?'

She slid her gin across the table, and Josephine was grateful for it. 'No, nothing like that. He was lovely, but I know now who hated Hester enough to hurt her.'

'Who?'

'Her name is Jane Peck. She's my solicitor's secretary.'

'In Inverness?'

'Yes.'

'But how . . .'

'Why didn't I come and see him earlier, Marta? All this time that woman was pretending to be so bloody respectful of Hester, making me feel as though I were the one behaving badly, sorting out Hester's will, for God's sake, and going to her funeral . . .'

The shock of the discovery had caught up with Josephine, and she knew she was making no sense. Marta put a hand gently on her arm. 'Calm down and tell me slowly, from the beginning.'

'All right, but can we go somewhere else? I can't talk to you in here.'

'Of course we can. Forget about dinner. We'll go back to Holly Place and I'll make us something to eat there. Lydia's going straight to the cottage after the show,' she added clairvoyantly. 'I told you we'd have the place to ourselves.'

It wasn't quite the evening that Josephine had had in mind, but she nodded and they found a taxi in the Strand to take them back to Hampstead. It was a year ago almost to the day that she had first made this journey, with every intention then of telling Marta that there could be nothing between them – but she had not been able to walk away. Twelve months later, she blessed her own weakness.

In spite of Marta's reassurances, she could not relax until she saw that the house really was in darkness. Marta put a match to the ready-laid fire and opened a bottle of wine, and Josephine looked round the sitting room, curious to see how it had changed since she was last here, when Marta had only recently moved in. She had lived alone then – even now, she and Lydia kept separate homes – and the house had been sparse but comfortable, a mirror of who Marta was and filled only with what was most important to her; now, the rooms were still beautiful and distinctive, but there were signs of compromise everywhere that Josephine looked – ornaments she knew Marta would never have chosen, books she did not read and spirits she did not drink, a play script left open on the chaise longue where Lydia had been learning her lines. Lydia did not have to be there in person to make her presence felt, and Josephine wished they could have gone back to Suffolk, or even to a hotel, where she would not have felt like an intruder.

Marta poured the wine and sat down. 'Right – tell me how this Peck woman is connected to Hester.'

'She's the secretary in my solicitor's office, and she's worked there on and off for years. She's lived in Inverness all her life – one of those people who's always been around, although I never got to know her very well. We even lived in the same street for a bit. She was younger than Hester and my mother, but the families all got along together – you know what it's like with tradesmen in a small town – so it made perfect sense to me that she would follow Hester's career and be interested in what happened to her, but I didn't know it was more personal than that.' She told Marta what Slaughter had said about the scene at the Little Theatre all those years ago. 'I knew Hester had jilted somebody to marry Walter Paget, and I knew Jane Peck had been caring for an invalid brother, but I never realised that it was one and the same person.'

'You *have* only got Slaughter's description to go on, though.'

287

'I can check to make sure. My mother talks about what happened in her letters to Hester. I can easily find out what the fiancé's name was.'

'All right, so assuming it *is* her, it doesn't necessarily follow that she had anything more to do with Hester after the scene at the theatre. Yes, she was hacked off with her lot and wanted to humiliate Hester in front of all her famous friends. I'm not sure I blame her. But there's no proof that she was ever in Suffolk, and certainly nothing to link her to Hester's death.'

'So why did she never tell me that they were connected in that way?'

'Why should she? Perhaps she was ashamed of what she did and wanted to forget it, or perhaps she was just being professional and separating her personal life from her job.'

'And she lied about the funeral. She told me she'd had a friendly conversation with Tod Slaughter when she hadn't and invented this other woman, and I'm sure she was the one who sold Lucy Kyte's diary to John Moore.'

'You don't know that.'

'Of course I do. He said the woman was like me – he meant she was Scottish. Then there was the business with my father. She implied on the telephone that he was at death's door, but it was only a sprained wrist. Why would she do that, if it wasn't to get me home and give me something other than Hester to worry about?'

'Jealousy, probably. I imagine she feels the same way about you as she did about Hester. A successful, attractive woman, able to come and go as she pleases, achieving things in her life that the Jane Pecks of this world could never do, invalid brother or not. It could just be spite, Josephine – taking the high and mighty Miss Tey down a peg or two, reminding you that life isn't all glamour and glory. It's vicious, I agree, but it's a long way short of what you're branding her with.'

Marta's level-headedness was beginning to get on Josephine's nerves, mainly because it was so convincing. Everything had seemed very clear to her in the heat of the moment, but now, away from the theatre and from the living, breathing Hester whom Slaughter had conjured up so beautifully for her, the conclusions she had drawn seemed less obvious. Even so, her determination to get justice for Hester did not allow her to give up easily. 'The money from Hester's treasures would have come in handy,' she continued defiantly. 'Her brother's treatment left her practically destitute. Everyone says so. She had to sell the house.'

Marta gave the point the scorn it merited. 'You of all people can't judge someone on the basis of idle gossip in Inverness. You haven't got a shred of evidence to link her with that.'

'Then I'll get some.'

'How?'

'I'll go and see her, ask her outright.'

'Jesus, Josephine, you can't go round accusing people of killing old ladies, especially when you don't even know that an old lady *has* been killed.'

'Then what do you suggest I do? She's a solicitor's secretary, for God's sake. She's got everybody's business in the palm of her hand. Who knows what else she might be planning?'

'So now she's a criminal mastermind? You're getting this completely out of proportion. If this is *anything* – and I do mean if – it's personal to Hester. You said so yourself.'

'You wouldn't think I was exaggerating if you'd been there when Bert Willis was describing Hester's body, or when Rose was talking about how frightened she was.'

'All right, I'm sorry, but how . . .'

'I don't know, Marta.' She put her glass down and took Marta's hands in her own, as if that might make her argument more convincing. 'I have no idea how any of this happened, but I know deep down that Jane Peck is in some way responsible for the way that Hester died, and I can't ignore it. Please try and understand that.'

Marta nodded reluctantly. 'Of course I understand. I'd be exactly the same. But I still say you need to be careful. You don't know what you're dealing with.'

A car pulled up in the street outside, and Josephine heard the sound of a key in the lock and laughter in the hallway. 'That's all we bloody need,' she said impatiently, giving Marta a look which suggested that the whole day was her fault. 'I thought Lydia was going straight to the cottage.'

'So did I.'

Marta stood up to get another drink and Josephine braced herself for the loss of peace and privacy. 'Change of plan,' Lydia announced, giving Josephine a hug and blowing a kiss to Marta. 'The damned car wouldn't start, so we had no choice but to get a taxi back here.'

'You could have stayed in town,' Marta said ungraciously, and Lydia's companions – two men and a woman, all of whom Josephine knew vaguely from past productions of her plays – looked uncomfortable.

'Don't be silly. I'm not really in the mood for the cottage this weekend, and anyway, I was dying to see Josephine – it's been ages.'

Lydia made drinks for everyone, and the evening descended rapidly into a round of theatre talk and bitchy speculation. Josephine tried to take part, if only for appearance's sake, but her mind was still on Hester and eventually she could stand it no longer. 'I have to go,' she said, with an apologetic glance at Marta. 'I need to get back to the club.'

'Well, next time we'll do it properly and have dinner,' Lydia insisted. 'And you must come to the cottage with us for Christmas.' Josephine opened her mouth to make an excuse, but Lydia was adamant. 'Marta said your father's going to be away this year, so there's no reason why you shouldn't come down, is there? Alec and Dodie will be there, and I'm hoping Caroline and Peggy will be able to make it, too.' The prospect was so horrific that it took Josephine a few seconds to compose an answer that was both firm and polite, but her delay proved fatal. 'Excellent. That's settled then. And perhaps we can drive over to see this cottage of yours while we're there. I've heard so much about it, and we're practically neighbours now.'

'Yes, I suppose we are.'

'Let me call you a cab,' Marta said, resigned to the end of the evening.

'Don't bother. I can pick one up in the high street.'

'All right. I'll walk you there.' She fetched their coats and followed Josephine out into the street. 'What a fucking disaster,' she said when the door was firmly closed behind them. 'I'm so sorry.'

'It's not your fault, but it does feel as though fate's trying to tell us something. I thought you were going to throw them all out at one point. Poor Ben looked mortified.'

Marta caught her eye, and somehow managed to laugh. 'Was I terribly rude?'

'Quite rude, yes. But don't think I wasn't cheering you on.' They stopped just before the end of the road, out of the glare of the street lamp, and Josephine pulled Marta close. 'We'll try again, I promise.' The tenderness of their kiss made her crave the evening they had planned; she shivered in the darkness, reminded of what it was like to feel Marta's skin against her own, to fall asleep to the smell and the taste of her. 'I'll even forgive you for Christmas,' she whispered.

'I just wanted to see you.'

'Even if it is across a war zone? Dodie and Lydia scoring points over a turkey – that doesn't quite work for me.'

'It's better than nothing.'

Josephine smiled. 'Yes, I suppose it is.'

'I'm coming with you, though. I've been thinking about it and I won't have any argument.'

'You want me to smuggle you through the back door of the Cowdray Club in the middle of the night?' It was a tempting idea: the last thing Josephine wanted tonight was to be parted from Marta. 'I suppose I could think of something.'

'I meant to Inverness. I'm not letting you go up there and confront this woman on your own. If you're right, God knows what might happen and I'd never forgive myself.'

Josephine drew back a little so that Marta could see her face. 'I can't be with you there,' she said seriously. 'We agreed. This has to be left behind when I go home.'

291

'You're going to see a woman who might have killed someone, and you're worried about your reputation? That makes no sense at all.'

'I know how silly it sounds, but I can't front that one out, Marta. I'm simply not brave enough.'

'But no one need know. You can have a friend, can't you?'

'You're forgetting who's the actress. I love you. I couldn't hide that any longer with Lydia just now, and I certainly wouldn't be able to hide it in Inverness.' She bit her lip, wondering how to explain. 'You're always true to yourself, more so than anyone else I know. I wish I could be more like you, but I'm someone different there and you'd hate me for it. I don't want you to see that. It would destroy us.'

To Josephine's relief, Marta seemed to understand, but she wouldn't give in. 'Take Archie, then. Or at least talk to him about it, see if he can help.'

'No, Marta – that would compromise him too much.' She was also afraid that Archie might tell her she was wrong, and she didn't want to hear that or even admit to Marta that she thought it was a possibility. 'I've asked too many favours of Archie already, and this is something *I* need to do – for Hester, and for myself.' She tried to look reassuring. 'You're right – this *is* personal.'

'So when will you go home?'

'Tomorrow. I need to face her while I'm still angry.'

'If you're leaving as soon as that, then you *are* going to have to smuggle me into the Cowdray Club.'

Josephine looked at her in disbelief, but she was serious. 'What will you tell Lydia?'

'The truth. That the last thing I need is a night with the West End. It's nothing she hasn't heard before.'

Something in her tone made Josephine stop walking. She waited for Marta to turn back, and studied her face for a moment. 'Lydia knows, doesn't she?'

'We've never talked about it.'

'That's not what I asked.' The thought that Marta and Lydia might have reached even an unspoken agreement about her – the freedom which that offered and the betrayal it laid bare – both elated and horrified Josephine.

'She would have said something if she were unhappy.'

It was the first naive thing that she had ever heard Marta say. 'I know how much you'd like that to be true, but I don't think there was anything wrong with Lydia's car tonight, do you?' She put her hand gently on Marta's cheek. 'You have no idea how badly I want to be with you now, but we can't do it – not like this, not in front of her friends. If you don't go back to the house now, Lydia will be utterly humiliated and that's not fair. You don't want that any more than I do.'

Marta sighed. 'No, of course I don't.'

A taxi drew up at the next junction, apparently summoned by their resolve. Reluctantly, Josephine waved it over. 'If I took the sleeper tomorrow night, I wouldn't have to be at Euston until six. We could spend the day together.'

She heard Marta's smile in her voice. 'I'd like that.'

'Yes, so would I.' The cab pulled in to the kerb and Josephine opened the door. 'I'll wait for you at the club. Come whenever you can.'

23

The Inverness air was thick with fog and gossip. Reports of the imminent abdication had broken in the press a few days earlier, and the story was well and truly out across Britain and the Empire. The newsstands were cleared in minutes and the papers were at war: *The Times*, the *Morning Post* and the *Telegraph* stood against the King; the *Mail*, the *Mirror* and the *Daily Sketch* adamantly for him – but all were united in packing their pages with as many photographs as possible, taken over a period of months and stored away until the embargo collapsed and it was decent to use them. At breakfast each morning, Josephine pored over pictures of Wallis Simpson – on yachts, in restaurants, at Ascot; the image that lingered in her mind, though, was of a woman on Felixstowe Promenade, anonymous and untroubled by anyone; a stranger to herself, no doubt, now that the peace of those last few weeks was lost and irretrievable.

Marta telephoned every day, still advocating caution where Jane Peck was concerned, and Josephine was at last able to admit that she had been in Felixstowe while Mrs Simpson was living there to fulfil the terms of her divorce – and that somewhere in the corner of an American newspaper there was probably a photograph of the wrong woman. Marta's descriptions of the atmosphere in London were dramatic and vivid: the silence on the Underground as everyone read their newspapers; bookshops and department stores eerily empty in the run-up to Christmas; crowds outside Buckingham Palace, waiting through the night, their eyes fixed on two or three lights burning in the upper windows. Whatever the bishops and politicians were doing behind the scenes, the people had come out to support their King: there were demonstrations at Marble Arch, Marta said, and the national anthem was not simply observed in theatres and cinemas, but applauded. Lydia, a staunch royalist, was practically in mourning. It wasn't an absurd reaction, Josephine thought; even in Inverness, further away from events and in a country where attitudes towards the British monarchy were more complex, there was a sense of shock among the townsfolk, a numbness and a disbelief that were not unlike the early stages of grief. She shared their astonishment: in Felixstowe, she had seen with her own eyes how seriously Wallis Simpson was treated, but she had never truly believed that it would come to this.

Marta's concern, coupled with a heavy cold that made Josephine listless and irritable, gave Jane Peck a few days' reprieve. By Thursday, she was feeling better and had had time to consider the most sensible way to approach the situation. There was no point in going to the office; she needed Miss Peck to be on her own and preferably off-guard, so she decided to call unannounced at her house that evening. They would be able to talk privately there, and if – God forbid – Josephine was wrong, she would not have humiliated anyone in public. The small matter of exactly what she was going to say was still unresolved by the time she left Crown Cottage and walked the short distance to Greenhill Terrace. It was probably best to play it by ear, and let the other woman set the tone of the conversation by her reaction to the unexpected visit.

Jane Peck still lived in her old family home, renting it now from the man she had sold it to after her brother's death. A wave of complex emotions washed over Josephine the minute she set foot in the street, and they had nothing to do with Hester – at least, not directly. She could not remember exactly what age she was when her family had moved here, but her youngest sister was not yet born, so she must have been six or seven. The house was bigger than the one they left behind in Crown Terrace, a reflection of her father's hard work and good fortunes, and she had loved it. She paused outside, allowing the memories to play in her head without effort or censor. Moments like this had ambushed her more often recently, and she put it down entirely to Red Barn Cottage. It was strange, but in a house full of other people's lives

– Lucy's and Maria's and especially Hester's – the past she had returned to most often was her own.

The number Josephine wanted was at the other end of the terrace. She wondered if she had left the secretary enough time to get home from work, but there was a light on in the front room and the door was answered before the chime of the bell had had time to die away. Miss Peck seemed different out of her customary environment – younger, somehow, and less severe, although most people would struggle to intimidate in a housecoat whose colour was best described as a dowdy salmon. She invited Josephine in without comment or question, and the absence of any flicker of guilt or suspicion was the first blow to Josephine's confidence: if she had expected Miss Peck to panic and confess at the very sight of her, she was obviously going to be disappointed. The house was identical in structure to the one she had grown up in and the thought disarmed her for a moment, but the decor was sufficiently different for her to recover quickly. It did not take her long to realise that these rooms were designed entirely for appearance's sake. The curtains at the front windows were good and the one solid piece of furniture – a round oak table, crowned by a vase of cheap flowers – stood at the head of the sitting room, where it could be seen from the road; further in, away from the judgemental glance of passers-by, the house was sparse and shabby, with everything either grey or beige. Even the chrysanthemums could only aspire to cream, and the lack of colour in the room – while it made the housecoat seem quite daring – depressed Josephine instantly.

Two cheap, oddly matched armchairs were huddled round the single bar of an electric fire, and the only other comfort was the low murmur of a wireless, soft and insistent in the background. A film magazine lay open on the floor – more economical, perhaps, than actually going to the cinema – and a plate with a half-eaten sandwich rested on the arm of the better chair. The scene reminded Josephine of how she had found Hester's room when she first walked into the cottage, the shrinking of a world to the most basic human necessities of food and warmth and another voice; what it did *not* suggest was a woman who had recently found fortune in the cruellest of ways, and she began to think that Marta was right. If Jane Peck was guilty of nothing more than screaming against the injustice of her life, then she, Josephine, shouldn't even be here: exposing pride as a lie was the unkindest thing she could have done. 'I'm sorry,' she said, aware that her thoughts were probably written all over her face. 'I've obviously interrupted your meal.'

The grandiose description of her supper brought the shadow of a smile to the other woman's lips. 'It will keep,' she said. 'Can I get you something, Miss Tey?'

'No, thank you.'

The answer obviously came as a relief, either because there was nothing much to get or because it implied that Josephine would not be staying. Miss Peck gestured to the chair opposite, and there was an awkward pause as she waited in vain for her guest to state her purpose. Josephine struggled to find a non-committal way to open the conversation, but it was in fact a news announcement that broke the silence and her host leaned forward to turn the wireless up. 'This is what we've all been waiting for, I suppose.' The voice was Stanley Baldwin's, speaking in the House of Commons, but the words he read were the King's: '*After long and anxious consideration I have determined to renounce the throne to which I succeeded on the death of my father, and I am now communicating this, my final and irrevocable decision.*' It seemed strange to be listening to something so momentous in the company of a stranger, and it made the situation more surreal than ever. Josephine watched Jane Peck as she listened intently, but her face was inscrutable. Baldwin followed the King's declaration with a speech of his own, but the wireless was snapped off abruptly before he could get very far. 'There we are,' Miss Peck said, apparently satisfied that her own fears had been proved correct. 'We can't expect a sense of duty from anyone these days – not even, it seems, from our King. You and I are a dying breed, Miss Tey.'

It was hard to say if the final comment was a compliment or a curse,

297

but again Josephine found the fellowship that it implied disturbing. 'I imagine that even kings feel a duty to the women they love,' she said.

'Duty and love are rarely connected, in my experience.' Deliberate or not, her response gave Josephine the perfect opportunity to raise the subject of Hester's broken engagement, but the moment was snatched from her before she opened her mouth. 'Did you resent it at first?'

The question wrong-footed her. 'Resent what?'

'The assumption that you would come running back and do *your* duty when your mother died.'

'I didn't come running back,' Josephine said, a little too quickly. 'I worked in England for three more years, finished what I wanted to do and came back when I was ready. So it wasn't really like that.'

'Oh, it's always like that, whether you admit it to yourself or not. Preferring not to marry, putting your work first – it's a dangerous choice, and you pay for it in the end.' She turned the fire off, although the room was anything but warm. 'I went away to college, just like you. Mine was secretarial, of course. I had hoped that I might go to Edinburgh after that, or even to London, work for a busy chambers, perhaps. Then Cameron had his stroke and my parents were too old to look after him, and my sister . . .' She laughed to herself, thinking back. 'Well, my sister couldn't get up the aisle quick enough. So it was all down to me. It's a shame, really. I was good at what I did. I've always been good at managing other people's lives. If I'd known it was at the expense of having one of my own, I might have chosen a different path.'

'They say it's never too late to make a fresh start.' Good God, Josephine thought, listening to herself; where on earth had that come from? She deserved the derisive sneer that came her way.

'I expect better than that from you, Miss Tey. I won't be patronised, and you of all people should know how it feels to be pitied.'

'That wasn't what I intended.'

'Good. Because it's all a sham. People are always saying how *good* we are to stay at home, aren't they? I get that all the time from my sister. I expect yours are the same – they treat you as a race apart, fill you with saintly qualities that make it easy to do what you do, when they never could. It's gratifying at first, isn't it? It gives you a sense of worth for a while, until you realise *why* they do it – to make sure you'll carry on. But I'm not a saint, are you, Miss Tey?'

'No.' Josephine did not trust herself to say any more. Everything that Jane Peck had said was true, and it frightened her that this woman should see so easily into her darkest soul, laying bare the anger and despair that she thought she had kept hidden, even from herself.

'No, you're not a saint. And yet people will look back at your life when you're gone and talk about the sacrifice you've made. They'll pity you for it, and what a blow that will be to your pride! You'll look down from wherever you are – or up, of course – and you'll want to scream at them to stop, but it will be too late by then. If you think they talk about you now, just wait until you're dead.' Something in the controlled calm of this speech told Josephine how carefully it had all been prepared; there was no doubt in her mind now that Jane Peck had known she would come, that she had waited here for days for the chance to bring Josephine face to face with her own demons; the only question was whether she had done it before with Hester, and how much she would admit. 'Still, at least that sacrifice *will* be recognised, because you're famous. Others make it, and just fade quietly away. Faded. That's how I've always felt.' Josephine's blush gave her away, and Jane Peck acknowledged it. 'I see that's how you think of me, too. And what was it all for? I wonder. Cameron wasn't even a war hero, for God's sake, just an invalid. Sometimes I used to think that would have been so much easier. I watched those women, caring for their heroic sick, united by some sort of collective tragedy, and I envied them that solidarity.'

'I'm not sure they would give it the nobility you seem to think it should have. A wasted life is a wasted life, no matter how worthwhile you're told the cause is.'

She refused to rise to the bait. 'But at least they knew they weren't alone. That's the point. I've *always* been alone. And it should never have been me, should it? We may as well get round to why you're here. It should have been Hester Larkspur.'

In the end, the question came easily to Josephine, and she matched Jane Peck's composure word for deadly word. 'Did you kill Hester?'

It was as though she had never spoken. 'She made a fool of Cameron from the very beginning. It wasn't hard to do, not to a man like him, but she achieved it with a certain panache, I must say. She came home less often from those theatre tours and it was obvious that she'd met someone else, but he wouldn't have it. Not his precious Hester. Even when she left him, he wouldn't have a word said against her. Is that love or foolishness, do you think? I could never tell, being a stranger to both.'

'I'm sure Hester didn't mean to humiliate your brother. She told my mother that . . .'

'Oh, I'm not saying she *meant* to humiliate him; I'm saying she was too selfish to care whether she did or not, or even to notice.' Hand on heart, from what she knew of Hester, Josephine would have found it hard to disagree. 'Let me tell you what Cameron said to me one day . . . well, not said exactly; slurred would be more accurate. His speech never really came back, thank God, but you know what I mean. He said that Hester had had a lucky escape, that she would never have wanted to be burdened with him, not a woman like her. It was fine for a woman like me, though. How do you think that made me feel, Josephine? Did I deserve that? Could he not understand that it was he who had turned me into that sort of woman?'

For the first time, Jane Peck seemed to be genuinely seeking some sort of reassurance from Josephine, rather than using their common situation as a weapon. 'I'm not surprised you were angry,' she said cautiously.

'Angry doesn't even begin to describe it. It's funny, isn't it, but not even a writer like you can find a word for what I was.' The scorn was already back in her voice. 'Cameron kept a photograph of Hester Larkspur by his bed until the day he died. I would have let it go then, you know – that's the truth. But when I was clearing out his things, ready to sell the house, I found a newspaper that he'd kept. It was just a small piece, but it said that Hester was about to star in a film. That was more than I could bear, I'm afraid. I suppose I'd felt better about it all since Walter died and she gave up what she loved. It seemed like justice of a sort. When things were bad with Cameron, I'd think of Hester growing old in that cottage and what utter loneliness would do to someone like her, someone who'd always been adored; how she'd cope when the fan letters began to dwindle and fewer people came to call, when she looked in the mirror and realised it was ridiculous to suppose that she would ever know passion again, that she would ever be needed. I knew how bitter she would become, and one of the worst things about bitterness is that it makes you paranoid. You stop trusting, and you see something tainted in even the purest friendship. You turn against everyone, and you end up being your own worst enemy.'

She had described Hester's gradual isolation so perfectly that it took Josephine's breath away. 'I thought she might finally have learned that she couldn't just take what she wanted. But no. Hester was making a comeback, the centre of attention all over again, because Hester had to be loved, damn it. Hester's God-given right on this planet was to be loved.' Her anger had got the better of her at last, and Josephine noticed how tightly she gripped the arm of her chair, how the colour had drained from her face; for the first time, she was afraid of more than what she might hear. 'And the casualty of that was never Cameron – he fooled himself right to the end. It was *my* life that Hester destroyed – my dreams, my independence, my right to love. I even had to give up my job in the end. Oh, I know you don't think it's much – I can see that in your face when you come into the office. But it's been everything to me – sanity, respite, money, and most important of all, self-respect. You see, I've never had much of that, Josephine. I've never turned heads. When Cameron was alive, I'd undress every night and look at my body in the mirror, touch myself just to imagine what it would be like to be loved. And in the end, I accepted that was all I would ever know.'

She ran her fingers over her breast, and Josephine could stand it no longer. 'This is sick,' she said, getting up to go. 'I don't have to listen to it.'

'Of course you don't – but you will, because you want to find out what I've done.' She was right, of course, and Josephine returned to her chair, despising her own meekness. 'I'll never forget that first visit to *your* cottage,' she said sarcastically. 'I'd gone for some money, that's all. A one-off payment for everything I'd given up. When I knocked on the door, I expected to be greeted by the same old Hester, the one who thought she had me eating out of her hand whenever she came to the office; the one who so generously forgave me for my little outburst at the theatre. I suppose you know about that?'

Josephine nodded. 'I went to see Tod Slaughter. He told me he recognised you at the funeral.'

'Quite the little sleuth. Good practice for your books, I suppose. But anyway, this Hester was very different – frail, and all but blind. It shocked me, I have to say. She didn't know who I was until I opened my mouth, and then she tried to bluff her way through it, but I could see how vulnerable she was. There was no fight when I asked her for money, you know. I took it and left, never imagining I'd see her again – but then I thought about how easy it had been, and how little I'd actually got for all those years, so I went back, supposedly to apologise and to make sure that we parted on good terms. I knew by then that the money wasn't enough, though. I wanted Hester to suffer like I had. I wanted to make her life a misery.'

'What did you do?' Josephine asked, dreading the answer but needing to know.

'Oh, made her home a little less comfortable. Moved things around so that she fell over them – furniture in the house, statues on the paths in her precious garden, the rope to the outhouse. I took the lid from the kettle so that the steam would burn her. Small things, really – all easy and quick to do while I was using her toilet or making her a cup of tea. It's not as though she was watching me.'

302

'Small things like taking the lid off the hotplate?' Josephine asked, remembering Rose's testimony to the burns on Hester's arms and allowing herself to imagine the agony they must have caused.

'Exactly. And changing things round in the cupboard so that her food would be disgusting – salt for sugar, that sort of thing. It never occurred to me that she'd stop eating because of it.'

Josephine recalled the chaos of those cupboards when she had first moved in, the bleach and the ant powder next to the food. 'It's a wonder she didn't poison herself.'

'Isn't it? And it was such a shame about the dog.' She smiled, and Josephine longed to wipe it from her face. 'But they were all things that could be put down to an old woman on her own, unable to cope. Hester needed someone to look after her, really, but I'd had enough of that.'

'How long *were* you there, for God's sake?'

'I came and went a few times – after all, Hester was effectively paying my rail fare and I had no responsibilities up here any more. It was nice to get out and see the countryside. But she went downhill so quickly. Too quickly, really.'

'Did she know what you were doing?'

'No, of course not. She blamed the girl who charred for her, or some children from the village. And this is going to sound ridiculous, perhaps, but she was convinced that the cottage was haunted.'

'So you started on her mind, as well. She'd hear you moving about the cottage and it terrified her. Were you there the day Rose went round to see her?'

'Yes, I was. She did me a favour, really, that girl. I was shocked when she just walked in. It made me realise that I'd been pushing my luck, that Hester wasn't quite as isolated as I thought. She was half out of her mind by then anyway, so I stepped things up a bit.' Josephine had no doubt that Jane Peck would be only too happy to be more specific, but she couldn't bear to hear the details. 'In the end, the mighty Miss Larkspur was so frightened that she crawled into a hole like an animal. All I had to do was wait to make sure that she never came out. I didn't lay a finger on her.'

She wore it almost as a badge of pride, a mark of her own achievement, and Josephine hated her for it. 'You didn't have to,' she said scathingly. 'You frightened her to death.'

'Yes, I suppose I did. It all goes back to that night at the theatre, now I think about it. There was a character called Daisy in one of the plays. She was an arrogant, insensitive little bitch, just like Hester, and she died of fright. Hester played the charwoman who found her body – not very convincingly, I must say – but I suppose that sowed the seed. Funny how those little things get stored away. It was called *The Person Unknown*, and I remember thinking at the time how appropriate a description that was for women like me.'

'Jesus, you disgust me.' Josephine stood up and walked across to the window, torn between her urge to get away from the house and her need to retaliate somehow on Hester's behalf.

'Do I, Josephine? I'm not sure I care. What matters to me is that Hester knew real fear before she died, the sort of fear that's been with me my whole life. You understand that, surely?'

She came over to join Josephine and stood quietly at her shoulder, their reflections side by side in the glass. The shadows of the room made each face pale and insubstantial, one a mirror image of the other, and the illusion of similarity gave Josephine a new strength, a determination to destroy once and for all the idea that there might be any sort of common ground between them. 'Don't even begin to suggest that I understand what you've done,' she said, her voice low and steady. 'You have no idea what real fear is. Anger, yes, and bitterness and regret, but we all have those. You're not the only person who's screamed against the unfairness of it all, who's longed to hurt the thing that's hurting them. But we don't do it – that's the difference. And neither of us has ever truly understood the fear that Hester felt in those last few hours, when she knew that her life was over.'

'Don't we?' She searched Josephine's eyes, and it was all Josephine could do not to flinch and look away. 'I do, and I'll admit that even if you won't. I understood it from the moment that Cameron had his stroke and they told me how serious it was, from that first night when I sat by his bed and watched him breathe my life away.'

Josephine could not speak for a moment. She remembered how she had felt as she sat by her mother's bedside during the final days of her illness, willing her to live, even though her face was contorted with pain and the morphia had ceased to make a difference. She had looked like a ghost under the sheets, a spirit who might drift away at any moment, and yet her hand had gripped Josephine's with a strength that would not have been possible but for her reluctance to leave her daughter. Josephine had clung to her – from love, yes, but also from a selfish fear of what this would mean to her own life, and she tried now to be honest with herself in the face of Jane Peck's accusation. She thought about the years that had passed since her mother's death, about her father's kindness and about the resentment that had faded, while the loss and the grief still had the power to engulf her, and she knew she had her answer. 'There's nothing to admit,' she said, 'because duty for me has *always* been about love. That's the difference between you and I.' For once, Jane Peck seemed silenced. Josephine had no appetite to continue the conversation any longer, but she needed to know everything. 'After Hester died, you took her things and sold them,' she said, although this hardly seemed to matter now.

'So what if I did? All that pious nonsense in the will about the important things in life not being of monetary value . . . that's easy enough to say when you've *got* money. What do you think it's like to pay rent for the house you grew up in, the house your father worked hard all his life to own?' She looked scornfully at Josephine. 'You can afford to be your mother's daughter when your father owns half of Castle Street, taking money off tenants like me, and you sit there in a fine house at the head of the town, looking down on the rest of us like God on His cloud. What makes you so special? I've worked whenever I could, just like you, and this house should be mine now. Shouldn't I be allowed a little pride in this town after what I've done for my family? But no. Everyone talks, I know they do. Sometimes people don't see you quite quickly enough, do they? They open their mouths and the poison's out there, and it eats away at you. You know what that's like.'

'Yes I do. So did Hester.'

'But Hester could run away. What choice did I have?' She looked round the room, as if involving the house in a conspiracy to hold her prisoner. 'You're right, though. I should have been more like her. Hester was the sort of woman who took whatever she wanted and was rewarded for it. Well, I thought I'd have a go at being *that* sort of woman for a change.'

'And where has it got you? You might scoff about Hester and her ghosts, but it's Lucy Kyte who'll make you pay. What a stupid mistake to make, selling that diary. Did you honestly think you'd get away with it?'

Miss Peck stared at her as though she were stupid. 'Of course I've got away with it. Do you really think I'd be standing here talking to you like this if I thought there was something you could do about it? If you repeat this, I'll deny it and no one will believe you. No one saw me at that cottage, and there's nothing to link me with any of those things, not even the diary. I was always paid in cash, and I never used my real name. Even if anyone were to identify me as having sold them something, they couldn't prove it was stolen.' They were Archie's words all over again, and Josephine's heart sank. 'I'll just say that Hester gave them to me to make up for what happened between us. They weren't listed in her will, so who can say what her intentions were regarding them? I'll say they were a thank you for taking her place, for fulfilling her responsibilities.' She laughed, sensing that the upper hand was hers again. 'Thank yous are important, Josephine. Cameron *never* thanked me. Does your father thank you?'

'He doesn't need to.'

'That's a no, then.' She pulled the curtains across the window and turned to face Josephine. 'Twenty-five years I cared for that man. I washed him and fed him and emptied his bedpan, things that only a wife should do, and not once did he even look grateful. You don't know what that's like yet, of course – your father can still fend for himself. But how old *is* he, Josephine? In his seventies?' Josephine walked over to the chair and picked up her bag, but Miss Peck caught her wrist and held it. 'Let me tell you how it was for me. It might help you understand what you've got to look forward to. There's a moment when the hatred takes over and you start to fight back. I got a little rougher when I moved Cameron, and sometimes I didn't hear him when he needed a bedpan. I ate my dinner in front of him, and put his down just a little too far out of reach. I found ways to humiliate him. I knew he was embarrassed when I washed him, so rather than chatting away to take his mind off it like I used to, I let him see me looking at him and I enjoyed his shame.'

'Let go of me.'

'Not until I've finished. This is the most important part. There'll be a time when you feel so tired and so desperate that you'll do anything to put a stop to it. You'll leave the window open a little bit longer than you should, forget his medication once in a while. Little things, as with Hester, but so easy in the end that you'll wonder why you didn't think of them years ago.'

Josephine stared at her in horror, too shocked to move now even though she had wrenched her arm free. 'You killed your brother?'

'No. You must get that right, even though this is strictly between us. I didn't kill Cameron. I simply withdrew my care.'

'I won't let you get away with this.'

'And who exactly do you think will believe you? They might pity me here, but they judge you. They think you're hard, Josephine – hard and aloof. The times I've heard someone say that there's nothing at all to like about you, that no one would ever guess you were your father's daughter, not with him being such a kind man. That you don't even care enough to visit your mother's grave.'

The violence took Josephine by surprise, and she watched the livid

307

red mark appear on Jane Peck's cheek as if it had had nothing to do with her. She took a step forward, enjoying the fear on the other woman's face as she backed against the wall, and put a hand against her throat, feeling the pulse quicken under her touch. 'You're right,' she said, watching Jane Peck's eyes widen in panic. 'It's much easier to hurt someone than I ever imagined it would be. But it takes a lot of effort to do what you did to Hester, and I really don't see how anyone could think you were worth it.'

Josephine released her grip and turned to go, leaving Jane Peck gasping for breath behind her. As she reached the hallway, Peck managed to find her voice again for one last jibe. 'All this and you didn't even know Hester Larkspur. Doesn't that make you the biggest fool of all?'

Her tone was much less confident now, but it was a hollow triumph and it shamed Josephine more than it comforted her. She slammed the door behind her, somehow managing to keep her tears in check until she was further down the street and out of sight.

24

It was still early when Josephine arrived at Stewart, Rule & Co. the next day, determined to have her say. She accepted that her chances of bringing Jane Peck to any sort of legal justice were slim, but her family had been with the firm for many years and she knew and trusted John MacDonald well enough to confide in him without too much risk of being treated like a lunatic. And if he doubted her word, then so be it; she had to try, for her own self-respect. At the very least, she could give his secretary a few nervous moments and remove her affairs to another solicitor; the thought of Jane Peck having anything further to do with her business, or her family's, sickened her.

The solicitor was already at work, searching through a filing cabinet in a bewildered fashion, and it looked as if he had been there for some time. He glanced up when he heard the door, and smiled at his visitor. 'I'm ashamed to admit it, Josephine, but I had absolutely no idea what she'd been doing all these years.'

'I'm sorry?' Josephine stared at him in confusion. After her defiance the night before, she hadn't for a moment imagined that Miss Peck would say something of her own accord.

'Jane. I didn't have a clue how hard she worked. She's only been gone a day and already I'm lost without her.'

Josephine looked at the desk by the door and noticed for the first time that it had been cleared of anything personal. 'She's left? Just like that?'

'I'm afraid so. It was all rather sudden, and she was very apologetic about it, but her sister was taken ill the day before yesterday and she's gone south to care for her. I offered to keep the post open again, but I gather it's a long-term affair and she doesn't expect to be back. Seems a bit rough on her to be landed with something like this so soon after Ronnie died, but you'd never guess it. She's a bloody martyr, that woman – an example to us all. I'll miss her.'

The testimonial was wasted on Josephine. 'When did she tell you this?'

'Yesterday morning, as soon as I got into work.'

'And she's definitely not coming back?'

'No, she made that very clear. So if you fancy a change of career, now might be the time to mention it.' He chuckled at his own joke and closed the drawer of the filing cabinet. 'Blast it! I give up. It'll turn up eventually. Now, what can I do for you? Is it something to do with Miss Larkspur?'

'It was, but it can wait. You look as though you've got enough on at the moment.' She turned to go before he could argue, but paused at the door. 'I don't suppose you have her sister's details, do you?'

'No, sorry. I'm not sure I could even tell you her name. But I dare say Jane will be in touch soon enough.'

Josephine doubted that very much, but she said nothing. There was no point in wasting any more time here; the horse had bolted with glowing references, and John MacDonald had convinced her that nothing she could say would make a difference. In any case, there was a part of her that was reluctant to share what had happened with any-one but Marta. It had been the same last night, when she had toyed with the idea of telephoning Archie to ask for his help; at the back of her mind, no matter how often she told herself that she was being ri-diculous, there was a tiny sliver of shame that threatened her soul, and it would not go away. Jane Peck's arrows had been deep and person-al, and she could only trust the person who knew her most intimately with their pain; only Marta could convince her that there was nothing to be ashamed of, and she would do it not through logic or through argument, but through love, through a simple refusal to acknowledge that it could be any other way.

She hurried back the way she had come, bypassing Crown Cottage to get to Greenhill Terrace. The curtains were still drawn, as they had been when she left the night before, and the house was quiet and lifeless – so much so that Josephine wondered fleetingly if Jane Peck had treated her own fate with the same terrible finality that she had given to others'. She knocked again, louder this time, but the only answer came from the house next door. 'You're too late, I'm afraid,' a woman called from the upstairs window. 'Her train was at half six.'

'Do you know where she's gone?' Josephine asked, although she already knew what the answer would be. She didn't for a moment believe that Jane Peck had gone to her sister: by now, she would be heading for a different town with a different name, starting a new life with Hester's money, and there wasn't a damned thing that anyone could do about it. 'She told me she'd come up on the pools,' the woman added with a laugh, 'but I think she was joking.'

'I wouldn't bet on it,' Josephine muttered, and the neighbour looked at her curiously.

'She mentioned you'd probably stop by, though. You are Miss Tey?' Josephine nodded. 'Hang on a minute – I'll come down.'

She waited, wondering what sort of forwarding message had been left for her. The door opened, and the woman pointed to a wooden trunk in the hallway. 'Jane said you'd have more use for this than she did. You're welcome to leave it here until you can have it collected.'

'Thank you.' Josephine bent down and opened Hester's clothes chest, given with love to her by Walter, the fake that Jane Peck had obviously not been able to sell. It was lined with red silk, but there was nothing inside.

'She was certainly travelling light when she left,' the neighbour offered good-naturedly, 'but I suppose that's the whole point of a new start, isn't it? Good for her, I say, after everything she's been through.'

'Yes,' Josephine said quietly. 'Good for her.'

25

The peace and solitude of the cottage were like a balm to Josephine after everything that had happened. She returned to Suffolk a few days before Christmas, relieved to put some distance between herself and her home town, where, before she was even born, the seeds of her god-mother's death had been sown. The taxi from Hadleigh dropped her at the top of the hill and she looked down at Hester's legacy to her, as apprehensive now as she had been on her very first visit. She had no idea how it would feel to walk into the cottage knowing exactly what had gone on there, and she could only hope that the images of fear and pain would fade with time.

It might have been her imagination, or simply a case of the wish fathering the thought, but, when she opened the front door and set her bags down inside, the house seemed more settled – its wrongs at least acknowledged, if not healed. And it was good to be there, to feel close again to the Hester she wanted to believe in: the friend her mother had loved; the actress Josephine admired; the wife who had grieved for her husband. She was still numb from her encounter with Jane Peck, and honest enough to see that some of the poison dripped in her ear had been justified – but she also remembered the original words of the will, the instruction to value what was important, to decide what had mean-ing: Red Barn Cottage and the life Hester had built there, her respect for its past and her willingness to honour women whom history had forgotten, seemed to Josephine to stand for all that was good about her godmother. Everything else, she had paid for.

Deaves and Son, or any combination of the above, had been as good as their word. The downstairs rooms were neatly packed away, just as she had left them, with no hint of a builder's talent for reaching places that had nothing to do with the actual work; and when she climbed warily up to the first floor, dreading what she might find, she could not have been more thrilled. Short of knocking this end of the cottage down and starting again, the room where Hester had died was as transformed as it could ever be. The old elm floorboards – coffin wood, as Josephine always thought of it – had been taken up and replaced with new oak, the walls had been replastered and painted, and the fireplace opened so that it now served both this room and her bedroom. Best of all, despite his doubts and protestations, Mr Deaves had found a way to incorporate Josephine's most difficult request into the work: the window in the gable end wall had been bricked up, and the light in the room now came from a new dormer built into the thatch, overlooking the garden and the farmland at the rear of the cottage; the window was finished off with an oak seat, its surface plain except for the grain of the wood. The slipper bath that Josephine had ordered stood in the middle of the floor and had obviously been brought in through the empty window space; it would never have come up the stairs, and she could see no way now of getting it out of the house if she ever changed her mind, but that seemed a very small price to pay. A reliable builder and a hot bath were appropriate to a season of miracles, and Josephine couldn't wait to see Marta's face when she found her Christmas present – and when she realised that, until modern life progressed a little further down the Stoke road, she would have to fill the bath by hand. She looked round the room, satisfied that she had done her best for Lucy's demons and for Hester's, and breathed in the smell of new wood, fresh paint, and peace.

There was a pile of something in the corner of the room, covered with a dust sheet. Deaves had left a note on top, explaining that he had found a box boarded into the old window seat; they had removed it as instructed, but he did not want to take it away or dispose of any of the wood until she had had a chance to look at it. Intrigued, she pulled back the sheet and found a chest similar to the one that Walter had bought for Hester, except that this one was older and in better condition. The chest was plainly made – solid oak with iron bands and a heavy padlock – but of a quality not to need adornment, and she felt a mixture of excitement and fear when she saw it. It was not beyond all possibility that Maria Marten's clothes chest had passed to her best friend after her death and, if so, that Lucy might have kept her own treasures inside – some later diaries, perhaps, or other things that would help Josephine to piece together the rest of her life. She held the padlock in her hand for a moment, tempted to break it open straight away, but reason got the better of her: if its contents proved exciting, then she would prefer to share them with Marta; if they testified to more pain for Lucy or for Maria, she would rather not be alone with them. She and Marta had planned to spend some time together at the cottage between Christmas and New Year; they could explore the trunk then. In the mean time, she saw with a heavy heart that she had still not managed to rid the cottage of the scarred wood that so disturbed her; the old window seat rested against the chest, and rather than try to wrestle it down the stairs on her own, she threw the sheet back over it and hoped that out of sight, out of mind would do.

It felt strange to be away from Scotland during the festive season. She had always spent Christmas with her family, and, as she looked ahead to Christmas Day, she half-wished that she had accepted her sister Moire's invitation to go to London; Lydia's parties were never restful, and the thought of sitting down to lunch with Dodie Smith and John Terry – joining in the gossip and trying not to look at Marta in the wrong way – filled her with dread. But she would not have missed the beauty of December in Suffolk for the world; the magic of the countryside, the remoteness of her rural life, made everything about the season somehow more real, and Josephine entered into the Christmas spirit as she never had before. She unpacked the cottage again and cleaned until it sparkled, went Christmas shopping in Bury and stocked up with every seasonal treat she could find, and – like a modern-day Scrooge with her own ghosts laid to rest – began to make amends with the villagers whom her concerns for Hester had kept at arm's length. She delivered a compendium of plays to Bert's children, knowing he would value that more than a gift for himself, thawed Elsie Gladding's heart with a Christmas card and a large order for mincemeat, and finally accepted a dinner invitation from Hilary and Stephen.

The days grew colder, and by Christmas Eve the trees around the cottage sparkled with a sharp, metallic crispness. Josephine took a pair of secateurs and a basket, and walked to Flaggy Pond to collect some greenery for the cottage. The air was exhilarating, the woods quiet and still, and she picked her way over winter-blackened brambles and pungent, dark leaf-mould, collecting armfuls of age-old scarlet. As she came out into the open fields again, her basket full of holly, she felt the ice on her face and marvelled at how the temperature had dropped, even in the short time she had been out. The sky was a sheet of pale greys and yellows, the surface of the pond frozen and expressionless. Sheep huddled against the fence, out of the cold, and she could hear the uneasy call of rooks overhead. The world was bracing itself for the weather to come, it seemed, and Josephine hurried back to the cottage to join it.

After lunch, she baked mince pies to take with her the next day, heavily laced with the brandy she thought she might need, then switched the wireless on and settled down in front of the fire to wrap some presents: a nice, ordinary book as her public gift to Marta; sherry, wine or whisky for the guests she knew less well; and a framed drawing of Ellen Terry as Juliet for Lydia – thoughtful, she hoped, but not extravagant enough to look like the product of a guilty conscience. The first few notes of 'Once in Royal David's City' drifted across the room from the beautiful candlelit chapel in Cambridge, bringing a lump to her throat as they always did – not from any particular spiritual conviction, but from an emotional response to the words and music that she sometimes found easy to confuse with a belief in God. As she listened to the lessons and carols, she thought about the people closest to her and felt connected to them through this shared celebration – then laughed at her own sentimentality: Archie would still be at his desk in Scotland Yard; her father, who was staying with his middle daughter, was far more likely to be sharing a single malt with his son-in-law than listening to the wireless; and Marta – well, Marta would have left her shopping until the last possible moment and was probably still having things gift-wrapped in Selfridge's. But for Josephine, isolated from the world and spending her first Christmas Eve alone, the familiarity of the service held a warmth and a solace that she cherished.

The choir was halfway through 'Hark! The Herald Angels Sing' when she noticed the snow, although it had obviously been falling for some time. She opened the front door and stood in the garden, just beyond the square of lamplight that followed her out from the house, and stared in wonder at the mournful, quiet beauty. Inside, the final notes of the organ died away, and she was left with the peculiar stillness of a silent land. The thatch was already swathed in a blanket of gleaming white, the bushes curled more sharply to the ground, and Josephine sensed that the sky was leaden with the weight of what was still to come. It would be a miracle if she could venture as far as the gate tomorrow, let alone the Essex borders, and she could not decide if she should bless or curse the prospect of a solitary Christmas. The snow was still falling at midnight, when she welcomed the day in and went up to bed. She blew out the lamp and drew the curtains back as wide as they would go. Outside, the landscape was a cacophony of blues, deep indigo for the sky and a pale, shimmering cyan where the moonlight hit the snow. Everything, it seemed, had been suspended, as though nature had deliberately chosen the most haunting and emotive night of the year to bring the world to a halt for a moment, to reflect on what really mattered.

When she woke on Christmas morning, the fields seemed to stretch for ever under the snow's gentle grace, a scene so different from the dramatic winter landscapes she was used to. The sun glistened on the ridges, the trees stood quiet under their burden of white and, in the distance, she could hear the peal of church bells, punctuated occasionally by the scraping of a shovel on tarmac or the chipping away of ice from the animals' water troughs. Josephine knew that she must try to let Marta and Lydia know that she was snowed in, so she dressed hurriedly and set out for the rectory to ask if she could use the telephone; if she went now, while the morning service was under way, she would not intrude on Hilary and Stephen's family Christmas, or be invited to stay and celebrate with them. The depth of the snow made for a punishing scramble to the top of the slope, and she looked back at her own footprints, struck by how – after delivering its initial blanket of concealment – snow stripped the earth of any right to secrecy; every movement of every creature was written on the fields and in the lanes, and they stood exposed and in sharp silhouette against an alien backcloth, robbed for the moment of their camouflage. When she reached the end of the track, at the junction with Marten's Lane, Josephine could see that even the short distance to the rectory was too ambitious: the roads were now rivers of snow, with drifts thrown like frozen waves against the hedgerows, and nothing in any direction looked passable. Reluctantly, she turned back, hoping that the snow would be widespread enough for Marta not to worry when she didn't arrive.

She stamped the snow off her boots in the porch and removed her outdoor clothes. Inside, the cottage was warm and welcoming, and she paused at the door, delighted by the image that greeted her, by the holly pinned to the beams and the presents piled expectantly onto the table. It wasn't quite the Christmas she had planned, but she was by her own fireside and determined to make the best of it. She stoked up the range, took a hammer to the water butt outside the back door, filling the air with a sound like breaking china, and prepared a pheasant to roast for lunch, along with bread sauce and all the trimmings. Before long, the cottage was filled with steam and with all the familiar smells and textures of past Christmases, evoked as a substitute for the company she would dearly have preferred. She switched the wireless on while she ate her lunch, hoping that the battery would outlast the snow, and listened as a strange, hesitant voice delivered his first seasonal message; how many of his subjects, Josephine wondered, would raise their glass to the King's health this Christmas, still thinking of the man who was now overseas?

Darkness came early, and with it the dancing of new snow against old. Her adventurous spirit faded a little more as she looked out of the window and saw the charcoal branches disappearing once again behind a soft gauze of white. She could only guess at how long her enforced solitude would last, and the evening brought with it a melancholy curiosity about the people she loved and what they might be doing; in her mind's eye, she watched them all without her, visiting each home with a Marleyesque knowing, and when she got to the fireside at Lydia's cottage, she knew she needed a distraction more compelling than an anonymous voice over the airwaves. She finished her drink and took a selection of candles and lamps upstairs, then went back to fetch the sturdiest knife she could find and the hammer she had used to break the ice. The room could be forgiven for its chill on a night like this, and she shivered as she looked at the trunk in the corner and the sheet that had slipped down to the floor. Shadows from the candlelight flickered playfully across the discarded window seat, bringing the words to life again in a shifting, staccato dance of regret, and Josephine hesitated, wondering if venturing up here really was the best way of entertaining herself when there was a whole bookshelf downstairs. But curiosity spurred her on – curiosity and, if she were honest, guilt: she still felt that she had failed Hester by not securing any form of justice for her death, and she was tired of loose ends; if the trunk offered the smallest insight into the rest of Lucy's life – the life Hester had so badly wanted to bring out into the open – something at least would have been achieved.

She slid the blade of her knife behind the rusted clasp and struck the handle hard with the hammer, surprised when the whole fitting came away in a single blow. The padlock clattered to the floor, absurdly loud in the silence of the room, and the now defenceless chest seemed to dare Josephine to violate it still further. She put her hand on the lid and raised it a few inches, and a stale, musty smell rose up to greet her, the scent of mould and damp and years of neglect. It was easy to see why: the trunk seemed to be packed with rotted clothes and linen that had failed the test of time, but her initial disappointment gave way to excitement when she saw what was resting on the very top of the pile. The book was a leather-bound journal, purpose-made and far grander than the makeshift volumes in which Lucy had recorded her earlier years, but filled with the same familiar handwriting. The pages were stained and fragile, but still legible, and Josephine felt a rush of excitement when she turned to the beginning and saw that it picked up again not long after the last diary had ended, at Lucy's Boxing Day wedding. There might be more books inside, but this would do for now and she took it downstairs, clutching it as tightly as a child with a favourite present.

She put a log on the fire, unwrapped the wine meant for Dodie and stood the bottle to warm, then settled down with the diary, just as she had a couple of months earlier.

27 December, 1828

This is the first day of my new life, and I will try to write down the joys as they come in this special book that Samuel gave me this mornin', my first in wakin' at Red Barn Cottage. He says he hopes I will need many more to hold all the happy days that are to come. Everyone has been kind, and Samuel is a sweet and gentle man. The Missis sent the most beautiful present of Irish linen. Samuel's new master provided a side of beef and more beer than we c'd drink for our weddin' party, and Molly was the prettiest girl at the weddin'. The Martins have given me Maria's clothes chest for a weddin' gift. Her father said she w'd have wanted me to have it, and that she c'd not have had a better friend. I shall treasure it all my days, but his words mean more. How I wish Maria had been there.

The first snow is startin', and Samuel has gone to fetch Molly from his sister, where she stay'd last night. Hannah filled the cottage with holly and mistletoe for our weddin' night. It has never look'd finer, but perhaps that is because it is now my home.

Josephine smiled to herself when she remembered her own pleasure at decorating the rooms, and the pride she had felt in how beautiful everywhere looked; it might be a century later, but life at Red Barn Cottage didn't seem to have changed very much, and the sense of tradition and continuity was satisfying. She moved on to the next entry, noticing that this was not a regular diary like its predecessors, but a more occasional record of a busy and happy life; as Samuel had said – a book for recording special days.

12 February, 1829

My birthday, and Samuel brought me snowdrops early this mornin'. Molly made me give her my book so that she c'd draw a picture of us all together, and I will treasure it. She has drawn us in the garden, which she loves. I have promis'd her that when the spring comes we will make a garden together. Samuel is away at market with the master's cattle. While he is gone, I am sewin' a quilt for our bed, which I will give him when it is finish'd.

As far as Josephine could remember, Lucy's needlework skills left a lot to be desired, but it was a moving gesture and, having learned in the churchyard that neither Samuel nor Molly were long-lived, she was glad to know that family life had been happy for Lucy while it lasted. She looked at Molly's drawing, saddened to think that she had died so young, and wondered how Lucy had borne the sorrow of it all.

25 March

Took Molly for a walk by Flaggy Pond. Spring is finally here, and everywhere I look the world is alive with somethin' new. I hope soon we will be bless'd with a brother or sister for Molly. Samuel says I must be patient. I am teachin' Molly her letters, and she is learnin' the names of the flowers in the garden. She is quick to learn and always askin' me questions, and she fills the house with laughter.

3 July
Nan Martin told me today that they have taken William's bones to a hospital in Bury, where people can see them for a few pennies. She said her father went yesterday to look, and put a shillin' in the box. It made me think of Maria, and I know she will come to me again tonight in my dreams. I have promis'd Samuel to try to forget, and I will not speak to him of Maria any longer, but I will not turn my back on my friend like the rest of the village has.

So the journal was not to be simply for special days, Josephine thought; even now, although Lucy's life was so different, the memory of Maria obviously threatened her relationship with Samuel. She remembered the cherry trees and the rose; it must have been hard for a husband to live in the shadow of that murder, to know that – whatever he did – he could never entirely dispel his wife's grief, or fill the hole left by the loss of her closest friend.

11 August
It is a year since they hang'd William. Some of the village folk say they have seen his ghost near Maria's cottage. They say he came in a dark shadow in the cloak he wore at his trial, but if anyone has the right to walk this earth, it is Maria's spirit they sh'd fear. She comes to me when I least expect her. The parson has agreed that she may have a stone on her grave at last, so folk will not forget her.

15 September
Took some of Maria's roses up to the churchyard, and c'd have

wept. People have chipp'd and broken her stone. Samuel says strangers have done it to make money, like they did with the barn. So the Reverend Whitmore is right, and it will not be long before he tells us so. Still they come to the field, dress'd in their Sunday finest, to see the barn where she lay. They will not let her rest.

Josephine didn't doubt that anyone living so close to the scene of a notorious murder would tire of the constant attention, but how much worse it must have been for someone who had loved Maria, who still missed her so desperately. The agricultural unrest that had led to the burning of the barn – while difficult for a farmer like Samuel – was surely a blessing for Lucy.

31 May, 1832

There is joy in our house. At last the day has come when I can write in my book that I am with child. Samuel will not say it, but I know he hopes for a boy. I am so happy that I do not mind as long as he or she is well.

The next few entries recorded Lucy's growing excitement over her pregnancy, and Josephine could barely read them, knowing as she did that Lucy and Samuel were to lose two daughters. She did not know, of course, if other children had survived, but by November her fears seemed justified.

25 November

Never have I known a winter to be so hard. Samuel works all the hours God sends to put food on the table and I try to help as I can but the child is a heavy burden and I am not as strong as I might be. Molly runs wild with no one to watch her and Samuel will not scold her when she disobeys me. I am so tired, and I fear our child will come before its time.

19 December

Hannah has come to help with my lyin' in, and has made a bed for me in Molly's old room so that Samuel can get his rest. It is strange to be away from him, and to see them all carry on without me and have another woman runnin' my home. I will be glad when the child is here and I can take my place again. I try not look out at the barn, but there is no help for it in this room.

6 January, 1833

We have a little girl. I have never known such pain and joy as she fought her way into the world. Samuel says that I am to name the girls and he will choose what the boys will be call'd. So she is Maria, and I hope she will have a long and happy life.

9 February

I can still barely write these words. My small, beautiful child was taken from me a week past. The ground is still frozen and we cannot bury her. She lies at the foot of my bed in the cradle that Samuel made for her. I want to look on her face, but my heart is broken. Samuel begs me to return to his bed where I will not be so sad, but I will not leave my little Maria until she is laid to rest.

Born in that room, carrying that name – it was hard to see how things could ever have turned out differently for Lucy's first-born, and the desperate sadness of both mother and child found Josephine easily across the years. She read on, and the diary became a mockery of its original purpose; there were very few precious days in Lucy's married life, and the pages recorded a series of miscarriages and bitter self-recrimination rather than happiness and fulfilment. Lucy's relationship with her husband and her stepdaughter seemed to deteriorate with each new loss, and Josephine felt desperately sorry for all of them. There were no villains here except circumstance and luck –

but Lucy's continued obsession with Maria blighted the whole house, making her overprotective of Molly's childhood and driving her and Samuel apart.

17 July, 1835

Samuel has taken Molly to the Cherry Fair as a birthday treat. She will be twelve next week, and I know that he will spend money we do not have and spoil her as he always does. I can do nothin' with her. The parson has said there is a place for her at the doctor's house in Layham, which is a good position, but Molly does not want to go and Samuel will not make her. She is a lazy girl and can play him for a fool whenever she chooses.

15 February, 1836

Phoebe Stowe call'd at the back door today and told me that the Missis is married again to a man called Harvey, and has been taken to court by William's wife. She is askin' for money for the child, who will never work because he has a wither'd hand. The court has said she must pay the boy what is due to him.

The description of William Corder's son jumped off the page at Josephine – it was the same genetic defect that she had noticed in John Moore – but she was too absorbed in Lucy's pain to give it much thought.

Hannah came later with a pie for dinner. I know she thinks I cannot feed my family and manage my house. She said Samuel needed lookin' after, as he is tired and worn out. We are all tired and worn out, and what she knows about keepin' a man happy when she c'd never get one is more than I can think of.

In the past, Josephine had enjoyed Lucy's barbed asides, but they carried a bitterness now that saddened her. She longed in vain for some joy, but she knew there would be no change of fortune with the next child. This time, out of superstition or resignation, Lucy did not even mark her pregnancy, and the child's name – Daisy, Josephine remembered from the parish register – was not recorded either.

21 June, 1837

Samuel says I held my baby, but I have no memory of her. I was taken with fever after she was born, and he told me today that she died three days ago, before she was even a week old. He has taken her to the churchyard to lie with her sister. I am no good to him as a wife, and I cannot bear him children.

From now on, the entries became sporadic and unconnected, as if Lucy could not bear to weave the bleakness of her life into a pattern, or to see it written down. Josephine knew that Molly and Samuel had less than two years to live after the next date, but the funeral that it recorded harked back to the past.

10 September, 1841

Went to the churchyard today to see the Missis laid to rest with her men. It was a sad day, as she was always good and fair to me, but most of the folk there were happy to see the last of the Corders put in the ground. Thomas Henry stood by the Gospel Oak, near his mother's grave, a fine lad of seventeen. She w'd have been so proud of him, but I wonder how much he remembers of her. I miss him comin' to the cottage as he used to when he was a boy. I hop'd once that he and Molly would grow to care for each other, but she will have nothin' to do with the Martins.

13 June, 1842

Molly has been sent to stay with Hannah. Samuel found her in the barn with Tabor's stable lad. After all that has happen'd, I cannot understand why she w'd go there, but she is not the only girl to do her courtin' in the Red Barn. It is time the master pull'd it down, as no one will learn from Maria's mistakes, but Samuel says it is needed. There will be no good come of this, but it is the first time that Samuel and I have agreed on anythin' to do with Molly for as long as I can remember. She will bring shame on us if no one puts a stop to her nonsense, and I will not let her go the same way as Maria. Samuel is thinkin' of sendin' her away to service now for her own good, and for ours. It cannot come a day too soon for me.

Josephine looked at the date and tried to remember exactly when the Red Barn was burned down. A thought had crossed her mind, but she dismissed it as too fanciful and read on.

23 July
I have fallen again, but there is no joy in it this time. I am too old, and if God had wanted me to have a child of my own, he w'd have bless'd me when I was young enough to bear it. Samuel still hopes for a son, as he grows old, too, and will not be able to go on for ever as he does. Then I do not know what will happen to us. We will not be able to keep our home if we cannot work for it.

There is much anger on the farms among the workers, who fear for their livelihoods. They have been settin' the hayricks alight and burnin' the farm buildings. I do not understand what is happenin'. It is no world to bring a child into. Molly has found a good place at last in Boxford, so that at least is a blessin' and one less mouth to feed.

1 October
Samuel brought Molly home today. She has lost her place for cheekin' her missis and makin' eyes at the master. Samuel is in a rage and will not trust himself to talk to her. She has lock'd herself in her room and will not come out.

3 November

Hannah has been laid low and I have sent Molly to sit with her.
The fields are full of water, and I doubt the rain will ever stop.
Samuel has caught a chill and is not fit to work, but says the master needs him to move the animals from the fields. It is all I can
do to drag myself from my bed. This child makes me so sickly,
worse even than before. It is a wicked thing to think, but I wish
nature would take her course as she has in the past. Then I c'd be
well again.

A loud thud outside the window startled Josephine until she realised
that it was just the snow, falling off the roof where the heat from the
chimney had melted it. The noise broke the spell for a moment, and
she poured another glass of wine and flicked back through the pages.
It was taking her much longer to decipher Lucy's actual entries than it
did to read Hester's transcript, but still she felt the rapid disintegration
of a life, of all the ordinary hopes and expectations that any woman
was entitled to have. Lucy was special to Josephine – as she had been
to Hester – because of her connection to Maria Marten, and because
she had faithfully testified to a series of extraordinary events; even so,
this part of her life was in no way unique, and it pleased Josephine to
think that – if and when her story was published – it would speak for
so many women whose struggles had gone unrecorded.

5 November

We are in mournin' again. Hannah was taken in the night, and
Samuel has gone to see the reverend about her buryin'. Molly was
with her when she went, and has surpris'd us all by carin' for her
aunt to the end. We have had our differences, but Hannah had
a good heart and I will miss her. I am fearful of havin' this child
without her, but am glad now that Molly is home.

12 November

The floods have gone but the air is full o' frost. Molly is courtin' the lad from the stables again. He came sniffin' round like a dog as soon as she was back, and I have seen them goin' to the Barn again. If she carries on so she will be ruin'd, but she will not listen to me and I dare not tell Samuel for fear of what he may do. He spends more time at the Cock than by his own hearth, and when he is in drink I do not know him. He is tired of me and this life, and I can neither help nor blame him.

2 December

I fear the child will not be long. I have gone to the small room again, as Samuel needs his rest. It is so cold, and there is no comfort.

9 December

It is late, and very cold. Samuel is not home, and Molly left her bed an hour ago to go to the barn. I watch'd her lantern move across the field, and thought of Maria. It is so long ago, and nothin' has chang'd. There is only one way this will end, and I cannot bear it.

13 December

Samuel says Mr Hoy's cottage has been raz'd to the ground. They think it is arson, and part of the recent troubles. The master has told us all to keep watch on the barns and cottages, for fear that it will happen again. God forgive me, but I wish they w'd set light to the Red Barn and take this evil from my sight once and for all.

In her heart, Josephine had known earlier that Lucy was going to do something terrible, and although she had suspected what it would be, the next entry still stunned her, its consequences more catastrophic than she could ever have imagined.

28 December

Two days on, the smell of smoke is still strong in the cottage and I cannot bear what I have done. Molly lies close to death, and I know that bathin' her wounds will make no difference. The men from the village did their best to save the barn, but the wind spread the flames faster than I c'd ever have thought, and in the end it was too fierce. It was ablaze in minutes, and burnt long into the night. Samuel and some of the others climb'd onto the roof of the cottage and threw off the burnin' embers as they lodg'd upon it. Molly and I pull'd the blankets from our beds and soak'd them in the pond to dampen the thatch. Then she went to help the lad from the stables with the barn, and Samuel c'd not stop her. She was caught in the flames and they brought her back cover'd in burns. And it is all my fault.

I cannot tell Samuel what I have done, and I pray for a miracle so that Molly may live. I thought that by burnin' the barn I would be savin' her, and my life with Samuel, but I have brought misery and sorrow on us all. There is nothin' left but blacken'd earth, but the grief is still here, worse than ever. And this time it is my doin'. Samuel can only watch as I tend his daughter. He thanks me for what I do, and I want to scream at him to stop.

So history was wrong. The Red Barn had not been destroyed by an anonymous hand in a political act, but by a woman whose personal pain had become too much to bear. Lucy had been damned from the moment that Maria Marten left her cottage to walk to the Red Barn, and although there was an inevitability about the sequence of events, Josephine was horrified at how many lives had been shattered by the murder. Samuel and Lucy might have borne the intimate tragedies of their life had they not been forever separated by Maria's shadow; Molly would have grown up as a carefree little girl, able to make her own mistakes without being continually reminded of others'; and the village could have moved on, creating its own ordinary, quiet history. Instead, on what should have been the happiest of days, the anniversary of her wedding, Lucy had taken fate into her own hands and confined the rest of her life to ashes along with the barn.

31 December

Molly lingers, but there is no savin' her. Phoebe Stowe came to sit with her while I tried to sleep, and brought some salve for the burns, but she cries with pain when we try to put it on her. Phoebe says they are offerin' a reward of a hundred pounds for the Boxin' Day fire at the Barn and for Mr Hoy's cottage. They think it is the same hand, but it is not. I may not answer to the law, but God knows what I have done.

Josephine knew that Molly would die, and could imagine that grief might have destroyed Samuel, but she still had no idea what Lucy's fate would be, and she feared the worst: if she had been hanged for what she had done, that would explain her absence from the churchyard. Or perhaps the guilt had forced her to take her own life. That, too, would deny her the peace of consecrated ground. She read on, conscious that very little of the diary was left and desperately hoping that it would not end without giving her the answers she needed.

2 January, 1843

The new year has brought grief, as I knew it w'd. Molly died early today, and she is at peace. Samuel has not left her side these past two nights, and this book that was so full of hope must now be my confession, for I cannot find the words to speak.

3 January

Nan Martin brought some holly thick with berries for Molly. They will bring her coffin tomorrow, and she is to be buried on Friday. I fear that Samuel will not let his daughter leave the house, he is so wretched with grief. He will not eat, and stares into a distant place where I cannot reach him.

2 *February*

The child is comin' now, I know. I cannot bring a new life into the world with this in my heart. I must tell him. Please God, let him forgive me.

Lucy's desperate plea marked the end of any coherence in the diary. There was nothing dated or ordered on the pages that followed, only single words or very short phrases, barely legible and obviously written while she was in great distress, physically and emotionally. Slowly, Josephine deciphered the scrawled, violent letters. *Samuel. He will not come to us. My beautiful boy. Cannot feed him. Too weak . . . There is no hope. Who will help us? Beg him . . . No one comes. Forgive for his sake.* The last thing that Lucy wrote was *please.* The ink was faint, a sign of how weak she had become, but to Josephine the word screamed from the page. It was all the narrative she needed to piece the story together image by dreadful image: she saw that bleak, desolate room in the depths of winter; Lucy terrified and in pain, struggling to bring a child into the world on her own, then watching him fade as her husband abandoned them both, unable or unwilling to forgive what she had done. For the most fleeting of moments, Josephine felt Lucy's grief – her wretchedness – in her own heart, not as a gesture of sympathy but as something that truly belonged to her, something that she had experienced for herself – and she knew, even before she turned to the last page of the journal, that the house had yet to reveal its final, dreadful secret.

Lucy's diary, her solace and her sanctuary for so many years, was completed by another hand, and that in itself seemed to Josephine a desecration. The words were poured onto the page with no sense of reason or control, and she could feel their anger, even after so many years. *You will rot in this room for what you have taken from me. I will not let you lie with Molly. You are not fit to share her earth. May your soul never rest, and God forgive me for the death of my son.* The desperate, raw emotion in the letters echoed the request for forgiveness on the window seat, and Josephine understood now that Samuel – not Lucy or Hester – had carved those words; she imagined his remorse when the red film of rage lifted and he faced what he had done to the wife he had loved. By Lucy's own testimony, he was a sweet and gentle man, and – although she could not be certain – Josephine found it easy to believe that he had punished himself in the way he had punished his wife, by simply allowing himself to die. She looked down at the journal in her hands, and wondered if Lucy had used it as her vehicle of confession, if she had found it easier to show Samuel her diary rather than speak the words herself. It was impossible to know now if Lucy had read her husband's response; if she had, Josephine could only begin to imagine the horror and fear that must have clawed at her heart in those final days, and she cried for her as she would have cried for a friend.

The cottage taunted her with its silence, goading her to open the chest again and prove herself right. She knew she had no choice – there was nowhere to turn for help on a night like this – but it took her a long time to find the courage to go back upstairs, and the only thing that forced her to her feet in the end was a dread of what might happen if she stayed where she was. Back in October, when she had felt Lucy's presence so strongly in the cottage, there had been no sense of anything to fear – but that was before she knew what had happened; now, as hard as she tried to picture that harmless face at the window, the Lucy that filled her mind was a malevolent force, the restless spirit of stories and nightmares, and her ghost frightened Josephine even more than the thought of her physical remains. She took another lamp, glad that she had left the candles burning upstairs, and returned to the room whose horrors she thought she had banished. Her courage left her completely the moment she stepped through the door. The chest, which she was sure she had closed, stood wide open now, its lid thrown back against the wall. The contents were in shadow, and Josephine made no attempt to illuminate them; without thinking, she stepped forward and slammed the lid shut again, feeling the tremor of her fear in the floorboards as she backed away. She stood rooted to the spot, reluctant to take her eyes off the trunk but unable to find the strength to face her fear and open it.

And then she smelt the smoke again. It was faint, but not so faint that she could blame it on her imagination, and she realised that it must be after midnight. Boxing Day – the anniversary of the fire at the Red Barn, the day on which those terrible events would be played out again in some other life or time that she didn't understand. Outside, she heard footsteps. She backed further into the corner of the room, doubting now her own sense of reality, but there it was again: the soft but unmistakable crunch of snow underfoot. Instinctively, she looked to the window that was no longer there, but now she did not need a view of the field where the barn had stood: she could see the silhouetted figure so clearly in her mind, hurrying back to the cottage in the darkness, oblivious still to the damage she had done. When it came, the thundering on the door was louder than anything she could have imagined. Josephine crouched to the floor, her hands over her ears, but still the pounding continued. Then suddenly it stopped, and the silence was worse. She heard Lucy moving about in the rooms below, heard her footsteps on the stairs, and wept tears of frustration and despair because she knew at any moment she would be brought face to face with the darkness that had lain dormant in the cottage for so long. Lost to everything but her own fear, she did not stop to question why the voice calling her name was somehow comforting.

'Jesus, Josephine, what on earth is going on? Didn't you hear me? Are you all right?'

Marta was beside her, holding her close, before Josephine's mind could catch up with her imagination; somehow, she seemed less real than the ghost Josephine had feared and it took her a moment to trust in what she saw. Then she clung to Marta as if her life depended on it, scarcely able to tell if the trembling that shook them both was the terror from her own body or the deathly cold from Marta's. There was snow on her coat and in her hair, and the shock of its chill brought Josephine to her senses a little. 'I thought you were Lucy,' she stammered, neither knowing nor caring how ridiculous she sounded.

'Why would she be knocking? God, a girl could freeze to death waiting for you to come to the door.' She spoke gently, trying to ease Josephine out of her panic with humour.

'But I thought it was the barn. I could smell smoke.'

'The room's full of smoke downstairs. When was the last time you had your chimneys swept?' Marta took Josephine's face in her hands. 'There's only one person stupid enough to come looking for you on a night like this. I might be as cold as the dead, but I'm not a ghost. What's happened, Josephine? Why were you so frightened?'

'It's Lucy Kyte. I think her body is in that chest. Her child, too, probably.'

'What?' Marta looked back over her shoulder. 'Good God, you're serious, aren't you?'

'Yes.' Marta listened while Josephine explained where the chest had come from and what she had read in the diary. 'She's been here all this time. I'm wandering round with Christmas decorations and she's up here in a box.'

The true horror of what she had been living with was only now beginning to dawn on Josephine, and Marta tried to calm her down. 'Hang on – we don't know that for sure. You haven't looked, have you?'

'No. I was going to, but then I came back up here and the lid was open. I know I closed it.'

'It can't just have opened by itself.'

'Who said anything about opening by itself?' Josephine snapped. 'You weren't here.' It wasn't meant to sound like an accusation; she still had no idea what miracle had brought Marta to her door – she was just happy that it had. 'I'm sorry. I didn't mean to bite your head off. But I'm sure I closed it.'

'All right.' Marta reached inside her coat and took out a hip flask. 'Thank God I brought this for the snow. Your festive hospitality leaves a lot to be desired so far.' She smiled and offered the flask to Josephine, then swallowed the rest of the whisky herself. 'Right. I'll look.'

'No you won't. I'll do it.'

Marta caught Josephine's arm. 'I'm not going to stand here and argue about who gets to see the bones first. We'll do it together.'

Marta moved some candles over to the corner to give more light, and Josephine took a deep breath and lifted the lid. The layers of material were faded and frayed, but one of them was still recognisable as a bedspread. Gently, Marta lifted the fabric and pulled it to one side. Lucy lay wrapped in the quilt that she had sewn with such love for her husband. Her body was doubled up, her head turned to the side, and Josephine stared down at the pathetic collection of bones, the strands of hair still matted to the skull, remembering how Lucy had felt when she saw Maria's remains in court. Lucy had never been flesh and blood to Josephine, only a voice speaking out from the past, but still she felt some of that pain and that anger at a life so easily cut short. The chest had been lined with sheets, stained dark with blood from the birth or discoloured later as her body rotted away, and some of Lucy's possessions – an inkstand and the trinket box Samuel had made for her – had been put in with her, a parody of a much grander burial. If they looked further, Josephine was sure that they would find the tiny body of Lucy's son, but she had seen all that she could bear and it had told them enough. She looked away, and Marta carefully covered Lucy's face.

Josephine closed the chest, then took a bunch of holly from one of the beams in the bedroom and laid it on the lid, a gesture of remembrance that was nearly a hundred years too late. It was a long time before either of them spoke. 'What do you think we should do?' Marta asked eventually.

'Wait until the morning, I suppose, then go to the rectory. I can telephone Archie from there. Someone will have to take Lucy away, but he'll know who to call. Then I'd like Stephen to come back and bless her body. I'm not sure I believe in any of that, but it seems the right thing to do.' Marta shivered, and Josephine took her hand. 'Come on. You need to get warm.'

She took the blankets off the bed and they went downstairs to the study, both of them glad to be out of the room and as far from it as possible. Josephine poured Marta a drink and built the fire up for her, then left her reading Lucy's diary while she warmed some soup. When she went back, the journal was put to one side and Marta had obviously been crying. 'What a wretched fucking life,' she said quietly. 'No wonder she needs peace. Do you think Hester knew?'

'I don't see how she could have.' Josephine put the tray down on the floor and sat next to Marta by the fire, pulling the blanket over them both. 'She would have done something about it, I'm sure. I don't know whether to wish she could have known the whole story when she felt so drawn to Lucy, or to be glad she was spared the grief.' She handed Marta a mug of soup. 'I don't know how you managed to get here, but I'm so relieved you did.'

'Well, I wasn't too worried at first. We didn't have much snow, but it can change so quickly within a few hundred yards. And anyway, I knew you'd use the slightest flurry as an excuse to miss the party.' Josephine smiled, but couldn't argue. 'Then I started thinking about that bloody Peck woman and what she'd done to Hester. I got it into my head that she might come back here and try to hurt you, so I had to know that you were all right.'

'You shouldn't have risked it, though.'

'Believe me – the bigger risk was to stay. I got out just as everyone else was moving on to Dodie's for a festive sing-song.'

Josephine laughed, mostly from relief at what she had missed. 'But what if you'd had an accident?'

'The snow wasn't very deep until Stoke, and even after that the main road had been cleared a bit. I got as far as I could, then dumped the car and walked the last mile or so.'

'Thank you – I mean that, Marta. I thought I was going mad. It must have been exactly how Hester felt.' Josephine stared into the flames, remembering everything that had happened. 'How ridiculous of me to think that I could gloss over all that pain with a bit of building work.' She smiled sadly. 'It wasn't quite the way you were supposed to get your Christmas present.'

'Nice bath, though.' Marta's grin faded, and she spoke more seriously. 'Look, Josephine – I'm not making light of this. God knows, I saw how frightened you were. But don't underestimate what you've done. You haven't glossed over anything – you wouldn't let Hester's death go, and now you're about to give Lucy the peace she's never had. This cottage will thank you for that, I know it will. It will make you happy.'

'Make *us* happy.'

Marta smiled. 'It occurred to me while I was reading the diary, though – will they bury Lucy in the churchyard if they know what she did?'

The thought had not crossed Josephine's mind. 'Why wouldn't they? What happened to Molly was an accident, and anyway, Stephen's not like that. He strikes me as a very compassionate man.'

'It might not be his decision, though. From what you say, there's been enough trouble about having Maria Marten in the graveyard, and she's the victim. Do you honestly think people will turn a blind eye to another murder? Or manslaughter, if we want to be pedantic about it. Perhaps we should make sure.'

'What are you suggesting?' She followed Marta's gaze to the final volume of the journal. 'Now that we've finally got to the truth, you think we should destroy it?'

'Only the end of it. The rest should stay with her body to help identify her. I'll do it, if you can't.'

'But if the diary's incomplete, everyone will think that Samuel killed her.'

'Not necessarily. We can't say for sure what really happened – how can they?'

'Even so, shouldn't we tell the truth and rely on people to understand why she did what she did?' Marta looked sceptical, and Josephine knew she was right. Lucy had suffered enough for her mistake. Without giving herself time to reconsider she tore the final pages from the diary and put them on the fire, watching as the flames refashioned a history and a justice of their own.

26

Lucy Kyte was laid to rest with her son in February, when the frost made the early spring flowers sparkle on the ground like coloured glass. The church was shrouded in silence, and only the birds in the ivy – sensing the end of a long winter – disturbed the stillness of the air as a band of mourners followed the coffin outside to the grave. Lucy's story seemed to have touched the village in a way that its more famous history could not, and Josephine was moved to see how many people had come to give her the respect she had waited so long for. Her grave was close to both Samuel's and Maria's, but Josephine hoped that she would not be torn between them in death as she had been in life, and that Lucy's peace – if that's what it now was – would prove enough for them all. She would bring roses in time, for Lucy and for Maria, but today she put snowdrops on the coffin, remembering what Lucy had written in her diary about their being either the last flower of winter or the first of spring. This time, she hoped they might stand for both an end and a beginning.

When the final prayers had been said, the mourners dispersed to visit their own dead. Josephine was not the only person to have brought flowers for Maria, she noticed, and she laid her snowdrops next to the daffodils that already graced the patch of ground that Stephen had pointed out to her on a foggy October morning. She looked round the churchyard, noticing how the sunlight bled across the sloping fields, touching the lower graves and blessing those who had fallen in the war, but refusing to reach as far as the Corders. The Gospel Oak was in shadow, too, and suddenly Josephine noticed a young woman standing close to its trunk, watching her. She took a few steps forward, but the woman turned and walked away in the direction of the village, disappearing for a moment behind a row of gravestones. Josephine waited for her to emerge again the other side and carry on down the path, but she was nowhere to be seen – and of all the possible explanations, Josephine knew which one she wanted to believe.

Smiling, she rescued Marta from Stephen and Hilary and they walked home along Marten's Lane, where banks of pink and yellow primroses shone in Maria's garden. The dead wood of winter already looked out of place, and as she opened her front gate, Josephine found herself looking forward to spring and summer at the cottage, free from all her old reservations about the future. She knew now that she would keep Hester's gift to her, and that she and Marta could be happy there when it was possible for them to be together, living always with those who had worked and died and made love there before them – but not, any longer, in their shadow. Marta had presented her with a new name-plate for the cottage, something she had had specially made to mark the start of another phase in its history; it stood just inside the door, waiting to be put up, and Josephine could not imagine a better day to say goodbye to the Red Barn once and for all. The old piece of wood came away easily in her hand, as though the house were breathing a sigh of relief. In its place, she proudly hung the sign to Larkspur Cottage.

Author's Note

I grew up with the story of Maria Marten and William Corder. As a
child in Suffolk, I remember summer days out in Polstead with my parents, walking past Maria's house, or William's, fascinated even then by
what had happened there and by the real people behind the legend. I
lived a stone's throw from Moyse's Hall and its macabre exhibits – so
thrilling and so horrifying to a little girl – and I passed the Gaol where
Corder was hanged every weekend on the way to my grandmother's
house. My father sings the ballad to this day. So the Red Barn murder is
the first crime story I ever knew, and I realised when I started this book
that I've always wanted to find a different way to tell it.

The character of Lucy Kyte was inspired by three lines of testimony
given at Maria Marten's inquest and reprised at William Corder's trial.
The witness was Lucy Baalham, a servant in the Corder household, but
there the similarity ends: the diary's account of the Red Barn murder
and its aftermath is based on fact, but Lucy Kyte's personal story, her
family, and all the events that take place at Red Barn Cottage are entirely
fictional.

After being stripped by souvenir hunters, the Red Barn was burned
down on Boxing Day, 1842, during a period of great agricultural unrest.
Local newspapers report sightings of a tramp in the area on the day of
the fire but, despite the offer of a generous reward, the culprit was never
caught. More than a hundred years later, Red Barn Cottage was also destroyed by fire.

The melodrama of Maria Marten was first staged in the summer of
1828, while William Corder was still alive, and has been frequently performed ever since; the story has also been the basis of five films and
a BBC drama. Norman Carter 'Tod' Slaughter (1885–1956) was the

finest Corder – and arguably the finest villain of any sort – on stage or screen; his many fans included Graham Greene, whose *Spectator* review of the 1939 film *The Face at the Window*, described him as 'one of our finest living actors'. Slaughter played Corder throughout his life, often opposite his wife, Jenny Lynn, and died in his sleep a few hours after strangling Maria Marten for the last time on stage in Derby.

James Curtis's 1828 book, *An Authentic and Faithful History of the Mysterious Murder of Maria Marten*, remains the most detailed account of the Red Barn murder, and was based on contemporary interviews in Polstead as well as time spent with Corder in Bury Gaol prior to his execution. In fact, Curtis became so synonymous with the case that his image was sometimes printed by mistake as the face of the killer. The murder continues to inspire new books, both fact and fiction, some of which question Corder's guilt, and the original ballad has been reinterpreted by musicians as diverse as The Albion Country Band and Tom Waits.

Moyse's Hall Museum still has on display a fascinating collection of artefacts relating to the Red Barn murder and its historical context, including Corder's death mask, his scalp, and a copy of Curtis's book bound in Corder's skin. Other relics have come and gone, including Maria Marten's hand, but her clothes chest is believed still to exist in private ownership. Corder's skeleton was put on display first at the West Suffolk Hospital and then at the Royal College of Surgeons, and was removed for cremation in 2004. Maria Marten is buried in St Mary's Church, Polstead, but her gravestone is no longer visible.

'Josephine Tey' is one of two pseudonyms created by Elizabeth MacKintosh (1896–1952) during a distinguished career as playwright and novelist; the name was taken from one of her Suffolk ancestors, and first appeared in 1936. *Claverhouse* was published a year later and is her only work of non-fiction, although she often used historical themes as the basis for her plays and novels, most notably in *The Daughter of Time*. In a number of Tey's letters, she expressed a wish for a cottage of her own;

sadly, she died before she was able to do anything about it, but I hope she would have enjoyed the one that I've chosen for her.

Acknowledgements

I'm indebted to Chris Mycock of Moyse's Hall, Bury St. Edmunds, for his generous help with research into the Red Barn murder and the life of the museum in the 1930s. Readers who would like to know more about the case can find images and contemporary sources at www.stedmundsburychronicle.co.uk. Works by Donald McCormick and Gareth Jenkins have also given insights into its different aspects. *Victorian Studies in Scarlet* by Richard Altick is a fascinating picture of peepshows, relics and the grislier side of collecting.

My thanks to Alan Riddleston for sharing memories of his childhood in William Corder's house, and for painting an invaluable picture of Polstead life; to Dennis and Paule Pym for a warm welcome at Maria Marten's cottage; to Miss Beattie Keeble for her recollections of Polstead and Stoke-by-Nayland between the wars, as well as some great ghost stories; and to Michael and Deborah at The Cock Inn.

H. F. Maltby's memoir *Ring Up the Curtain* brought colour to the character of Hester Larkspur, and *London's Grand Guignol and the Theatre of Horror* by R. Hand and M. Wilson gave her an interesting later career. Jeffrey Richards's *The Unknown 1930s: An Alternative History of the British Cinema 1929–1939*, Jacqueline Finesilver, and numerous film magazines of the 1930s provided valuable information on Tod Slaughter and Jenny Lynn; Slaughter's films have been reissued in the Best of British Collection.

Suffolk is a magical place, and I'm for ever grateful to my parents for showing me its beauty as well as its darker history. Two authors in particular brought the county to life for me in the 1930s: Ronald Blythe, in *Akenfield* and in personal interviews; and Julian Tennyson in *Suffolk Scene*. Thanks to Jenny and Alan Bradley for information on old Bury, and to everyone else who has contributed to my research, directly or through their books: Anne Fraser of the Highland Council; Dr Peter Fordyce; Sue Lambert of Mrs Simpson's Café; Susan Williams in *The People's King*; and Liz Stanley in *The Diaries of Hannah Cullwick*. From Lucy's surname to Hester's cottage, the late Irene Cranwell has helped more than she will ever know, and I appreciate the continued support of everyone who looks after each book: Véronique Baxter and all at David Higham Associates; and Walter Donohue, Alex Holroyd and Katherine Armstrong at Faber.

And to Mandy, who has brought so much to every stage – the initial ideas and development of the story, the writing of Lucy's diary and the creation of her voice, even an early Christmas. It's been lovely to share a story that we came to individually, and you've made it a joy to write, as well as a much better book. Thank you.

Also by Nicola Upson

An Expert in Murder

Death is not a rehearsal . . .

'A new and assured talent.' **P. D. James**

'An ingenious concept, beautifully realised.' **Reginald Hill**

It is 1934, and celebrated Scottish crime writer Josephine Tey is on her way to London to see her own hit West End play – but her trip is interrupted by the grisly murder of a young woman she meets on the train.

Detective Inspector Archie Penrose is convinced that the killing is connected to Tey, and that somewhere in the flamboyant theatre world lurks a ruthless and spiteful killer who is out to ensure Josephine becomes a victim of her own success.

Cleverly blending elements of Josephine Tey's real life with a gripping murder mystery, *An Expert in Murder*, is both a tribute to one of the most popular writers of crime's Golden Age and a richly atmospheric detective novel in its own right.

'A playful, cleverly constructed affair in which it is as much fun trying to guess the true identities of Upson's fictional characters as it is her demented killer.' *Daily Telegraph*

ff

Angel with Two Faces

Two can keep a secret if one of them is dead

'Packed with lust and illicit passion.' *Sunday Times*

When Inspector Archie Penrose invites Josephine Tey to his
family home in Cornwall, she seizes the opportunity
to get away from London and work on her second mystery
novel. The landscape is inspiring: a lake on Archie's
estate which is said to claim a life every seven years,
and an open-air theatre near the sea.

But death clouds the holiday from the start. Josephine arrives
on the day of the funeral of a young estate worker and, soon
after, a local boy disappears. Archie and Josephine are
forced to turn their attentions to the violent reality which
lies beneath a seemingly idyllic community – a community
with one face turned to the present and another looking
back at the crimes of the past.

'The portrayal of Tey is both sympathetic and perceptive . . . Upson
is chillingly effective at showing how good intentions may lead to evil
consequences . . . A fine addition to a promising series.'
Andrew Taylor, *Spectator*

ff

Two for Sorrow

Old sins cast long shadows . . .

'Psychologically compelling.' *Sunday Times*

When Josephine Tey sets out to write a novel about the notorious Finchley baby farmers hanged for their crimes in 1903, she has little idea of the relevance of her research to the modern-day murder of a young seamstress. Moving between the decadence and glamour of a private women's club in 1930s London and the claustrophobia of Holloway Prison, Tey discovers how crimes of the past destroy those left behind – long after justice is done.

'With a well-made plot and a fascinating cast of female characters, this is an assured addition to an excellent series.' *Guardian*

'Any crime aficionado should make room for Nicola Upson's novels in which the real-life author Josephine Tey, one of the grandes dames of the Golden Age of detective fiction, investigates murders in the thirties.' *Daily Telegraph*

ff

Fear in the Sunlight

The final cut is the deepest

'A smart, playful pleasure in an increasingly adventurous series.'
Financial Times

Summer, 1936. Josephine Tey joins her friends in the holiday
village of Portmeirion to celebrate her fortieth birthday and
to sign a deal with Alfred Hitchcock to film one of her novels.
But then one of their party is brutally slashed to death.

The following day, fear and suspicion escalate as another of
the guests is savagely murdered. Josephine Tey and Chief
Inspector Archie Penrose find themselves on the trail of the
most sadistic killer they have yet encountered . . .

'The novel injects new life into the serial killer genre, as well as
offering an elegiac commentary on Tey's sadly truncated life.'
Sunday Times

'[Upson's] choice of sleuth was a masterstroke of literary theft . . .
a novel that charms until the dagger strikes and then, as Hitchcock
once explained, it provides the public with beneficial shocks.'
Independent on Sunday

'An absolute delight . . . Upson has created a fine series of cosy
but intelligent mysteries.' *Catholic Herald*